MOB JUSTICE

"I will not give over a man to a lynch mob," said Curtis. "If one of the Tetongs killed your herder, he will be punished. Give me three days in which to act."

"No way!" said Sheriff Yarbe. "That crowd will not be satisfied unless we bring them an Indian. If I can't get the man I want, I'll take old Crawling Elk himself and hold him until the tribe produces the killer."

"You'll leave," said Curtis, "or I'll put you in irons!"

"Like hell!" sputtered Yarbe. He reached for his gun but Curtis stopped him with a cold look.

"What do you suppose would be the consequence of firing on a captain of the United States Army in the discharge of his duty, by a sheriff acting outside the law?"

THE CAPTAIN OF THE GRAY-HORSE TROOP

Hamlin Garland

FORGE®

A TOM DOHERTY ASSOCIATES BOOK
NEW YORK

This is a work of fiction. All the characters and events portrayed in this book are either products of the author's imagination or are used fictitiously.

THE CAPTAIN OF THE GRAY-HORSE TROOP

A Forge Book
Published by Tom Doherty Associates, Inc.
175 Fifth Avenue
New York, NY 10010

Forge® is a registered trademark of Tom Doherty Associates, Inc.

ISBN: 0-812-58042-7

First Forge edition: February 1999

Printed in the United States of America

0 9 8 7 6 5 4 3 2 1

CONTENTS

Contents

CHAPTER I

A Camp in the Snow

WINTER IN the upper heights of the Bear Tooth Range is a glittering desolation of snow with a flaming blue sky above. Nothing moves, nothing utters a sound, save the cony at the mouth of the spiral shaft, which sinks to his deeply buried den in the rocks. The peaks are like marble domes, set high in the pathway of the sun by day and thrust amid the stars by night. The firs seem hopeless under their ever-increasing burdens. The streams are silenced—only the wind is abroad in the waste, the tireless, pitiless wind, fanged like ingratitude, insatiate as fire.

But it is beautiful, nevertheless, especially of a clear dawn, when the shadows are vividly purple and each rime-wreathed summit is smit with ethereal fire, and each eastern slope is resplendent as a highway of powdered diamonds—or at sunset, when the high crests of the range stand like flaming milestones leading to the Celestial City, and the lakes are like pools of pure gold caught in a robe of green velvet. Yet always this land demands youth and strength in its explorer.

King Frost's dominion was already complete over all the crests, over timber-line, when young Captain Curtis set out to cross the divide which lay between Lake Congar and Fort Sherman—a trip to test the virtue of a Sibley tent and the staying qualities of a mountain horse.

Bennett, the hairy trapper at the head of the lake, advised against it. "The snow is soft—I reckon you better wait a week."

But Curtis was a seasoned mountaineer and took pride in assaulting the stern barrier. "Besides, my leave of absence is nearly up," he said to the trapper.

"Well, you're the doctor," the old trapper replied. "Good luck to ye, Cap."

It was a sunrise of a crisp, clear autumn morning when they started, and around them the ground was still bare, but by noon they were wallowing mid-leg deep in new-fallen snow. Curtis led the way on foot—his own horse having been packed to relieve the burdens of the others—while Sergeant Pierce, resolute and uncomplaining, brought up the rear.

"We must camp beside the sulphur spring to-night," Curtis said, as they left timber-line and entered upon the bleak, wind-swept slopes of Grizzly Bear.

"Very well, sir," Pierce cheerily replied, and till three o'clock they climbed steadily toward the far-off glacial heights, the drifts ever deepening, the cold ever intensifying. They had eaten no food since dawn, and the horses were weak with hunger and weariness as they topped the divide and looked down upon the vast eastern slope. The world before them seemed even more inhospitable and wind-swept than the land they had left below them to the west. The air was filled with flying frost, the sun was weak and pale, and the plain was only a pale-blue sea far, far below to the northeast. The wind blew through the pass with terrible force, and the cold nipped every limb like a famishing white wolf.

"There is the sulphur spring, sir," said Pierce, pointing towards a delicate, strand of steam which rose from a clump of pines in the second basin beneath them.

"Quite right, sergeant, and we must make that in an hour. I'd like to take an observation here, but I reckon we'd better slide down to camp before the horses freeze."

The dry snow, sculptured by the blast in the pass, made the threadlike path an exceedingly elusive line to keep, and trailing narrowed to a process of feeling with the feet; but Curtis set his face resolutely into the northeast wind and led the way down the gulch. For the first half-mile the little packtrain crawled slowly and hesitatingly, like a bewildered worm, turning and twisting, retracing its way, circling huge bowlders, edging awful cliffs, slipping, stumbling, but ever moving, ever descending; and, at last, while yet the sun's light glorified the icy kings behind them, the Captain drew into the shelter of the clump of pines from which the steam of the warm spring rose like a chimney's cheery greeting.

"Whoa, boys!" called Curtis, and with a smile at Pierce, added, "Here we are, home again!"

It was not a cheerful place to spend the night, for even at this level the undisturbed snow lay full twelve inches deep and the pines were bowed with the weight of it, and as the sun sank the cold deepened to zero point; but the sergeant drew off his gloves and began to free the horses from their packs quite as if these were the usual conditions of camping.

"Better leave the blankets on," remarked the young officer. "They'll need 'em for warmth."

The sergeant saluted and continued his work, deft and silent, while Curtis threw up a little tent on a cleared spot and banked it snugly with snow. In a very short time a fire was blazing and some coffee boiling. The two men seemed not to regard the cold or the falling night, except in so far as the wind threatened the horses.

"It's hard luck on them," remarked Curtis, as they were finishing their coffee in the tent; "but it is unavoidable. I don't think it safe to try to go down that slide in the dusk. Do you?"

"It's dangerous at any time, sir, and with our horses weak as they are, it sure would be taking chances."

"We'll make Tom Skinner's by noon to-morrow, and be out of the snow, probably." The young soldier put down his tin cup and drew a map from his pocket. "Hold a light, sergeant; I want to make some notes before I forget them."

While the sergeant held a candle for him, Curtis rapidly traced with a soft pencil a few rough lines upon the map. "That settles that water-shed question;" he pointed with his pencil. "Here is the dividing wall, not over there where Lieutenant Crombie drew it. Nothing is more deceptive than the relative heights of ranges. Well, now take a last look at the horses," he said, putting away his pencil, "and I'll unroll our blankets."

As they crawled into their snug sleeping-bags Curtis said again, with a sigh, "I'm sorry for the ponies."

"They'll be all right now, Captain; they've got something in their stomachs. If a cayuse has any fuel in him he's like an engine—he'll keep warm," and so silence fell on them, and in the valley the cold deepened till the rocks and the trees cried out in the rigor of their resistance.

The sun was filling the sky with an all-pervading crimson-and-orange mist when the sergeant crawled out of his snug nest and started a fire. The air was perfectly still, but the frost gripped each limb with benumbing fury. The horses, with blankets awry, stood huddled close together in the shelter of the pines not far away. As the sergeant appeared they whinnied to express their dependence upon him, and when the sun rose they turned their broadsides to it gratefully.

The two men, with swift, unhesitating action, set to work to break camp. In half an hour the tent was folded and packed, the horses saddled, and then, lustily singing, Curtis led the way down upon the floor of the second basin, which narrowed towards the north into a deep and wooded valley leading to the plains. The grasp of winter weakened as they descended; December became October. The snow thinned, the streams sang clear, and considerably before noon the little train of worn and hungry horses came out upon the grassy shore of a small lake to bask in genial sunshine. From this point the road to Skinner's was smooth and easy, and quite untouched of snow.

As they neared the miner's shack, a tall young Payonnay, in the dress of a cowboy, came out to meet them, smiling broadly.

"I'm looking for you, Captain."

"Are you, Jack? Well, you see me. What's your message?"

"The Colonel says you are to come in right off. He told me to tell you he had an order for you."

A slouching figure, supporting a heap of greasy rags, drew near, and a low voice drawled, weakly: "Jack's been here since Friday. I told him where you was, but he thought he'd druther lay by my fire than hunt ye."

Curtis studied the squat figure keenly. "You weren't looking for the job of crossing the range yourself, were you?"

The tramplike miner grinned and sucked at his pipe. "Well, no—I can't say that I was, but I like to rub it into these lazy Injuns."

Jack winked at Curtis with humorous appreciation. "He's a dandy to rub it into an Injun, don't you think?"

Even Skinner laughed at this, and Curtis said: "Unsaddle the horses and give them a chance at the grass, sergeant. We can't go into the fort to-night with the packs. And, Skinner, I want to hire a horse of you, while you help Pierce bring my outfit into the fort to-morrow. I must hurry on to see what's in the wind."

"All right, Captain, anything I've got is yours," responded the miner, heartily.

The bugles were sounding "retreat" as the young officer rode up to the door of Colonel Quinlan's quarters and reported for duty.

"Good-evening, Major," called the Colonel, with a quizzical smile and a sharp emphasis on the word major.

"Major!" exclaimed Curtis; "what do you mean—"

"Not a wholesale slaughter of your superiors. Oh no! You are Major by the grace of the Secretary of Indian Affairs. Colonel Hackett, of the War Department, writes me that you have been detailed as Indian agent at Fort Smith. You'll find your notification in your mail, no doubt."

Curtis touched his hat in mock courtesy. "Thanks, Mr. Secretary; your kindness overwhelms me."

"Didn't think the reform administration could get along without you, did you?" asked the Colonel, with some humor. He was standing at his gate. "Come in, and we'll talk it over. You seem a little breathless."

"It does double me up, I confess. But I can't consistently back out after the stand I've made."

"Back out! Well, not if I can prevent it. Haven't you hammered it into us for two years that the army was the proper instrument for dealing with these redskins? No, sir, you can't turn tail now. Take your medicine like a man."

"But how did they drop onto me? Did you suggest it?"

The Colonel became grave. "No, my boy, I did not. But I think I know who did. You remember the two literary chaps who camped with us on our trail march two years ago?"

The young officer's eyes opened wide. "Ah! I see. They told me at the time that they were friends of the Secretary. That explains it."

"Your success with that troop of enlisted Cheyennes had something to do with it, too," added the Colonel. "I told those literary sharps about that experience, and also about your crazy interest in the sign-language and Indian songs."

"You did? Well, then you *are* responsible, after all."

The Colonel put his hand on his subordinate's shoulder. "Go and do the work, boy! It's better than sitting around here waiting promotion. If I weren't so near retirement I'd resign. I have lived out on these cursed deserts ever since 1868—but I'll fool 'em," he added, with a grim smile. "I'm going to hang on to the last, and retire on half-pay. Then I'll spend all my time looking after my health and live to be ninety-five, in order to get even."

Curtis laughed. "Quite right, Colonel," and, then becoming serious, he added, "It's my duty, and I will do it." And in this quiet temper he accepted his detail.

Captain George Curtis, as the Colonel had intimated, was already a marked man at Fort Sherman—and, indeed, throughout the western division of the army. He feared no hardship, and acknowledged no superior on the trail except Pierce, who was as invincible to cold and snow as a grizzly bear, and his chief diversions were these trips into the wild. Each outing helped him endure the monotony of barrack life, for when it was over he returned to the open fire of his study, where he pored over his maps, smoking his pipe and writing a little between bugle-calls. In this way he had been able to put together several articles on the forests, the water-sheds, and the wild animals of the region he had traversed, and in this way had made himself known to the Smithsonian Institution. He was considered a crank on trees and Indians by his fellow-officers, who all drank more whiskey and played a better hand at poker than he; "but, after all, Curtis is a good soldier," they often said, in conclusion. "His voice in command is clear and decisive, and his control of his men excellent." He was handsome, too, in a firm, brown, cleanly outlined way, and though not a popular officer, he had no enemies in the service.

His sister Jennie, who had devotedly kept house for him during his garrison life, was waiting for him at the gate of his little yard, and cried out in greeting:

"How *did* you cross the range this weather? I was frightened for you, George. I could see the storm raging up there all day yesterday."

"Oh, a little wind and snow don't count," he replied, carelessly. "I thought you'd given up worrying about me."

"I have—only I thought of poor Sergeant Pierce

and the horses. There's a stack of mail here. Do you know what's happened to you?"

"The Colonel told me."

"How do you like it?"

"I don't know yet. At this moment I'm too tired to express an opinion."

From the pile of mail on his desk he drew out the order which directed him to "proceed at once to Fort Smith, and as secretly as may be. You will surprise the agent, if possible—intercepting him at his desk, so that he will have no opportunity for secreting his private papers. You will take entire charge of the agency, and at your earliest convenience forward to us a report covering every detail of the conditions there."

"Now that promises well," he said, as he finished reading the order. "We start with a fair expectancy of drama. Sis—we are Indian agents! All this must be given up." He looked round the room, which glowed in the light of an open grate fire. The floor was bright with Navajo blankets and warm with fur rugs, and on the walls his books waited his hand.

"I don't like to leave our snug nest, Jennie," he said, with a sigh.

"You needn't. Take it with you," she replied, promptly.

He glanced ruefully at her. "I knew I'd get mighty little sympathy from you."

"Why should you? I'm ready to go. I don't want you trailing about over these mountains till the end of time; and you know this life is fatal to you, or any other man who wants to do anything in the world. It's all very well to talk about being a soldier, but I'm not so enthusiastic as I used to be. I don't think sitting around waiting for some one to die is very noble."

He rose and stood before the fire. "I wish this

whole house could be lifted up and set down at Fort Smith; then I might consider the matter."

She came over, and, as he put his arm about her, continued earnestly: "George, I'm serious about this. The President is trying to put the Indian service into capable hands, and I believe you ought to accept; in fact, you can't refuse. There is work for us both there. I am heartily tired of garrison life, George. As the boys say, there's nothing in it."

"But there's danger threatening at Smith, sis. I can't take you into an Indian outbreak."

"That's all newspaper talk. Mr. Dudley writes—"

"Dudley—is he down there? Oh, you are a masterful sly one! Your touching solicitude for the Tetongs is now explained. What is Dudley doing at Smith besides interfering with my affairs?"

"He's studying the Tetong burial customs—but he isn't there at present!"

"These Smithsonian sharps are unexpectedly keen. He'd sacrifice me and my whole military career to have you study skulls with him for a few days. Do you know, I suspect him and Osborne Lawson of this whole conspiracy—and you—you were in it! I've a mind to rebel and throw everything out o' gear."

Jennie gave him a shove. "Go dress for dinner. The Colonel and his wife and Mr. Ross are coming in to congratulate you, and you must pretend to be overjoyed."

As he sat at the head of his handsome table that night Curtis began to appreciate his comforts. He forgot the dissensions and jealousies, the cynical speculations and the bitter rivalries of the officers—he remembered only the pleasant things.

His guests were personable and gracious, and Jennie presided over the coffee with distinction. She was a natural hostess, and her part in the conversation which followed was notable for its good sense, but Mr. Ross, the young lieutenant, considered her delicate color and shining hair even more remarkable than her humor. He liked her voice, also, and had a desire to kick the shins of the loquacious Colonel for absorbing so much of her attention. Mrs. Quinlan, the Colonel's wife, was, by the same token, a retiring, silent little woman, who smiled and nodded her head to all that was said, paying special attention to the Colonel's stories, with which all were familiar; even Mr. Ross had learned them.

At last the Colonel turned to Curtis. "You'll miss this, Curtis, when you're exiled down there at old Fort Smith among the Tetongs. Here we are a little oasis of civilization in the midst of a desert of barbarians; down there you'll be swallowed up."

"We'll take civilization with us," said Jennie. "But, of course, we shall miss our friends."

"Well, you'll have a clear field for experiment at Smith. You can try all your pet theories on the Tetongs. God be with them!—their case is desperate." He chuckled gracelessly.

"When do you go?" asked Mrs. Quinlan.

"At once. As soon as I can make arrangements," replied Curtis, and then added: "And, by-the-way, I hope you will all refrain from mentioning my appointment till after I reach Fort Smith."

The visitors did not stay late, for their host was plainly preoccupied, and as they shook hands with him in parting they openly commiserated him. "I'm sorry for you," again remarked the Colonel, "but it's a just punishment."

After they were gone Curtis turned to his sister. "I must leave here to-morrow morning, sis."

"Why, George! Can't you take time to breathe and pack up?"

"No, I must drop down on that agent like a hawk on a June-bug, before he has a chance to bury his misdeeds. The Colonel has given out the news of my detail, and the quicker I move the better. I must reach there before the mail does."

"But I want to go with you," she quickly and resentfully replied.

"Well, you can, if you are willing to leave our packing in Pierce's hands."

"I don't intend to be left behind," she replied. "I'm going along to see that you don't do anything reckless. I never trust a man in a place requiring tact."

Curtis laughed. "That's your long suit, sis, but I reckon we'll need all the virtues that lie in each of us. We are going into battle with strange forces."

CHAPTER II

The Streeter Gun-rack

THERE IS a good wagon-road leading to old Fort Smith from Pinon City, but it runs for the most part through an uninteresting country, and does not touch the reservation till within a few miles of the agency buildings. From the other side, however, a rough trail crosses a low divide, and for more than sixty miles lies within the Tetong boundaries, a rolling, cattle country rising to grassy hills on the west.

For these reasons Curtis determined to go in on horseback and in civilian's dress, leaving his sister to follow by rail and buckboard; but here again Jennie promptly made protest.

"I'll not go that way, George. I am going to keep with you, and you needn't plan for anything else—so there!"

"It's a hard ride, sis—sixty miles and more. You'll be tired out."

"What of that? I'll have plenty of time to rest afterwards."

"Very well. It is always a pleasure to have you with me, you stubborn thing," he replied, affectionately.

It had been hard to leave everything at the Fort, hard to look back from the threshold upon well-ordered books and furniture, and harder still to know that rude and careless hands would jostle them into heaps on the morrow, but Jennie was accustomed to all the hardships involved in being sister to a soldier, and, after she had turned the key in the lock, set her face to the south cheerfully. There was something of the missionary in her, and she had long burned with a desire to help the red people.

They got off at a squalid little cow-town called "Riddell" about noon of the second day, and Curtis, after a swift glance around him, said: "Sis, our chances for dinner are poor."

The hotel, a squat, battlemented wooden building, was trimmed with loafing cowboys on the outside and speckled with flies on the inside, but the landlord was unexpectedly attractive, a smiling, courteous host, to whom flies and cowboys were matters of course. It was plain he had slipped down to his present low level by insensible declinations.

"The food is not so bad if it were only served decently," said Jennie, as they sat at the table eying the heavy china chipped and maimed in the savage process of washing.

"I hope you won't be sorry we've left the army, sis."

"I would, if we had to live with these people," she replied, decisively, looking about the room, which was filled with uncouth types of men, keen-eyed, slouchy, and loud-voiced. The presence of a pretty woman had subdued most of them into something

like decorum, but they were not pleasant to look at.
They were the unattached males of the town, a mob
of barkeepers, hostlers, clerks, and railway hands,
intermixed with a half-dozen cowboys who had ridden in to "loaf away a day or two in town."

"The ragged edge of the cloth of gold," said Curtis, as he glanced round at them. "Civilization has
its seamy side."

"This makes the dear old Fort seem beautiful,
doesn't it?" the girl sighed. "We'll see no more
green grass and well-groomed men."

An hour later, with a half-breed Indian boy for a
guide, they rode away over the hills towards the
east, glad to shake the dust of Riddell off their feet.

The day was one of flooding sunlight, warm and
golden. Winter seemed far away, and only the dry
grass made it possible to say, "This is autumn." The
air was without dust or moisture—crystalline, crisp,
and deliciously invigorating.

The girl turned to her brother with radiant face.
"This is living! Isn't it good to escape that horrid little town?"

"You'd suppose in an air like this all life would be
clean and sweet," he replied. "But it isn't. The trouble is, these people have no inner resource. They
lop down when their accustomed props are removed. They come from defective stock."

The half-breed guide had the quality of his Indian
mother—he knew when to keep silence and when to
speak. He led the way steadily, galloping along on
his little gray pony, with elbows flapping like a
rooster about to take flight.

There was a wonderful charm in this treeless
land, it was so lonely and so sinister. It appealed
with great power to Curtis, while it appalled his sister. The solitary buttes, smooth of slope and grotesque of line; the splendid, grassy hollows, where
the cattle fed; the burned-up mesas, where nothing

lived but the horned toad; the alkaline flats, leprous and ashen; the occasional green line of cottonwood-trees, deep sunk in a dry water-course—all these were typical of the whole vast eastern water-shed of the continental divide, and familiar to the young officer, for in such a land he had entered upon active service.

It was beautiful, but it was an ill place for a woman, as Jennie soon discovered. The air, so dry, so fierce, parched her skin and pinched her red lips. The alkali settled in a gray dust upon her pretty hair and entered her throat, increasing her thirst to a keen pain.

"Oh, George! here is a little stream," she cried out.

"Courage, sis. We will soon get above the alkali. That water is rank poison."

"It looks good," she replied, wistfully.

"We'll find some glorious water up there in that clump of willows," and a few minutes' hard riding brought them to a gurgling little brook of clear, cold water, and the girl not merely drank—she laved away all traces of the bitter soil of the lower levels.

At about four o'clock the guide struck into a transverse valley, and followed a small stream to its source in a range of pine-clad hills which separate the white man's country from the Tetong reservation. As they topped this divide, riding directly over a smooth swell, Curtis drew rein, crying out, "Wait a moment, Louie."

They stood on the edge of a vast dip in the plain, a bowl of amethyst and turquoise. Under the vivid October sun the tawny grass seemed to be transmuted into something that shimmered, was translucent, and yet was firm, while the opposite wall, already faintly in shadow, rose by two degrees to snow-flecked mountains, faintly showing in the west and north. On the floor of this resplendent amphitheatre a flock of cattle fed irregularly, luminous as red and white and deep-purple beads. The landscape was silent—as silent as the cloudless sky above. No bird or beast, save the cattle, and the horses the three travellers rode, was abroad in this dream-world.

"Oh, isn't it beautiful!" exclaimed Jennie.

Curtis sat in silence till the guide said: "We must hurry. Long ways to Streeter."

Then he drew a sigh. "That scene is typical of the old time. Nothing could be more moving to me. I saw the buffaloes feed like that once. Whose are the cattle?" he asked of the boy.

"Thompson's, I think."

"But what are they doing here—that's Tetong land, isn't it?"

The guide grinned. "That don't make no difference to Thompson. All same to him whose grass he eats."

"Well, lead on," said Curtis, and the boy galloped away swiftly down the trail. As they descended to the east the sun seemed to slide down the sky and the chill dusk rose to meet them from the valley of the Elk, like an exhalation from some region of icy waters. Night was near, but Streeter's was in sight, a big loghouse, surrounded by sheds and corrals of various sorts and sizes.

"How does Mr. Streeter happen to be so snugly settled on Indian land?" asked Jennie.

"He made his location before the reservation was set aside. I believe there are about twenty ranches of the same sort within the lines," replied Curtis, "and I think we'll find in these settlers the chief cause of friction. The cattle business is not one that leads to scrupulous regard for the rights of others."

As they clattered up to the door of the ranch-house a tall young fellow in cowboy dress came out to meet them. He was plainly amazed to find a pretty girl at his door, and for a moment fairly gaped with lax jaws.

"Good-evening," said Curtis. "Are you the boss here?"

He recovered himself quickly. "Howdy—howdy! Yes, I'm Cal Streeter. Won't you 'light off?"

"Thank you. We'd like to take shelter for the night if you can spare us room."

"Why, cert. Mother and the old man are away just now, but there's plenty to eat." He took a swift stride towards Jennie. "Let me help you down, miss."

"Thank you, I'm already down," said Jennie, anticipating his service.

The young man called shrilly, and a Mexican appeared at the door of the stable. "Hosy, come and take these horses." Turning to Jennie with a grin, he said: "I can't answer for the quality of the grub, fer Hosy is cooking just now. Mother's been gone a week, and the bread is wiped out. If you don't mind slapjacks I'll see what we can do for you."

Jennie didn't know whether she liked this young fellow or not. After his first stare of astonishment he was by no means lacking in assurance. However, she was plains-woman enough to feel the necessity of making the best of any hospitality when night was falling, and quickly replied: "Don't take any trouble for us. If you'll show me your kitchen and pantry I'll be glad to do the cooking."

"Will you? Well, now, that's a sure-enough trade," and he led the way into the house, which was a two-story building, with one-story wings on either side. The room into which they entered was large and bare as a guard-room. The floor was uneven, the log walls merely whitewashed, and the beams overhead were rough pine boles. Some plain wooden chairs, a table painted a pale blue, and covered with dusty newspapers, comprised the visible furniture, unless a gun-rack which filled one entire wall could be listed among the furnishings. Curtis brought a keen gaze to bear on this arsenal, and estimated that it contained nearly a score of rifles—a sinister array.

Young Streeter opened a side door. "This is where you are to sleep. Just make yourself to home, and I'll rub two sticks together and start a fire."

After Jennie left the room, the young fellow turned abruptly. "Stranger, what might I call you?"

"My name is Curtis. I'm going over to visit the agency."

"She your wife?" He pointed his thumb in Jennie's direction.

"No, my sister."

"Oh! Well, then, you can bunk with me in this room." He indicated a door on the opposite side of the hall. "When she gets ready, bring her out to the kitchen. It's hard lines to make her cook her own grub, but I tell you right now I think she'd better."

As Jennie met her brother a few moments later, she exclaimed, "Isn't he handsome?"

"M—yes. He's good-looking enough, but he's just a little self-important, it seems to me."

"Are you going to let him know who you are?"

"Certainly not. I want to draw him out. I begin to suspect that this house is a rendezvous for all the interests we have to fight. These guns are all loaded and in prime order."

"What a big house you have here," said Jennie, ingratiatingly, as she entered the kitchen. "And what a nice kitchen."

"Oh, purty fair," replied the youth, busy at the stove. "Our ranch ain't what we'd make it if these Injuns were out o' the way. Now, here's the grub—if you can dig up anything you're welcome."

He showed her the pantry, where she found plenty of bacon and flour, and some eggs and milk.

"I thought cattlemen never had milk?"

"Well, they don't generally, but mother makes us milk a cow. Now, I'll do this cooking if you want me to, but I reckon you won't enjoy seein' me do it. I can't make biscuits, and we're all out o' bread, as I say, and Hosy's sinkers would choke a dog."

"Oh, I'll cook if you'll get some water and keep a good fire going."

"Sure thing," he said, heartily, taking up the water-pail to go to the spring. When he came back Jennie was dabbling the milk and flour. He stood watching her in silence for some minutes as she worked, and the sullen lines on his face softened and his lips grew boyish.

"You sure know your business," he said, in a tone of conviction. "When I try to mix dough I get all strung up with it."

She replied with a smile. "Is the oven hot? These biscuit must come out just right."

He stirred up the fire. "A man ain't fitten to cook; he's too blame long in the elbows. We have an old squaw when mother is home, but she don't like me, and so she takes a vacation whenever the old lady does. That throws us down on Hosy, and he just about poisons us. We get spring-poor by the time the old lady comes back." Jennie was rolling at the dough and did not reply to him. He held the door open for her when she was ready to put the biscuit in the oven, and lit another bracket-lamp in order to see her better.

"Do you know, you're the first girl I ever saw in this kitchen."

"Am I?"

"That's right." After a pause he added: "I'm mighty glad I didn't get home to eat Hosy's supper. I want a chance at some of them biscuit."

"Slice this bacon, please—not too thick," she added, briskly.

He took the knife. "Where do you hail from, anyway?" he asked, irrelevantly.

"From the coast," she replied.

"That so? Born there?"

"Oh no. I was born in Maryland, near Washington."

"There's a place I'd like to live if I had money enough. A feller can have a continuous picnic in Washington if he's got the dust to spare, so I hear."

"Now you set the table while I make the omelette."

"The how-many?"

"The omelette, which must go directly to the table after it is made."

He began to pile dishes on the table, which ran across one end of the room, but found time to watch her as she broke the eggs.

"If a feller lives long enough and keeps his mouth shut and his eyes open he'll learn a powerful heap, won't he? I've seen that word in the newspaper a whole lot, but I'll be shot if I ever knew that it was jest aigs."

Jennie was amused, but too hungry to spend much time listening. "You may call them in," she said, after a glance at the biscuit.

The young man opened the door and said, lazily, "Cap, come to grub."

Curtis was again examining the guns in the rack. "You're well heeled."

"Haff to be, in this country," said the young fellow, carelessly. "Set down anywhere—that is, I mean anywhere the cook says."

Jennie didn't like his growing familiarity, but she dissembled. "Sit here, George," she said, indicating a chair at the end. "I will sit where I can reach the coffee."

"Let me do that," said Calvin. "Louie, I guess

you're not in this game," he said to the boy looking wistfully in at the door.

"Oh, let him come—he's as hungry as we are. Let him sit down," protested Jennie.

Young Streeter acquiesced. "It's all the same to me, if *you* don't object to a 'breed," he said, brutally. Louie took his seat in silence, but it was plain he did not enjoy the insolence of the cowboy.

Curtis was after information. "You speak of needing guns—there isn't any danger, I hope?"

"Well, not right now, but we expect to get Congress to pass a bill removing these brutes, and then there may be trouble. Even now we find it safer to go armed. Every little while some Injun kills a beef for us, and we want to be prepared to skin 'em if we jump 'em up in time. I wouldn't trust one of 'em as far as you could throw a yearling bull by the tail."

"Are they as bad as that?" asked Jennie, with widely open eyes.

"They're treacherous hounds. Old Elk goes around smiling, but he'd let a knife into me too quick if he saw his chance. Hark!" he called, with lifted hand.

They all listened. The swift drumming of hoofs could be heard, mingled with the chuckle of a carriage. Calvin rose. "That's the old man, I reckon," and going to the door he raised a peculiar whoop. A voice replied faintly, and soon the buggy rolled up to the door and the new-comer entered the front room. A quick, sharp voice cried out:

"Whose hat is that? Who's here?"

"A feller on his way to visit the agent. He's in there eatin' supper."

A rapid, resolute step approached the door, and Curtis looked up to meet the keen eyes of a big, ruddy-faced man of fifty, with hair and beard as white as wool. His eyes were steel-blue and penetrating as fire.

"Good-evening, sir. Good-evening, madam. Don't rise. Keep your seats. I'll just drop my coat and sit down with you."

He was so distinctly a man of remarkable quality that Curtis stared at him in deep surprise. He had expected to see a loose-jointed, slouchy man of middle-age, but Joseph Streeter was plainly a man of decision and power. His white hair did not betoken weakness or age, for he moved like one in the full vigor of his late manhood. To his visitors he appeared to be a suspicious, irascible, and generous man.

"Hello!" he called, jovially, "biscuit! Cal, you didn't do these, nor Hosy, neither."

Cal grinned. "Well, not by a whole row o' dogs. This—lady did 'em."

Streeter turned his vivid blue eyes on Jennie. "I want to know! Well, I'm much obliged. When did you come?" he asked of Curtis.

"About an hour ago."

"Goin' far?"

"Over to the agency."

"Friend of the agent?"

"No, but I have a letter of introduction to him."

Streeter seemed to be satisfied. "You'll find him a very accommodating gentleman."

"So I hear," said Curtis, and some subtle inflection in his tone caused Streeter to turn towards him again.

"What did I understand your name was?"

"Curtis."

"Where from?"

"San Francisco."

"Oh yes. I think I heard Sennett speak of you. Those biscuit are mighty good. I'll take another. Couldn't persuade you to stay here, could I?" He turned to Jennie.

Jennie laughed. "I'm afraid not—it's too lonesome."

Cal seized the chance to say: "It ain't so lonesome as it looks now. We're a lively lot here sometimes."

Streeter gave him a glance which stopped him. "Cal, you take Hosy and go over to the camp and tell the boys to hustle in two hundred steers. I want to get 'em passed on to-morrow afternoon, or next day sure."

Calvin's face fell. "I don't think I need to go. Hosy can carry the orders just as well as me," he said, boyishly sullen.

"I want *you* to go!" was the stern answer, and it was plain that Streeter was commander even of his reckless son.

As he rose from the table, Calvin said, in a low voice, to Jennie, "I'll be here to breakfast all right, and I'll see that you get over to the agency."

Streeter the elder upon reflection considered that his guests had not sufficiently accounted for themselves, and, after Calvin left, again turned a penetrating glance on Curtis, saying, in a peculiar way, "Where did you say you were from?"

"San Francisco," replied Curtis, promptly, and cut in ahead with a question of his own. "You seem to be well supplied with munitions of war. Do you need all those guns now?"

"Need every shell. We're going to oust these devils pretty soon, and they know it, and they're ugly."

"What do you mean by ousting 'em?"

"We're pushing a bill to have 'em removed."

"Where to?"

"Oh, to the Red River reservation, or the Powder Valley; we're not particular, so that we get rid of 'em."

Jennie tingled with indignation as Streeter outlined the plans of the settlers and told of his friction with the redmen, but Curtis remained calm and smiling.

"You'll miss their market for your beef, won't you?"

"Oh, that's a small item in comparison with the extra range we'll get," and thereupon he entered upon a long statement of what the government ought to do.

Jennie rose wearily, and the old man was all attention.

"I suppose you are tired and would like to go to bed?"

"We are rather limp," confessed Curtis, glad to escape the searching cross-examination which he knew would follow Jennie's retirement.

When they were alone the two young people looked at each other in silence, Jennie with big, horrified eyes, Curtis with an amused comprehension of his sister's feeling. "Isn't he a pirate? He doesn't know it, but his state of mind makes him indictable for murder on the high seas."

"George, I don't like this. We are going to have trouble if this old man and his like are not put off this reservation."

"Well, now, we won't put him off to-night, especially as he is a gallant host. But this visit here has put me in touch with the cattlemen. I feel that I know their plans and their temper very clearly."

"George, I will not sleep here in this room alone. You must make up a cot-bed or something. These people make me nervous, with their guns and Mexican servants."

"Don't you worry, sis, I'll roll up in a blanket and sleep across your door-sill," and this he did, acknowledging the reasonableness of her fears.

CHAPTER III

Curtis Assumes Charge of the Agent

DURING THE night Curtis was quite sure he heard a party of men ride up to the door, but in the morning there remained no signs of them.

They were early on their feet, and Calvin, true to his promise, was present to help get breakfast. He had shaved some time during the night, and wore a new shirt with a purple silk handkerchief looped about his neck, and Jennie found it hard to be as cold and severe with him as she had resolved upon. He was only a big, handsome boy, after all.

"I'm going to send that half-breed back and take you over to the fort myself," he said to Curtis.

"No, I can't have that," Curtis sharply replied. "If you care to ride with us over to the fort I've no objection, but Louie will carry out his contract with us." The truth was, he did not care to be under any further obligation to the Streeters.

Breakfast was a hurried and rather silent meal. As they rose, Jennie said, apologetically: "I fear I can't stop to do up the dishes. It is a long, hard ride to the fort."

"That's right," replied Calvin, "it's close on thirty-five miles. Never you mind about the dishes. Hosy will swab 'em out."

As they were mounting, the elder Streeter said, hospitably: "If you return this way, Mr. Curtis, make my ranch your half-way house." He bowed to Jennie. "My wife will be here then, miss, and you will not be obliged to cook your own meals."

"Oh, I didn't mind; I rather enjoyed it," responded Jennie.

Calvin was delayed at the start, and came thundering after with a shrill, cowboy yell, his horse running close to the ground with ears viciously laid back. The boy made a fine figure as he swept past them with the speed of an eagle. His was the perfection of range horsemanship. He talked, gesticulated, rolled cigarettes, put his coat on or off as he rode, without apparent thought of his horse or of the ground he crossed.

He knew nothing but the life of a cattleman, and spoke quite frankly of his ignorance.

"The old man tried to send me to school once. Packed me off to St. Joe. I stayed a week. 'See here, old man, don't do that again,' I says. 'I won't stand for it.' Hell! You might as well tie up a coyote as shut me in a school-room."

He made a most picturesque guide as he rode ahead of them, always in view, completing a thousand typical combinations of man and horse and landscape—now suppling in his saddle to look down and a little backward at some "sign," now trotting straight towards a dark opening among the pines, now wheeling swiftly to mount a sudden ascent on the trail. Everything he did was as graceful and as self-unconscious as the movements of a panther. He was a living illustration of all the cowboy stories the girl had read. His horse, his saddle, his peculiar, slouching seat, the roll of clothing behind his saddle, his spurs, his long-heeled boots—every detail was as it should be, and Jennie was glad of him, and of Louis, too.

"Yes, it's all here, Jennie," replied Curtis—"the wild country, the Indian, the gallant scout, and the tender maiden."

"I'm having a beautiful ride. Since we left the wagon-road it really seems like the primitive wilderness."

"It is. This little wedge of land is all these brave people have saved from the flood. They made their last stand here. The reflux from the coast caught them here, and here they are, waiting extinction."

The girl's eyes widened. "It's tragic, isn't it?"

"Yes, but so is all life, except to Calvin Streeter, and even he wants what he can't get. He told me this morning he wanted to go to Chicago and take a fall out of a judge who fined him for carrying a gun. So even he has his unsatisfied ambition. As he told me about it he snarled like a young tiger."

At about one o'clock, Calvin, who was riding ahead, halted on the crest of a timbered ridge and raised a shout.

"He's topped the divide!" called Curtis to Jennie, who was riding behind. "We'll soon be in."

"I'm glad of it. I'm tired."

When they reached the spot where Calvin waited they could look down into the main valley of the Elk, and the agency, a singular village of ancient barracks, sheds, corrals, and red-roofed storehouses was almost beneath them. All about on the low hills the criss-crossing trails gave evidence that the Tetongs were still a nation of horsemen. Theirs was a barren land, a land of pine-clad, precipitous hills and deep valleys, which opened to the east—a region of scant rains and thin, discouraged streams.

The sight of the officers' whitewashed quarters and the parade-ground brought a certain sadness to Curtis.

"The old garrison don't look as it did when I was here in 188–," he said, musingly. "Army days in the West are almost gone. The Indian war is over. What a waste of human life it was on both sides! Yes, Louie, go ahead."

As they alternately slid and trotted down the trail, native horsemen could be seen coming and going, their gay blankets sparkling in the clear air. Others on foot were clustered about the central building, where the flag hung droopingly on a tall staff. As they passed the corral, groups of young Tetongs smiled and nudged each other, but offered no greeting. Neither did the older men, though their keen eyes absorbed every detail of the stranger's dress and bearing. It was plain that they held every white man in suspicion, especially if he came attended by a cowboy.

Calvin was elaborately free and easy with them all, eager to show his wide acquaintanceship. "Hello, Two Horns; hello, Hawk," he called to a couple of fine-looking men of middle age. They did not reply. "Hello, Gray Wolf, you old sardine; want to try another horse-race?"

Gray Wolf, evidently something of a wag, smilingly replied: "You bet. Got new pony—heap fast."

Calvin wheeled and spurred into the bunch of young fellows, who scattered with shouts of laughter, while the Captain and Jennie followed Louie, their guide, to the agency gate.

They were met at the fence before the office by two men, one a middle-aged man, with a dirty-gray beard and fat, bloated cheeks, who said, blandly: "Good-morning, sir. Good-morning, miss; nice day."

Curtis dismounted. "Are you Mr. Sennett?"

"I am—what can I do for you?" He turned to his

companion, a tall young man, with innocent gray eyes and a loose, weak mouth: "This is my son Clarence. Clarence, take the lady's horse."

"Thank you," said the Captain, as he stepped inside the gate. "I am Captain Curtis, of the cavalry, detailed to take charge of this agency. You have just left the office—have you the keys in your pocket? If so, please surrender them to me. It is an unpleasant duty, but I am ordered to assume absolute control at once."

The man's red skin faded to a yellow-gray—the color of his beard. For a moment he seemed about to fall, then the blood came surging back; his cheeks grew purple with its weight.

"I'll be damned if I submit. It is an outrage!"

"You can't afford to make any trouble. I am sorry to do this, but I am under orders of the department to take you unawares, and on no account to let you return to your office."

Sennett began to bluster. "Show me your authority."

"My authority is in this paper." He drew the order from his pocket. "If you think a moment you will see that instant acquiescence is best."

While Sennett stormed, the two chiefs, Elk and Two Horns, drew near, and lifting his hand, Curtis, using the sign language swiftly, said to them:

"I am your new agent. The Great Father has heard that the old agent is bad. I am here to straighten matters out. I am Swift Eagle—don't you remember? I came with Bear Robe. I was only second lieutenant then."

The faces of the old chiefs lit up with pleasure. "Ay, we remember! We shake your hands. We are glad you have come."

Curtis then asked: "Who is your interpreter—one you can trust, one who can read this paper."

The two men looked at each other for a moment. Elk said, "Joe?"

Two Horns shook his head; then, catching sight of a man who was regarding the scene from a doorway not very distant, he said, in English: "Him—Nawson. Hay, my friend," he called, "come here!"

This observer at once responded to Two Horns' sign. As he came up the chief said: "My friend, here is a paper from Washington; read it for us."

Curtis said: "I am Captain Curtis, of the cavalry, detailed to act as agent here. This is my commission."

The stranger extended his hand. "I'm glad to meet you, Captain Curtis, very glad, indeed." As they shook hands he added: "I've read your articles on the sign language, et cetera, with great pleasure. My name is Lawson."

Curtis smiled. "Are you Osborne Lawson? I'm mighty glad to meet you. This is my sister, Mr. Lawson."

Mr. Lawson greeted Jennie with grace, and she liked him at once. His manner was direct and his voice pleasing. He was tall, lean, and a little stooping, but strong and brown. "Now, Captain, what can I do for you?" he asked, turning briskly.

"I want you to read this paper to the chiefs here, and then I intend to put a guard on the door. Mr. Sennett is not to be permitted to re-enter his office. These are harsh measures, but I am not responsible for them."

Lawson looked thoughtful. "I see." After reading the paper he said to the chiefs: "It is as this man has said. The Great Father has sent him here to take charge of the office. The old agent is cut off—he is not allowed to go back to his office for fear he may hide something. Have Crow put a guard on the door. The new agent will try to find out why you have not received your rations. This is the secret of this paper, and here is the signature of the Secretary. This is a true thing, and you must now obey Captain Curtis. I know him," he said, looking round him. "He is my friend; you can trust him. That is all."

"Good! Good!" said the chiefs. "We understand."

A short, dark Tetong in a frayed captain's uniform came up. "I am chief of the police," he signed. "What shall I do?"

"Guard the door of the office and of the issue house. Let no one but those I bring enter. Will you do as I say?" he asked.

"Ay!" replied the officer, whose name was Crow.

"Then all is said: go guard the door."

Sennett and his son had withdrawn a little from the scene and were talking in low voices. They had placed themselves in the worst possible light, and they felt it. As Curtis reached this point in his orders, Sennett started to cross the road.

"Wait a moment, gentlemen," called Curtis. "My orders are very strict. I must precede you. There is a certain desk in your library, Mr. Sennett, which I must search."

Sennett flamed out into wild oaths. "You shall not search my private papers."

"Silence!" called Curtis. "Another oath and I'll put you in the guard-house."

"Do you suppose I'm going to submit to this without protest? You treat me like a criminal."

"So far as my orders go, that's what you are," said Curtis. "I give you the benefit of the doubt so long as you act the gentleman, but you must respect the presence of my sister, or I'll gag you." After a pause he added, in a gentler tone: "I don't pretend to judge your case. I am merely obeying the orders of the department."

"I have powerful friends in Washington. You will regret this," snarled Sennett. But his son was like one smitten dumb; his breathing was troubled, and his big, gray eyes were childish in their wide appeal.

Lawson then spoke. "Can I do anything further, Captain? Command me freely."

"No, I think not, except to see that my horses are taken care of and my guide fed. I suppose there is a mess or boarding-house where my sister can get something to eat."

"Won't you come to dinner with me?" asked Lawson. "Mrs. Wilcox, some artist friends, and I are messing over in one of the old quarters, and our mid-day dinner is waiting."

Curtis smiled grimly. "Thank you, I am on duty. I must dine with Mr. Sennett. Jennie will accept your invitation thankfully."

As Curtis walked over to the agency house with Sennett and his son, Jennie looked anxious. "They may do something to him."

Lawson smiled. "Oh no, they won't. They are quite cowed, but I'll suggest a guard." He turned to Two Horns and said, in Dakota: "Father, the old agent is angry. The new agent is a brave man, but he is only one against two."

"I understand," said the old man, with a smile, and a few minutes later a couple of policemen were sitting on the door-step of the agent's house. It was a sunny place to sit, and they enjoyed being there very much. One of them understood English, and the other was well able to tell an angry word when he heard it spoken.

The drowsy hush of mid-day again settled down upon the little cluster of buildings—news, even when it passes swiftly among Indians, makes no noise. It walks with velvet foot, it speaks in a murmur; it hastens, but conceals its haste.

CHAPTER IV

The Beautiful Elsie Bee Bee

As Jennie entered the mess-house she uttered a little cry of amazement. Outwardly, it was a rude barrack of whitewashed cottonwood logs, but its interior glowed with color and light. Bright rugs were on the floor, and a big divan in one corner displayed a monstrous black bear-skin. A capacious fireplace, which dated back to the first invasion of the army, filled one end of the hall, which had been enlarged by the removal of a partition. Oil-paintings, without frames, were tacked against the walls, and the odor of fresh pigments lingered in the air.

"This is our general meeting-place," explained Lawson.

"It smells like a studio," Jennie replied, after a glance around her.

A plain, quiet little woman, with a look of inquiry on her face, appeared at the dining-room door, and Lawson called out:

"Mrs. Wilcox, this is Miss Curtis, who will stay

with us for a few days." As they greeted each other
he added: "There is a story to tell, but we are late,
and it can wait. Where is Elsie?"

"Still at work. She never *would* come to her meals
if we didn't call her."

"I'm disposed to try it some day. Will you take
charge of Miss Curtis while I go fetch the delin-
quent?"

Under Mrs. Wilcox's direction Jennie prepared for
luncheon in an adjoining room, wondering still at
the unexpected refinement of the furnishings, and
curious to see the artist.

As she re-entered the sitting-room a tall girl rose
languidly to meet her, and Lawson said: "Miss Curtis, this is Miss Brisbane, the painter of the pictures
you see about."

Miss Brisbane bowed in silence, while Jennie
cried out: "Oh! did you do them? I think they are
beautiful!"

The sincerity of her voice touched the young artist, and she said: "I'm glad you like them—
sometimes I think they're pretty 'bum.' "

A slang word on the red lips of the handsome girl
seemed wofully out of place to Jennie, who stared
at her with the eager curiosity of a child. She was
slender and dark, with an exquisite chin, and her
hands, though slim and white, were strong and capable. Her eyes were very dark, of a velvety brown-
black, and her hair was abundant and negligently
piled upon her small head. Altogether she had a
stately and rather foreign presence, which made
Jennie feel very dowdy and very commonplace.

Mrs. Wilcox hurried them all out into the dining-
room, where a pretty table was spread for six people. Jennie's attention was absorbed by the walls,
which were also lightened with sketches of small,
red babies in gay cradles, and of glowing bits of
tawny plain and purple butte.

"Did you do all of these beautiful things?" she asked.

Lawson interposed. "She did, Miss Curtis. Be not deceived. Miss Brisbane's languid manner springs from her theory of rest. When work is finished she 'devitalizes'—I think that is the word—and becomes a rag. But she's a horrible example of industry, spineless as she now appears."

Miss Brisbane remained quite unmoved by Lawson's words; smiling dreamily, her red lips, as serene as those of a child, softly shaped themselves to say: "The strung bow needs relaxation."

"I think you are right," said Jennie, with sudden conviction.

Elsie opened her eyes wide and murmured, "Thank you."

Jennie went on: "Now my trouble is just that. I'm always nerved up. I can't relax. Won't you teach me how?"

"With pleasure. Are you going to live here?" asked Elsie, with faint accession of interest.

"As long as my brother does."

"I suppose you've come to teach these ragamuffins?"

Lawson here answered for Jennie. "Miss Curtis is a sister to Captain Curtis, who has come to displace your uncle."

Miss Brisbane looked up blankly. "I don't understand."

Lawson became explicit, and as she listened the girl's hands clinched.

"How abominable!" she cried, with eyes aflame.

"Not at all. If Mr. Sennett is an honest employé of the government, he should be willing to be searched—if he isn't, then no measure is too harsh. He'll get a thorough raking over, if my impression of the new agent is correct."

"My father would not put a dishonest man in this

place," insisted Elsie, "and I don't believe Uncle Sennett has done wrong."

"Well, now, we'll suspend judgment," retorted Lawson, who knew just when to change his tone. "Captain Curtis is an officer of known ability, and no one can accuse him of prejudice. His living doesn't depend upon pleasing either Mr. Sennett or your father. Undoubtedly the government has good reasons for sending him here, and I for one am willing to accept his judgment."

Elsie rose in swift resolution. "I say it is an outrage! I am going to see that Uncle Sennett is not persecuted."

Lawson laid his hand on her arm and his voice was sternly quiet. "I think you would better finish your tea. Whatever protest you feel called upon to make can be made later. If you like," he added, in a gentler voice, "I will represent you in the matter and go with you to see Captain Curtis during the afternoon. I don't think we should trouble him now."

Elsie resumed her seat without either accepting or rejecting his offer, and the meal continued in some constraint, although Lawson summoned his best humor to cover Elsie's passionate outburst.

A few minutes later Elsie sullenly retired to her studio, and Lawson said: "I am going out to see what is going on, Miss Curtis; please make yourself at home here."

When the door closed behind him Jennie turned to Mrs. Wilcox. "Why does Mr. Lawson use that tone with Miss Brisbane—are they engaged?"

Mrs. Wilcox laughed. "That's just what none of us knows. Sometimes I think they are husband and wife—he lectures her so."

When Curtis joined the mess in the evening he was weary and a little sombre. Vastly preoccupied with his difficult task at the office, he had given but little attention to Jennie's announcement of having been taken into the bosom of an artistic family messing at the barracks, and when Elsie met him in a regal gown, glittering and changeful, he pulled himself up in surprise and admiration.

Elsie, on her part, was eager to see him and ready to do battle, but as he faced her, abrupt, vigorous of movement, keen-eyed and composed—almost stern of countenance—she was a little daunted. He was handsomer than she had expected, and older. His head was impressive, his frame muscular, and his movements graceful. Plainly he was a man of power, one it would be polite to treat with respect.

As they took up their napkins at the table Lawson opened out: "Well, Captain, we don't want to seem inquisitive, but we are dying to know what you've been doing this afternoon. We feel on the outside of it all."

"Yes," Elsie quickly added, "we want to know whether there is to be a revolution, or only a riot."

Curtis turned to her smilingly and replied: "You'll all be disappointed. I've been looking over accounts and holding humdrum audience with my clerks—a very busy but very quiet afternoon—nothing doing, as the phrase goes."

"Where is Uncle Sennett?" inquired Elsie. "I tried to find him, but your men would not let me into the office."

"You shouldn't have tried," interjected Lawson.

"Is he your uncle?" asked Curtis.

"He's my father's sister's husband—but that doesn't matter; I'd defend him if he were a stranger. I think he has been shamefully treated. The idea of searching his private desk!"

Curtis looked at her keenly. "I am under orders," he said. "Mr. Sennett is nothing to me, one way or the other. The question for answer is—has he abused his office?"

"He has not!" exclaimed Elsie. "I *know* he has not. He is not a man to cheat and steal; he is not a strong man, but he is kind and generous."

"Too kind and too generous," muttered Lawson.

"I'm sorry to say that the records are against him," replied Curtis, "and his action is against him. He and his son have gone to Pinon City—riding very like fugitives. I had no orders to hold them; indeed, I was glad to let them go."

Elsie bit her lips. "He has gone to get aid," she said at last, "and when he comes back you will take a different tone with him."

Curtis laughed. "I believe he did say he'd have my hide, or something like that."

Lawson put in a word. "He'll do it, too, if the cattle interest can influence the Secretary. Don't tell us any more than is proper, Captain, but—how do you find his accounts?"

"In very bad shape. The chiefs say he has been holding back rations and turning in bad beef for some time."

"You'd take the word of an Indian against my uncle, or *any* white man, I can see that," said Elsie, in withering scorn.

Curtis turned upon her a most searching glance. "Miss Brisbane, I don't understand your attitude towards me. As a soldier on special duty, detailed almost against my will, I have no prejudice in this affair. It is my duty to see that the treaties of the government are carried out. You seem to think I am started on a line of persecution of your uncle—" he checked himself. "I beg you will not pursue the subject any further." He turned to Lawson with an effort to put aside unpleasant conversation. "Please don't ask me disagreeable questions when I am curious to know the meaning of this artistic invasion of my territory. Who is responsible for these pictures?"

Lawson hastened to explain. "This plague of art-ists is due to me entirely, Captain Curtis. I am doing some studies of the Tetongs, and Miss Brisbane came out to make some illustrations for me. In fact, she suggested coming here rather than to the upper agencies, because of her uncle's presence. Our com-ing brought others."

"I am very glad you came," said Curtis, heartily, "and I will do all in my power to further your work. Please do not allow my coming to change your plans in the slightest degree."

Lawson continued: "Intending to stay some months, we concluded to set up a mess and be comfortable—and permit me to say, we hope you'll eat with us until your own goods arrive."

"Thank you; I accept with pleasure, for I don't en-joy camping in the tent of my angry predecessor—this company is more to my mind."

Elsie's red lips were tremulous with indignation. "You can't blame Mr. Sennett for being angry. You would be if treated in the same way. There is no jus-tice in it. *I* would never have surrendered those keys to you."

Curtis patiently repeated, "My orders were pe-remptory."

"You can't take shelter behind that plea. Your acts are atrocious, and I shall write to my father in Washington and have you investigated." She was beautiful as flame in the glow of her wrath.

Curtis seemed struck with a new idea. "Are you the daughter of ex-Senator Brisbane?"

She braced herself. "Well, suppose I am?"

"Oh, nothing at all—only it explains."

"What does it explain?"

"Your attitude. It is quite natural for a daughter of Andrew Brisbane to take sides against these peo-ple." He was not in a mood to be gallant, and his glance quelled the angry girl.

With flushed face and quivering lips she sprang to her feet. "I will not stay to be insulted," she said.

Curtis rose as she swept from the room, but checked his instinctive words of apology and returned to his seat in silence.

Mrs. Wilcox relieved the painful pause by saying, "Captain Curtis, you must not misjudge Elsie. She is a much better girl than she seems."

Lawson was troubled as he said, "She has lashed herself into a great rage over this affair, but as a matter of fact she don't care a hang for Sennett."

"I can't apologize for doing my duty," said Curtis, "even to Miss Brisbane."

"Certainly not," replied Lawson, though he was deeply hurt by Elsie's display of unreason.

As soon as he decently could, he followed her to her studio, where he found her lying in sullen dejection on the big divan. "Bee Bee, you are missing a good dinner," he began, gently.

She was instantly ready to fight. "I suppose you blame me for this scene."

"I think you are hasty, and a little unreasonable. I know Curtis by reputation, and he is above any petty malice."

"You are taking his side against me!"

"Not at all, Bee Bee, I am merely trying to show you—"

"He looked at me as no man ever dared to look before, and I hate him. He thinks because he has a little authority he can lord it over us all here. I shall write to father at once, telling him just how this little prig of a lieutenant—"

"Captain," interrupted Lawson—"for distinguished service."

His smile made her furious. She flung herself back on the divan. "Go away. I hate you, too."

Lawson, at the end of his patience, went out and

closed the door behind him. "What is the matter with the girl?" he said to Mrs. Wilcox. "I've seen her in temper, but never like this. She has taken the most violent antagonism to Curtis."

"She'd better let that young man alone," replied Mrs. Wilcox, sagely. "He has a very firm mouth."

CHAPTER V

Caged Eagles

THE WORD had gone out among all the Indians that the old agent was entirely "cut off," and that a soldier and a sign-talker had come to take his place, and so each little camp loaded its tepees on wagons or lashed them to the ponies and came flocking in to sit down before the Little Father and be inspired of him.

The young men came first, whirling in on swift ponies, looking at a distance like bands of cowboys—for, though they hated the cattlemen, they formed themselves on Calvin Streeter as a model. Each wore a wide, white hat and dark trousers, and carried a gay kerchief slung round his neck. All still wore moccasins of buckskin, beautifully beaded and fringed, and their braided hair hung low on their breasts.

The old men, who jogged in later in the day, still carried blankets, though they, too, had adopted the trousers and calico shirts of the white man. Several of the chieftains preserved their precious peace-pipes, and their fans and tobacco pouches, as of old, and a few of those who had been in Washington came in wrinkled suits of army-blue. The women dressed in calico robes cut in their own distinctive style, with wide sleeves, the loose flow of the garment being confined at the waist with a girdle. As this was a time of great formality, several of the young girls returned to their buckskin dresses trimmed with elk teeth, which they highly prized.

As a race they were tall and strong, but the men, from much riding, were thin in the shanks and bowed out at the knee. They had lost the fine proportions for which they were famed in the days when they were trailers a-foot. "Straight as an Indian" no longer applied to them, but they were all skilled and picturesque horsemen. Lacking in beauty and strength, they possessed other compensating qualities which still made them most interesting to an artist. Their gestures were unstudiedly graceful, and their roughhewn faces were pleasant in expression. Ill words or dark looks were rare among them.

In all external things they were quite obviously half-way from the tepee to the cabin. Their homes consisted of small hovels of cotton-wood logs, set round with tall tepees and low lodges of canvas, used for dormitories and kitchens in summer. A rack for drying meat rations was a part of each family's possessions. They owned many minute ponies, and their camps abounded in dogs of wolfish breed which they handled not at all, for they were, as of old, merely the camp-guard.

Such were the salient characteristics of the Tetongs, westernmost representatives of a once powerful race of hunters, whose home had been far to the east, in a land of lakes, rivers, and forests. They were not strangers to the young soldier; he knew their history and their habits of thought. He now studied them to detect change and found deterioration. "I am your friend," he said to them each and all. "I come to do you good, to lead you in the new road. It is a strange road to me also, for I, too, am a soldier and a hunter; but together we will learn to make the earth produce meat for our eating. Put your hand in mine."

He was plunged at once into a wilderness of work, but in his moments of leisure the face of Elsie Brisbane came into his thought and her resentment troubled him more than he cared to acknowledge. He well knew that her birth and her training put her in hopeless opposition to all he was planning to do for the Tetongs, and yet he determined to demonstrate to her both the justice and the humanity of his position.

He knew her father's career very well. He had once travelled for two days on the same railway train with him, and remembered him as a boastful but powerful man, whose antagonism no one held in light esteem. Andrew Brisbane had entered the State at a time when its mineral wealth lay undeveloped and free to the taker, and having leagued himself with men less masterly than himself but quite as unscrupulous, had set to work to grasp and hold the natural resources of the great Territory—he laid strong fists upon the mines and forests and grass of the wild land. Once grasped, nothing was ever surrendered.

It mattered nothing to him and his kind that a race of men already lived upon this land and were prepared to die in defence of it. By adroit juggling, he and his corporation put the unsuspecting settler forward to receive the first shock of the battle, and, when trouble came, loudly called upon the government to send its troops "in support of the pioneers." In this way, without danger to himself, the shrewd old Yankee had acquired mineral belts, cattle-ranges, railway rights, and many other good things, and at last, when the Territory was made a State, he became one of its senators.

Naturally, he hated the Indians. They were pestilential because, first of all, they paid no railway charges, and also for the reason that they held the land away from those who would add to his unearned increment and increase the sum total of his tariff receipts. His original plan was broadly simple. "Sweep them from the earth," he snarled, when asked "What will we do with the Indians?" But his policy, modified by men with hearts and a sense of justice, had settled into a process of remorseless removal from point to point, from tillable land to grazing land, from grazing land to barren waste, and from barren waste to arid desert. He had no doubts in these matters. It was good business, and to say a thing was *not* good business was conclusive. The Tetong did not pay—remove him!

Elsie in her home-life, therefore, had been well schooled in race hatred. Tender-hearted where suffering in a dog or even a wolf was concerned, she remained indifferent when a tribe was reported to be starving. Nothing modified her view till, as an art student in Paris, she came into contact with men who placed high value on the Indian as "material." She found herself envied because she had casually looked upon a few of these "wonderful chaps," as Newt Penrose called them, and was often asked to give her impressions of them. When she returned to New York she was deeply impressed by Maurice Stewart's enormous success in sculpturing certain types of this despised race. A little later Wilfred J. Buttes, who had been struggling along as a painter of bad portraits, suddenly purchased a house in a choice suburb on the strength of two summers' work among the mountain Utes.

Thereupon Elsie opened her eyes. Not that money was a lure to her, for it was not, but she was eager for notice—for the fame that comes quickly, and with loud trumpets and gay banners. In conversation with Lawson one day she learned that he was about to do some pen-portraits of noted Tetong chieftains, and at once sprang to her opportunity. She admired and trusted Lawson. His keen judgment, his definiteness of speech awed her a little, and with him she was noticeably less assertive than with the others of her artist acquaintances. So here now she sat, painting with rigor and immense satisfaction the picturesque rags and tinsel ornaments of the Tetongs. To her they were beggars and tramps, on a scale with the lazzaroni of Rome or Naples. That they were anything more than troublesome models had not been borne in on her mind.

She had never professed special regard for her uncle the agent—in fact, she covertly despised him for his lack of power—but, now that the issue was drawn, she naturally flew to the side of those who would destroy the small peoples of the earth. She wrote to her father a passionate letter.

"Can't you stop this?" she asked. "No doubt Uncle Henry will go direct to Washington and make complaint. This Captain Curtis is insufferable. I would leave here instantly only I am bound to do some work for Mr. Lawson. We must all go soon, for winter is coming on, but I would like to see this upstart humbled. He treats me as if I were a schoolgirl—'declines to argue the matter.' Oh! he is provoking. His sister is a nice little thing, but she sides with him, of course—and so does Lawson, in a sense; so you see I am all alone. The settlers are infuriated at Uncle Sennett's dismissal, and will support you and Uncle Henry."

In the days that followed she met Curtis's attempts at modifying her resentment with scornful silence, and took great credit to herself that she did not literally fly at his head when he spoke of his work or his wards. Her avoidance of him became so painful that at the end of the third day he said to his sister: "Jennie, I think I will go to the school mess after this. Miss Brisbane's hostility shows no signs of relenting, and the situation is becoming decidedly unpleasant."

"George!" said Jennie, sternly. "Don't you let that snip drive you away. Why, the thing is ridiculous! She is here on sufferance—your sufferance. You could order them all off the reservation at once."

"I know I could, but I won't. You know what I mean—I can't even let Miss Brisbane know that she has made me uncomfortable. She's a very instructive example of the power of environment. She has all the prejudices and a good part of the will of her father, and represents her class just as a little wild-cat represents its species. She's a beautiful girl, and yet she is to me one of the most unattractive women I ever knew."

Jennie looked puzzled. "You are a little hard on her, George. She *is* unsympathetic, but I think she says a lot of those shocking things just to hurt you."

"That isn't very nice, either," he said, quietly. "Well, our goods are on the way, and by Thursday we'll be independent of any one. But maybe you are right—it would excite comment if I left the mess. I will join you all at meals until we are ready to light our own kitchen fire."

Thereafter he saw very little of the artists. By borrowing a few necessaries of his head farmer he was able to camp down in the house which Sennett had so precipitately vacated. He was busy, very busy, during the day; but when his work was over and he sat beside his fire, pipe in hand, Elsie's haughty face troubled him. His life had not taken him much among women, and his love fancies had been few. His duties as an officer and his researches as a forester and map-builder had also aided to keep him a bachelor. Once or twice he had been disturbed by a fair face at the post, only to have it whisked away again into the mysterious world of happy girlhood whence it came.

And now, at thirty-four, he was obliged to confess that he was as far from marriage as ever—farther, in fact, for an Indian reservation offers but slender opportunity in way of courtship for a man of his exacting tastes.

He was not quite honest with himself, or he would have acknowledged the pleasure he took in watching Elsie's erect and graceful figure as she rode past his office window of a morning. It was pleasant to pause at the open door of her studio for a moment and say "Good-morning," though he received but a cold and formal bow in return. She was more alluring at her easel than in any other place, for she had several curious and very pretty tricks in working, and seemed like a very intent child, with her brown hair loosening over her temples, her eyes glowing with excitement, while she dabbed at the canvas with a piece of cheese-cloth or a crumb of bread. She dragged her stool into position with a quick, amusing jerk, holding her brush in her teeth meanwhile. Her blouses were marvels of odd grace and rich color.

The soldier once or twice lingered in silence at the door after she had forgotten his presence, and each time the glow of her disturbing beauty burned deeper into his heart, and he went away with drooping head.

Mrs. Wilcox took occasion one day to remonstrate with her niece. "Elsie, you were very rude to Captain Curtis again to-day. He was deeply hurt."

"Now, aunt, don't *you* try to convert me to a belief in that tin soldier. He gets on my nerves."

"It would serve you right if he ordered us off the reservation. Your remarks to-day before that young Mr. Streeter were very wrong and very injudicious, and will be used in a bad cause. Captain Curtis is trying to keep the peace here, and you are doing a great deal of harm by your hints of his removal."

"I don't care. I intend to have him removed. I have taken a frightful dislike to him. He is a prig and a hypocrite, and has no business to come in here in this way, setting his low-down Indians up against the settlers."

"That's just what he is trying *not* to do, and if you weren't so obstinate you'd see it and honor him for his good sense."

"Aunt, don't *you* lecture me," cried the imperious girl. "I will not allow it!"

In truth, Mrs. Wilcox's well-meant efforts at peacemaking worked out wrongly. Elsie became insufferably rude to Curtis, and her letters were filled with the bitterest references to him and his work.

Lawson continued most friendly, and Curtis gladly availed himself of the wide knowledge of primitive psychology which the ethnologist had acquired. The subject of Indian education came up very naturally at a little dinner which Jennie gave to the teachers and missionaries soon after she opened house, and Lawson's remarks were very valuable to Curtis. Lawson was talking to the principal of the central school. "We should apply to the Indian problem the law of inherited aptitudes," he said, slowly. "We should follow lines of least resistance. Fifty thousand years of life proceeding in a certain way results in a certain arrangement of brain-cells which can't be changed in a day, or even in a generation. The red hunter, for example, was trained to endure hunger, cold, and prolonged exertion. When he struck a game-trail he never left it. His pertinacity was like that of a wolf. These qualities do not make a market-gardener; they might not be out of place as a herder. We must be patient while the Indian makes the change from the hunter to the herdsman. It is like mulching a young crab-apple and expecting it to bear pippins."

"Patience is an unknown virtue in an Indian agent," remarked the principal of the central school—"present company excepted."

"Do you believe in the allotment?" asked Miss Colson, one of the missionaries for kindergarten work, an eager little woman, aflame with religious zeal.

"Not in its present form," replied Lawson, shortly. "Any attempt to make the Tetong conform to the isolated, dreary, lonesome life of the Western farmer will fail. The Indian is a social being—he is deeply dependent on his tribe. He has always lived a communal life, with the voice of his fellows always in his ears. He loves to sit at evening and hear the chatter of his neighbors. His games, his hunting, his toil, all went on with what our early settlers called a 'bee.' He seldom worked or played alone. His worst punishment was to be banished from the camping circle. Now the Dawes theorists think they can take this man, who has no newspaper, no books, no letters, and set him apart from his fellows in a wretched hovel on the bare plain, miles from a neighbor, there to improve his farm and become a citizen. This mechanical theory has failed in every case; nominally, the Sioux, the Piegans, are living this abhorrent life; actually, they are always visiting. The loneliness is unendurable, and so they will not cultivate gardens or keep live-stock, which would force them to keep at home. If they were allowed to settle in groups of four or five they would do better."

Miss Colson's deep seriousness of purpose was evident in the tremulous intensity of her voice. "If they had the transforming love of Christ in their hearts they would feel no loneliness."

A silence followed this speech; both men mentally shrugged their shoulders, but Jennie came to the rescue.

"Miss Colson, did you ever live on a ranch, miles from any other stove-pipe?"

"No, but I am sure that with God as my helper I could live in a dungeon."

"You should have been a nun," said Lawson. "I don't mind your living alone with Christ, but I think it cruel and unchristian to force your solitary way of life on a sociable Indian. Would Christ do that? Would He insist on shutting the door on their mythology, their nature lore, their dances and ceremonies? Would He not go freely among them, glad of their joy, and condemning only what was hurtful? Is there any record that He ever condemned an innocent pleasure? How do you know but they are as near the Creator's design as the people of Ohio?"

The teacher's pretty face was strained and white, and her wide-set eyes were painful to see. She set her slim hands together. "Oh, I can't answer you now, but I know you are wrong—wickedly wrong!"

Jennie again broke the intensity of the silence by saying: "Two big men against one little woman isn't fair. I object to having the Indian problem settled over cold coffee. Mr. Lawson, stop preaching!"

"Miss Colson is abundantly able to take care of herself," said Slicer, and the other teachers, who had handed over their cause to their ablest advocate, chorused approval.

Curtis, who sat with deeply meditative eyes fixed on Miss Colson, now said: "It all depends on what we are trying to do for these people. Personally, I am not concerned about the future life of my wards. I want to make them healthy and happy, here and now."

"Time's up!" cried Jennie, and led the woman out into the safe harbor of the sitting-room.

After they had lighted their cigars, Lawson said privately to Curtis: "Now there's a girl with too much moral purpose—just as Elsie is spoiled by too little. However, I prefer a wholesome pagan to a morbid Christian."

"It's rather curious," Curtis replied. "Miss Colson is a pretty girl—a very pretty girl; but I can't quite imagine a man being in love with her. What could you do with such inexorable moral purpose? You couldn't put your arm round it, could you?"

"You'd have to hang her up by a string, like one of these toy angels the Dutch put atop their Christmas-trees. The Tetongs fairly dread to see her coming—they think she's deranged."

"I know it—the children go to her with reluctance; she doesn't seem wholesome to them, as Miss Diehl does. And yet I can't discharge her."

"Naturally not! You'd hear from the missionary world. Think of it! 'I find Miss Colson too pious, please take her away.'" Both men laughed at the absurdity of this, and Lawson went on: "I wished a dozen times during dinner that Elsie Bee Bee had been present. It would have given her a jolt to come in contact with such inartistic, unshakable convictions."

"She would have been here, only her resentment towards me is still very strong."

"She has it in for you, sure thing. I can't budge her," said Lawson, smiling. "She's going to have you removed the moment she reaches Washington."

"I have moments when I think I'd like to be removed," said Curtis, as he turned towards Mr. Slicer and his other guests. "Suppose we go into the library, gentlemen."

CHAPTER VI

Curtis Seeks a Truce

"Our artists are going to flit," remarked Jennie, one evening, as they were taking seats at luncheon.

He looked up quickly. "Are they?"

"Yes, Miss Brisbane is going back to Washington, and Mr. Lawson will follow, no doubt."

He unfolded his napkin with unmoved countenance. "Well, they are wise; we are likely to have a norther any day now."

The soldier had all the responsibilities and perplexities he could master without the addition of Elsie Brisbane's disturbing lure. The value of her good opinion was enormously enhanced by the news of her intended departure, and for a day or two Curtis went about his duties with absent-minded ineffectiveness; he even detected himself once or twice sitting with his pen in his hand creating aimless markings on his blotting-pad. Wilson, the clerk, on one occasion waited full five minutes for an answer while his chief debated with himself whether to call upon Miss Brisbane at the studio or at the house. He began to find excuses for her—"A man who is a villain in business may be a very attractive citizen in private life—and she may have been very fond of Sennett. From her point of view—anyhow, she is a lovely young girl, and it is absurd to place her among my enemies." The thought of her face set in bitter scorn against him caused his heart to contract painfully. "I've been too harsh. These people are repugnant to one so dainty and superrefined. There are excuses for her prejudice. I can't let her go away in anger." And in this humble mood he stopped at the door of her studio one morning, prepared to be very patient and very persuasive.

"Good-morning, Miss Brisbane. May I come in?"

"Certainly, if my work will interest you," she replied; "you'll excuse my going on. I want to finish this portrait of Little Peta to-day."

"By all means—I do not intend to interrupt." He took a seat to the front and a little to the left of her, and sat in silence for a few moments. Her brown hair, piled loosely on her head, brought out the exquisite fairness of her complexion, and the big, loose sleeve of her blouse made her hand seem like a child's, but it was strong and steady. She was working with her whole mind, breathing quickly as she mixed her colors, holding her breath as she put her brush against the canvas. She used the apparently aimless yet secure movement of the born painter. With half-closed eyes and head a little to one side, with small hand lifted to measure and compare, she took on a new expression, a bewitching intentness, which quite transformed her.

"I hear you are going away," said Curtis at last, speaking with some effort, uncertain of her temper.

"Yes, we break up and vacate to-morrow."

"Why break up? You will want to come back next spring. Leave the place as it is."

She gave him a quick, keen glance, and put her head again on one side to squint.

"I have no intention of returning."

"Have you exhausted Indian subjects?"

"Oh no!" she exclaimed, with sudden, artistic enthusiasm. "I have just begun to see what I want to do."

"Then why not come back?" She did not reply, and he resumed, with tender gravity: "I hope I haven't made it so unpleasant for you that you are running away to escape *me*?"

She turned with a sharp word on her tongue, but he was so frank and so handsome, and withal so humble, that she instantly relented. She was used to this humility in men and knew the meaning thereof, and a flush of gratified pride rose to her face. The proud soldier had become a suitor like the others.

"Oh no—you have nothing to do with it," she replied, carelessly.

"I am glad of that. I was afraid you might think me unsympathetic, but I am not. I am here this morning to offer you my cordial assistance, for I am eager to see this people put into art. So far as I know, they have never been adequately treated in painting or in sculpture."

"Thank you," she said, "I don't think I shall go very far with them. They are very pleasant on canvas, but there are too many disagreeable things connected with painting them. I don't see how you endure the thought of living here among them." She shuddered. "I hate them!"

"I don't understand that hardness in you, Miss Brisbane," he replied.

"I'm sure it isn't mysterious. I hate dirt and rags, even when painted. Now Little Peta here is quite different. She is a dear little thing. See her sigh—she gets so tired, but she's patient."

"You are making a beautiful picture of her. Your skill is marvellous." His method of approach was more adroit than he realized; she softened yet again.

"Thank you. I seem to have hit her off very well."

"Will you exhibit in Washington this winter?" he asked, with boyish eagerness.

"I may—I haven't quite decided," she said, quite off guard at last.

"If you do I wish you would let me know. I may be able to visit the exhibition and witness your triumph."

She began to suspect his motives. "Oh, my little row of paintings couldn't be tortured into a triumph. I've stolen the time for them from Mr. Lawson, whose illustrations I have neglected." She was again cold and repellent.

"Miss Brisbane, this whole situation has become intolerable to me." He rose and faced her, very sincere and deeply earnest. "I do not like to have you go away carrying an unpleasant impression of me. What can I do to change it? If I have been boorish or presuming in any way I sincerely beg your pardon."

She motioned to Peta. "You can go now, dear, I've done all I can to-day."

Curtis took up his hat. "I hope I have not broken up your sitting. It would be unpardonable in me."

She squinted back at the picture with professional gravity. "Oh no; I only had a few touches to put in under the chin—that luminous shadow is so hard to get. I'm quite finished."

She went behind a screen for a few moments, and when she reappeared without her brushes and her blouse she was the society young lady in tone and manner.

"Would you like to look at my sketches?" she asked. "They're jolly rubbish, the whole lot, but they represent a deal of enthusiasm."

Her tone was friendly—too friendly, considering the point at which he had paused, and he was a little hurt by it. Was she playing with him?

His tone was firm and his manner direct as he said: "Miss Brisbane, I am accustomed to deal directly with friends as well as enemies, and I like to have people equally frank with me. I know you are angry because of my action in the case of your uncle. I do not ask pardon for that; I was acting there in line of my duty: But if I have spoken harshly or without due regard to your feelings at any time I ask you to forgive me."

He made a powerful appeal to her at this moment, but she willfully replied: "You made no effort to soften my uncle's disgrace."

"I didn't know he was your uncle at that time," he said, but his face grew grave quickly. "It would have made no difference if I had—my orders were to step between him and the records of the office. So far as my orders enlightened me, he was a man to be watched." He turned towards the door. "Is there anything I can do to help you reach the station tomorrow? My sister and I would gladly drive you down."

She was unrelenting, but very lovely as she replied: "Thank you; you are very kind, but all arrangements are made."

"Good-afternoon, Miss Brisbane."

"Good-bye, Captain Curtis."

"She is hard—hard as iron," he said, as he walked away. "Her father's daughter in every fibre."

He was ashamed to acknowledge how deeply he felt her rejection of his friendship, and the thought of not seeing her again gave him a sudden sense of weakness and loneliness.

Elsie, on her part, was surprised to find a new nerve tingling in her brain, and this tremor cut into the complete self-satisfaction she expected to feel over her refusal of the peace-pipe. Several times during the afternoon, while superintending her packing, she found herself standing in an attitude of meditation—her inward eye reverting to the fine, manly figure he made, while his grave, sweet voice vibrated in her ears. She began to see herself in an unpleasant light, and when at the dinner-table Lawson spoke of Curtis, she listened to him with more real interest than ever before.

"He is making wonderful changes here," Lawson was saying. "Everywhere you go you see Tetongs working at fence-building, bridge-making, cabin-raising, with their eagle feathers fluttering in the winds, their small hands chapped with cold. They are sawing boards and piling grain in the warehouse and daubing red paint on the roofs. They are in a frenzy of work. Every man has his rations and is happy. In some way he has persuaded the chiefs to bring in all the school-children, and the benches are full of the little ones, wild as colts."

"A new broom, etc.," murmured Elsie.

"His predecessor never was a new broom," retorted Lawson, quickly. "Sennett always had a nasty slaunch to him. He never in his life cleaned the dirt from the corners, and I don't see exactly why you take such pains in defending him."

"Because he is my uncle," she replied.

"Uncle Boot-jack! That is pure fudge, Bee Bee. You didn't speak to him once a week; you privately despised him—anybody could see that. You are simply making a cudgel of him now to beat Curtis with—and, to speak plainly, I think it petty of you. More than this, you'd better hedge, for I'm not at all sure that Sennett has not been peculating."

Elsie stopped him with an angry gesture. "I'll not have you accusing him behind his back."

Lawson threw out his hands in a gesture of despair. "All right! But make a note of it: you'll regret this taking sides with a disreputable old bummer against an officer of Captain Curtis's reputation."

"You are not my master!" she said, and her eyes were fiercely bright. "I do not wish to hear you use that tone to me again! I resent it!" and she struck the floor with her foot. "Henceforth, if we are to remain friends, you will refrain from lecturing me!" and she left the room with a feeling of having done two men a wrong by being unjust to herself, and this feeling deepened into shame as she lay in her bed that night. It was her first serious difference with Lawson and she grew unhappy over it. "But he shouldn't take sides against me like that," she said, in an attempt to justify her anger.

On the second morning thereafter Lawson came into the office and said: "Well, Captain, we leave you this morning."

Curtis looked up into his visitor's fine, sensitive face, and exclaimed, abruptly—almost violently: "I'm going to miss you, old man."

"My heart's with you," replied Lawson. "And I shall return next spring."

"Bring Miss Brisbane with you."

"I'd like to do so, but she is vastly out of key—and I doubt. Meanwhile, if I can be of any use to you in Washington let me know."

"Thank you, Lawson, I trust you perfectly," Curtis replied, with a glow of warm liking.

As he stood at the gate looking up into Elsie's face, she seemed very much softened, and he wished to reach his hand and stay her where she sat; but the last word was spoken, and the wagon rolled away with no more definite assurance of her growing friendship than was to be read in a polite smile.

Jennie was tearful as she said: "After all, they were worth while."

Curtis sighed as he said: "Sis, the realities of our position begin to make themselves felt. Play-spells will be fewer now that our artists are gone."

"They certainly broke our fall," replied Jennie, soberly. "Osborne Lawson is fine, and I don't believe Elsie Bee Bee is as ferocious as she pretends to be."

"It's her training. She has breathed the air of rapacity from childhood. I can't blame her for being her father's child."

Jennie looked at him as if he were presented from a new angle of vision. "George, there *is* a queer streak in you—for a soldier; you're too soft-hearted. But don't you get too much interested in Elsie Bee Bee; she's dangerous—and, besides, Mr. Lawson wears an air of command."

CHAPTER VII

Elsie Relents a Little

THE FEELING against the redmen, intensified throughout the State by the removal of Sennett, beat against Curtis like a flood. Delegations of citizens, headed by Streeter and Johnson, proceeded at once to Washington, laden with briefs, affidavits and petitions, and there laid siege to Congress as soon as the members began to assemble. The twenty original homesteaders were taken as the text for most impassioned appeals by local orators, and their melancholy situation was skilfully enlarged upon. They were described as hardy and industrious patriots, hemmed in by sullen savages, with no outlet for trade and scant pasturage for their flocks—in nightly fear of the torch and the scalping-knife.

To Curtis, these settlers were by no interpretation martyrs in the cause of civilization—they were quite other. His birth, his military training, and his natural refinement tended to make him critical of them. They were to him, for the most part, "poor whites," too pitiless to be civilized, and too degenerate to have the interest of their Indian neighbors. "The best of them," he said to Jennie, "are foolhardy pioneers who have exiled their wives and children for no good reason. The others are cattlemen who followed the cavalry in order to fatten their stock under the protection of our guidon."

The citizens of Pinon City wondered why their delegates made so little impression on the department, but Streeter was not left long in doubt.

The Secretary interrupted him in the midst of his first presentation of the matter.

"Mr. Streeter, you are a cattleman, I believe?"

Streeter looked a little set back. "I am—yes, sir, Mr. Secretary."

The Secretary took up a slip of paper. "Are you the Streeter located on the reservation itself?"

"Yes, sir."

"Well, you are an interested witness. How can you expect me to take your word against that of Captain Curtis? He tells me the Tetongs are peaceful, and quick to respond to fair treatment. The department has absolute confidence in Captain Curtis, and you are wasting time in the effort to discredit him. The tribe will *not* be removed. Is there any other question you would like to raise?"

Streeter took his dismissal hard. He hurried at once to Brisbane, his face scarlet with rage. "He turned me down," he snarled, "and he's got to suffer for it. There's a way to get at him, and you must find it."

Brisbane was too crafty to promise any definite thing. "Now wait a minute, neighbor; never try to yank a badger out of his den—wait and watch him on the open plain. We must sound the Committee on Indian Affairs, and then move on the House. If we can't put through our removal bill we'll substitute the plan for buying out the settlers. If that don't work I've a little scheme for cutting down the reservation. We must keep cool—and don't mention my name in the matter. What we want to do is to pave the way for my return to the Senate next fall; then I can be of some real service to you. I am now entirely out of it, as you can see, but I'll do what I can."

Streeter went away with a feeling that Brisbane was losing his vigor, and a few days later returned to the West, very bitter and very inflammatory of speech. "The bill is lost. It will be smothered in committee," he said to Calvin.

Brisbane, after leaving Streeter that day, went home to dinner with an awakened curiosity to know more about this young man in whom the department had such confidence. Lawson was dining at his table that night, and it occurred to him to ask a little more fully about Curtis.

"See here, Lawson, you were out there on the Fort Smith reservation, weren't you? Wasn't that where you and Elsie camped this summer?"

Elsie replied, "Yes, papa. We were there when Uncle Sennett was dismissed."

Brisbane started a little. "Why, of course you were; my memory is failing me. Well, what about this man Curtis—he's a crank on the Indian question, like yourself, isn't he?"

Lawson smiled. "We believe in fair play, Governor. Yes, he's friendly to the Indians."

· "And a man of some ability, I take it?"

"A man of unusual ability. He is an able forester, a well-read ethnologist, and has made many valuable surveys for the War Department."

"His word seems to have great weight with the department."

"Justly, too, for he is as able a man as ever held an agent's position. A few men like Curtis would solve the Indian problem."

Elsie, who had been listening in meditative silence, now spoke. "Nevertheless, his treatment of Uncle Sennett was brutal. He arrested him and searched all his private papers—don't you remember?"

Brisbane looked at Lawson solemnly and winked the eye farthest from his daughter. Lawson's lips quivered with his efforts to restrain a smile. Turning then to Elsie, Brisbane said: "I recall your story now—yes, he was pretty rigorous, but I'm holding up the department for that; the agent wasn't to blame. He was sent there to do that kind of a job, and from all accounts he did it well."

Elsie lifted her eyebrows. "Does that excuse him? He kept repeating to me that he was under orders, but I took his saying so to be just a subterfuge."

"Mighty little you know about war, my girl. To be a soldier means to obey orders from general down to corporal. Moreover, your uncle has given me a whole lot of trouble, and I wouldn't insist on a relationship which does us no credit. I've held his chin above water about as long as I'm going to."

Elsie was getting deeper into the motives and private opinions of her father than ever before, and as he spoke, her mind reverted to the handsome figure of the young soldier as he stood before her in the studio, asking for a kindlier good-bye. His head was really beautiful, and his eyes were deep and sincere. She looked up at her father with frowning brows. "I thought you liked Mr. Sennett? He told me you got him his place."

Brisbane laughed. "My dear chicken, he was a political choice. He was doing work for our side, and had to be paid."

"Do you mean you knew the kind of a man he was when you put him there?"

Brisbane pulled himself up short. "Now see here, my daughter, you're getting out of your bailiwick."

"But I want to understand—if you knew he was stealing—"

"I didn't know it. How should I know it? I put him there to keep him busy. I didn't suppose he was a sot and a petty plunderer. Now let's have no more of this." Brisbane was getting old and a trifle irritable, but he was still master of himself. "I don't know why I should be taken to task by my own daughter."

Elsie said no more, but her lips straightened and her eyes grew reflective. As the coffee and cigars came in, she left the two men at the table and went out into the music-room. It seemed very lonely in the big house that night, and she sat down at the piano to play, thinking to cure herself of an uneasy conscience. She was almost as good a pianist as a painter, and the common criticism of her was on this score. "Bee does everything *too* well," Penrose said.

She played softly, musingly, and, for some reason, sadly. "I wonder if I have done him an injustice?" she thought. And then that brutal leer on her father's face came to disturb her. "I wish he hadn't spoken to me like that," she said. "I don't like his political world. I wish he would get out of it. It isn't nice."

In the end, she left off playing and went slowly up to her studio, half determined to write a little of apology. Her "work-shop," which had been added to the house since her return from Paris, was on a level with her sitting-room, which served as a reception hall to the studio itself. Her artist friends declared it to be too beautiful to work in, and so it seemed, for it was full of cosey corners and soft divans—a glorious lounging-place. Nevertheless, its walls were covered with pictures of her own making. Costly rugs and a polished floor seemed not to deter her from effort. She remained a miracle of industry in spite of the scoffing of her fellows, who were stowed about the city in dusty lofts like pigeons.

'Proud and wilful as she seemed, Elsie had always prided herself on being just, and to be placed in the position of doing an honorable man a wrong was intolerable. The longer she dwelt upon her action the more uneasy she became. Her vision clarified. All that had been hidden by her absurd prejudice and reasonless dislike—the soldier's frank and manly firmness, Lawson's reproaches, her aunt's open reproof—all these grew in power and significance as she mused.

Taking a seat at her desk, she began a letter, "Captain Curtis, Dear Sir—" But this seemed so palpably a continuance of her repellent mood that she tore it up, and started another in the spirit of friendliness and contrition which had seized upon her:

"DEAR CAPTAIN CURTIS,—I have just heard something which convinces me that I have done you an injustice, and I hasten to beg your pardon. I knew my uncle Sennett only as a child knows a man of middle age—he was always kind and good and amusing to me. I had no conception of his real self. My present understanding of him has changed my feeling towards your action. I still think you were harsh and unsympathetic, but I now see that you were simply doing the will of the department. So far I apologize. If you come to Washington I hope you will let us know."

As she re-read this it seemed to be a very great concession indeed; but as she recalled the handsome, troubled face of the soldier, she decided to send it, no matter what he might think of her. As she sealed the letter her heart grew lighter, and she smiled.

When she re-entered the library her father was

saying: "No, I don't expect to get him removed. The present administration and its whole policy must be overthrown. Curtis is only a fly on the rim of the wheel. He don't count."

"Any man counts who is a moral force," Lawson replied, with calm sincerity. "Curtis will bother you yet."

CHAPTER VIII

Curtis Writes a Long Letter

THE STAGE-DRIVER and mail-carrier to Fort Smith was young Crane's Voice, and this was his first trip in December. He congratulated himself on having his back to the wind on the fifty-mile ride up the valley. A norther was abroad over the earth, and, sweeping down from arctic wildernesses, seemingly gathered power as it came. It crossed two vast States in a single night and fell upon the Fort Smith reservation with terrible fury about ten o'clock in the morning.

Crane's Voice did not get his mail-sack till twelve, but his ponies were fed and watered and ready to move when the bag came. He did not know that it contained a letter to warm the heart of his hero, the Captain, but he flung the sack into his cart and put stick to his broncos quite as manfully as though the Little Father waited. The road was smooth and hard and quite level for thirty miles, and he intended to cover this stretch in five hours. Darkness would come early, and the snow, which was hardly more than a frost at noon, might thicken into a blizzard. So he pushed on steadily, fiercely, silently, till a sinister dusk began to fall over the buttes, and then, lifting his voice in a deep, humming, throbbing incantation, he sang to keep off spirits of evil.

Crane's Voice was something of an aristocrat. As the son of Chief Elk he had improved his opportunities to learn of the white man, and could speak a little English and understand a good deal more than he acknowledged, which gave him a startling insight at times into the words and actions of the white people. It was his report of the unvarying kindliness and right feeling of Captain Curtis which had done so much to make the whole tribe trust and obey the new agent.

Crane's Voice was afraid of spirits, but he shrank from no hardship. He was proud of his blue uniform, and of the revolver which he was permitted to wear to guard the mail. No storm had ever prevented him from making his trip, and his uncomplaining endurance of heat, cold, snow, and rain would have been counted heroic in a military scout. His virtues were so evident even to the cowboys that they made him an exception by saying, "Yes, Crane is purty near one of us," and being besotted in their own vanity, they failed to see the humor of such a phrase in the mouth of a drunken, obscene, lawless son of a Missouri emigrant. As a matter of fact there were many like Crane in the tribe, only the settlers never came in personal contact with them.

Crane found his road heavy with drifts as he left the main valley and began to climb, and he did not reach the agency till long after Curtis had gone to bed, but he found his anxious mother waiting for him, together with the captain of police, who took the bag of mail to the office. As he drove into the big corral out of the wind the boy said, in his quaint

English: "Me no like 'um blizzard. Fleeze ears like buffalo horn."

Curtis came to the office next morning with a heavy heart. He knew how hard the bitter cold pressed upon his helpless wards, and suffered acutely for sympathy. He spoke to all of those he met with unusual tenderness, and asked minutely after the children, to be sure that none were ill or hungry.

As Wilson, his clerk, laid the big package of letters and papers on his table, the pale-blue, square envelope which bore Elsie's handwriting was ostentatiously balanced on top. Wilson, the lovelorn clerk, sighed to think he had no such missive in his mail that gloomy morning. Looking in, a half-hour later, he found Curtis writing busily in answer to that letter, all the rest of his mail being untouched. "I thought so," said he; "I'd neglect any business for a sweet little envelope like that," and he sighed again.

Curtis had opened the letter eagerly, but with no expectation of comfort. As he read he forgot the storm outside. A warm glow crept into his blood. Lover-like, he got from the letter a great deal more than Elsie had intended to say. He seized his pen to reply at once—just a few lines to set her mind at rest; but his thought ran on so fast, so full of energy, that his writing became all but illegible:

"DEAR MISS BRISBANE,—You have given me a great pleasure by your letter, and I am replying at once to assure you that I did not lay your words up against you, because I felt you did not fully understand the situation. Your letter gives me courage to say that I think you are unjust in your attitude towards these people—and I also hope that as fuller understanding comes you will change your views.

"Here they are, fenced in on the poorest part of

this bleak reservation, on the cold slope of the range, exposed to the heat and drought of summer and the storms of winter. This morning, for example, the wind is rushing up the converging walls of this valley—which opens out to the northeast, you remember—and the cold is intense. I am just sending out messengers to see that no children are freezing. Everything is hard as iron, and the Indians, muffled in their blankets, are sitting beside their fires glum as owls, waiting the coming of the sunshine.

"I must tell you something which happened since you went away—it may correct your views of the Tetongs. It is my policy to give all hauling and wood contracts to the Indian instead of the white man, and when I told the white who has been putting in the wood that I was about to let the contract to the reds he laughed and said, 'You can't get 'em to do that work!' But I felt sure I could. I called them together and gave them fifty axes and told them how much wood I wanted. A few days later I thought I'd ride over to see how they were getting along. As I drew near I heard the most astonishing click-clack of axe-strokes, shouts, laughter, the falling of trees, and when I came in sight I 'trun up both hands.' They had hundreds of cords already cut—twice as much, it seemed, as I could use. I begged them to stop, and finally got them to begin to haul. In the end I was obliged to take sixty cords more than I needed.

"You cannot understand what a pleasure it is for me to see ancient lies about these people destroyed by such experiences as this. It was pathetic to me to find the Two Horns, the Crawling Elk, and other proud old warriors toiling awkwardly with their axes, their small hands covered with blisters; but they laughed and joked about it, and encouraged each other as if they were New-Englanders at a husking-bee. My days and nights are full of trouble, because I can do so little for them. If they were on tillable land I could make them self-supporting in two years, but this land is arid as a desert. It is fair to look upon, but it will not yield a living to any one but a herder.

"Your attitude towards the so-called *savage* races troubles me more than I have any right to mention. The older I grow the less certain I am that any race or people has a monopoly of the virtues. I do not care to see the 'little peoples' of the world civilized in the sense in which the word is commonly used. It will be a sorrowful time to me when all the tribes of the earth shall have cottonade trousers and derby hats. You, as an artist, ought to shrink from the dead level of utilitarian dress which the English-speaking race seems determined to impose on the world. If I could, I would civilize only to the extent of making life easier and happier—the religious beliefs, the songs, the native dress—all these things I would retain. What is life for, if not for this?

"My artist friends as a rule agree with me in these matters, and that is another reason why your unsympathetic attitude surprises and grieves me. I know your home-life has been such as would prejudice you against the redman, but your training in Paris should have changed all that. You consider the Tetongs 'good material'—if you come to know them as I do you will find they are *folks*, just like anybody else, with the same rights to the earth that we have. Of course, they *are* crude and unlovely—and sometimes they are cruel; but they have an astonishing power over those who come to know them well.

"Pardon this long letter. You may call me a crank or any hard name you please, but I am anxious to have you on the right side of this struggle, for it is a struggle to the death. The tragedy of their certain extinction overwhelms me at times. I found a little scrap of canvas with a sketch of Peta on it—may I keep it? My sister is quite well and deep in 'the work.' She often speak of you and we are both hoping to see you next year."

It was foolish for him to expect an immediate reply to this epistle, but he did—he counted the days which lay between its posting and a possible date for return mail. Perhaps, had he been in Washington, diverted by Congress, cheered by the Army and Navy Club, and entertained by his friends, he would not have surrendered so completely to the domination of that imperious girl-face; but in the dead of winter, surrounded by ragged, smoky squaws and their impatient, complaining husbands, with no companionship but his sister and Wilson, the love-sick clerk, his thought in every moment of relaxation went back to the moments he had spent in Elsie's company. Nature cried out, "It is not good for man to be alone," but the iron ring of circumstance held him a prisoner in a land where delicate women were as alien as orange blossoms or tea-roses.

Outwardly composed, indefatigable, stern in discipline and judicial of report, he was inwardly filled with a mighty longing to see again that slim young girl with the big, black, changeful eyes. He made careful attempt to conceal his growing unrest from Jennie, but her sharp eyes, accustomed to every change in his face, detected a tremor when Elsie's name was mentioned, and her ears discovered a subtle vibration in his voice which instructed her, though she did not attain complete realization of his absorbing interest. She was sympathetic enough to search out Elsie's name in the social columns of the Washington papers, and it was pitiful to see with what joy the busy Indian agent listened to the brief item concerning "Miss Brisbane's reception on

Monday," or the description of her dress at the Mc-
Cartney ball.

Jennie sighed as she read of these brilliant assem-
blages. "George, I wonder if we will ever spend
another winter in Washington?"

"Oh, I think so, sis—some time."

"Some time! But we'll both be so old we won't enjoy it. Sometimes I feel that we are missing everything that's worth while."

He did not mention Elsie's letter, and as the
weeks passed without any reply he was very glad
he had kept silence. Jennie had her secret, also,
which was that Elsie was as good as engaged to
Lawson. No one knew this for a certainty, but Mrs.
Wilcox was quite free to say she considered it a settled thing.

Jennie was relieved to know how indifferent her
brother was to Miss Colson, the missionary, who
seemed to be undergoing a subtle transformation.
With Jennie she was always moaning and sighing,
but in the presence of her lord, the agent, she relaxed and became quite cheerful and dangerously
pretty. The other teachers—good, commonplace
souls!—went their mechanical way, with very little
communication with the agent's household, but
Miss Colson seized every opportunity to escape her
messmates. "They are so material," she said,
sighfully; "they make spiritual growth impossible to
me."

Jennie was not deceived. "You're a cat, that's
what you are—a nice, little, scared cat; but you're
getting over your scare," she added, as she watched
the devotee in spirited conversation with her
brother.

Elsie's reply to Curtis's long letter was studiedly
cool but polite. "I feel the force of what you say, but
the course of civilization lies across the lands of the
'small peoples.' It is sorrowful, of course, but they

must go, like the wolves and the rattlesnakes." In this phrase he recognized the voice of Andrew J. Brisbane, and it gave him a twinge to see it written by Elsie's small hand. The letter ended by leaving matters very adroitly at an equipoise. It was friendlier than she had ever been in conversation, yet not so womanly as he had hoped it might be. As he studied it, however, some subtler sense than sight detected in its carefully compounded phrases something to feed upon, and though he did not write in answer to it, he had a feeling that she expected him to do so.

Meanwhile the tone of the opposition grew confident. The settlers were convinced that Congress would accede to their wishes and remove the Tetongs, and they began to treat the redmen with a certain good-natured tolerance, as if to say, "Well, you'll soon be settled for, anyway."

Calvin Streeter came often to the agency, and not infrequently stayed to dinner with Curtis, paying timid court to Jennie, who retained enough of her girlhood's coquetry to enjoy the handsome cowboy's open-eyed admiration, even though she laughed at him afterwards in response to her brother's jesting. Calvin vastly improved under the stress of his desire to be worthy of her. He caught up many of the Captain's nice mannerisms, and handled his fork and napkin with very good grace indeed. He usually came galloping across the flat, his horse outstretched at full speed, his hat-rim uprolled by the wind, his gay neckerchief fluttering, his hands holding the reins high—a magnificent picture of powerful young manhood. As he reached the gate it was his habit to put his horse on his haunches with one sudden, pitiless wrench on the Mexican bit and drop to the ground, and in dramatic contrast with his approach call out in smooth, quiet voice:

"Howdy, folks, howdy! Nice day."

These affections pleased Jennie very much, though she finally complained of his cruelty in reining in his horse so sharply.

"All right, miss, I won't do it no more," he said, instantly.

He quite regularly invited them to the dances given round about, and Jennie was ready to go, but Curtis, being too deeply occupied, could not spare the time, and that debarred Jennie, though Calvin could see no good reason why it should. "I'll take care of you," he said, but the girl could not trust herself to his protection.

His was not a secretive nature, and he kept Curtis very well informed as to the feeling of the settlers, reporting, as he did, their conversations as well as their speeches, with great freedom and remarkable accuracy.

In this way the agent learned that the cattlemen had agreed to use caution in dealing with him. "He's a bad man to monkey with," was the sentiment Calvin reported to be current among the settlers on the West Fork. Young Crane's Voice also circulated this phrase, properly translated into Dakota, to his uncles Lame Paw and Two Horns, and so the tribe came to understand that they had a redoubtable defender in Swift Eagle, as they called the agent in their own tongue.

From every source they heard good things of him, and they came to love him and to obey him as they had never loved and obeyed even their best-regarded chief. The squaws made excuse to come in and shake hands with him and hear his laughter, and the children no longer hid or turned away when he came near—on the contrary, they ran to him, crying "Hello, Hagent!" and clung to his legs as he walked. The old men often laid their arms across his shoulders as they jokingly threatened to pull out the hairs of his face, in order to make him a redman. His lightest wish was respected. The wildest young dare-devil would dismount and take a hand at pushing a wagon or lifting a piece of machinery when Curtis asked it of him.

"If I only had the water that flows in these three little streams," he often said to Jennie, "I'd make these people self-supporting."

"We'll have things our own way yet," replied Jennie, always the optimist.

CHAPTER IX

Called to Washington

ONE DAY Curtis announced, with joyful face: "Sis, we are called to Washington. Get on your bonnet!"

She did not light up as he had expected her to do. "I can't go, George," she replied, decisively and without marked disappointment.

He seemed surprised. "Why not?"

"Because I have my plans all laid for giving my little 'Ingines' such a Christmas as they never had, and you must manage to get back in time to be 'Sandy Claws.'"

"I don't see how I can do it. I am to appear before the Committee on Indian Affairs relative to this removal plan, and there may be other business requiring me to remain over the holidays."

"I don't like to have you away. I suppose you'll see Mr. Lawson and Miss Brisbane," she remarked, quietly, after a pause.

"Oh yes," he replied, with an assumption of carelessness. "I imagine Lawson will appear before the committee, and I hope to call on Miss Brisbane—I want to see her paintings." He did not meet his sister's eyes as squarely as was his wont, and her keen glance detected a bit more color in his face than was usual to him. "You must certainly call," she finally said. "I want to know all about how they live."

Many things combined to make this trip to Washington most pleasurable to the soldier. He was weary with six weeks of most intense application to a confused and vexatious situation, and besides he had not been East for several years, and his pocket was filled with urgent invitations to dinner from fellow-officers and co-workers in science, courtesies which he now had opportunity to accept; but back of all and above all was the hope of meeting Elsie Brisbane again. He immediately wrote her a note, telling her of his order to report at the department, and asking permission to call upon her at her convenience.

It was a long ride, but he enjoyed every moment of it. He gave himself up to rest. He went regularly to his meals in the dining-car; he smoked and dreamed and looked out with impersonal, shadowy interest upon the flying fields and the whizzing cities. He slept long hours and rose at will. Such freedom he had known only on the trail; here luxury was combined with leisure. In Chicago a friend met him and they lunched at a luxurious club, and afterwards went for a drive. That night he left the Western metropolis behind and Washington seemed very near.

As the train drew down out of the snows of the hill country into the sunshine and shelter of the Potomac Valley his heart leaped. This was home! Here were the little, whitewashed cabins, the red soil, the angular stone houses—verandaed and shuttered—of his native town. It was pleasant to meet the dark-skinned porters swarming around the train. They shadowed forth a warmer clime, a less insistent civilization than that of the West, and he was glad of them. They brought up in his mind a thousand memories of his boy-life in an old Maryland village not far from the great city, which still retained its supremacy in his mind. He loved Washington; to him it was the centre of national life.

The great generals, the great political leaders were there, and the greatest ethnologic bureau in all the world was there, and when the gleaming monument came into view over the wooded hills he had only one regret—he was sorrowful when he thought of Jennie far away in the bleak valley of the Elk.

It was characteristic of him that he took a cab to the Smithsonian Society rather than to the Army and Navy Club, and was made at home at once in the plain but comfortable "rooms of the Bug Sharps." He had just time to report by telephone to the Department of the Interior before the close of the official day. Several letters awaited him. One was from Elsie, and this he read at once, finding it unexpectedly cordial:

"My father is writing you an invitation to come to us immediately. You said you would arrive in Washington on the 17th, either on the 11 a.m. train or the one at 3 p.m. In either case we will look for you at 6:30 to dine with us before you get your calendar filled with engagements. I shall wait impatiently to hear how you are getting on out there. It is all coming to have a strange fascination for me. It is almost like a dream."

This letter quickened his pulse in a way which should have brought shame to him, but did not. The Senator's letter was ponderously polite. "I hope, my dear Captain Curtis, you will be free to call at once. My daughter and Lawson—"

At that word a chill wind blew upon the agent's hope. Lawson! "I had forgotten the man!" he said, almost aloud. "Ah! that explains her frank kindliness. She writes as one whose affections are engaged, and therefore feel secure from criticism or misapprehension." That explained also her feeling for the valley—it was the scene of her surrender to Lawson. The tremor went out of his nerves, his heart resumed its customary beating, steady and calm, and, setting his lips into a straight line, he resumed the Senator's letter, which ended with these significant words: "There are some important matters I want to talk over in private."

A note from Lawson urged him to take his first breakfast in the city with him. "I want to post you on the inside meaning of certain legislation now pending. I expect to see you at the Brisbanes'."

Curtis made his toilet slowly and with great care, remitting nothing the absence of which would indicate a letting down of military neatness and discipline. He wore the handsome undress uniform of a captain, and his powerful figure, still youthful in its erectness, although the lines were less slender than he wished, was dignified and handsome—fit to be taken as a type of mature soldier. He set forth, self-contained but eager.

The Brisbane portico of rose granite was immensely imposing to a dweller in tents and cantonments, such as Curtis had been for ten years, but he allowed no sign of his nervousness to appear as he handed his overcoat and cap to the old black man in the vestibule.

As he started down the polished floor of the wide hall, stepping over a monstrous tiger-skin, he saw Elsie in the door of the drawing-room, her back against the folded portière. Her slender figure was exquisitely gowned in pale-green, and her color was iridescent in youthful sparkle. He thought once again—"Evening dress transforms a woman." She met him with a smile of welcome.

"Ah, Captain, this is very good of you, to come to us so soon."

"Not at all," he gallantly replied. "I would have come sooner had opportunity served."

"Father, this is Captain Curtis," she said, turning her head towards a tall man who stood within.

Brisbane came forward, greeting Curtis most cordially. He was grayer than Curtis remembered him, and a little stooping from age. His massive head was covered with a close-clipped bristle of white hair, and his beard, also neatly trimmed, was shaped to a point, from the habit he had of stroking it with his closed left hand in moments of deep thought. His skin was flushed pink with blood, and his urbane manner denoted pride and self-sufficiency. He was old, but he was still a powerful personality, and though he shook hands warmly, Curtis felt his keen and penetrating glance as palpably as an electric shock.

Lawson's voice arose. "Well, Captain, I hardly expected to see you so soon."

As the two men clasped hands Elsie again closely compared them. Curtis was the handsomer man, though Lawson was by no means ill-looking, even by contrast. The soldier more nearly approached the admirable male type, but there was charm in the characteristic attitudes and gestures of the student, who had the assured and humorous manner of the onlooker.

A young woman of indeterminate type who was seated in conversation with Mrs. Wilcox received Curtis with impassive countenance, eying him closely through pinch-nose glasses. Mrs. Wilcox beamed with pleasure, and inquired minutely concerning the people at the agency, and especially she wished to know how little Johnny and Jessie Eagle were. "I quite fell in love with the tots, they were so cunning. I hope they got the toys I sent."

Brisbane gave Curtis the most studious attention, lounging deep in his big chair. Occasionally he ponderously leaned forward to listen to some remark, with his head cocked in keen scrutiny—actions which did not escape the Captain's notice. "He's sizing me up," he thought. "Well, let him."

Elsie also listened, curiously like her father in certain inclinations of the head—intent, absorbed; only Lawson seemed indifferent to the news the agent guardedly recited.

Brisbane broke his silence by saying: "I infer you're on the side of the Indian?"

"Decidedly, in this connection."

"Quite aside from your duty?"

"Entirely so. My duty in this case happened to be my inclination. I could have declined the detail, but being a believer in the army's arrangement of Indian affairs, I couldn't decently refuse."

Brisbane settled back into his chair and looked straight at his visitor.

"You think the white man the aggressor in this land question?"

Curtis definitely pulled himself up. "I am not at liberty to speak further on that matter."

Mrs. Wilcox interrupted smilingly. "Andrew, don't start an argument now. Dinner is served, and I know Captain Curtis is hungry."

Elsie rose. "Yes, papa, leave your discussion till some other time, when you can bang the furniture."

Curtis expected to take Miss Cooke in to dinner, but Elsie delighted him by saying, "You're to go in with me, Captain."

"I am very glad of the privilege," he said, with deliberate intent to please her; his sincerity was unquestionable.

Curtis would have been more profoundly impressed with the spaciousness of the hall and the dining-room had they been less like the interior of a hotel. The whole house, so far as its mural decoration went, had the over-stuffed quality of a Pullman car (with the exception of the pictures on the wall, which were exceedingly good), for Brisbane had successfully opposed all of Elsie's new-fangled notions with regard to interior decoration; he was of those who insist on being masters in their houses as well as in their business offices, and Elsie's manner was that of an obedient daughter deferring to a sire who had not ceased to consider her a child.

Seated at Elsie's right hand, with Mrs. Wilcox between himself and the head of the table, Curtis was fairly out of reach of Brisbane, who was dangerously eager to open a discussion concerning the bill for the removal of the Tetongs.

Elsie turned to him at once to say: "Do you know, Captain Curtis, I begin to long to return to the West. All my friends are enthusiastic over the studies I made last year, and I've decided to go back next spring. How early could one come out?"

"Any time after the first of May—in fact, that is the most beautiful month in the year; the grass is deliciously green then. I'm glad to know you think of returning. Jennie will also rejoice. It seems too good to be true. Will Mr. Lawson also return?"

"Oh yes. In fact, I go to complete his work—to do penance for neglecting him last summer." And in her tone, he fancied, lay a covert warning, as though she had said: "Do not mistake me; I am not coming out of interest in you."

He needed the word, for under the spell of her near presence and the charm of her smile, new to him, the soldier was beginning to glow again and to soften, in spite of his resolution to be very calm.

She went on: "I am genuinely remorseful, because

Mr. Lawson has not been able to bring his paper out as he had planned."

"I will see that you have every possible aid," he replied, matter-of-factly. "The work must be done soon."

"How handsome he is!" the girl thought, as she studied his quiet face. "His profile is especially fine, and the line of his neck and shoulders—" an impulse seized her, and she said:

"Captain, I'd like to make a sketch of you. Could you find time to sit for me?"

"That's very flattering of you, but I'm afraid my stay in Washington is too short and too preoccupied."

Her face darkened. "I'm sorry. I know I could make a good thing of you."

"Thank you for the compliment, but it is out of the question at present. Next summer, if you come out, I will be very glad to give the time for it. And that reminds me, you promised to show me your pictures when I came, and your studio."

"Did I? Well, you shall see them, although they are not as good as I shall do next year. One has to learn to handle new material. Your Western atmosphere is so different from that of Giverney, in which we all paint in Paris; then, the feeling of the landscape is so different; everything is so firm and crisp in line—but I am going to get it! 'There is the mystery of light as well as of the dark,' Meunnot used to say to us, and if I can get that clear shimmer, and the vibration of the vivid color of the savage in the midst of it—"

She broke off as if in contemplation of the problem, rapt with question how to solve it.

"There speaks the artist in you, and it is fine. But I'd like you to see the humanitarian side of life, too," he replied.

"There is none," she instantly replied, with a curious blending of defiance and amusement. "I belong to the world of Light and Might—"

"And I to the world of Right—what about that?"

"Light and Might make right."

"Your team is wrongly harnessed—Light and Right are co-workers. Might fears both Light and Right."

Mrs. Wilcox, who had been listening, fairly clapped her hands. "I'm glad to have you refute her arguments, Captain. She is absolutely heartless in her theories—in practice she's a nice girl."

Elsie laughed. "What amuses me is that a soldier, the embodiment of Might, should dare to talk of Right."

Curtis grew grave. "If I did not think that my profession at bottom guarded the rights of both white men and red, I'd resign instantly. Our army is only an impartial instrument for preserving justice."

"That isn't the old-world notion," put in Lawson from across the table.

"It is *our* notion," stoutly replied Curtis. "Our little army to-day stands towards the whole nation as a police force relates itself to a city—a power that interferes only to prevent aggression of one interest on the rights of another."

Brisbane's big, flat voice took up the theme.

"That's a very pretty theory, but you'll find plenty to claim that the army is an instrument of oppression."

"I'll admit it is sometimes wrongly used," Curtis replied. "We who are in the field can't help that, however. We are under orders. Of course," he added, modestly, "I am only a young soldier. I have seen but ten years of service, and I have taken part in but one campaign—a war I considered unavoidable at that time."

"You would hold, then, that an officer of the army has a right to convictions?" queried Brisbane, in the tone of the lawyer.

"Most certainly. A man does not cease to think upon entering the army."

"That's dangerous doctrine."

"It's the American idea. What people would suffer by having its army intelligent?"

Lawson coughed significantly. "Bring forth the black-swathed axe—treason has upreared her head."

It was plain that Brisbane was lying in wait for him. Curtis whispered to Elsie:

"Rescue me! Your father is planning to quiz me, and I must not talk before I report to the department."

"I understand. We will go to my studio after dinner." And with Lawson's aid she turned the conversation into safe channels.

It was very great pleasure to the young soldier to sit once more at such a board and in pleasant relation to Elsie. It was more than he had ever hoped for, and he surprised her by his ability to take on her interests. He grew younger in the glow of her own youth and beauty, and they finished their ices in such good-fellowship that Mrs. Wilcox was amazed.

"We will slip away now," Elsie said, in a low tone to Curtis, and they both rose. As they were about to leave the room Brisbane looked up in surprise. "Where are you going? Don't you smoke, Captain? Stay and have a cigar."

Elsie answered for him. "Captain Curtis can come back, but I want him to see my studio now, for I know if you get to talking politics he will miss the pictures altogether."

"She has a notion I'm growing garrulous," Brisbane retorted, "but I deny the charge. Well, let me see you later, Captain; there are some things I want to discuss with you."

"Grace, you are to come, too," Elsie said to her girl friend, and led the way out into the hall.

Miss Cooke stepped to Curtis's side. "You've been in Washington before?" she asked, with an inflection which he hated.

"Oh yes, many time. In fact, I lived here till I was sixteen. I was born in Maryland, not far from here."

"Indeed! Then you know the city thoroughly?"

"Certain sides of it. Exteriorly and officially I know it; socially, I am a stranger to it. My people were proud and poor. A good old family in a fine old house, and very little besides."

Elsie led the way slowly up the big staircase, secretly hoping Miss Cooke would find it too cool for her thin blood. She wished to be alone with Curtis, and this wish, obscure as it was, grew stronger as she set a chair for him and placed a frame on an easel.

"You really need daylight to see them properly."

"Am I to make remarks?"

"Certainly; tell me just what you think."

"Then let me preface my helpful criticisms by saying that I don't know an earthly thing about painting. We had drawing, of a certain kind, at the academy, and I used to visit the galleries in New York when occasion served. Now you know the top and the bottom of my art education."

"It's cold in here, Elsie," broke in Miss Cooke, whom they had quite forgotten. "Is the steam turned on?"

"Wrap my slumber-robe around you," Elsie carelessly replied. "Now here is my completed study of Little Peta. What do you think of that? Is it like her?"

"Very like her, indeed. I think it excellent," he said, with unaffected enthusiasm. "She was a quaint little thing. She is about to be married to young Two Horns—a white man's wedding."

Elsie's eyes glowed. "Oh, I wish I could see that!

But don't let her wear white man's clothing. She'd be so cunning in her own way of dress. I wish she had not learned to chew gum."

"None of us quite live up to our best intentions," he replied, laughing. "Peta thinks she's gaining in grace. Most of the white ladies she knows chew gum."

The pictures were an old story to Miss Cooke, who shivered for a time in silence and at last withdrew. Elsie and Curtis were deep in discussion of the effect of white man's clothing on the Tetongs, but each was aware of a subtle change in the other as the third person was withdrawn. A delicious sense of danger, of inward impulse warring with outward restraint, added zest to their intercourse. He instantly recalled the last time he stood in her studio feeling her frank contempt of him. "I am on a different footing now," he thought, with a certain exultation. It was worth years of hardship and hunger and cold to stand side by side with a woman who had not merely beauty and wealth but talent, and a mysterious quality that was more alluring than beauty or intellect. What this was he could not tell, but it had already made life a new game to him.

She, on her part, exulted with a sudden sense of having him to herself for experiment, and every motion of his body, every tone of his voice she noted and admired.

He resumed: "Naturally, I can say nothing of the technique of these pictures. My praise of them must be on the score of their likeness to the people. They are all admirable portraits, exact and spirited, and yet—" He hesitated, with wrinkled brows.

"Don't spare me!" she cried out. "Cut me up if you can!"

"Well, then, they seem to me unsympathetic. For example, the best of them all is Peta, because you liked her, you comprehended her, partly, for she was a child, gentle and sweet. But you have painted old Crawling Elk as if he were a felonious mendicant. You've delineated his rags, his wrinkled skin, his knotted hands, but you've left the light out of his eyes. Let me tell you something about that old man. When I saw him first he was sitting on the high bank of the river, motionless as bronze, and as silent. He was mourning the loss of his little grandchild, and had been there two days and two nights wailing till his voice had sunk to a whisper. His rags were a sign of his utter despair. You didn't know that when you painted him, did you?"

"No, I did not," she replied, softly.

"Moreover, Crawling Elk is the annalist and storyteller of his tribe. He carries the 'winter count' and the sacred pipe, and can tell you of every movement of the Tetongs for more than a century and a half. His mind is full of poetry, and his conceptions of the earth and sky are beautiful. He knows little that white men know, and cares for very little that the white man fights for, but his mind teems with lore of the mysterious universe into which he has been thrust, and which he has studied for seventy-two years. In the eyes of God, I am persuaded there is no very wide difference between old Crawling Elk and Herbert Spencer. The circle of Spencer's knowledge is wider, but it is as far from including the infinite as the redman's story of creation. Could you understand the old man as I do, you would forget his rags. He would loom large in the mysterious gloom of life. Your painting is as prejudiced in its way as the description which a cowboy would give you of this old man. You have given the color, the picturesque qualities of your subjects, but you have forgotten that they are human souls, groping for happiness and light."

As he went on, Elsie stared at the picture fixedly, and it changed under her glance till his deeply passionate words seemed written on the canvas. The painting ceased to be a human face and became a mechanical setting together of features, a clever delineation of the exterior of a ragged old man holding a beaded tobacco-pouch and a long red pipe.

"This old 'beggar,'" Curtis continued, "never lights that pipe you have put in his hands without blowing a whiff to the great spirits seated at the cardinal points of the compass. He makes offerings for the health of his children—he hears voices in the noonday haze. He sits on the hill-top at dawn to commune with the spirits over his head. As a beggar he is picturesque; as a man, he is bewildered by the changes in his world, and sad with the shadow of his children's future. All these things, and many more, you must learn before you can represent the soul of the redman. You can't afford to be unjust."

She was deeply affected by his words. They held conceptions new to her. But his voice pierced her, strangely subdued her. It quivered with an emotion which she could not understand. Why should he care so much whether she painted her subjects well or ill? She was seized with sudden, bitter distrust.

"I wish I had not shown you my studies," she said, resentfully.

His face became anxious, his voice gentle. "I beg your pardon; I have presumed too far. I hope, Miss Brisbane, you will not take what I say too much to heart. Indeed, you must not mind me at all. I am, first of all, a sort of crank; and then, as I say, I don't know a word about painting; please forget my criticisms."

She understood his mood now. His anxiety to regain her good-will was within her grasp, and she seized the opportunity to make him plead for himself and exonerate her.

"You have torn my summer's work to flinders,"

she said, sullenly, looking down at a bit of charcoal she was grinding into the rug beneath her feet.

He was aghast. "Don't say that, I beg of you! Good Heavens! don't let my preachment discourage you. You see, I have two or three hobbies, and when I am once mounted I'm sure to ride right over somebody's garden wall." He rose and approached her. "I shall never forgive myself if I have taken away the smallest degree of your enthusiasm. My aim—if I had an aim—was to help you to understand my people, so that when you come out next summer—"

"All that is ended now," she said, sombrely. "I shall attempt no more Indian work!"

This silenced him. He took time to consider what this sudden depression on her part meant. As he studied her he saw her lip quiver, and anxiety suddenly left him. His tone was laughter-filled as he called: "Come, now, Miss Brisbane, you're making game of me by taking my criticisms so solemnly. I can see a smile twitching your lips this moment. Look at me!"

She looked up and broke into a laugh. He joined in with her, but a flush rose to his face.

"You fooled me completely. I reckon you should have been an actress instead of a painter."

She sobered a little. "Really, I *was* depressed for a moment. Your tone was so terribly destructive. Shall we go down?"

"Not till you say you'll forgive me and forget my harangue."

She gave him her hand. "I'll forgive you, but I'm going to remember the harangue. I—rather liked it. It made me think. Strange to say, I like people who make me think."

Again his heart leaped with the blood of exultant youth. "She is coming to understand me better!" he thought.

"You must see my other pictures by daylight,"

she was saying. "Mr. Lawson likes this one particularly." They had moved out into the little reception-room. "I did it in Giverney—we all go down sooner or later to paint one of Monet's pollard willows. These are my 'stunts.'"

Lawson! Yes, there was the secret of her increasing friendliness. As the fiancée of Lawson she could afford to lessen her reserve towards his friend.

And so it happened that, notwithstanding her cordial welcome and her respectful consideration of his criticism, he went away with a feeling of disappointment. That her beauty was more deeply enthralling than he had hitherto realized made his disquiet all the greater. As he stepped out upon the street, she seemed as insubstantial as a dream of his imaginative youth, far separated from any reality with which he had any durable association.

CHAPTER X

Curtis at Headquarters

CURTIS WAS frankly exclamatory at the size and splendor of Lawson's apartments. He had accepted the invitation to take breakfast with him without much thought as to the quality of the breakfast or where it would be eaten, until he found himself entering the hall of a superb apartment hotel.

"Why, see here, Lawson," he exclaimed, as he looked about his friend's suite, "this is too much for any bachelor—it's baronial! I must revise my judgments. I had a notion you were a hard-working ethnologic sharp."

"So I am," replied Lawson, smiling with frank enjoyment of his visitor's amazement. "I've been at work two hours at my desk. If you don't believe it, there's the desk."

The room was filled with books, cases of antique pottery, paintings of Indians, models of Pueblo dwellings, and other things in keeping, and was made rich in color by a half-dozen very choice Na-

vajo blankets in the fine old weaves with the vege-
table dyes so dear to the collector. The long table
was heaped with current issues of the latest maga-
zines, and dozens of books, with markers set to
guard some valuable passages, were piled within
reach. It was plainly the library of a student and
man of letters.

Lawson's lean, brown face at once assumed a different aspect to Curtis. It became more refined,
more scholarly, and distinctly less shrewd and quizzical, and the soldier began to understand the writ-
er's smiling defiance of Western politicians and
millionaire cattle-owners. Plainly a man of large for-
tune, with high social connections, what had Lawson to fear of the mountain West? The menace of
the greedy cattlemen troubled him no more than
the howl of the blizzard.

In the same measure that Lawson's power was revealed to him the heart of the agent sank. He could
not but acknowledge that here was the fitting husband and proper home for Elsie—"while I," he
thought, "have only a barrack in a desolate Indian
country to offer her," and he swung deep in the
trough of his sea of doubt.

A map on the wall, lined with red, caught his eye,
and he seized upon it for diversion.

"What is this?" he asked.

"That's my trail-map," replied Lawson. "The red
lines represent my wanderings."

Curtis studied it with expert eyes. "You have
ploughed the Arizona deserts pretty thoroughly."

"Yes, I've spent three summers down in that
country studying cliff-dwellings. It's a mighty alluring region. Last summer I broke away and got back
into the north, but I am greatly taken with the hot
sunshine and loneliness of the desert."

Curtis turned sharply. "What I can't understand,
Lawson, is this: How can you pull up and leave such

a home?"—he indicated the room with a sweep of his hand—"and go out on the painted desert or down the Chaco and swelter in the heat like a horned toad?"

Lawson smiled. "It *is* absurd, isn't it? Man's an unaccountable beast. But come! Breakfast is waiting, and I hope you're hungry."

The dining-room was built on a scale with the library, and the mahogany table, sparsely covered with dishes, looked small and lonely in the midst of the shining floor. This feature of the beautiful room impressed Curtis, and as they took seats opposite each other he remarked, "If I were not here you would be alone?"

"Yes, quite generally I breakfast alone. I entertain less than you would think. I'm a busy man when at home."

"Well, the waste of room is criminal, Lawson, that's all I have to say—criminal. You'll be called upon to answer for it some time."

"I've begun to think so myself," replied the host, significantly.

They talked mountain ranges and Pueblo dwellers, and the theoretical relation of the mound-builders to the small, brown races of the Rio Grande Valley, touching also on the future of the redman; and all the while Curtis was struggling with a benumbing sense of his hopeless weakness in the face of a rival like Lawson. He gave up all thought of seeing Elsie again, and resolutely set himself to do the work before him, eager to return to his duties in the Western foot-hills.

Lawson accompanied him to the Interior Department and introduced him to the Secretary, who had the preoccupied air of a business man rather than the assumed leisure of the politician. He shook hands warmly, and asked his visitors to be seated while he finished a paper in hand. At last he turned and pleasantly began:

"I'm glad to meet you, Captain. Yours is a distinguished name with us. We fully recognize the value of your volunteer service, and hope to make the best use of you. Our mutual friend, Lawson here, threatens to make you Secretary in my stead." Here he looked over his spectacles with a grave and accusing air, which amused Lawson greatly.

"Not so bad as that, Mr. Secretary," he laughed. "I merely suggested that Captain Curtis would make an excellent President."

"Oh, well, it all comes to the same thing." He then became quite serious. "Now, Captain, I would suggest that you put this whole matter as you see it, together with your recommendations, into the briefest, most telling form possible, and be ready to come before the committee to-morrow. Confer with the commissioner and be ready to meet the queries of the opposition. Brisbane is behind the cattlemen in this controversy, and he is a strong man. I agree entirely with you and Lawson that the Tetongs should remain where they are and be helped in the way you suggest. Be ready with computations of the cost of satisfying claims of the settlers, building ditches, etc. Come and see me again before you return. Good-morning," and he bent to his desk with instant absorption.

Lawson again led the way across the square in search of the commissioner's office. The large, bare waiting-room was filled with a dozen or more Indians, all wearing new blue suits and wide black hats. They were smoking in contemplative silence, with only an occasional word spoken in undertone. It was plain they were expecting an audience with the great white chief.

Several of them knew Lawson and cried out: "Ho! Ho!" coming up one by one to shake hands, but they glowed with pleasure as Curtis began to sign-talk with them.

"Who are you?" he asked of one. "Oh! Northern Cheyenne—I thought so. And you—you are Apache?" he said to another. "I can tell that, too. What are you all waiting for? To see the commissioner? Have you had a good visit? Yes, I see you have nice new suits. The government is good to you—sometimes." They laughed at his sharp hits. "Well, don't stay too long here. The white man will rob you of your good clothes. Be careful of fire-water."

One old man, whose gestures were peculiarly flowing and dignified, thereupon signed: "When the white man come to buy our lands we are great chiefs—very tall; when we ask for our money to be paid to us, then we are small, like children." This caused a general laugh, in which Curtis joined. They all wanted to know who he was, and he told them. "Ah! we are glad for the Tetongs. They have a good man. Tell the commissioner we are anxious to council and go home—we are weary of this place."

Lawson, meanwhile, had entered the office and now reappeared. "Mr. Brown will see you at once, Captain."

The acting commissioner wore the troubled look of a man sorely overworked and badly badgered. He breathed a sigh of ostentatious relief as he faced his two visitors, who came neither to complain nor to ask favors. He studied Curtis contemplatively, his pale face set in sad lines.

"I'm leaning on you in this Tetong business," he began. "I have so many similar fights all over the West, I can't give you the attention you deserve. It seems as though our settlers were insane over Indian lands. I honestly believe, if we should lay out a reservation on the staked plains there'd be a mad rush for it. 'The Injun has it—let's take it away from him,' seems to be the universal cry. I am pestered to death with schemes for cutting down reservations and removing tribes. It would seem as if these poor, hunted devils might have a thumb-nail's breadth of the continent they once entirely owned; but no, so long as an acre exists they are liable to attack. I'm worn out with the attempt to defend them. I'll have nervous prostration or something worse if this pressure continues. Yesterday nearly finished me. What kind of pirates do you raise out there, anyway?"

Curtis listened with amazement to his frank avowal, but Lawson only laughed, saying, in explanation: "This is one of the commissioner's poor days. He'll fight till the last ditch—"

"Irrigating ditch!" supplemented the commissioner. "Yes, there's another nightmare. Beautiful complication! The government puts the Indian on a reservation so dry that water won't run down hill, and then Lawson or some other friend of the Indian comes in here and insists on irrigating ditches being put in, and then I am besieged by civil engineers for jobs, and wild-eyed contractors twist my door-knobs off. Captain Curtis, keep out of the Indian service if you have any conscience."

"That's exactly why I recommended him," said Lawson—"because he *has* a conscience."

"It'll shorten his life ten years and do no material good. Well, now, about this Tetong imbroglio."

Immediately he fell upon the problem with the most intense application, and Curtis had a feeling that his little season of plain speaking had refreshed him.

Lawson went his way, but Curtis spent the remainder of the day in the commissioner's office, putting together his defence of the Tetongs, compiling figures, and drawing maps to show the location of grass and water. He did not rise from his work till the signal for closing came, and even then he gathered his papers together and took them home to his room in the club in order to put the finishing touches to them.

While dressing for his dinner with Lieutenant Kirkman, a classmate and comrade, he began to wonder how soon he could decently make his dinner-call on the Brisbanes. It was shameful in him, of course, but he had suddenly lost interest in the Kirkmans. The day seemed lost because he had not been able to see Elsie. There was a powerful longing in his heart, an impatience which he had not experienced since his early manhood. It was a hunger which had lain dormant—scotched but not killed—for now it rose from its mysterious lair with augmented power to break his rest and render all other desires of no account.

That night, after he returned from the Kirkmans', where he had enjoyed an exquisite little dinner amid a joyous chatter reviving old-time memories, he found himself not merely wide-awake, but restless. His brain seemed determined to reveal itself to him completely. Pictures of his early life and the faces and homes of his friends in the West came whirling in orderless procession like flights of swift birds—now a council with the Sioux; now a dinner of the staff of General Miles; visions of West Point, a flock of them, came also, and the faces of the girls he had loved with a boy's fancy; and then, as if these were but whisks of cloud scattering, the walls of great mountain ranges appeared behind, stern and majestic, sunlit for a moment, only to withdraw swiftly into gray night; and when he seized upon these sweeping fragments and attempted to arrange them, Elsie's proud face, with its dark, changeful eyes and beautiful, curving lips, took central place, and in the end obscured all the rest.

The Kirkman home, the cheer, the tenderness of

the husband towards his dainty little wife, the obvious rest and satisfaction of the man, betokening that the ultimate of his desires had been reached, also came in for consideration by the restless brain of the soldier-mountaineer. "I shall never be at peace till I have wife and child, that I now realize," he acknowledged to himself in the deep, solitary places of his thought.

Then he rose and took up the papers which he had been preparing, and as he went over them again he came to profounder realization than ever before of the mighty tragedy whose final act he seemed about to witness. His heart swelled with a great tenderness towards that fragment of a proud and free people who sat in wonder before the coming of an infinite flood of alien races, helpless to stay it, appalled by the breadth and power of the stream which swept them away. He felt himself in some sense their chosen friend—their Moses, to lead them out of the desolation in which they sat bewildered and despairing. Thinking of them and of plans to help them, he grew weary at last, his brain ceased to grind, and he slept.

CHAPTER XI

Curtis Grapples with Brisbane

THE HEARING took place at ten o'clock, but Curtis had opportunity for a little helpful consultation with Lawson before the chairman called the committee-men to order. The session seemed unimportant—perfunctory. The members sat for the most part silent, ruminating, with eyes fixed on the walls or upon slips of paper which they held abstractedly in their hands. Occasionally some one of them would rouse up to ask a question, but, in general, their attitudes were those of bored and preoccupied business men. They came and went carelessly in response to calls of their clerks, and Curtis perceived that they had very little real interest in the life or death of the redmen. He would have been profoundly discouraged had not the chairman been alert and his questions to the point. After his formal statement had been taken and the hearing was over, the chairman approached Curtis informally and showed a very human sympathy for the Tetongs.

"Yes, I think we can hold this raid in check," he said, in answer to Curtis, and added, slowly, "I am very glad to find a man of your quality taking up this branch of service." He paused, and a smile wrinkled his long, Scotch face. "They accuse me of being a weak sentimentalist, because I refuse to consider the redman in the light of a reptile. I was an abolitionist"—the smile faded from his eyes and his thin lips straightened—"in days when it meant something to defend the negro, and in standing for the rights of the redman I am merely continuing my life-work. It isn't a question of whether I know the Indian or not, though I know him better than most of my critics; it's a question of his dues under our treaties. We considered him a man when we bought his land, and I insist he shall be treated the same now. I should like to hear from you—unofficially, of course—whenever you have anything to say. Lawson's testimony"—he laid a caressing hand on Lawson's shoulder—"is worth more to me than that of a thousand land speculators. He's a comfort to us, for we know he is disinterested, and has nothing to gain or lose in any question which concerns the reds, and we find very much the same about you, Captain Curtis, and I am determined that you shall have free hand."

Curtis shook hands with the old man with a sense of security. Here, at least, was a senator of the old school, a man to be depended upon in time of trouble. He began also to realize Lawson's power, for he seemed to be the personal friend of every honest official connected with the department.

As the two young men stepped out into the hall they came face to face with Elsie and her father.

"Are we too late?" cried the girl. "Is the hearing over?"

"My part of it is," answered Curtis—"at least for to-day. They may recall me to-morrow."

Brisbane was visibly annoyed. "I didn't suppose you would come on till eleven; that's the word I got over the 'phone. I particularly wanted to hear your deposition," he added, sourly.

"Papa has an idea your opposition to this bill is important," Elsie said, lightly, as Curtis edged away from Brisbane.

Brisbane followed him up. "Well, now that your hearing is over, suppose you get into our carriage and go home with us to lunch?"

"Please do!" said Elsie, with flattering sincerity.

Curtis hesitated, and was made captive. "It is a great temptation," he said, looking at Lawson.

Elsie saw him yielding and cried out: "Oh, you must come—and you, too, Osborne."

Lawson was plainly defeated. "I can't do it. I have a couple of New York men to lunch at the club, and I couldn't think of putting them off."

"Oh, I'm so sorry; we would have made a nice little lunch party."

"There are other days coming!" he replied, as lightly as possible.

As they drove away Curtis had a premonition that his impending interview would be disagreeable, for Brisbane sat in silence, his keen eyes full of some sinister resolution. He was, in fact, revolving in his mind a plan of attack. He realized the danger of attempting to bribe such a man even indirectly, but a poor and ambitious soldier might be removed by gentler means, through promotion; and friendly pressure might be brought to bear on the War Department to that effect. Having set himself to the task of clearing the reservation of the Tetongs, a man of Brisbane's power did not hesitate long over the morality of methods, and having decided upon promotion as his method of approaching Curtis, the old man distinctly softened, and made himself agreeable by extending the drive and affably pointing out the recent improvements in the city. "Our Capitol is as good as any now," he said. "Our new buildings are up to the standard."

The young soldier refused to be drawn into any blood-heating discussions, begin quite content to sit facing Elsie, feeling obscurely the soft roll of the wheels beneath him, and absorbing the light and color of the streets. "This is my city," he said; "I spent my boyhood here. I went to West Point from here."

"It *is* beautiful," replied Elsie, and at the moment a spark of some mysterious flame sprang from each to the other. They were young, and the air was soft and sweet. Thereafter everything gave the young soldier pleasure. The whistling of the men, the gay garments of the shoppers, the glitter of passing carriages, the spread of trees against the bright sky—everything assumed a singular grace. His courage rose, and he felt equal to any task.

As they entered the big house Elsie said: "You're to come right up to the studio. I want to show you a canvas I finished yesterday. I had an inspiration—I think you brought it to me."

As she led the way up the wide and splendidly carved stairway the soldier's elation sank away, for each step emphasized the girl's pride and power, and by contrast threw the poor Indian agent into hopeless shadow. He hardly heard what she said, till she led him before her easel and said:

"There is yesterday's work. I've been trying for days to get a certain effect of color, and, behold! I caught it flying this morning. What puzzles me in your country is the enormously high value of your earth in reference to the sky. The sky is so solid."

As he took in the significance of the canvas Curtis exclaimed:

"It is very beautiful. It is miraculous. How do you do it?"

"I'm glad you like it. My problem there was to represent the difference in value between Chief Elk, who is riding in the vivid sunlight, and his wife and Little Peta, who are just in the edge of that purple cloud-shadow. The difference between white in sunlight and white in shadow is something terrific in your dry air. Contrasts are enough to knock you down. This gray, Eastern studio light makes all my sketches seem false, but I know they are not."

"They are very true, it seems to me."

"When I close my eyes and hark back to the flooding light of the valley of the Elk, then I can do these things; I can't if I don't. I have to forget all my other pictures. This is nearer my impression than anything else I've done."

"It has great charm," he said, after a pause, "and it also reminds me of my duty. I must return at once to the West."

"When do you go—actually?"

"Actually, I leave to-morrow at three o'clock; unless I receive word to the contrary, to-morrow morning."

"So soon? You are making a very short stay. Can't you remain over the holidays? Some friends of mine are coming on from New York. I'd like you to meet them."

"I think I must return. Jennie is preparing to give her little 'Ingines' a Christmas-tree, and I am told that my 'Sandy Claws' would add greatly to their joy, so I am making special effort to reach there on the 23d."

She looked at him musingly. "You really are interested in those ugly creatures? I don't understand it."

"To be really frank, I don't understand your lack of sympathy," he replied, smiling a little. "It isn't at all feminine."

She took a seat on the divan before she spoke

again. "Oh, women are such posers. You think I am quite heartless, don't you?"

"No, I don't think that, but I do think you are a little unjust to these people, whose thought you have made very little effort to comprehend."

"Why should I? They are not worth while."

"Do you speak now as an artist?" he asked, gravely.

"But they are so gross and so cruel!"

"I don't deny but they are, sometimes, both gross and cruel, but so are civilized men. The scalp-dance no more represents them than a bayonet charge represents us. It isn't just to condemn all for the faults of a few. You wouldn't destroy servant-girls because some of them are ugly and untidy, would you?"

"The cases are not precisely similar."

"I'll admit that, but the point is here: as an artist you can't afford to dispose of a race on the testimony of their hereditary enemies. You wouldn't expect a sympathetic study of the Greek by the Saracen, would you?"

"It isn't that so much, but they are so perfectly unimportant. They have no use in the world. What does it matter if they die, or don't?"

"Perhaps not so much to them; but to me, if I can help them and fail to do it, it matters a great deal. We can't afford to be unjust, for our own sake. The bearer of the torch should not burn, he should illumine."

"I don't understand that," she said, genuinely searching for his meaning.

"There is where you disappoint me," he retorted. "Most women quiver with altruistic passion the moment they see helpless misery. If you saw a kitten fall into a well what would you do?"

"I should certainly try to save it."

"Your heart would bleed to see it drown?"

She shivered at the thought. "Why, of course!"

"And yet you can share in your father's exterminating vengeance as he sweeps ten thousand redmen into their graves?"

"The case is different—the kitten never did any harm."

"The wrong is by no means all on the redman's side. But even if it were, Christ said, 'Love them that hate you,' and as a Christian nation we should not go out in vindictive warfare against even those who despitefully use us. I haven't a very high seat in the synagogue. I have a soldier's training for warfare, but I acknowledge the splendor of Christ's precepts and try to live up to them. I always liked Grant's position as regards the soldier. But more than that—I like these red people. They are a good deal more than rude men. It is a great pleasure to feel their trust and confidence in me. It touches me deeply to have them come and put their palms on me reverently, as though I were superhuman in wisdom, and say: 'Little Father, we are blind. We cannot see the way. Lead us and we will go.' At such times I feel that no other work in the world is so important. If human souls are valuable anywhere on earth they are valuable here; no selfish land-lust should blind us to see that."

As he spoke, the girl again felt something large and sweet and powerful, like a current of electrical air which came out of wide spaces of human emotion and covered her like a flood. She was humbled by the high purpose and inexplicable enthusiasm of the man before her.

"I suppose you consider me cruel and heartless!" she cried out. "But I am not to blame for being what I am."

"If you are not free, who is? You have it all—youth, wealth, beauty. Nothing enslaves you but indifference."

She was thinking that Lawson had never moved her so, and wishing Curtis were less inexorable in his logic, when he checked himself by saying: "I beg your pardon again. I came to see your pictures, not to preach forgiveness of sins. I here pull myself up short."

"I think you could make me feel personal interest in brickbats or—or spiders," she said, with a quaint, relaxing smile. "You were born to be a preacher, not a soldier."

"Do you think so? I've had a notion all along that I was a fairly good commander and a mighty poor persuader; what I don't intend to be is a bore." He rose and began to walk slowly round the walls, studying the paintings under her direction. He was struggling with obscure impulses to other and more important speech, but after making the circuit of the room he said, as though rendering a final verdict:

"You have great talent; that is evident. What do you intend to do with it? It should help some one."

"You are old-fashioned," she replied. "In our modern day, art is content to add beauty to the world; it does not trouble itself to do good. It is *un*-moral."

"Perhaps I *am* a preacher, after all, for I like the book or picture that has a motive, that stands for something. Your conception of art's uses is French, is it not?"

"I suppose it is; clearly, it isn't Germanic. What would you have me do—paint Indians to convince the world of their sufferings?"

"Wouldn't that be something like the work Millet did? Seems to me I remember something of that sort in some book I have read."

She laughed. "Unfortunately, I am not Millet; besides, he isn't the god of our present idolatry. He's a dead duck. We paint skirt-dancers and the singers in the cafés now. Toiling peasants are 'out.' "

"You are a woman, and a woman ought—"

"Please don't hand me any of that stupid rot about what a woman *ought* to be, and isn't. What I am I am, and I don't like dirty, ragged people, no matter whether they are Roman beggars or Chinese. I like clean, well-dressed, well-mannered people, and no one can make me believe they are less than a lot of ill-smelling Indians."

"Miss Brisbane, you must not do me an injustice," he earnestly entreated. "It was not my intention to instruct you to-day. I am honestly interested in your pictures, and had no thought of renewing an appeal. I was tempted and fell. If you will forgive me this time, I'll never preach again."

"I don't say I object to your preachment. I think I rather like it. I don't think I ever met a man who was so ready to sacrifice his own interest for an idea. It's rather amusing to meet a soldier who is ready to knock one down with a moral war-club." She ended with a mocking inflection of voice.

His face lost its eager, boyish expression. "I'm delighted to think I have amused you," he said, slowly. "It makes amends."

"Please don't be angry," she pleaded. "I didn't mean to be flippant."

"Your words were explicit," he replied, feeling at the moment that she was making a mock of him, and this duplicity hurt him.

She put forth her sweetest voice. "Please forgive me! I think your work very noble, only I can't understand how you can exile yourself to do it. Let us go down; it is time for lunch, and papa is waiting for you, I know."

It was unaccountable that a mocking tone, a derisive smile from this chance acquaintance, should so shake the soldier and so weaken him, but he descended the stairway with a humiliating consciousness of having betrayed his heart to a fleering, luring daughter of wealth.

At the door of the library the girl paused. "Papa, are you asleep?"

The abrupt rustle of a newspaper preceded Brisbane's deep utterance. "Not at all—just reading the *Star*. Come in, Captain. Is lunch nearly ready?" he asked of Elsie.

"I think so. They are a little late. I'll go see."

As she left the room Brisbane cordially rumbled on. "Sit down, Captain. I'm sorry I missed your talk to-day. I am curious to know what your notion is about the Tetongs. Of course, I understood you couldn't go into the case the other night, but, now that your testimony is all in, I hope you feel free to give me your reasons for opposing our plan for a removal of the tribe."

Curtis took a seat, while Brisbane stretched himself out in a big chair and fixed his cold, gray-blue eyes on the soldier, who hesitated a moment before replying, "I don't think it wise to go into that matter, Senator."

"Why not?"

"Well, we differ so radically on the bill, and your interests make it exceedingly difficult for you to be just in the case. Nothing would be gained by argument."

"You think you know what my interests are?" There was a veiled sarcasm in the great man's smile.

"I think I do. As a candidate for re-election to the Senate you can't afford to antagonize the cattle and mining interests of your State, and, as I am now officially the representative of the Tetongs, I sincerely hope you will not insist on a discussion of the motives involved." The young officer spoke firmly, but with impressive dignity and candor.

Brisbane's ambiguous manner took a sudden shift to cordiality, and, leaning forward, he said:

"Curtis, I like you. I admire your frankness. Let me be equally plain. You're too able a man to be shelved out there on a bleak reservation. What was your idea of going into the Indian service, anyway?"

The young officer remained on guard despite this genial glow. "I considered it my duty," he replied. "Besides, I was rusting out in garrison, and—but there is no need to go into my motives. I am agent, and shall stand firmly for the right of my wards so long as I am in position to do so."

"But you're wasting your life. Suppose you were offered a chance to go to—well, say West Point, as an instructor on a good salary?"

"I would decline the appointment."

"Why?"

"Because at this time I am needed where I am, and I have started on a plan of action which I have a pride in finishing."

Brisbane grew distinctively less urbane. "You are bent on fighting me, are you?"

"What do you mean?" asked Curtis, though he knew.

"You are dead set against the removal of the Tetongs?"

"Most certainly I am!"

Elsie re-entered the room during this rapid interchange of phrase, but neither of the men heard her, so intent were they upon each other.

"Young man, do you know who you are fighting?" asked Brisbane, bristling like a bear and showing his teeth a little. Curtis being silent, he went on: "You're lined up against the whole State! Not only the cattlemen round about the reservation, but a majority of the citizens are determined to be rid of those vagabonds. Anybody that knows anything about 'em knows they're a public nuisance. Why should they be allowed to camp on land which they can't use—graze their mangy ponies on lands rich in minerals—"

"Because they are human beings."

"Human beings!" sneered Brisbane. "They are nothing but a greasy lot of vermin—worthless from every point of view. Their rights can't stand in the way of civilization."

"It is not a question of whether they are clean or dirty, it is a question of justice," Curtis replied, hotly. "They came into the world like the rest of us, without any choice in the matter and so far as I can see have the same rights to the earth—at least, so much of it as they need to sustain life. The fact that they make a different use of the soil than you would do isn't a sufficient reason for starving and robbing them."

"The quicker they die the better," replied Brisbane, flushing with sudden anger. "The only good Injun is a dead Injun."

At this familiar phrase Curtis took fire. "Yes, I expected that accursed sentence. Let me tell you, Mr. Brisbane, I never knew a redman savage enough to utter such a sentiment as that. The most ferocious utterance of Geronimo never touched the tigerish malignity of that saying. Sitting Bull was willing to live and let live. If your view represents civilization, I want none of it. The world of the savage is less cruel, less selfish."

Brisbane's face writhed white, and a snarling curse choked his utterance for a moment. "If you weren't my guest," he said, reaching a clutching hand towards Curtis, "I'd cut your throat."

Elsie, waiting in strained expectancy, cried out: "Father! What are you saying? Are you crazy?"

Curtis hastily rose, very white and very quiet.

"I will take care not to put myself in your way as guest again, sir."

"You can't leave too quick!" roared the old man, his face twitching with uncontrollable wrath. "You are a traitor to your race! You'd sacrifice the settlers to the interests of a greasy red vagabond!"

"Father, be quiet! You are making a scene," called Elsie, and added, sadly: "Don't go, Captain Curtis; I shall be deeply mortified if you do. Father will be sorry for this."

Brisbane also rose, shaking with a weakness pitiful to see. "Well, sir, you can go, for I know now the kind of sneak you are. Let me tell you this, young man: you'll feel my hand before you are a year older. You can't come into my house and insult me in the presence of my daughter. Get out!" His hands were moving uncontrollably, and Elsie discovered with a curious pang that she was pitying him and admiring the stern young soldier who stood quietly waiting for an opportunity to speak. At last he said:

"Miss Brisbane, I beg your pardon; I should not have said what I did." He turned to Brisbane. "I am sorry I spoke so harshly, sir. You are an older man than I, and—"

"Never mind my age," replied Brisbane, his heat beginning to cool into self-contained malice. "I desire no terms of friendship with you. It's war now—to the knife, and the knife to the hilt. You think you are safe from me, but the man that lines up against me generally regrets it to the day of his death."

"Very well, sir, I am not one to waste words. I shall do my duty to the Tetongs regardless of you or your friends." He turned to Elsie. "Miss Brisbane, I ask you to remember that I honestly tried to avoid a controversy."

Six months before Elsie would have remained passive while her father ordered Curtis from the door, but now she could not even attempt to justify his anger, and the tears glistened on her lashes as she said: "Father, why can't you accept Captain Curtis's hand? These ragamuffin Indians aren't worth quarrelling about. No one ever went away from us like this, and it breaks my heart to have it so. Don't go, Captain Curtis. Father, ask his pardon."

The old man turned towards her. "Go to your room. I will see that this young squirt finds the door!"

Elsie shrank from the glare of his eyes. "Father, you are brutal! You hurt me."

"Do as I say!" he snarled.

"I will *not*!" She faced him, tall and resolute. "I am not a child. I am the mistress of this house." She turned and walked towards the door. "Captain Curtis, I beg *your* pardon; my father has forgotten himself."

Brisbane took a step towards Curtis. "Get out! And you, girl, leave the room."

The girl's face whitened. "Have you no sense of decency?" she said, and her voice cut deep down into his heart and he flinched. "Captain Curtis is my guest as well as yours." She extended her hand. "Please go! It is best."

"It is the most miserable moment of my life," he replied, as they moved down the hall, leaving Brisbane at the door of the study. "I will do any honorable thing to regain your good-will."

"You have not lost it," she replied. "I cannot blame you—as I should," she added, and the look on her face mystified him.

"May I see you again before I leave for the West?"

"Perhaps," she softly replied. "Remember he is old—and—"

"I will try not to bear anger," he replied.

And as he turned away it seemed that she had leagued herself with him against her own father, and this feeling deepened as she ran up the stairs heedless of the voice whose commands had hitherto been law to her.

The young officer walked down the sunny avenue towards the White House with a curious feeling of having just passed through a bitter and degrading dream. He was numb and cold. Around him the little negro newsboys were calling the one-o'clock editions of the *"Styah,"* and the pavements were swarming with public servants hastening to lunch, punctual as clocks, while he, having been ordered from the house of his host, was mechanically returning to his club.

There was something piercingly pathetic in the thought of the good cheer he had anticipated, and the lost pleasure of sitting opposite Elsie made his heart ache. At the moment his feet stumbled in the path of duty. Surely he was a long way from the single-minded map-builder who had crossed the Sulphur Spring Divide.

CHAPTER XII

Spring on the Elk

SPRING CAME early in that latitude, and Curtis was profoundly thankful that his first winter had proven unusually short and mild, for it enabled him to provide for his people far better than he had dared to hope. The rations were insufficient at best, and for several days of each alternate week the grown people were hungry as well as cold, though no one actually perished from lack of food. Beyond the wood contract and the hauling of hides each month there was very little work to be done during the winter, not enough to buy the tobacco the men longed for.

They believed in Swift Eagle, however, for he visited every cluster of huts each month, and became acquainted with nearly every family during the winter. No agent had ever taken the like pains to shake the old women by the hand, or to speak as kindly to the old men who sat beside the fire, feeble and bent with rheumatism. The little children all ran to him when he came near, as if he were a friend, and that was a good sign, too. Some of the old chiefs complained, of course—there was so little else for them to do; but they did not blame the LIttle Father. They were assured of his willingness to do whatever lay within his power to mitigate their poverty. Jennie, who was often at the beds of those who suffered, had won wide acceptance of her lotions by an amused tolerance of the medicine-men, whose mystic paraphernalia interested her exceedingly. The men of magic came at last to sing their curious songs and perform their feats of healing in her presence. "Together we will defeat the evil spirits," they said, and the health of the tribe continued to be very good, in spite of unsanitary housing and the evil influence of the medicine-men. When the missionaries came to have the native doctors suppressed Curtis said: "My policy is to supplant, not to suppress."

The bill which called for the removal of the Tetongs to another reservation was reported killed. The compromise measure for buying out the settlers was "hung up" in the committee-room, and this delay on the part of Congress exasperated the settlers beyond reason, and at a convention held early in April at Pinon City, Joseph Streeter brazenly shouted, "If the government does not remove these Indians before the first of July we'll make it hot for all concerned," and his threat was wildly cheered and largely quoted thereafter as the utterance of a man not afraid of Congress or anybody else.

Seed-time came without any promise of change, and the white settlers on the reservation went sullenly to their planting, and the cattlemen drove their herds across the boundaries upon the Tetong range as they had been doing for many years. "We are in for another season of it," they said, with the air of being martyrs in the cause of civilization.

Curtis immediately sent warning commands to all

the outside ranchers to keep clear of the reservation, and also notified Streeter, Johnson, and others of the settlers on the Elk and the Willow that their cattle must not be allowed to stray beyond certain lines, which he indicated. These orders, according to Calvin, made the settlers "red-headed as woodpeckers. They think you're drawin' the lines down pretty fine."

"I mean to," replied Curtis. "You original settlers are here by right and shall have full opportunity to graze your stock, but those on the outside must keep out. I will seize and impound all stock that does not belong on this land."

Calvin reported this statement to the outside men, and its audacity provoked the most violent threats against the agent, but he rode about unaccompanied and unarmed; but not without defence, for Calvin said to one of the loudest of the boasters, "The man who jerks a gun on Curtis runs a good chance of losing a lung or two," and the remark took effect, for Calvin had somehow acquired a reputation for being "plumb sassy when attack-ted."

Curtis had the army officer's contempt of personal injury, and, in pursuance of his campaign against the invading stockmen, did not hesitate to ride into their round-up camps alone, or accompanied only by Crow Wing, and no blusterer could sustain his reputation in the face of the agent's calm sense of command.

"I am not speaking personally," he said once, to an angry camp of a dozen armed men. "I am here as an officer of the United States army, detailed to special duty as an Indian agent, and I am in command of this reservation. It is of no use to bluster. Your cattle *must* be kept from the Tetong range."

"The grass is going to waste there," the boss argued.

"That does not concern you. It is not the fault of

the Tetongs that they have not cattle enough to fill the range."

In the end he had his way, and though the settlers and ranchers hated him, they also respected him. No one thought of attempting to bribe or scare him, and political "pull" had no value in his eyes.

Jennie, meanwhile, had acquired almost mythic fame as a marvelously beautiful and haughty "queen." Calvin was singularly close-mouthed about her, but one or two of the cowboys who had chanced to meet her with the agent spread the most appreciative reports of her beauty and of the garments she wore. She was said to be a singer of opera tunes, and that she played the piano "to beat the Devil." One fellow who had business with the agent reported having met her at the door. "By mighty! she's purty enough to eat," he said to his chum. "Her cheeks are as pink as peaches, and her eyes are jest the brown I like. She's a 'glad rag,' all right."

"Made good use o' your time, didn't ye?" remarked his friend.

"You bet your life! I weren't lettin' nothin' git by me endurin' that minute or two."

"I bet you dursn't go there again."

"I take ye—I'll go to-morrow."

"Without any business, this time? No excuse but jest to see her? You 'ain't got the nerve."

"You'll see. I'm the boy. There ain't no 'rag' gay enough to scare me."

It became a common joke for some lank, brown chap to say carelessly, as he rose from supper, "Well, I guess I'll throw a saddle onto my bald-faced sorrel and ride over and see the agent's sister." In reality, not one of them ever dared to even knock at the door, and when they came to the yards with a consignment of cattle they were as self-conscious as school-boys in a parlor and uneasy as wolves in a trap, till they were once more riding down the trail; then they "broke loose," whooping shrilly and racing like mad, in order to show that they had never been afraid. Calvin continued to call, and his defence of the agent had led to several sharp altercations with his father.

The red people expanded and took on cheer under the coming of the summer, like some larger form of insect life. They were profoundly glad of the warmth. The old men, climbing to some rounded hill-top at dawn, sat reverently to smoke and offer incense to the Great Spirit, which the sun was, and the little children, seeing the sages thus in deep meditation, passed quietly by with a touch of awe.

As the soft winds began to blow, the dingy huts were deserted for the sweeter and wholesomer life of the tepee, which is always ventilated, and which had also a thousand memories of battle and the chase associated with its ribbed walls, its yellowed peak, and its smouldering fires. The sick grew well and the weak became strong as they passed once more from the foul air of their cabins to the inspiriting breath of the mountains, uncontaminated by any smoke of white man's fire. The little girls went forth on the hills to gather flowers for the teachers, and the medicine-men, taking great credit to themselves, said: "See! our incantations again prevailed. The sun is coming back, the grass is green, and the warm winds are breathing upon the hills."

"Ay, but you cannot bring back the buffalo," said those who doubted, for there are sceptics among the redmen as elsewhere. "When you do that, then we will believe that you are really men of magic."

But the people did not respond cheerfully to Curtis when he urged them to plant gardens. They said: "We will do it, Little Father, but it is of no use. For two years we tried it, and each year the hot sun dried our little plants. Our corn withered and our potatoes came to nothing. Do not ask us to again plough the hard earth. It is all a weariness to no result."

To Jennie, Curtis said: "I haven't the heart to push them into doing a useless thing. They are right. I must wait until we have the water of the streams for our own use."

The elder Streeter was very bitter, Calvin reported. "But he ain't no idyot. He won't make no move that the law don't back him up in; but some o' these other yaps are talkin' all kinds of gun-play. But don't you lose any flesh. They got to git by me before they reach you."

Curtis smiled. "Calvin, you're a loyal friend, but I am not a bit nervous."

"That's all right, Captain, but you can't tell what a mob o' these la-hees will do. I've seen 'em make some crazy plays—I sure have; but I'll keep one ear lapped back for signs of war."

CHAPTER XIII

Elsie Promises to Return

ONE BEAUTIFUL May day Curtis came into the house with shining face.

"Sis, our artists are coming back," he called to Jennie from the hall.

"Are they? Oh, isn't that glorious!" she answered, running to meet him. "When are they to reach here? Whom did you hear from?"

"Lawson. They can't come till some time in June, however."

Jennie's face fell. "In June! I thought you meant they were coming now—right away—this week."

"Lawson furthermore writes that he expects to bring a sculptor with him—a Mr. Parker. You remember those photographs he showed us of some statues of Indians? Well, this is the man who made the figures. His wife is coming as chaperon for Miss Brisbane."

"She still needs a chaperon, does she?"

"It would seem so. Besides, Mrs. Parker goes everywhere with her husband."

"I hope she'll be as nice as Mrs. Wilcox."

"I don't think Lawson would bring any crooked timber along—there must be something worth while in them."

"Well, I am delighted, George. I confess I'm hungry for a message from the outside world; and during the school vacation we can get away once in a while to enjoy ourselves."

The certainty of the return of the artistic colony changed Curtis's entire summer outlook. Work had dragged heavily upon him during February and March, and there were moments when his enthusiasm ebbed. It was a trying position. He began to understand how a man might start in his duties with the most commendable desire, even solemn resolution, to be ever kindly and patient and self-respecting, and end by cursing the redmen and himself most impartially. Misunderstandings are so easy where two races are forced into daily contact, without knowledge of each other's speech, and with only a partial comprehension of each other's outlook on the world. Some of the employes possessed a small vocabulary of common Tetong words, but they could neither explain nor reason about any act. They could only command. Curtis, by means of the sign language, which he had carried to marvellous clearness and swiftness, was able to make himself understood fairly well on most topics, but nevertheless found himself groping at times in the obscure caverns of their thinking.

"Even after a man gets their thought he must comprehend the origin of their motives," he said to Wilson, his clerk. "Everything they do has meaning and sequence. They have developed, like ourselves, through countless generations of life under relatively stable conditions. These material conditions are now giving way, are vanishing, but the mental traits they formed will persist. Think of this when you are impatient with them."

Wilson took a pessimistic view. "I defy the angel Gabriel to keep his temper if he should get himself appointed clerk. If I was a married man I could make a better mark; but there it is—they can't see me." He ended with a deep sigh.

Curtis took advantage of Lawson's letter to write again to Elsie, and though he considered it a very polite and entirely circumspect performance, his fervor of gladness burned through every line, and the girl as she read it fell to musing on the singularity of the situation. He was in her mind very often, now; the romance and the poetry of the work he was doing began at last to appeal to her, and the knowledge that she, in a sense, shared the possibilities with him, was distinctly pleasurable. She had perception enough to feel also the force of the contrast in their lives, he toiling thanklessly on a barren, sun-smit land, in effort to lead a subject race to self-supporting freedom, while she, dabbling in art for art's sake, sat in a secure place and watched him curiously.

"How well he writes," she thought, returning to his letter. His sentences clutched her like strong hands, and she could not escape them. As she read she drew again the splendid lines of his head in profile, and then, a sentence later, it seemed that he was looking straight into her eyes, grave of countenance, involved in some moral question whose solution he considered essential to his happiness and to the welfare of his people. Surely he was a most uncommon soldier. When she had finished reading she was sincerely moved to reply. She had nothing definitely in mind to say, and yet somehow she visualized him at his desk waiting an answer. "The worst of it is, we seem to have no topic in common except his distressing Indians," she said, as she returned to her work. "Even art to him means painting the redmen sympathetically."

But he could not be put aside. He was narrow and one-sided, but he was sincere and manly—and handsome. That was the very worst of it; he was too attractive to be forgotten. Therefore she took up her pen again, being careful to keep close to artistic motives. She spoke of the success of her spring exhibition, and said: "It has confirmed me in the desire to go on valiantly in the same line. That is the reason I am coming back to the Tetongs. I feel that I begin to know them—artistically, I mean; not as you know them—and I need your blazing sunlight to drink up the fogs that I brought from Holland and Belgium. The prismatic flare of color out there pleases me. It's just the white ray split into its primary colors, but I can get it. I'm going to do more of those canvases of the moving figure blended with the landscape; they make a stunning technical problem in vibration as well as in values; and then the critics shout over them, too. I sold the one you liked so well, and also five portraits, and feel vastly encouraged. Owen Field was over from New York and gave me a real hurrah. I am going to exhibit in New York next fall if all goes well with me among the Tetongs."

CHAPTER XIV

Elsie Revisits Curtis

JENNIE THOUGHT her brother the handsomest man in the State as they walked up and down the station platform waiting for the express train which was bringing Elsie and Lawson and a famous Parisian-American sculptor and his wife. Curtis was in undress uniform, and in the midst of the slouching crowd of weather-beaten loafers he seemed a man of velvet-green parade grounds and whitewashed palings, commanding lines of polished bayonets.

He was more profoundly stirred at the thought of Elsie's coming than he cared to admit, but Jennie's delight was outspoken. "I didn't know how hungry for a change I was," she said. "They will bring the air of the big city world with them."

The whistle of the far-off train punctuated her sentences. "Oh, George, doesn't it seem impossible that in a few moments the mistress of that great Washington home will descend the car-steps to meet us?"

"Yes, I can't believe it," he replied, and his hands trembled a little as he nervously buttoned his coat.

The train came rapidly to a stop, with singing rods, grinding brakes, and the whiz of escaping steam. Some ordinary mortals tumbled out, and then the wonderful one!

"There they are!" cried Jennie. "And, oh—aren't her clothes maddening!"

Lawson, descending first, helped Elsie to the platform with an accepted lover's firm touch. She wore a blue-cloth tailored suit which fitted marvellously, and her color was more exquisite than ever. Admiring Jennie fairly gasped as the simple elegance of Elsie's habit became manifest, and she had only a glance for the sculptor and his wife.

Elsie, with hands extended, seized upon them both with cordial intensity. A little flurry of handshakings followed, and at last Mr. and Mrs. Jerome Parker were introduced. He was a tall man with a bush of yellow beard, while she was dark and plain; but she had a pleasant smile, and her eyes were nice and quiet.

"Do you know, I'm overjoyed to get back!" said Elsie to Curtis. "I don't know why I should be, but I've been eagerly looking for the Cleft Butte all day. Jerome will tell you that I expressed a sort of proprietorship in every prairie-dog."

"We are very glad to have you here again," replied Curtis. "And now that you *are* here, we must get your belongings together and get away. We are to camp to-night at the Sandstone Spring."

"A real camp?"

"A real camp. We could drive through, of course, but it would be tiresome, and then I thought you'd enjoy the camp."

"Of course we shall. It's very thoughtful of you."

"Everything will be ready for us. I left Two Horns to look after it."

"Then it will be *right*," said Lawson, who was beaming with placid joy. "Isn't it good to breathe this air again? It was stifling hot in Alta City. I never knew it to be hotter in the month of June."

While they talked, Crane's Voice was collecting the trunks, and in a few minutes, with Elsie by his side, Curtis drove his three-seated buckboard out upon the floor of the valley, leaving the squalid town behind. Lawson and Mrs. Parker occupied the middle seat, and Jennie and the tall sculptor sat behind. They were all as merry as children. Elsie took off her hat and faced the sun with joyous greeting.

"Isn't this glorious? I've dreamed of this every night for a month."

"That's one thing the Tetong has—good, fresh air, and plenty of it," said Lawson.

"A thin diet, sometimes," Curtis replied. He turned to Elsie. "Your studio is all ready for you, and I have spoken to a number of the head men about you. You'll not lack sitters. They are eager to be immortalized at your convenience."

"You are most kind—I am going to work as never before."

"You mustn't work too hard. I have a plan for an outing. One of my districts lies up in the headwaters of the Willow. I propose that we all go camping up there for a couple of weeks."

"Do you hear that, Osborne?" she called, turning her head.

"I did not—what is it?"

Curtis repeated his suggestion, and Parker shouted with joy. "Just what I want to do," he said.

Curtis went on: "We'll find the redman living there under much more favorable conditions than down in the hot valley. We have a saw-mill up in the pines, and the ladies can stay in the superintendent's house—"

"Oh no!" interrupted Elsie. "We must camp. Don't

think of putting us under a roof." A little later she said, in a low voice: "Father is in Chicago, and expects to be out here later. I mean, he's coming to make a tour of the State."

"How is his health?" Curtis asked, politely.

Her face clouded. "He's not at all well. He is older than he realizes. I can see he is failing, and he ought not to go into this senatorial fight." After a pause she said: "He was quite ill in March, and I nursed him; he seemed very grateful, and we've been very good friends since."

"I'm glad of that," he replied, and bent closely to his driving.

"You drive well, Captain."

"An Indian agent needs to be able to do anything."

"May I drive?"

"You will spoil your gloves."

"Please! I'll take them off. I'm a famous whip." She smiled at him with such understanding as they had never before reached, as she stripped her gloves from her hands and dropped them at her feet. "Now let me take the reins," she said. He surrendered them to her unhesitatingly.

"I believe you can drive," he said, exultantly.

Her hands were as beautiful as her face, strong and white, and exquisitely modelled; but he, looking upon them with keen admiration, caught the gleam of a diamond on the engagement finger. This should not have chilled him, but it did. Then he thought: "It is an engagement ring. She is now fairly bound to Lawson," and a light that was within him went out. It was only a tiny, wavering flame of hope, but it had been burning in opposition to his will all the year.

As she drove, they talked about the grasses and flowers, the mountain range far beyond, the camping trip, and a dozen other impersonal topics which did not satisfy Curtis, though he had no claim to more intimate phrase. She, on her part, was perfectly happy, and retained her hold of the reins and the whip in spite of his protest.

"You must not spoil your beautiful hands," he protested; "they are for higher things. Please return the lines to me."

"Oh no! Please! Just another half-hour—till we reach that butte. I'm stronger than you think. I am accustomed to the whip."

She had her way in this, and drove nearly the entire afternoon. When he took the reins at last, her fingers were cramped and swollen, but her face was deeply flushed with pleasure.

"I've had a delicious drive," she gratefully remarked.

At the foot of a tall butte Curtis turned his team and struck into a road leading to the left. This road at once descended upon a crescent-shaped, natural meadow enclosed by a small stream, like a babe in a sheltering arm. All about were signs of its use as a camping-ground. Sweat lodges, broken tepee-poles, piles of blackened stones, and rings of bowlders told of the many fires that had been built. Willows fringed the creek, while to the south and west rose a tall, bare hill, on which a stone tower stood like a sentinel warrior.

Elsie cried out in delight of the place. "Isn't it romantic!" Already the sun, sinking behind the hill, threw across the meadow a mysterious purple gloom, out of which a couple of tents gleamed like gray bowlders.

"There is your house to-night," said Curtis. "See the tents?"

"How tiny they look!" Elsie exclaimed, in a hushed voice, as though fearing to alarm and put them to flight.

"They are small, but as night falls you will be

amazed to discover how snug and homelike they can become."

Two Horns came to meet them, and Parker cried out, "Hello! see the big Indian!"

The chief greeted Lawson with a deep and hearty "Hah! Nawson—my friend. How! How!" And Lawson, with equal ceremony, replied, in Dakota:

"I am well, my brother; how is it with you?"

"My heart is warm towards you."

Elsie gave him her hand, and he took it without embarrassment or awkwardness. "I know you; you make pictures," he said, in his own tongue.

"Jerusalem, but he's a stunner!" said Parker. "Hello, old man! How you vass, ain't it?" and he clapped the old man on the shoulder.

Two Horns looked at him keenly, and the smile faded from his face. "Huh! Big fool," he said to Lawson.

"You mustn't talk to an Indian like that, Parker, if you expect to have his friendship," said Lawson. "Two Horns hates over-familiarity."

"Oh, he does, does he?" laughed Parker. "Kind of a Ward McAllister, hey?"

Lawson, a little later, said, privately: "That was a bad break, Parker; you really must treat these head men with decent respect or they'll hoodoo you so you can't get any models. Two Horns is a gentleman, and you must at least equal him in reserve and dignity or he will report you a buffoon."

Parker, who had done his figures from models procured in Paris from Buffalo Bill's show, opened his eyes wide.

"Lawson, you're joking!"

"You'll find every word I tell you true. I advise you to set to work now and remove your bad impression from Two Horns, who is one of the three principal chiefs. You can't come out here and clap these people on the back and call 'em 'old hoss.'

That will do in some of the stories you read, but realities are different. You'll find money won't command these people, either."

"I thought they liked to be treated as equals?"

"They do, but they don't like to have a stranger too free and easy. You haven't been introduced yet."

While Crane's Voice attended to the teams, Jennie and Two Horns worked at getting supper. Their comradeship was charming to see, and the Parkers looked on with amazement. Two Horns, deft, attentive, careful, anticipated every want. Nothing could be finer than the perfectly cheerful assistance he rendered the pretty cook. His manner was like that of an elder brother rather than that of a servant.

"I didn't suppose Indians ever worked around a camp, and especially with a woman," remarked Parker.

"What you don't know about Indians is still a large volume, Parker," retorted Lawson. "If you stay around with this outfit for a few weeks you'll gather a great deal of information useful for a sculptor of redmen."

Elsie took Lawson mildly to task for his sharp reply.

Lawson admitted that it made him impatient when a man like Parker opened his mouth on things he knew nothing about. "You never can tell what your best friend will do, can you? Parker is decidedly fresh. If he keeps on he'll become tiresome."

Elsie presumed on her enormous experience of three months on the reservation, and gave Parker many valuable hints of how to wheedle the Tetongs in personal contact.

"It seems I'm being schooled," he complained.

"You need it," was Lawson's disconcerting reply.

As night fell, and the fire began to glow in the cool, sweet dark with increasing power, they all sat round the flame and planned the trip into the mountains.

"I have some Tetongs up there who are disposed to keep very clear of the agency. Red Wolf is their head man. You may all go with me and see my council with him if you like."

"Oh! that will be glorious fun!" cried Elsie.

But Parker asked, a little anxiously, "You think it safe?" which amused Curtis, and Parker hastened to explain: "You've no idea what a bad reputation these Tetongs have. Anyhow, I would not feel justified in taking Mrs. Parker into any danger."

"She is quite safe," replied Curtis. "I will answer for the action of my wards."

"Well, if you are quite sure!"

"How far away Washington seems now!" remarked Elsie, after a silence. "I feel as if I had gone back to the very beginning of things."

"It seems the end of things for the Tetongs," replied Lawson. "We forget that fact sometimes when we are anxious to have them change to our ways. Barring out a few rudenesses, their old life was a beautiful adaptation of organism to environment. Isn't that so, Curtis?"

"It certainly had its idyllic side."

"But they must have been worried to death for fear of getting scalped," said Parker.

"Oh, they didn't war much till the white man came to disturb them, by crowding one tribe into another tribe's territory. Their 'wars' were small affairs—hardly more than skirmishes. That they were infrequent is evident from the importance given small forays in their 'winter counts.' "

One by one the campers began to yawn, and Jennie and Mrs. Parker withdrew into the tent reserved for the women, but Lawson and Elsie and Curtis still remained about the fire. The girl's eyes were wide with excitement. "Isn't it delicious to be a little speck of life in this limitless world of darkness? Osborne, why didn't we camp last year?"

"I proposed it, but Mattie would not hear to it. I have a notion that you also put my suggestion aside with scorn."

She protested that he was mistaken. "It is the only way to get close to these people. I begin to understand them as I sit here beside this fire. What do you suppose Two Horns is thinking about as he sits over there smoking?"

As they talked, Lawson began to yawn also, and at last said: "Elsie Bee Bee, I am sleepy, and I know Curtis is."

"Not at all," protested Curtis. "I'm just coming to myself. As the camp-fire smoulders the night is at its best. Besides, I'm in the midst of a story."

"Well, I didn't sleep very well last night," began Lawson, apologetically. "I think—if you don't mind—"

"Go to bed, Sleepy Head," laughed Elsie. "We'll excuse you."

"I believe I will," and off he went, leaving the two young people alone.

"Go on!" cried Elsie. "Tell me all about it."

Curtis glowed with new fire at this proof of her interest. "Well, there we were, Sergeant Pierce, Standing Elk, and myself, camped in Avalanche Basin, which at that time of the year is as full of storms as a cave is of bats." A yelping cry on the hill back of them interrupted him. "There goes a coyote! Now the night is perfect," he ended, with a note of exultant poetry.

She drew a little nearer to him. "I don't enjoy that cry as well as you do," she said, with a touch of delicious timidity in her voice. "That's the woman of it, isn't it?"

"I know how harmless he is." After a pause, he slowly said: "This is the farthest reach of the imaginable—that you should sit here beside my fire in this wild land. It must seem as much of a dream to you as your splendid home was to me."

"I didn't suppose these things could shake me so. How mysterious the world is when night makes it lone and empty! I never realized it before. That hill behind us, and the wolf—and see those willows by the brook. They might be savages creeping upon us, or great birds resting, or any silent, threatening creature of the darkness. If I were alone my heart would stand still with awe and fear of them."

"They are not mysterious to me," he made answer. "Only in the sense that space and dusk are inexplicable. After all, the wonder of the universe is in our brains, like love, rather than in the object to which we attribute mystery or majesty. To the Tetong, the simplest thing belonging to the white race is mysterious—a button, a cartridge, a tinplate. 'How are they made? What are they built for?' he asks. So, deeply considered, all nature is inexplicable to us also. We white children of the Great Ruler push the mystery a little further back, that is all. Once I tried to understand the universe; now I am content to enjoy it."

"Tell me, how did you first become interested in these people?"

He hesitated a little before he replied. "Well, I was always interested in them, and when I got out among the Payonnay I tried to get at their notions of life; but they are a strange people—a secretive people—and I couldn't win their confidence for a long time. One day while on a hunting expedition I came suddenly upon a crew of wood-choppers who had an old man tied to a tree and were about to burn him alive—"

"Horrible! Why?"

"No reason at all, so far as I could learn. His wife sat on the ground not far away, wailing in deep despair. What treatment she had suffered I do not know. Naturally, I ordered the men to release the old man, and when they refused I cut his bands. The ruffians were furious with rage, and threatened to tie me up and burn me, too. By this time I was too angry to fear anything. 'If you do, you better pulverize the buttons on my uniform, for the United States government will demand a head for every one of them.' Had I been a civilian they would have killed me."

"They wouldn't have dared!" Elsie shuddered.

"Such men dare do anything when they are safe from discovery—and there is always the Indian to whom a deed of that sort can be laid."

"Did they release the old man?"

"Yes; and he and his wife camped along with me for several days, and their devotion to me was pathetic. Finally I came to understand that he considered himself dead, so far as his tribe was concerned. 'My life belongs to you,' he said. I was just beginning the sign language at that time and I couldn't get very far with him, but I made him understand that I gave his life back to him. He left me at last and returned to the tribe. Thereafter, every redman I met called me friend, and patiently sat while I struggled to learn his language. As I grew proficient they told me things they had concealed from all white men. I ceased to be an enemy. I became an adviser, a chief."

"Did you ever see the old man again?"

"Oh yes. He was my guide on several hunting expeditions. Poor old Siyeh, he died of small-pox. 'The white man's disease,' he called it, bitterly. He wanted to see me, but when he understood that I would be endangered thereby, he said: 'It is well—I will die alone; but tell him I fold my hands on my breast and his hand is between my palms.' " The soldier's voice grew hard and dry as the memory of the old man's death returned upon him.

Elsie shuddered with a new emotion. "You make my head whirl—you and the night. Did that determine your course with regard to them?"

"Yes. I resolved to get at their hearts—their inner thoughts—and my commanders put me forward from time to time as interpreter, where I could serve both the army and the redman. In some strange way all the Northwest tribes came to know of me, and I could go where few men could follow me. It is curious, but they never did seem strange to me. From the first time I met an Indian I felt that he was a man like other men—a father, a son, a brother, like anybody else. Naturally, when the plan for enlisting redmen into the cavalry came to be worked out, I was chosen to command a troop of Shi-an-nay. I received my promotion at that time. My detail as Indian agent came from the same cause, I suppose. I was known to be a friend of the redman, and the department is now experimenting with 'Curtis of the Gray-Horse Troop,'" he added, with a smile. "Such is the story of my life."

"How long will you remain Indian agent?"

"Till I can demonstrate my theory that, properly led, these people can be made happy."

"I am afraid you will live here until you are old," she said, and there was a note of undefinable regret in her voice. "I begin to feel that you really have a problem to solve."

"It lies with us, the dominant race," he said, slowly, "whether the red race shall die or become a strand in the woof of our national life. It is a question of saving our own souls, not of making them grotesque caricatures of American farmers. I am not of those who believe in teaching creeds that are dying out of our own life; to be clean, to be peaceful, to be happy—these are the precepts I would teach them."

"I don't understand you, and I think I would better go to bed," she said, with a return to her ordinary manner. "Good-night."

"Good-night," he replied, and in the utterance of those words was something that stirred her unaccountably.

"He makes life too serious, and too full of responsibility," she thought. "I don't like to feel responsible. All the same, he is fine," she added, in conclusion.

CHAPTER XV

Elsie Enters Her Studio

ELSIE, BEING young and of flamelike vitality, was up and ready for a walk while Two Horns was building the fire, and was trying to make him understand her wish to paint him, when Curtis emerged from his tent.

"Good-morning, Captain," she called. "I'm glad you've come. Please tell Two Horns I want to have him sit for me."

Curtis, with a few swift gestures, conveyed her wishes to Two Horns, who replied in a way which made Curtis smile.

Elsie asked, "What does he say?"

"He says, 'Yes, how much?' "

"Oh, the mercenary thing!"

"Not at all," replied Curtis. "His time is worth something. You artists think the redmen ought to sit for nothing."

Two Horns ran through a swift and very graceful series of signs, which Curtis translated rapidly.

"He says: 'I have heard of you. You painted Elk's daughter. I hear you sell these pictures and catch a great pile of money. I think it is right you pay us something when we stand before you for long hours, while you make pictures to sell to rich men in Washington. Now, I drive a team; I earn some days two dollars driving team. If I stop driving team, and come and sit for you, then I lose my two dollars.'"

As he finished, Two Horns smiled at Elsie with a sly twinkle in his eyes which disconcerted her. "You sabbe?" he ended, speaking directly to her.

"I sabbe," she said, in reply.

"Good!" He held out his hand and she took it, and the bargain was sealed. He then returned to his work about the camp.

"Isn't it glorious!" the girl cried, as she looked about her. "It's enough to do an artist all over new." The grass and the willows sparkled with dew-drops. The sky, cloudless save for one long, low, orange-and-purple cape of glory just above the sunrise, canopied a limitless spread of plain to the north and east, while the high butte to the back was like the wall of a temple.

"Oh, let's take a run up that hill," Elsie said, with sudden change of tone. "Come!" and, giving Curtis no time to protest, she scuttled away, swift as a partridge. He followed her, calling:

"Wait a moment, please!"

When he overtook her at the foot of the first incline she was breathless, but her eyes were joyous as a child's and her cheeks were glowing.

"Let me help you," he said; "and if you slip, don't put your hand on the ground; that is the way men get snake-bitten."

"Snakes!" She stopped short. "I forgot—are there rattlesnakes here?"

"There is always danger on the sunny side of

these buttes at this time of the year, especially where the rocks crop out."

"Why didn't you tell me?"

"You didn't give me time."

"Do you really think there is danger?"

"Not if you walk slowly and follow me; I'll draw their poison. After they bite me they'll have no virus left for you."

She began to smile roguishly. "You are tired—you want an excuse to rest."

"If I thought you meant that, I'd run up to the summit and back again to show you that I'm younger than my years."

She clapped her hands. "Do it! It will be like the knight in the story—the glove-and-lion story."

"No. On reflection, I will not run; it would compromise my dignity. We will climb soberly, side by side, like Darby and Joan on the hill of life."

With a demure countenance she took his hand, and they scrambled briskly up the slope. When they reached the brow of the hill she was fairly done up, while he, breathing easily, showed little fatigue, although she had felt his powerful arm sustaining her many times on the steeper slopes. She could not speak, and he smilingly said, "I hope I haven't hurried you?"

"You—are—strong," she admitted, brokenly. "I'm not tired, but I can't get breath."

At length they reached the summit and looked about. "What is the meaning of those little towers of stone?" she asked, after a moment's rest.

"Oh, they have different meanings. Sometimes they locate the springs of water, sometimes they indicate the course of a trail. This one was put here by a young fellow to mark the spot from whence he saw a famous herd of buffalo—what time he made a wonderful killing."

"I suppose all this land has been the hunting-ground of these people for ages. Do you suppose they had names for hills like this, and were fond of them like white people?"

"Certainly. They had a geography of their own as complete in its way as ours, and they are wonderfully sure of direction even now. They seldom make a mistake in the correlative positions of streams or mountains, even when confused by a white man's map."

"It *is* wonderful, isn't it—that they should have lived here all those years without knowing or caring for the white man's world?"

"They don't care for it now—but I see Two Horns signaling that breakfast is ready, so we had better go."

"Let's run down!"

"Wait!" He caught her. "It will lame you frightfully, I warn you."

"Oh no, it won't."

"Very well, experience is a fine school. If you must run down, we'll go down the shadowed side. Now I'll let you get half-way down and beat you in, after all. One, two, three—go!"

With her skirt caught up in her hand, she started down the hill in reckless flight. She heard his shout and the thud of his prodigious leaps, and just as she reached the level he overtook her and relentlessly left her far behind. Discouraged and panting, she fell into a walk and waited for him to return, as she knew he would.

"Oh, these skirts!" she said, resentfully. "What chance has a woman with yards of cloth binding her? I nearly tumbled headlong."

He did not make her suffer for her defeat, and they returned to camp gay as a couple of children. Lawson smiled benevolently, like an aged uncle, while Elsie told him of their climb. Said he: "When you're as old as I am you will wait for wonders to come your way; you will not seek them."

The breakfast was made merry by Jennie, who waged gentle warfare on Parker, whose preconceived ideas of the people resident on an Indian reservation had been shaken.

"Why, you're very decent," he admitted at last.

"They are all like us—nit," replied Jennie. "We're marked 'special.'"

"Couldn't be any more like you, sis," said Curtis.

"*You* shouldn't say that."

"Well, it needed saying, and no one else seemed ready to do it. If Calvin had been here!"

"Who is Calvin?" asked Mrs. Parker.

"I know!" cried Elsie. "He's one of the handsomest young cowboys you ever saw. If you want to do a cow-puncher, Parker, he's your model."

"I certainly must see him. If I don't do a cowboy or a bucking bronco I'm a failure."

As they were ready to start, Elsie again took her place beside Curtis, but Lawson insisted on sitting behind with Jennie. "It's hard luck, Parker, to have to sit with your wife," he said, compassionately.

"Oh, well! I'm used to disappointments," Parker replied, in resigned calm.

Elsie felt the need of justifying herself. "Are you complaining? Am I the assistant driver, or am I not? If I am, here is where I belong."

"When I was coaching in Scotland once—" began Lawson.

"Oh, never mind Scotland!" interrupted Elsie. "See that chain of peaks? Aren't they gorgeous! Do we camp there?"

"Yes," replied Curtis. "Just where that fanshaped belt of timber begins, I hope to set our tent. The agency is just between those dark ridges."

"It is strange," Elsie said, after a pause. "Last year

I was *wondering* at everything; now I am looking for familiar things."

"That is the second stage," he answered. "The third will be sympathy."

"What will the fourth be?"

"Affection."

"And the fifth?"

"Devotion."

She laughed. "You place too high a value on your Western land."

"I admit there is to me great charm in these barren foot-hills and the great divide they lead up to," he soberly answered.

As they talked, the swift little horses drummed along the hard road, and by the time the agency flagpole came in view they had passed over their main points of difference, and were chatting gayly on topics not controversial. Elsie was taking her turn with the reins, her face flushed with the joy and excitement of it, while Jennie and Mrs. Parker, shrieking with pretended fear, clung to their seats with frenzied clasp.

Curtis was as merry as a boy, and his people, seeing him come in smiling and alert, looked at each other in amazement, and Crow Wing said:

"Our Little Father has found a squaw at last."

Whereas, as her lover, Curtis had been careful to consider the effect of every word, he now went to Elsie's service as frankly as Lawson himself, and his thoughtfulness touched her deeply. Her old studio had been put in order, and contained all needful furniture, and her sleeping apartment looked very clean and very comfortable indeed.

Jennie apologized. "Of course, it's like camping compared to your own splendid home, but George said you wouldn't mind that, being an artist. He has an idea an artist can sleep in a palace one night and a pigsty the next, and rejoice."

"He isn't so very far wrong," Elsie valiantly replied. "Of course, the pigsty is a little bit extreme. This is good enough for any one. You are very kind," she added, softly. "It was good of him to take so much trouble."

"George is the best man I ever knew," replied Jennie. "That's why I've never been able to leave him for any other man." She smiled shrewdly. "I'll admit that eligible men have been scarce, and my chances have been few. Well, I must run across and look after dinner. You're to eat with us till you get settled. *We* insist on being hosts this time."

"Surely," said Curtis, as they rose from the table, "being Indian agent is not the grim, vexatious experience I once considered it. If the charm of such company should get reckoned in as one of the perquisites of the office, the crush of applicants would thicken into a riot. I find it hard to return to my work in the office."

"Don't be hasty; we may turn out to be nuisances," responded Elsie.

CHAPTER XVI

The Camp Among the Roses

During the remainder of the day the agent found office work most difficult. His mind wandered to other and pleasanter things, and at last he began to make out a list of the necessaries for the camping trip.

The next day, about four o'clock, Crow Wing and Crawling Elk came into his office bringing a young Tetong, who said he had been struck on the head by a sheep-herder.

Curtis was instantly alert. "Sit down—all of you!" he commanded. "Now, Yellow Hand, tell your story."

Yellow Hand, a tall and sinister-looking fellow, related his adventure sullenly. "I was riding the line of the reservation, as Crawling Elk had told me and as you commanded, when I came upon this sheepman driving his flocks across the river. I hollered to him to keep away, but he kept on pushing the sheep into the river; then I tried to drive them back. This made him angry and he threw a rock at me, and struck me here." He touched his bandaged head. "I had no gun, so I came away."

"Did you throw rocks at him?" asked Curtis.

"No, I was on my horse."

"You rode among his sheep?"

"Yes."

"Well, that was wrong. You should have reported to me and I would have sent a policeman. You must not make trouble with these men. Come to me or report to Grayman, your head man over there. The ranchers are angry at Washington, and we must be careful not to make them angry at us. I will send Crow back with you and he will remove this man."

As they went out Curtis said to Wilson: "This is the second assault they have made on our boys. They seem determined to involve us in a shooting scrape, in order to influence Congress. We must be very careful. I am afraid I ought not to take this camping trip just now."

"Don't put too much importance on these little scraps, Major. Yellow Hand is always getting into trouble. He's quarrelsome."

"I'd disarm a few of these reckless young fellows if it would do any good."

"It wouldn't. They'd simply borrow a gun of some one, and it won't do to disarm the whole tribe, for if you do these cowboys will swarm in here and run us all out."

"Well, caution everyone to be careful. I'm particularly anxious just now, on account of our visitors."

"I don't think you need to be, Major. You take your trip with your friends. I'll guarantee nothing serious happens down here. And as you are not to leave the reservation, I don't see as the department can have any roar coming."

Nevertheless, it was with some misgiving that Curtis made his final arrangements for the start. Crane's Voice and Two Horns had interested Elsie very much; therefore he filled their places with other men, and notified them to be in readiness to accompany the expedition, an order which pleased them mightily. Mary, the mother of Crane's Voice, was to go along as chief cook, under Jennie's direction, while Two Horns took general charge of the camp.

Elsie burdened herself with canvases. "I don't suppose I'll paint a picture while I'm gone, but I'm going to make a bluff at it on the start," she said, as she came out and took her place with the driver amid the mock lamentations of Lawson and Parker and Jennie.

"Can any of you drive—no!" replied Elsie, in German fashion. "Then I am here."

"I like her impudence," said Lawson.

As they drove up the valley, Curtis outlined his plan for using the water on a huge agency garden. "I would lay it out in lots and mark every lot with the name of a family, and require it to be planted and taken care of by that family. There are sites for three such gardens, enough to feed the entire tribe, but so long as a few white men are allowed to use up all the water nothing can be done but continue to feed the Tetongs in idleness, as we are now doing."

As they rose the grass grew greener, and at last Elsie began to discover wild roses growing low in damp places, and at noon, when they stopped for lunch, they were able to eat in the shade of a murmuring aspen, with wild flowers all about them. The stream was swift and cold and clear, hardly to be classed with the turbid, sluggish, discouraged current which seeped past the agency.

"It is a different world up here," Elsie said, again and again. "I can't believe we are only a half-day's drive from the agency. I never saw more delicious greens."

Mrs. Parker, being an amateur botanist, was filled with delight of the thickening flowers. "It is exactly as if we had begun in August and were moving backward towards spring. I feel as though violets were near. It is positively enchanting."

"You'll camp beside violets to-night," replied Curtis.

Lawson pretended to sleep. Parker smoked a pipe while striding along behind the wagon. Elsie drove, and of course Curtis could not leave her to guide the team alone. Necessarily, they talked freely on many topics, and all restraint, all reserve, were away at last. It is difficult to hold a formal and carefully considered conversation in a jolting buckboard climbing towards a great range of shining peaks, and every frank speech brought them into friendlier relation. Considered in this light, the afternoon assumed vast importance.

At last, just on the edge of a small lake entirely enclosed by sparse pines, they drew into camp. To the west the top of a snow mountain could be seen, low down, and against it a thin column of blue smoke was rising. The water, dark as topaz and smooth as oil, reflected the opposite shore, the yellow sky, and the peak with magic clearness, and Elsie was seized with a desire to do something.

"Where is my paint-box? Here is the background for some action—I don't know what—something primeval."

"An Indian in a canoe, *à la* Brush; or a bear coming down to drink, *à la* Bierstadt," suggested Parker.

"Don't mention that old fogy," cried Elsie.

Lawson interposed. "Well, now, those old chaps had something to say—and that's better than your modern Frenchmen do."

She was soon at work, with Lawson and Parker standing by her side, overlooking her panel and offering advice.

"There's no color in that," Parker said, finally. "It's a black-and-white merely. Its charm is in things you can't paint—the feel of the air, the smell of pine boughs."

"Go away—both of you," she commanded, curtly, and they retreated to the camp, where Curtis was setting the tents, and Jennie, old Mary, and Two Horns, with swift and harmonious action, were bringing appetizing odors out of various cans and boxes, what time the crackle of the fire increased to a gentle roar. There they sat immovably, shamelessly waiting till the call for supper came.

They were all hungry, and Jennie's cooking received such praise as comes from friends who speak and devour—Parker nearly devoured without speaking, so lank and empty was he by reason of his long walk. Elsie seemed to have forgotten her life of luxury, and was reverted to a primitive stage of culture wherein she found everything enjoyable. Her sketch, propped up against a basket by Curtis, was admired unreservedly. Altogether, the trouble and toil of civilized life were forgotten tyrants, so far as these few souls were concerned. They came close to the peace and the care-free tranquility of the redman, whose ideals they had come to destroy.

As soon as supper was eaten and the men had lighted their cigars, the whole party walked out to the edge of the little pond and lounged about on blankets, and watched the light go out of the sky. Talk grew more subdued as the beauty and the mystery of the night deepened. Elsie listened to every sound, and asked innumerable questions of Curtis. She insisted on knowing the name of every bird or beast whose call could be heard. The young soldier's wood-craft both pleased and astonished her. Mrs. Parker, with her lap full of botanical specimens, was absorbed in the work of classifying them. Parker was a gentleman of leisure, with nothing to do but watch the peaceful coming of the dusk and comment largely on the universe.

It was natural that, as host, Curtis should enjoy a large part of Elsie's company, but neither of them seemed to realize that Lawson was being left quite unheeded in the background, but Jennie was aware of this neglect, and put forth skilful effort to break the force of it. Lawson himself seemed to be entirely unconscious of any loss or threatening disaster.

A little later, as they sat watching the fire grow in power in the deepening darkness, Curtis suddenly lifted his hand.

"Hark!"

All listened. Two Horns spoke first. "One man come, on horse."

"Some messenger for me, probably," said the Captain, composedly. "He is coming fast, too."

As the steady drumming of the horse's hoofs increased in power, Elsie felt something chill creep beneath the roots of her hair. Perhaps the Indians had broken out in war against the whites! Perhaps—

A tall young Tetong slipped from his tired horse and approached the Captain. In his extended hand lay an envelope, which gleamed in the firelight. As Curtis took this letter the messenger, squatting before him, began to roll a cigarette. His lean and powerful face was shadowed by a limp sombrero and his eyes were hidden, but his lips were grave and calm. A quirt dangled from his right wrist, and in the two braids of his hair green eagle-plumes were twisted. The star on the lapel of his embroidered vest showed him to be a police-officer. From the intensity of his attitude it was plain he was studying his agent's face in order to read thereon the character of the message he had brought.

Curtis turned the paper slowly and without excitement. With rapid signs he dismissed the courier.

"I have read it. You will camp with Two Horns. Go get some food. Mary will give you meat."

Turning to his guests, he then said: "It is nothing special—merely some papers I forgot to sign before leaving."

"By George! what a picture the fellow made, sitting there!" said Parker. "It was like an illustration in a novel. Why don't you paint that kind of thing, Bee Bee?"

"Because I can't," she replied. "Don't you suppose I saw it? I'd need the skill of Zorn to do a thing as big and mysterious as that. Did you see the intensity of his pose? He expected Captain Curtis to show excitement or alarm. He was very curious to know what it was all about—don't you think so?"

Curtis was amused. "Yes, I suppose he thought the paper more important than it was. The settlers have kept the tribe guessing all the spring by threats of running them off the reservation. Of course they wouldn't openly resort to violence, but there are several irresponsibles who would strike in the dark if they found opportunity."

In spite of his reassuring tone, a vague fear fell over the camping party. Parker was frankly alarmed.

"If you think there is any danger, Captain, I want to get out o' here quick. I'm not here to study the Tetong with his war-paint on."

"If there had been any danger, Mr. Parker, I would not have left my office. I shall have a report similar to this every day while I am away, so please be composed."

The policeman came back, resumed his squatting position before the fire, and began a series of vigorous and dramatic gestures, to which the Captain replied in kind, absorbed, intent, with a face as inscrutable as that of the redman himself. The contrast between the resolute, handsome young white man and the roughhewn Tetong was superb.

"There's nothing in it for me," said Parker, "but it's great business for a painter."

Elsie seized a block of paper, and with soft pencil began to sketch them both against the background of mysterious blackness, out of which a pine bole gleamed ashy white.

Suddenly, silently, as though one of the tree-trunks had taken on life, another Tetong appeared in the circle of the firelight and stood with deep-sunk eyes fastened on the Captain's face. Another followed, and still others, till two old men and four young fellows ranged themselves in a semicircle before their agent, with Crane's Voice and Two Horns at the left and a little behind. The old men smoked a long pipe, but the young men rolled cigarettes, taking no part in the council, listening the while with eyes as bright as those of foxes.

It was all sinister and menacing to the Parkers, and all wondered till Curtis turned to say: "They are my mill-hands—good, faithful boys, too."

"Mill-hands!" exclaimed Parker. "They looked uncommonly like a scalping party."

"That is what imagination can do. I thought your faces were extra solemn," remarked Curtis, dryly; but Lawson knew that the agent was not so untroubled as he pretended, for old Crow Killer had a bitter story to relate of the passage of a band of cowboys through his camp. They had stampeded his ponies and shot at him, one bullet passing so close to his ear that it burned the skin, and he was angry.

"They wish to kill us, these cattlemen," he said, sombrely, in conclusion. "If they come again we will fight."

Happily, his vehemence did not reach the comprehension of the women nor the understanding of Parker, and Lawson smoked on as calmly as if these telltale gestures were the flecking of shadows cast by the leaping flames. At last the red visitors rose and vanished as silently as they came. They seemed to pass through black curtains, so suddenly they disappeared.

In spite of all reassurance, the women were a little reluctant to go to bed—at least Mrs. Parker and Elsie were.

"I wish the men's tent were not so far off," Mrs. Parker said to Elsie, plaintively.

"I'll ask them to move it, if you wish," returned Elsie, and when Jennie came in she said: "Aren't you a little nervous to-night?"

Jennie looked surprised. "Why, no! Do you mean about sleeping in a tent?"

"Yes," replied Mrs. Parker. "Suppose a wolf or a redman should come?"

Jennie laughed. "You needn't worry—we have a powerful guard. I never am afraid with George."

"But the men are so far away! I wish their tent were close beside ours. I'm not standing on propriety," Mrs. Parker added, as Jennie hesitated. "I'm getting nervous, and I want Jerome where he can hear me if I call to him."

Perceiving that Elsie shared this feeling in no small degree, Jennie soberly conveyed their wish to Curtis.

"Very well, we'll move over. It will take but a moment."

As she heard the men driving the tent-pegs close beside her bed Mrs. Parker sighed peacefully.

"*Now* I can sleep. There is no comfort like a man in case of wolves, Indians, and burglars," and the fact that the men were laughing did not disturb her.

With a little shock, Elsie realized that Curtis and not Lawson was in her mind as her defender. Of course, he was in command; that accounted for it.

Nevertheless, as she listened to the murmur of their voices she detected herself waiting for Curtis's crisp, clear bass, and not for the nasal tenor of the man whose ring she wore. Her mind was filled, too, with the dramatic figure the young officer made as he sat in gesture-talk with his Tetong wards. In case of trouble the safest place on all the reservation would be by his side, for his people loved and trusted him. She did not go to sleep easily; the excitement, the strangeness of being in a tent, kept her alert long after Jennie and Mrs. Parker were breathing tranquilly on their cots.

One hears everything from a tent. It seems to stand in the midst of the world. It is like being in a diving-bell under water. Life goes on almost uninterruptedly. The girl heard a hundred obscure, singular, sibilant sounds, as of serpents conferring. Mysterious footsteps advanced, paused, retreated. Whispered colloquies arose among the leaves, giving her heart disquiet. Every unfamiliar sound was a threat. The voices of birds and beasts no longer interested her—they scared her; and, try as she would to banish these fancies, her nerves thrilled with every rush of the wind. It was deep night before she dropped asleep.

CHAPTER XVII

A Flute, a Drum, and a Message

ELSIE DREAMED she was at the theatre. The opera was "Il Trovatore," and at the moment when the prison song—that worn yet ever-mournful cry—should have pulsed forth; but in its stead another strain came floating from afar, a short phrase equally sad, which sank slowly, as a fragment of cloud descends from sky to earth to become tears of dew on the roses. Over and over again it was repeated, so sad, so sweet, so elemental, it seemed that the pain of all love's vain regret was in it, longing and sorrow and despair, without relief, without hope, defiant of death.

Slowly the walls of the theatre faded. The gray light of morning crept into the dreamer's eyes, and she was aware of the walls of her tent and knew she had been dreaming. But the sorrowful song went on, with occasional slight deviations of time and tone, but always the same. Beginning on a high key, it fell by degrees, hesitating, momentarily swooping upward, yet ever falling, till at last it melted in with the solemn moan of the pines stirring above her head. Then she drowsed again, and seemed to be listening to the wailing song with some one whose hand she held. As she turned to ask whence the music came a little shudder seized her, for the eyes looking into hers were not those of Lawson. Curtis faced her, grave and sweet.

With the shock she wakened, but the song had ceased. She waited in silence, hoping to hear it again. When fully aroused to her surroundings, she was convinced that she had dreamed the music as well as the hand-clasp, and a flush ran over her. "Why should I dream in that way of *him*?"

She heard the soft lisp of moccasined feet outside the tent, and immediately after the sound of an axe. Presently the fire began to crackle, and the rising sun threw a flood of golden light against the canvas wall. Jennie lifted her arms and yawned, and at last sat up and listened. Catching Elsie's eye she said: "Good-morning, dear. How did you sleep?"

"Deliciously—but did you hear some one singing just before sunrise?"

"No—did you?"

"I thought I did; but perhaps I dreamed it."

"Where did it seem to come from?"

"Oh, from away off and high-up—the saddest song—a phrase constantly repeated."

"Oh, I know. It was some young Tetong lover playing the flute. They often do that when the girls are going for water in the morning. Isn't it beautiful?"

"I never heard anything so sad."

"All their songs are sad. George says the primitive love-songs of all races are the same. But Two Horns has the fire going, and I must get up and superintend breakfast. You need not rise till I call."

Mrs. Parker began to stir. "Jerome! What time is it?"

The girls laughed as Jerome, in the other tent, replied, sweetly:

"Time to arise, Honey Plum."

Mrs. Parker started up and stared around, her eyes still misty with slumber. "I slept the whole night through," she finally remarked, as if in answer to a question, and her voice expressed profound astonishment.

"Didn't hear the wolves, did you, pet?" called Parker.

"Wolves! No. Did they howl?"

"Howl is no name for it. They tied themselves into double bow-knots of noise."

"I don't believe it."

Elsie replied: "I didn't hear anything but the music. Did you hear the singing?"

Lawson spoke. "You people have the most active imaginations. All I heard was the wind in the pines, and an occasional moose walking by."

"Moose!" cried Mrs. Parker. "Why, they're enormous creatures!"

Jennie began to laugh. "You people will need to hurry to be ready for breakfast. I'm going to put the coffee on." She slipped outside. "Oh, girls! Get up at once, it's glorious out here on the lake!"

Curtis was busy about the camp-fire. "Good-morning, sis. Here are some trout for breakfast."

"Trout!" shouted Lawson, from the tent.

"Trout!" echoed Parker. "We'll be there," and the tent bulged and flapped with his hasty efforts at dressing.

In gay spirits they gathered round their rude table, Parker and Jennie particularly jocular. Curtis was puzzled by some subtle change in Elsie. Her gaze was not quite so frank, and her color seemed a little more fitful; but she was as merry as a child, and enjoyed every makeshift as though it were done for the first time and for her own amusement.

"What's the programme for to-day?" asked Parker.

"After I inspect the saw-mill we will hook up and move over the divide to the head-waters of the Willow and camp with Red Wolf's band."

Parker coughed. "Well, now—of course, Captain, we are depending on you."

Curtis smiled. "Perhaps you'd like to go back to the agency?"

"No, sirree, bob! I'm sticking right to your coat-tails till we're out o' the woods."

Lawson interposed. "You wouldn't infer that Parker had ever had a Parisian education, would you?"

Parker was not abashed. "I know what you mean. Those are all expressions my father used. They stick to me like fly-paper."

"I've tried and tried to break him of his plebeian phrases, but I cannot," Mrs. Parker said, with sad emphasis.

"I wouldn't try," replied Jennie. "I like them."

"Thank you, lady, thank you," Parker fervently made answer.

Curtis hurried away to look at the saw-mill. Lawson and Parker went fishing, and Elsie got out her paint-box and started another sketch. The morning was glorious, the air invigorating, and she painted joyously with firm, plashing strokes. Never had she been so sure of her brush. Life and art were very much worth while—only now and then a disturbing wish intruded—it was only a vague and timid longing; but it grew a little in power each time. Once she looked steadily and soberly at the ring whose jewel sparkled like a drop of dew on the third finger of her left hand.

A half-hour later Curtis came back, walking rapidly. Seeing her at work he deflected from the straight trail and drew near.

"I think that is wonderful," he said, as he looked

at her sketch. "I don't see how you do so much with so few strokes."

"That always puzzles the layman," she replied. "But it's really very simple."

"When you know how. I hope you're enjoying your trip with us?"

She flashed a smile that was almost coquettish upon him. "It is glorious. I am so happy I'm afraid it won't last."

"We always feel that way about any keen pleasure," he replied, soberly. "Now I can't keep the thought of your going out of my mind. Every hour or two I find myself saying, 'It'll be lonesome business when these artists leave us.'"

"You mustn't speak of anything sorrowful this week. Let's be as happy as we can."

He pondered a fitting reply, but at last gave it up and said: "If you are satisfied with your sketch, we'll start. I see the teams are ready."

"Oh yes, I'm ready to go. I just wanted to make a record of the values—they are changing so fast now," and she began to wipe her brushes and put away her panel. "I don't care where we go so we keep in the pines and have the mountains somewhere in sight."

It must have been in remorse of her neglect of Lawson the preceding day that Elsie insisted on sitting beside him in the back seat, while Mrs. Parker took her place with the driver. The keen pang of disappointment which crossed his heart warned Curtis that his loyalty to his friend was in danger of being a burden, and the drive was robbed of all the blithe intercourse of the day before. Parker and Jennie fought clamorously on a variety of subjects in the middle distance, but Curtis was hardly more than courteous to Mrs. Parker—so absorbed was he in some inner controversy.

Retracing their course to the valley the two wagons crossed the stream and crawled slowly up the divide between the Elk and the Willow, and at one o'clock came down upon a sparse village of huts and tepees situated on the bank of a clear little stream—just where it fell away from a narrow pond which was wedged among the foot-hills like an artificial reservoir. The year was still fresh and green here, and the air was like May.

Dogs were barking and snarling round the teams, as a couple of old men left the doors of their tepees and came forward. One of them was gray-haired, but tall and broad-shouldered. This was Many Coups, a famous warrior and one of the historians of his tribe. He greeted the agent soberly, expressing neither fear nor love, asking: "Who are these with you? I have not seen them before."

To this Curtis replied: "They are my friends. They make pictures of the hills and the lakes and of chieftains like Many Coups."

Many Coups looked keenly at Elsie. "My eyes are old and poor," he slowly said. "But now I remember. This young woman was at the agency last year," and he put up his hand, which was small and graceful even yet—the hand of an artist. "I make pictures also," he said.

When this was translated, Elsie said: "You shall make a picture of me and I will make one of you."

At this the old man smilingly answered: "It shall be so."

"Where is Red Wolf?" asked Curtis.

"He is away with Tailfeathers to keep the cowboys from our land. We are growing afraid, Little Father."

"We will talk more of that by-and-by—we must now camp. Call your people together and at midafternoon we will council," replied Curtis.

Driving a little above the village, Curtis found a sheltered spot behind some low-growing pines and not far from the lake, and there they hastened to camp. The news flew from camp to camp that the Little Father was come, but no one crowded unseasonably to look at him. "We will council," Many Coups announced, and began to array himself for the ceremony. Horsemen galloped away to call Red Wolf and others who lived down the valley. Never before had an agent visited them in their homes, and they were disposed to make the most of it.

By the time the white people had eaten their lunch all the red women were in their best dresses. The papooses were shining with the scrubbing they had suffered and each small warrior wore a cunning buckskin coat elaborate with beads and quills. A semicircular wall of canvas was being erected to shield the old men from the mountain wind, and a detail of cooks had started in upon the task of preparing the feast which would end the council.

Said Curtis: "You will find in this camp the Tetong comparatively unchanged. Red Wolf's band is the most primitive encampment I know." A few minutes later he added, "Here comes Many Coups and his son in official garb."

The two chieftains greeted their visitors as if they had not hitherto been seen—with all the dignity of ambassadors to a foreign court.

"Please treat them with the same formality," warned Curtis. "It will pay you for the glimpse of the old-time ceremony."

The younger man was unpainted, save for some small blue figures on his forehead. On his head he wore a wide Mexican hat which vastly became him. His face was one of the handsomest and most typical of his race.

"This young man is the son of Many Coups, and is called Blue Fox, or 'The Southern Traveller,' because he has been down where the Mexicans are.

His hat he got there, and he is very proud of it," explained Curtis.

Jennie gave each of them a cup of coffee and a biscuit, of which they partook without haste, discussing meanwhile the coming council.

"We did not know you were coming; some of our people will not get here in time," said Many Coups.

"To-night, after the council, we wish to dance," said Blue Fox, meaning it as a request.

"It is forbidden in Washington to dance in the old way."

"We have heard of that, but we will dance for your wives. They will be glad to see it."

"Very well, you may dance, but not too long. No war-dance—only the visitors' dance."

"Ay, we understand," said Many Coups as he rose and drew his blanket about him. "In one hour we will come to council. Red Wolf will be there, and Hump Shoulder and his son. It may be others will return in time."

The women were delighted at the promise of both a council and a dance, and Lawson unlimbered his camera in order to take some views of both functions, though he expressed some dissatisfaction.

"The noble redman is thin and crooked in the legs," he said to Curtis. "Why is this?"

"All the plains Indians, who ride the horse almost from their babyhood, are bow-legged. They never walk, and they are seldom symmetrically developed."

"They are significant, but not beautiful," said Lawson.

As they walked about the camp Elsie exclaimed: "This is the way all redmen should live," and, indeed, the scene was very beautiful. They were far above the agency, and the long valleys could be seen descending like folds in a vast robe reaching to the plain. The ridges were dark with pines for a space, but grew smooth and green at lower levels, and at last melted into haze. The camp was a summer camp, and all about, in pleasant places among the pines, stood the tepees, swarming with happy children and puppies. Under low lodges of canvas or bowers of pine branches the women were at work boiling meat or cooking a rude sort of cruller. They were very shy, and mostly hung their heads as their visitors passed, though they soon yielded to Jennie, who could speak a few words to them.

"There's nothing in them for sculpture," said Parker, critically. "At least not for beauty. They might be treated as Raffaelle paints—for character."

"They grow heavy early," Jennie added, "but the little girls are beautiful—see that little one!"

The crier, a tall old man, toothless and wrinkled and gray, began to cry in a hollow, monotonous voice, "Come to the council place," and Curtis led his flock to their places in the midst of the circle.

The council began with all the old-time forms, with gravity and decorum. Red Wolf was in the centre, with Many Coups at his left. The pipe of peace went round, and those whose minds were not yet prepared for speech drew deep inspirations of the fragrant smoke in the hope that their thoughts might be clarified, and when they lifted their eyes they seemed not to perceive their visitors or those who passed to and fro among the tepees. The sun, westering, fell with untempered light on their heads, but they faced it with the calm unconcern of eagles.

To please his guests, Curtis allowed the utmost formality, and did not hasten, interrupt, or excise. The speeches were translated into English by Lawson, and at each telling point or period in Red Wolf's speech the women looked at each other in surprise.

"Did he really say that?" asked Elsie. "Didn't you make it up?"

"Rather good for a ragamuffin, don't you think?" said Lawson, as the old man took his seat.

Many Coups spoke slowly, sadly, as though half communing with himself, with nothing of the bombast the visitors had expected, and he grew in dignity and power as his thought began to make itself felt through his interpreter.

"He is speaking for his race," remarked Lawson to Elsie.

"By Jove! the old fellow is a good lawyer!" cried Parker. "I don't see any answer to his indictment."

Curtis sat listening as though each point the old man made were new—and this attitude pleased the chieftains very much.

The speech, in its general tenor, was similar to many others he had heard from thoughtful redmen. Briefly he described the time when the redmen were happy in a land filled with deer and buffalo, before the white man was. "We lived as the Great Spirit made us. Then the white man came—and now we are bewildered with his commands. Our eyes are blinded, we know not where to go. We know not whom to believe or trust. I am old, I am going to my grave troubled over the fate of my children. Agents come and go. The good ones go too soon—the bad ones stay too long, but they all go. There is no one in whose care to leave my children. It is better to die here in the hills than to live the slave of the white man, ragged and spiritless, slinking about like a dog without a friend. We do not want to make war any more—we ask only to live as our fathers lived, and die here in the hills."

As he spoke these final tragic words his voice grew deep and trembled, and Elsie felt some strong force gripping at her throat, and burning tears filled her eyes. In the city it was easy to say, "The way of civilization lies over the graves of the primitive races," but here, under the sun, among the trees, when one of those about to die looked over and beyond her to the hills as though choosing his grave—the utterance of the pitiless phrase was difficult in any tone—impossible in the boasting shout of the white promoter. She rose suddenly and walked away—being ashamed of her tears, a painful constriction in her throat.

The speakers who followed spoke in much the same way—all but Blue Fox, who sharply insisted that the government should help them. "You have put us here on barren land where we can only live by raising stock. You should help us fence the reservation, and get us cattle to start with. Then by-and-by we can build good houses and have plenty to eat. This is right, for you have destroyed our game—and you will not let us go to the mountains to hunt. You must do something besides furnish us ploughs in a land where the rain does not come."

In answer to all this, Curtis replied, using the sign language. He admitted that Red Wolf was right. "The Tetongs have been cheated, but good days are coming. I am going to help you. I am going to stay with you till you are safely on the white man's road. We intend to buy out the settlers, and take the water in the streams so that you may raise potatoes for your children, and you will then be glad because your gardens will bear many things good to eat. Do not despair, the white people are coming to understand the situation now. You have many friends who will help."

As Many Coups rose and shook hands with the agent he was smiling again, and he said, "Your words are good."

The old crier went forth again calling: "Come to the dance-hall. The white people desire to see you dance. Come clothed in your best garments."

Then the drum began to utter its spasmodic signal, and the herald's voice sounded faint and far off as he descended the path to the second group of tepees.

"Shall we go now?" asked Mrs. Parker.

"Oh no, it will be two hours before they begin. The young men must go and dress. We have time to sup and smoke a pipe."

"Oh! I'm so glad we're going to see a real Indian dance. I didn't suppose it could be seen now—not the real thing."

Lawson smiled. "You'll think this is the real thing before you get inside the door. I've known tenderfeet to weaken at the last moment."

Parker pretended to be a little nervous. "Suppose they should get hold of some liquor."

"This band is too far away from the white man to have his vices," replied Curtis, with a slight smile. He had wondered at Elsie's going, but concluded she had grown weary of the old chief's speech.

"There is great charm in this life," said Lawson, as they all gathered before their tent and sat overlooking the village and the lake. "I sometimes wonder whether we have not complicated life without adding to the sum of human happiness."

"I'm thinking of this in winter," said Elsie. "O-o-o! It must be terrible! No furnace, no bath-tubs."

The others laughed heartily at the sincerity of her shudder, and Curtis said:

"Well, now, you'd be surprised to know how comfortable they keep in their tepees. In the old skin tepee they were quite warm even on the coldest days. They always camp in sheltered places out of the wind, and where fuel is plenty."

"At the same time I prefer my own way of living to theirs—when winter comes."

"I know something of your logic," replied Curtis. "But I think I understand the reluctance of these people when asked to give up the old things. I love their life—their daily actions—this man coiling a lariat—that child's outline against the tepee—the smell of their fresh bread—the smoke of their little fires. I can understand a Tetong when he says: 'All this is as sweet to me as your own life—why should I give it up?' Feeling as I do, I never insist on their giving up anything which is not an impediment. I argue with them, and show that some of their ways are evil or a hinderance in the struggle for life under new conditions, and they always meet me halfway."

"Supper is ready," called Jennie, and his audience rose.

While still at meat, the drum, which had been sounding at intervals, suddenly took on a wilder energy, followed immediately by a high, shrill, yelping call, which was instantly augmented by a half-dozen others, all as savage and startling as the sudden burst of howling from a pack of wolves. This clamor fell away into a deep, throbbing chant, only to rise again to the yelping, whimpering cries with which it began.

Every woman stiffened with terror, with wide eyes questioning Curtis. "What is all that?"

"The opening chorus," he explained, much amused. "A song of the chase."

The dusk was beginning to fall, and the tepees, with their small, sparkling fires close beside, and the shadowy, blanketed forms assembling slowly, silently, gave a wonderful remoteness and wildness to the scene. To Curtis it was quite like the old-time village. The husky voice of the aged crier seemed like a call from out of the years primeval before the white race with its devastating energy and its killing problems had appeared in the east. The artist in Elsie, now fully awake, dominated the daughter of wealth. "Oh, this is beautiful! I never expected to see anything so primitive."

Knowing that his guests were eager to view it all, Curtis led the way towards the dance-lodge. Elsie was moved to take her place beside him, but checked herself and turned to Lawson, leaving Mrs. Parker to walk at the Captain's elbow.

To the ears of the city dwellers the uproar was appalling—full of murder and sudden death. As they approached the lodge the frenzied booming of the drum, the wild, yelping howls, the shrill whooping, brought up in their minds all the stories of dreadful deeds they had ever read, and Parker said to Jennie:

"Do you really think the Captain will be able to control them?"

Jennie laughed. "I'm used to this clamor; it's only their way of singing."

Elsie said: "They must be flourishing bloody scalping-knives in there; it is direful."

"Wait and see," said Lawson.

The dance-house was a large octagonal hut built of pine logs, partly roofed with grass and soil. It was lighted by a leaping fire in the centre, and by four lanterns on the walls, and as Curtis and his party entered, the clamor (in their honor) redoubled. In a first swift glance Elsie apprehended only a confused, jingling, fluttering mass of color—a chaos of leaping, half-naked forms and a small circle of singers fiercely assaulting a drum which sat on the floor at the right of the door.

Then Red Wolf, calm, stately, courtly, came before them carrying his wand of office and conducted them to seats at the left of the fire, and the girl's heart ceased to pound so fiercely. Looking back she saw Jennie shaking hands with one of the fiercest of the painted and beplumed dancers, and recognized him as Blue Fox. Turning, she fixed her eyes on a middle-aged man who was dancing as sedately as Washington might have led the minuet, his handsome face calm of line and the clip of his lips genial and placid. Plainly the ferocity did not extend to the dancers; the singers alone seemed to express hate and lust and war.

The music suddenly ceased, and in an instant the girl's mind cleared. She perceived that the singers were laughing as they rolled their cigarettes, and that the savage warrior dancers were gossiping together as they rested, while all about her sat plump young girls in gay dresses, very conscious of the eyes of the young men. In her early life Elsie had attended a country dance, and her changed impressions of this mad, blood-thirsty revel was indicated in her tone as she said:

"Why, it's just an old-fashioned country hoedown."

Curtis laughed. "I congratulate you on your penetration," he mockingly said.

The old men came up to shake hands with the agent, and on being presented to Elsie smiled reassuringly. Their manners were very good, indeed. Several of them gravely made a swift sign which caused Curtis to color and look confused, and when his answering sign caused them all to look at Lawson, Elsie demanded to know what it was all about.

"Do you think you'd better know?" he asked.

"Certainly, I insist on knowing," she added, as he hesitated again.

He looked at her, but a little unsteadily. "They asked if you were my bride, and I replied no, that you came with Lawson."

It was her turn to look confused. "The impudent things!" was all she could find to say at the moment.

Red Wolf called out a few imperative words, the song began with its imitation of the wolves at war as before, then settled into a pounding chant—

deep, resonant, and inspiriting. The dancers sprang forth—not all, but a part of them—as though their names had been called, while a curious little bent and withered old man crept in like a gnome and built up the fire till it blazed brightly. As they danced the younger men re-enacted with abrupt, swift, violent, yet graceful gestures the drama of wild life. They trailed game, rescued lost warriors, and defeated enemies.

"You see it proceeds with decorum," said Curtis to Elsie and Mrs. Parker, as the dancers returned to their seats. "They enjoy it just as white people enjoy a cotillion, and, barring the noise of the singers, it is quite as formal and harmless."

A little boy in full dancing costume now came on with the rest, and the visitors exclaimed in delight of his grace and dignity. He could not have been more than six years of age. His companion, an old man of seventy, was a good deal of a wag, and danced in comic-wise to make the on-lookers laugh.

Parker was fairly hooking his chin over Curtis's shoulder to hear every word uttered and to see all that went on, and Curtis was in the midst of an explanation of the significance of the drama of the dance, when a short, sturdy, bow-legged Tetong, dressed in a policeman's uniform, pushed his way in at the door and thrust a letter at his agent's hand.

Instantly every eye was fixed on Curtis's bent head as he opened the letter. The dancers took their seats, whispering and muttering, the drum ceased, and the singers, turned into bronze figures, stared solemnly. A nervous chill ran though Elsie's blood and Parker turned pale and cold.

"What's up—what's up?" he asked, hurriedly. "This is a creepy pause."

Lawson laid a hand on his arm and shut down on it like a vice.

Red Wolf brought a lantern and held it at the Captain's shoulder.

Jennie, leaning over, caught the words, "There's been a row over on the Willow—"

Curtis calmly folded the paper, nodded and smiled his thanks to Red Wolf, and then lifting his hand he signed to the policeman, in full view of all the dancers:

"Go back and tell Wilson to issue just the same amount of flour this week that he did last, and that Red Wolf wants a new mowing-machine for his people. You need not return till morning." Then, turning to Red Wolf, he said: "Go on with the dance: my friends are much pleased."

The tension instantly gave way, every one being deceived but Jennie, who understood the situation and tried to help on the deception, but her round face was plainly anxious.

Elsie, as she ceased to wonder concerning the forms and regulations of the dance, grew absorbed in the swirling forms, the harsh clashing of colors, the short, shrill cries, the gleam of round and polished limbs, the haughty fling of tall head-dresses, and the lightness of the small and beautifully modelled feet drumming upon the ground; but most of all she was moved by the aloofness of expression on the faces of many of the dancers. For the most part they seemed to dream—to revisit the past— especially the old men. Their lips were sad, their eyes pensive—singularly so—and mentally the girl said: "I must paint my next portrait of this quality—an old man dreaming of the olden time. I wonder if they really were happy in those days— happier than our civilization can make them?" and thoughts came to her which shook her confidence in the city and the mart. For the first time in her life she doubted the sanctity of the steam-engine and the ore-crusher.

As they took their seats from time to time the older men smoked their long pipes; only the young men rolled their cigarettes. To them the past was a child's recollection, not the irrevocable dream of age. They were the links between the old and the new.

As the time came to go, Curtis rose and addressed his people in signs. "We are glad to be here," he said. "All my friends are pleased. My heart is joyous when you dance. I do not forbid it. Sometimes Washington tells me to do something, and I must obey. They say you must not dance the wardance any more, and so I must forbid it. This dance was pleasant—it is not bad. My heart is made warm to be with you. I am visiting all my people, and I must go to-morrow. Do not quarrel with the white man. Be patient, and Washington will do you good."

Each promise was greeted by the old men with cries of "Ay! Ay!" and the drummers thumped the drums most furiously in applause. And so the agent said, "Good-night," and withdrew.

CHAPTER XVIII

Elsie's Ancient Love Affair

As THEY walked back to their camp Jennie took her brother's arm:

"What is it, George?"

"I must return to the agency."

"That means we must all go?"

"I suppose so. The settlers seemed determined to make trouble. They have had another row with Gray Man's band, and shots have been fired. Fortunately no one was hurt. We must leave here early. Say nothing to any of our guests till we are safely on the way home."

Elsie, walking with Lawson, was very pensive. "I begin to understand why Captain Curtis is made Indian agent. He understands these people, sympathizes with them."

"No one better, and if the department can retain him six years he will have the Tetongs comfortably housed and on the road to independence and self-respect."

"Why shouldn't he be retained?"

"Well, your father may secure re-election to the Senate next winter."

"I know," she softly answered, "he dislikes Captain Curtis."

"More than that—in order to be elected, he must pledge himself to have Curtis put out o' the way."

"That sounds like murder," she said.

"Oh no; it's only politics—politics and business. But let's not talk of that—let us absorb the beauty of the night. Did you enjoy the dance?"

"Very much. I am hopeless of ever painting it though—it is so full of big, significant shadows. I wish I knew more about it."

"You are less confident than you were last year." He looked at her slyly.

"I see more."

"And feel more?" he asked.

"Yes—I'm afraid I'm getting Captain Curtis's point of view. These people aren't the mendicants they once seemed. The expression of some of those faces to-night was wonderful. They are something more than tramps when they discard their rags."

"I wish you'd come to my point of view," he said, a little irrelevantly.

"About what?"

"About our momentous day. Suppose we say Wednesday of Thanksgiving week?"

"I thought you were going to wait for me to speak," she replied.

He caught his breath a little. "So I will—only you won't forget my gray hairs, will you?"

"I don't think I will—not with your broad daily hints to remind me. But you promised to be patient and—just friendly."

He ignored her sarcasm. "It would be rather curious if I *should* become increasingly impatient, wouldn't it? I made that promise in entire good faith, but—I seem to be changing."

"That's what troubles me," she said. "You are trying to hurry me."

At this moment they came close to the Parkers and she did not continue. He had given her another disturbing thought to sleep on, and that was, "Would it hurt him much if I should now return his ring?"

Mrs. Parker was disposed to discuss the dance, but Jennie said:

"We must all go to sleep. George says we are to move early to-morrow."

The walls of the tent could hardly be seen when the sound of the crackling flames again told that faithful Two Horns was feeding the camp-fire. Crane's Voice could be heard bringing in the horses, and in a few moments Curtis called out in a low, incisive voice:

"Everybody turn out; we must make an early start across the range."

The morning was gray, the peaks hidden in clouds, and the wind chill as the women came from their beds. Two Horns had stretched some blankets to keep off the blast, but still Elsie shivered, and Curtis roundly apologized. "I'm sorry to get you up so early. It spoils all the fun of camping if you're obliged to rise before the sun. An hour from now and all will be genial. Please wait for my explanation."

Breakfast was eaten in discomfort and comparative silence, though Parker, with intent to enliven the scene, cut a few capers as awkward as the antics of a sand-hill crane. Almost before the smoke of the tepee fires began to climb the trees the agent and his party started back over the divide towards the mill, no one in holiday mood. There was a certain pathos in this loss of good cheer.

Once out of sight of the camp, Curtis turned and said: "Friends, I'm sorry to announce it, but I must return to the agency to-night and I must take you all with me. Wilson has asked me to hasten home, and of course he would not do so without good reason."

"What is the matter?' asked Elsie.

"The same old trouble. The cattlemen are throwing their stock on the reservation and the Tetongs are resenting it."

"No danger, I hope," said Parker, pop-eyed this time with genuine apprehension.

"Oh no—not if I am on hand to keep the races apart. Now I'm going to drive hard, and you must all hang on. I want to pull into the agency before dark."

The wagon lurched and rattled down the divide as Curtis urged the horses steadily forward. With his foot in the brake, he descended in a single hour the road which had consumed three long hours to climb. Conversation under these conditions was difficult and at times impossible.

Jennie, intrepid driver herself, clutched her brother's arm at times, as the vehicle lurched, but Curtis made it all a joke by shouting, "It is always easy to slide into Hades—the worst is soon over."

Once in the valley of the Elk the road grew better, and Curtis asked Elsie if she wished to drive. She, being very self-conscious for some reason, shook her head, "No, thank you," and rode for the most part in silence, though Lawson made a brave effort to keep up a conversation.

By eleven o'clock not even Curtis and Lawson together could make the ride a joke. The women were hungry and tired, and distinctly saddened by this sudden ending of their joyous outing.

"I wish these rampant cowboys could have

waited till we had our holiday," Jennie grumbled, as she stretched her tired arms.

"Probably they were informed of the Captain's plans and seized the opportunity," suggested Parker.

"I wonder if Cal is a traitor?" mused Jennie.

Two Horns and Crane's Voice came rattling along soon after Curtis stopped for noon at their first camping-place, and in a few minutes lunch was ready. Conversation still lagged in spite of inspiriting coffee, and the women lay out on their rugs and blankets, resting their aching bones, while the men smoked and speculated on the outcome of the whole Indian question.

The teams were put to the wagons as soon as their oats were eaten and the homeward drive begun, brisk and business-like, and for some mysterious reason Curtis recovered his usual cheerful tone.

It was mid-afternoon when the agency was sighted, and the five-o'clock bell had just rung as they drove slowly and with no appearance of haste into the yard.

Wilson came out to meet them. "How-de-do? You made a short trip."

"How are things?" inquired Curtis.

"Nothing doing—all quiet," replied the clerk, but Curtis detected something yet untold in the quiver of his clerk's eyelid.

"Well, I'm glad we got in."

Supper was eaten with little ceremony and very languid conversation, and the artists at once sought their rooms to rest. The Parkers were too tired to be nervous, and Curtis was absorbed with some private problem.

As Lawson and Elsie walked across the square in the twilight he announced, meditatively:

"I'm going to be more and more impatient—that is now certain."

"Osborne, don't! Please don't take that tone; I don't like it."

"Why not, dear?" he asked, tenderly.

"Because—because—" She turned in a swift, overmastering impulse. "Because if you do, I must give you back your ring." She wrung it from her finger. "'I think I must, anyhow."

As she crowded the gem into his lax hand he said: "Why, what does this mean, Elsie Bee Bee?" His voice expressed pain and bewilderment.

"I don't know *what* it means yet, only I feel that it isn't right now to wear it. I told you when you put it on that it implied no promise on my part."

"I know it, and it doesn't imply any now."

"Yes, it does. Your whole attitude towards me implies an absolute engagement, and I can't rest under that. Take back your ring till I can receive it as other girls do—as a binding promise. You *must* do this or I will hate you!" she added, with a sudden fury.

"Why, certainly, dearest—only I don't see what has produced this change in you."

"I have not changed—you have changed."

He laughed at this. "The woman's last word! Well, I admit it. I have come to love you as a man loves the woman he wishes to make his wife. I'm going to care a great deal, Elsie Bee Bee, if you do not come to me some time."

"Don't say that!" she cried, and there was an imploring accent in her voice. "Don't you see I must not wear your ring till I promise all you ask?"

They walked on in silence to the door. As they stood there he said: "I feel as though I were about to say good-bye to you forever, and it makes my heart ache."

She put both hands on his shoulders, then, swift as a bird, turned and was gone. He felt that she had thought to kiss him, but he divined it would have been a farewell kiss, and he was glad that she had turned away. There was still hope for him in that indecision.

As for Elsie, life seemed suddenly less simple and less orderly. She pitied Osborne, she was angry and dissatisfied with herself, and in doubt about Curtis. "I'm not in love with him—it is impossible, absurd; but my summer is spoiled. I shall go home at once. It is foolish for me to be here when I could be at the seashore."

After a moment she thought: "Why am I here? I guess the girls were right. I *am* a crank—an irresponsible. Why should I want to paint these malodorous tepee dwellers? Just to be different from any one else."

As she sat at her open window she heard again the Tetong lover's flute wailing from the hill-side across the stream, and the sound struck straight in upon her heart and filled her with a mysterious longing—a pain which she dared not analyze. Her mind was active to the point of confusion—seething with doubts and the wreckage of her opinions. Lawson's action had deeply disturbed her.

They had never pretended to sentiment in their relationship; indeed, she had settled into a conviction that love was a silly passion, possible only to girls in their teens. This belief she had attained by passing through what seemed to her a fiery furnace of suffering at eighteen, and when that self-effacing passion had burned itself out she had renounced love and marriage and "devoted herself to art," healing herself with work. For some years thereafter she posed as a man-hater.

The objective cause of all this tumult and flame and renunciation seemed ridiculously inadequate in the eyes of others. He was the private secretary of Senator Stollwaert at the time, a smug, discreet, pretty man, of slender attainment and no great ambition. Happily, he had afterwards removed to New York, or Washington would have been an impossible place of residence for Elsie. She had met him once since her return—he had had the courage to call upon her—and the familiar pose of his small head and the mincing stride of his slender legs had given her a feeling of nausea. "Is it possible that I once agonized over this trig little man?" she asked herself.

To be just to him, Mr. Garretson did not presume in the least on his previous intimacy; on the contrary, he seemed timid and ill at ease in the presence of the woman whose beauty had by no means been foreshadowed in her girlhood. He was not stupid; the splendor of her surroundings awed him, but above all else there was a look on her face which too plainly expressed contempt for her ancient folly. Her shame was as perceptible to him as though expressed in spoken words, and his visit was never repeated.

Of this affair Elsie had spoken quite freely to Lawson. "It only shows what an unmitigated idiot a girl is. She is bound to love some one. I knew quantities of nice boys, and why I should have selected poor Sammy as the centre of all my hopes and affections I don't know. I dimly recall thinking he had nice ears and hands, but even they do not now seem a reasonable basis for wild passion, do they?"

Lawson had been amused. "Love at that age isn't a creature of reason."

"Evidently not, if mine was a sample."

"Ours now is so reasonable as to seem insecure and dangerous."

Her intimacy with Lawson, therefore, had begun on the plane of good-fellowship while they were in Paris together, and for two years he seemed quite satisfied. Of late he had been less contained.

After her outburst of anger at her father's ejectment of Curtis, she met Lawson with a certain re-

serve not common to her. At the moment, she more
than half resolved that the time had come to leave
her father's house for Lawson's flat, and yet her will
wavered. She said as little as possible to him concerning that last disgraceful scene, as much on her
own account as to spare Curtis, but her restless-
ness was apparent to Lawson and puzzled him. Two
or three times during the summer he had openly,
though jocularly, alluded to their marriage, but she
had put him off with a keen word. Now that her father seemed intolerable, she listened to him with a
new interest. He became a definite possibility—a
refuge.

Encouraged by this slight change in her attitude
towards him, Lawson took a ring from his pocket
one night and said, "I wish you'd wear this, Elsie
Bee Bee."

She drew back. "I can't do that. I'm not ready to
promise anything yet."

"It needn't bind you," he pleaded. "It needn't
mean any more than you care to have it mean. But
I think our understanding justifies a ring."

"'That's just it,'" she answered, quickly. "I don't
like you to be so solemn about our 'understanding.'
You promised to let me think it all out in my own
way and in my own time."

"I know I did—and I mean to do so. Only"—he
smiled with a wistful look at her—"I would have
you observe that I have developed three gray hairs
over my ears."

She took the ring slowly, and as she put the tip of
her finger into it a slight premonitory shudder
passed over her.

"You are sure you understand—this is no binding
promise on my part?"

"It will leave you as free as before."

"Then I will wear it," she said, and slipped it to its
place. "It is a beautiful ring."

He bent and kissed her fingers. "And a beautiful hand, Elsie Bee Bee."

Now, lying alone in the soundless deep of the night, she went over that scene, and the one through which she had just passed. "He's a dear, good fellow, and I love him—but not like that." And the thought that it was all over between them, and the decision irrevocably made, was at once a pain and a pleasure. The promise, slight as it was, had been a burden. "Now I am absolutely free," she said, in swift, exultant rebound.

CHAPTER XIX

The Sheriff's Mob

THE NEXT day was cloudless, with a south wind, and the little, crawling brook which watered the agency seemed about to seethe. The lower foothills were already sere as autumn, and the ponies came down to their drinking-places unnaturally thirsty; and the cattle, wallowing in the creek-bed, seemed at times to almost stop its flow. The timid trees which Curtis had planted around the schoolhouse and office were plainly suffering for lack of moisture, and the little gardens which the Indians had once more been induced to plant were in sore distress.

The torrid sun beat down into the valley from the unclouded sky so fiercely that the idle young men of the reservation postponed their horse-racing till after sunset. Curtis felt the heat and dust very keenly on his guests' account, and was irritated over the assaults of the cattlemen. "If they had but kept the peace we would still be in the cool, sweet hills," he said to Lawson.

"This will not last," Lawson replied. "We'll get a mountain wind to-night. The girls are wisely keeping within doors and are not yet aware of the extreme heat."

"I hope you are a true prophet. But at this moment it seems as if no cool wind could arise out of this sun-baked land."

"Any news from the Willow?"

"The trouble was in the West Fort. Some cowboys raided a camp of Tetongs. No one was injured, and so it must pass for a joke."

"Some of those jokes will set something afire some of these hot days."

"But you know how hard it is to apprehend the ruffians; they come and go in the night like wolves. They spoiled our outing, but I hope we may get away again next week."

In the days which followed, Curtis saw little of Elsie, and when they met she seemed cold and pre-occupied. In conversation she seemed listening to another voice, appeared to be pondering some abstract subject, and Curtis was puzzled and vaguely saddened. Jennie took a far less serious view of the estrangement. "It's just a mood. We've set her thinking; she's 'under conviction,' as the revivalists used to say. Don't bother her and she'll 'come through.' "

Curtis was at lunch on Wednesday when Wilson came to the door and said, "Major, Streeter and a man named Jenks are here and want to see you."

"More stolen cattle to be charged up to the Indians, I suppose."

"I reckon some such complaint—they didn't say."

"Well, tell them to wait—or no—ask them to come over and lunch with me."

Wilson soon returned. "They are very glum, and say they'll wait at the office till you come."

"As they prefer. I will have finished in a few moments."

He concluded not to hasten, however, and the ranchers had plenty of time to become impatient. They met him darkly.

"We want a word in private, Major," said Jenks, a tall, long-bearded man of most portentous gravity.

Curtis led the way to an inner office and offered them seats, which they took in the same oppressive silence.

The agent briskly opened the hearing. "What can I do for you, gentlemen?"

Jenks looked at Streeter—Streeter nodded. "Go ahead, Hank."

Jenks leaned over aggressively. "Your damned Injuns have murdered one o' my herders."

Curtis hardened. "What makes you think so?" he sharply asked.

"He disappeared more than a week ago, and no one has heard of him since. I know he has been killed, and your Injuns done it. No one—"

"Wait a moment," interrupted Curtis. "Who was he?"

"His name is Cole—he was herdin' my sheep."

"Are you a sheep-man?"

"I am."

"Where do you live?"

"My sheep ranch is over on Horned Toad Creek."

"Where was this man when he disappeared?"

Jenks grew a little uneasy. "He was camped by the Mud Spring."

Curtis rose and called Wilson in. "Wilson, where is the Mud Spring?"

"Just inside our south line, about four miles from the school."

"I thought so," replied Curtis. "Your sheep were on the reservation. Are you sure this man was murdered?"

"Him and the dog disappeared together, and hain't neither of 'em been seen since."

"How long ago was this?"

"Just a week to-morrow."

"Have you made a search for him? Have you studied the ground closely?"

Streeter interposed. "We've done all that could be done in that line. I *know* he's killed. He told Cal about two weeks ago that he had been shot at twice and expected to get wiped out before the summer was over. There isn't a particle of doubt in my mind about it. The thing for you to do is to make a demand—"

"I am not in need of instructions as to my duty," interrupted Curtis. "Wilson, who is over from the Willow Creek?"

"Old Elk himself."

"Send him in. I shall take all means to help you find this herder," Curtis said to the ranchers, "but I cannot allow you to charge my people with his death without greater reason than at present. We must move calmly and without heat in this matter. Murder is a serious charge to make without ample proof."

The Elk, smiling and serene, entered the door and stood for a moment searching the countenances of the white men. His face grew grave as the swift signs of his agent filled his mind with the story of the disappearance of the herder.

"I am sorry; it is bad business," he said.

"Now, Crawling Elk, I want you to call together five or six of your best trailers and go with these men to the place where the herder was last seen and see if you can find any trace of him;" then, turning to Streeter, he said: "You know Crawling Elk; he is the one chief against whom you have no enmity. If Cole was murdered, his body will be found. Until you have more proof of his death I must ask you to give my people the benefit of the doubt. Good-day, gentlemen."

As they turned to go, two young reds were seen leaving the window. They had watched Curtis as he signed the story to Crawling Elk. As the white men emerged these young fellows were leaning lazily on the fence, betraying no interest and very little animation, but a few minutes later they were mounted and riding up the valley at full gallop, heavy with news of the herder's death and Streeter's threats.

"Now, Elk," signed Curtis, "say nothing to any one but your young men and the captain of police, whom I will send with you to bring me word."

After they had all ridden away, Curtis turned to Wilson and said, "I didn't suppose I should live to see a sheep-man and a cattleman riding side by side in this amicable fashion."

"Oh, they'll get together against the Indian, all right. They're mighty glad of a chance to make any kind of common cause. That lazy herder has jumped the country. He told me he was sick of his job."

"But the dog?"

"Oh, he killed the dog to keep him from being traced. There isn't a thing in it, Major."

"I'm inclined to think you're right, but we must make careful investigation; the people are very censorious of my policy."

Next morning Crawling Elk brought word that no trace of the man could be found. "The grass is very dry," he explained, "and the trail is old. We discovered nothing except some horses' hoof-marks."

"Keep searching till every foot of land is covered," commanded Curtis. "Otherwise the white man will complain."

On Friday, just after the bell had called the people to resume work at one o'clock, Crow, the police captain, rode into the yard on a pony covered with ridges of dried sweat. His face was impassive, but his eyes glittered as he lifted his hand and signed:

"The white man's body is found!"

"Where?" asked Curtis from the door-way.

"On the high ground near the spring. He has three bullet-holes in him. Three cartridge-shells were found where the horses' hoof-marks were. The ones who shot dismounted there and fired over a little knoll. There are many white men over there now; they are very angry. They are coming here—"

"Be silent! Come in here!" Once within the office, Curtis drew from Crow Wing all he knew. He was just in the midst of giving his orders when Wilson opened the door and said, quietly, though his voice had a tremulous intensity:

"Major, step here a moment."

Curtis went to the door. He could not restrain a smile, even while a cold chill went to his heart. Nothing could exceed the suddenness of the change which had swept over the agency. As he had stood in the office door ten minutes before, his ears had been filled with the clink-clank of the blacksmiths' hammers, the shouts of drivers, and the low laughter of young women on their way to the store. Crane's Voice was hitching up his team, while Lost Legs and Turkey Tail were climbing to the roof of the warehouse with pots of red paint. Peter Wolf was mending a mowing-machine, and his brother Robert was cutting wood behind the agency kitchen. All about he had observed groups of white-blanketed Indians smoking cigarettes in the shade of the buildings, while a crowd of nearly twenty others stood watching a game of duck-on-the-rock before the agency store.

Now as he looked over the yards not a man could be seen at his work. On every side the people, without apparent haste, but surely, steadily, and swiftly, were scattering. The anvil no longer cried out, the teamsters were silent, all laughter had ceased, the pots of paint sat scorching in the sun. There was something fiercely ominous as well as uncanny in this sudden, silent dispersion of a busy, merry throng, and Curtis, skilled in Indian signs, appreciated to the full the distrust of the white man here expressed. He understood this panic. The settlers had long threatened war. Now the pretext had come, and the sound of guns was about to begin.

"Wilson," said Curtis, calmly, "if the settlers fire a shot they will regret it. See Crane's Voice, if you can find him, and send him to me." He turned to Crow and signed: "Go tell your people I will not let the cowboys hurt them. Hurry! Call them all back. Tell them to go to work. I will call the soldiers, if necessary, to keep the white man away. There is no danger."

Crow was a brave and loyal man, and, weary as he was, hastened to carry out his orders. The call for "assembly" was rung on the signal-bell, and a few of the red employés responded. To them Curtis spoke reassuringly, but his words were belied by Thomas Big Voice, the official interpreter, who was so scared his knees shook.

Curtis sent Wilson to quiet the teachers and hurried immediately to the studio, where Elsie was at work painting a portrait of old Chief Black Bull. The old man sprang to his feet the instant he caught sight of his agent's face.

"Friend, what is the matter?" he asked.

To Elsie, Curtis said: "Do not be alarmed."

"There is no danger," he signed to Black Bull. "The white man's body has been found near the spring. He was shot by two men with horses. The white men are coming to see me about it, but there is no need of alarm. Tell your people to go quietly to their camps. I will protect them."

The old chief's face grew sterner as he flung his blanket over his arm. "I go to see," he said, "The white men are very angry."

"Wait!" called Curtis. "Keep your people quiet right where they are. You must help me. I depend on you. You must not alarm them."

"I will do as you command," Bull replied, as he went away, but it was plain he apprehended violence.

"What is the matter?" inquired Elsie.

"The settlers have discovered the body of the herder who was killed, and Crow brings word they are angry. I don't think there is any danger, but I wish you and Jennie were at the fort for a few days. I don't like to have you disturbed by these things."

It was their first meeting alone since their return from the camping-trip, but Elsie was too much concerned with the serious expression of his face to feel any embarrassment.

"You don't think there will be trouble?"

"No, only a distracting wrangle, which may prevent your getting models. The Indians are nervous, and are even now getting out for the hills. But I hope you will not be alarmed."

"I'm not a nervous person."

"I know you're not—that is the reason I dared to come and tell you what was going on. I deeply regret—"

Wilson rapped on the door. "Major, you are needed. Bow-legs reports two bodies of armed men riding up the valley; the dust of their horses' hoofs can be seen. There are at least twenty men in the two squads," Wilson continued; "one came across from the West Fork, the other came from the south. It looks like a prearranged invasion."

"Very well, Wilson, I'll be at the office in time to meet them."

Curtis turned on Elsie a look which went to her heart. His voice was low as he said: "Let me take you over to Jennie. I presume these men are coming to make a demand on me for the murderers. They may or may not know who the guilty ones are, but their coming in force by prearrangement has alarmed the people."

As she laid down her brushes and took up her hat she said, gleefully: "Father won't be able to ask me what I know about war—will he? Will they begin shooting at once?"

"I don't think they are likely to do anything as a body, but some reckless cowboy may do violence to some Tetong, which will rouse the tribe to retaliation. The settlers have too much sense to incite an outbreak." At the door he said: "I wish you would go to Jennie. Tell her not to get excited. I will let you know what it is all about as soon as I find out myself. It may be all a mistake."

As he was crossing the road Lawson joined him, and when they reached the gate before the office, several of the invaders had dismounted and were waiting the agent's coming. There were eleven of them; all were deeply excited, and two or three of the younger men were observably drunk and reckless. Streeter, stepping forward, introduced a short, sullen-faced man as "Sheriff Winters, of Pinon County."

"What name?" said Curtis, as he shook hands pleasantly.

"Sheriff Winters," repeated Streeter.

"What is the meaning of all this?" queried Curtis.

"We have come for the man that killed Ed Cole. We are a committee appointed by a convention of three hundred citizens who are holding an inquest over the body," said Winters. "We have come for the murderer."

"Do you know who committed the murder?"

"No, but we know it was an Indian."

"How do you know it?" They hesitated. "Do you come as an officer of the law? Have you a warrant?"

"No, I have not, but we are determined—"

"Then I deny your right to be here. Your coming is an armed invasion of federal territory," said Curtis, and his voice rang like steel.

"Here comes the other fellers," called some one in the crowd. Turning his head, Curtis saw another squad of men filing down over the hill from the north. He counted them and made out fifteen. Turning sharply to the sheriff, he asked: "Who are those men?"

"I don't know."

"Are you responsible for their coming?"

"No, sir, I am not!" the sheriff replied, plainly on the defence.

As the second squad came galloping up, the sheriff's party greeted them with nods and low words. Curtis heard one man ask: "Where's Charley? I thought he was coming," and became perfectly certain that this meeting had been prearranged. The new-comers mingled with the sheriff's party quite indistinguishably and made no further explanation of their presence.

The young officer burned hot with indignation. "Sheriff Winters, order these men to retire at once. They have no business here!"

A mutter of rage ran over the mob and several hands dropped ostentatiously upon pistols.

One loud-voiced young whelp called out an insulting word. "You go to—! We'll retire when we get an Injun, not before!"

"Shut up, you fool!" called the sheriff, and, turning to Jenks, began to mutter in consultation. Curtis advanced a step, and raising his voice addressed the entire mob.

"As commander fo this reservation, I order you to withdraw. Your presence here is unlawful and menacing. Retire to the boundary of the reservation, and I will use every effort to discover the murderer.

If he is in the tribe I will find him and deliver him to the county authorities."

At this one of the same young ruffians who had challenged him before spurred his horse close to Curtis, and with his pistol in his hand shouted: "Not by a d—— sight. We come to take it out o' these thieves, and we're goin' to do it. Go ahead, Winters—say the word and we'll clean out the whole tribe."

Curtis looked the youth in the eye. "My boy, I advise you to make war slowly, even with your mouth."

Calvin Streeter, with his teeth clinched, crowded his horse forward and struck the insolent hoodlum in the face with his hat. "Shut up, or I'll pinch your neck off! Think you're sheriff?" The belligerent retired, snarling wild curses.

Curtis addressed himself again to Winters, assuming a tone of respect and confidence which he did not feel. "Mr. Winters, you are here as a representative of the courts of Pinon County. I call upon you, as sheriff, to disperse all these men, who are here without warrant of law!"

The sheriff hesitated, for the cattlemen were now furious and eager to display their valor. Many of them were of the roughest types of cowboys, the profane and reckless renegades of older communities, and being burdened with ammunition, and foolhardy with drink, they were in no mood to turn tail and ride away. They savagely blustered, flourishing their revolvers recklessly.

The sheriff attempted to silence them, and said, petulantly, to Curtis: "If I hadn't come you'd 'a' had a mob of two hundred armed men instead of twenty. I had hard work to keep 'em back. I swore in these ten men as my deputies. This second crowd I don't know anything about. They just happen to be here."

Curtis knew this to be a lie, but proceeded to cajole the sheriff by recognizing him and his authority.

"In that case I shall act." Addressing the leader of the second party, he said: "Sheriff Winters is the legal representative of the county; you are an unlawful mob, and I once more command you to leave the reservation, which is federal territory, under my command."

"No, you don't! We stay right here!" shouted several.

"We'll see whether the people of this State have any rights or not," said Jenks, deeply excited. "We won't allow you to shield your murdering redskins under such a plea; we'll be judge and jury in this case."

Curtis turned sharply to the sheriff: "Officer, do your duty! Dispose of this mob!" His tone was magnificently commanding. "I shall hold you responsible for further trouble," said Curtis, turning a long look on Winters, which stung.

The sheriff angrily addressed the crowd. "Get out o' this, boys. You're twisting me all up and doing no good. Vamoose now! I've got all the help I need. I'm just as much obliged, but you'd better clear out." Then to his deputies, "Round 'em up, boys, and send 'em away."

Calvin's face wore a smile of wicked glee as he called out:

"Now you fellers git!" and spurring his horse into their midst he hustled them. "Hunt your holes! You're more bother than you are worth. Git out o' here!"

While the sheriff and his deputies alternately pleaded and commanded the mob to withdraw, Lawson touched Curtis on the arm and pointed to the crests of the hills to the west. On every smooth peak a mounted sentinel stood, silent and motionless as a figure on a monument—watching the struggle going on before the agency gate.

"Behind every hill young warriors are riding," said Lawson. "By sundown every man and boy will be armed and ready for battle. If these noble citizens knew what you have saved them from they would bless you."

The mob of cattlemen retreated slowly, with many fierce oaths and a jangle of loud debate which Curtis feared each moment might break into a crackle of pistol shots.

"That was a good stroke," said Lawson. "It sets up division, and so weakens them. You will be able to handle the sheriff now."

CHAPTER XX

Feminine Strategy

HAVING SEEN the horsemen ride away, Jennie and Elsie came across the road tense with excitement.

"Tell us all about it? Have they gone?"

"Who are they?"

"We hope they are gone," Curtis replied, as lightly as he could. "It was the sheriff of Pinon County and a lynching party. I have persuaded one mob to drive away the other. They were less dangerous than they seemed."

"See those heads!" exclaimed Lawson, pointing out several employés who were peering cautiously over roofs and around corners. "Not one has retained his hat," he added. "If the danger sharpens, off will come their shirts and trousers, and those belligerent white men will find themselves contending with six hundred of the best fighters in the world."

"We must temporize," said Curtis. "A single shot

now would be disaster." He checked himself there, but Lawson understood as well as he the situation.

Jennie was not yet satisfied. "Has the sheriff come for some one in particular?"

"No, he has no warrant, hasn't even a clew to the murder. He is really at the lead of a lynching party himself, and has no more right to be here than the men he is driving away."

"What ought he to do?" asked Elsie.

"He should go home. It is my business as agent to make the arrest. I have only a half-dozen police, and I dare not attempt to force him and his party to leave the reservation."

"The whole situation is this," explained Lawson. "They've made this inquest the occasion for bringing all the hot-headed fools of the country together, and this is a bluff which they think will intimidate the Indians."

"They wouldn't dare to begin shooting, would they?" asked Elsie.

"You can't tell what such civilized persons will do," said Lawson. "But Curtis has the sheriff thinking, and the worst of it is over."

"Here they come again!" exclaimed Wilson, who surprised Curtis by remaining cool and watchful through this first mutiny.

At a swift gallop the sheriff and his posse came whirling back up the road—a wild and warlike squad—hardly more tractable than the redoubtables they had rounded up and thrown down the valley.

"I think you had better go in," said Curtis to Elsie. "Jennie, take her back to the house for a little while."

"No, let us stay," cried Elsie. "I want to see this sheriff myself. If we hear the talk we'll be less nervous."

Curtis was firm. "This is no place for you. These

cowboys have no respect for God, man, or devil; please go in."

Jennie started to obey, but Elsie obstinately held her ground.

"I will not! I have the right to know what is threatening me! I always hated to go below in a storm."

In a cloud of dust—with snorting of excited horses, the posse, with the sheriff at its head, again pulled up at the gate. The young men stared at the two daintily dressed girls with eyes of stupefaction. Here was an unlooked-for complication. A new element had entered the controversy. The sheriff slid from his horse and gave a rude salute with his big brown fist.

"Howdy, ladies, howdy." It was plain he was deeply embarrassed by this turn of affairs.

Elsie seized Curtis by the arm and whispered: "Introduce me to him—quick! Tell him who I am."

Curtis instantly apprehended her plan. "Sheriff Winters, this is Miss Brisbane, daughter of ex-Senator Brisbane, of Washington."

The sheriff awkwardly seized her small hand, "Pleased to make your acquaintance, miss," he said. "I know the Senator well."

Curtis turned to Jennie, who came forward—"And this is my sister."

"I've heard of you," the sheriff said, regaining his self-possession. "I'm sorry to disturb you, ladies—"

Elsie looked at him and quietly said: "I hope you will not be hasty, sheriff; my father will not sanction violence."

"Your being here makes a difference, miss—of course—I—"

Jennie spoke up: "You must be hungry, Mr. Sheriff," she said, and smiling up at Calvin, added, "and so are your men. Why not picket your horses and have some lunch with us?"

Curtis took advantage of the hesitation. "That's

the reasonable thing, men. We can discuss measures at our ease."

The cowboys looked at each other with significant glances. Several began to dust themselves and to slyly swab their faces with their gay kerchiefs, and one or two became noticeably redder about the ears as they looked down at their horses' bridles.

Calvin broke the silence. "I don't let this chance slip, boys. I'm powerful keen, myself."

"So 'm I," echoed several others.

The sheriff coughed. "Well—really—I'm agreeable, but I'm afeerd it'll be a powerful sight o' trouble, miss."

"Oh no, let us attend to that," cried Jennie. "We shall expect you in fifteen minutes," and taking Elsie by the arm, she started across the road.

As the cowboys followed the graceful retreating figures of the girls, Lawson and Curtis looked at each other with eyes of amazement; Lawson acknowledged a mighty impulse to laugh. "How unmilitary," he muttered.

"But how effective," replied Curtis, his lips twitching.

The cowboys muttered among themselves. "Say, is this a dream?"

"Who said pork-and-beans?"

"Does my necktie kiver my collar-button?" asked a third.

"Come, boys!" called Curtis, cheerily. "While the sheriff and I have a little set-to, you water your ponies and dust off, and be ready for cold potatoes. You're a little late for a square meal, but I think we can ease your pangs."

With a patter of jocose remarks the cowboys rode off down towards the creek, taking the sheriff's horse along with them.

Curtis turned to Lawson. "I wish you'd bring that

code over to the house, Lawson. I want to show that special clause to the sheriff."

Turning to Winters, he said: "Come, let's go across to my library and talk our differences over in comfort."

The sheriff dusted his trousers with the broad of his hand. "Well, now, I'm in no condition to sit down with ladies."

"I'll give you a chance to clean up," replied Curtis, who plainly saw that the girls had the rough bordermen "on the ice and going," as Calvin would say. A man can brag and swear and bluster out of doors, or in a bare, tobacco-stained office; but in a library, surrounded by books, in the hearing of ladies, he is more human—more reasonable. Jennie's invitation had turned impending defeat to victory.

Curtis took Winters into his own bedroom and put its toilet articles at his service and left him. As the sheriff came out into the Captain's library five minutes later, it was plain he had washed away a large part of his ferocity; his hair, plastered down smooth, represented the change in his mental condition—his quills were laid. He was, in fact, fairly meek.

Curtis confidentially remarked, in a low voice: "You see, sheriff, we must manage this thing quietly. We mustn't endanger these women, and especially Miss Brisbane. If the old Senator gets a notion his daughter is in danger—"

Winters blew a whiff. "Great God, he'd tear the State wide open! No, the boys were too hasty. As I say, I saw the irregularity, but if I hadn't consented to lead a posse in here that whole inquest would have come a-rampin' down on ye. I said to 'em, 'Boys,' I says, 'you can't do that kind of thing,' I says. 'These Tetongs are fighters,' I says, 'and you'll have a sweet time chasin' 'em over the hills—just go slow and learn to peddle,' I says—"

Lawson, entering with the code, cut him short in his shameless exculpation, and Curtis said, suavely: "Mr. Winters, I think you know Mr. Lawson."

"We've crossed each other's trail once or twice, I believe," said Lawson. "Here is the clause."

Curtis laid the book before the sheriff, who pushed a stubby forefinger against the letters and read the paragraph laboriously. His thick wits were moved by it, and he said: "Seems a clear case, and yet the reservation is included in the lines of Pinon County. 'Pears like the county dought 'o have some rights."

"Well, here comes the posse," said Curtis: "we'll talk it all over with them after lunch. Come in, boys!" he called cheerily to the straggling herders, who came in sheepishly, one by one, their spurs rattling, their big, limp hats twisted in their hands. They had pounded the alkali from each other's shirt, and their red faces shone with the determined rubbing they had received. All the wild grace of their horsemanship was gone, and as they sidled in and squatted down along the wall they were anything but ferocious in manner or speech.

"Ah, now, this is all right," each man said, when Curtis offered chairs. "You take the chair, Jim; you take it, Joe—this suits me."

Lawson was interested in their cranial development, and their alignment along the wall gave a fine opportunity for comparison. "They were, for the most part, shapeless and of small capacity," he said afterwards—"just country bumpkins, trained to the horse and the revolver, but each of them arrogated to himself the judicial mind of the Almighty Creator."

The sheriff, leaning far back in the big Morris chair, wore a smirking smile which seemed to say: "Boys, I'm onto this luxury all right. Stuffed chair don't get me no back-ache. Nothing's too rich for *my* blood—if I can get it."

The young fellows were transfixed with awe of Calvin, for, though the last to enter the house, he walked calmly past the library door on into the dining-room, and a moment later could be heard chatting with the girls, "sassy as a whiskey-jack."

One big, freckled young fellow nudged his neighbor and said: "Wouldn't that pull your teeth? That wall-eyed sorrel has waltzed right into the kitchen to buzz the women. Say, his neck needs shortening."

"Does he stand in, or is it just gall?"

"It's nerve—nothing else. We ain't onto our job, that's all."

"Oh, he knows 'em all right. I heered he stands in with the agent's sister."

"The hell he does! Lookin' that way? Well, I don't think. It's his brass-bound cheek. Wait till we ketch him alone."

Cal appeared at the door. "Well, fellers, come in; grub's all spread out."

"What you got to say about it?" asked Green.

"Think you're the boy that rings the bell, don't ye?" remarked Galvin. "We're waitin' for the boss to say 'when.'"

Not one of them stirred till Curtis rose, saying to the sheriff, "Well, we'll take time later to discuss that; come right out and tame the wolf."

The fact that Curtis accepted Calvin's call impressed the crowd deeply.

"You'd think he was one o' the fambly," muttered Galvin. "Wait till we get a rope 'round his neck."

The table, looking cool and dainty in its fleckless linen, was set with plates of cold chicken and ham, with pots of jelly and white bread at each end of the cloth, beside big pitchers of cool milk. To the cowboys, accustomed only to their rude camps and the crude housekeeping of the settlers round about, this dainty cleanliness of dining-room was marvellously subduing. They shuffled into their seats noisily, with only swift, animal-like glances at the girls, who were bubbling over with the excitement of feeding this band of Cossacks.

As they drank their milk and fed great slices of bread and jelly into their mouths, fighting Indians seemed less necessary than they had supposed. Whiskey and alkali dust, and the smell of sweating ponies, were all forgotten in the quiet and sweetness of this pretty home. The soft answer had turned wrath into shamefaced wonder and awkward courtesy.

Curtis, sitting at the head of the board as host, plied the sheriff with cold chicken, discussing meanwhile the difficulties under which the Tetongs labored, and drew from that sorely beleaguered officer admissions which he afterwards regretted. "That's so, I don't know as I'd do any better in their places, but—"

Jennie, with a keen perception of her power over her guests, went from one to the other, inquiring, in her sweetest voice: "Won't *you* have another slice of bread? Please do!"

Elsie, less secure of manner, followed her with the pitcher of milk, while the young men bruised each other's shins beneath the table in their zealous efforts to diminish the joy each one took in the alluring presence of his cup-bearer.

Calvin sat near the end of the table, and his assured manner made the others furious. "Look at that stoatin' bottle," growled Green, out of the corner of his mouth; "he needs killin'."

"Ah, we'll fix that tommy-cod!" replied Galvin.

While the girls were at the upper end of the table the men on Calvin's right leaned over and said:

"Say, Cal, 'pears like you got the run o' the house here."

Calvin, big with joy and pride, replied: "Oh, I ride round and picket here once in a while. It pays."

"Well, I should say yes—carry all your cheek right with ye, don't ye?"

As the boys began to shove back, Curtis brought out a box of cigars and passed them along the line.

"Take hearty, boys; they don't belong to the government; they're mine, and you'll find them good."

As they were all helping themselves, the sheriff coughed loudly and called out: "Boys, the Major and me has fixed this thing up. I won't need but three of you; the rest can ride back and tell the gang on the West Fork it's all right. Cal, you and Tom and Green stay with me. The rest of you can go as soon as your dinner's settled."

The ones not chosen looked a little disappointed, but they made no protest. As they rose to go out they all made powerful effort to do the right thing; they lifted their eyes to the girls for a last glance and grumbled:

"Much obliged, ladies!"

And in this humble fashion the ferocious posse of the sheriff retreated from the house of their enemy.

Once outside, they turned on each other with broad grins. They straightened—took on grace and security of manner again. They were streaming with perspiration, and their neckerchiefs were moist with the drip of it, but they lit their cigars nonchalantly, flung their hats rakishly on their heads, and turned to take a last look at the house.

Elsie appeared at the door. "Boys!" she called, and her clear voice transfixed every soul of them. "You mustn't do anything reckless. You won't, will you?"

Galvin alone was able to reply. "No, miss, we

won't. We won't do nothing to hurt you nor the Major's sister—you needn't be scart."

"You can trust Captain Curtis; he will do what is right, I'm sure of that. Good-bye."

"Good-bye," they answered, one by one. Nothing further was said till they had crossed the road. Then one of the roughest-looking of the whole gang turned and said: "Fellers, that promise goes. We got to keep that mob from goin' to war while these girls are here. Ain't that right?"

"That's right!"

"Say, fellers, I'll tell you a job that would suit me—"

"Hain't got any work into it if it does."

"What is it?"

"I'd like to be detailed to guard these 'queens' from monkeys like you."

The others fell upon this reckless one with their hats and gloves till he broke into a run, and all disappeared down the road in a cloud of dust.

CHAPTER XXI

In Stormy Councils

MEANWHILE THE sentinels on the hills missed little of the movement in the valley. They quivered with rage as the horsemen dismounted and entered the agent's house, for that seemed a defeat for their friend; but when the strangers remounted and rode away all were reassured, and Two Horns said, "I will go down and see what it all means."

One by one the principal native employés reappeared. Crane's Voice came out of the barn, where he had lain with his eyes to a crack in the wall, and Peter Big-Voice and Robert Wolf stepped cautiously into view from behind the slaughter-pen. Old Mary, the cook, suddenly blocked the kitchen door-way, and, with tremulous lips, asked: "Cowboys gone?"

"Yes, all gone," replied Jennie, much amused.

"Good, good," replied the old woman.

"Where have you been, Mary?"

Her white teeth shone out in a sudden smile. "Ice-house—heap cold."

"What did you go in there for?"

"Cowboy no good—mebbe so shoot."

"They won't hurt you," said Jennie, gently. "Go to work again. The Captain will take care of you."

"Little Father no got gun—cowboy heap gun."

"Little Father don't need gun now; you are all right," Jennie said, and the old woman went to her work again, though nervously alert to every sound.

From nowhere in particular, two sharp-eyed lads sauntered up the road to play under the office window, so that if any loud word should be spoken the tribe might know of it.

Jennie and Elsie discussed the situation while sitting at the library window with a view of the agency front door.

"I can't for the life of me take a serious view of this episode," said Jennie. "These cowboys wouldn't be so foolish as to fire a first shot. They are like big, country school-boys."

"The Parkers!" cried Elsie, suddenly. "Where are the Parkers?"

Jennie gasped. "True enough! I had forgotten all about them. I don't believe they have got back from their ride."

"They will be scared blue. We must send for them."

"I'll have Crane's Voice go at once," said Jennie. "I will go with him."

"Don't do that—not without letting the Captain know. How far is it?"

"Just over the hill—not more than five miles."

But even as she was hurrying across to the corral to find an angel for this mission of mercy, she saw the Parkers coming down the hill-side, moving slowly, for both were very bad riders. It was plain they had heard nothing, and as she watched them approach Jennie cried:

"Don't say a word. They won't see anything suspicious."

There was something irresistibly funny in the calm stateliness of the blond Parker as he led the way past the store which was deserted of its patrons, past the school-house where the students were quivering with excitement, and close beside the office behind whose doors Curtis was still in legal battle with the sheriff.

Jennie met her visitors at the gate, her hands clinched in the effort to control her laughter. "You are late. Are you hungry?" she asked.

"Famished!" said Parker. "I had to ride slow on Mrs. Parker's account."

"I like that!" cried Jennie. "As if any one could be a worse rider than you are."

"How do women get off, anyway?" asked Parker, as he approached his wife's pony.

"Fall off," suggested Jennie, and this seemed so funny that she and Elsie went off into simultaneous hysterical peals of laughter.

"You are easily amused," remarked Parker, eying them keenly. "Laugh on; it is good for digestion. Excuse me from joining; I haven't anything to digest."

Putting his angular shoulder to Mrs. Parker's waist, he eased her to the ground awkwardly but tenderly. Upon facing the girls again and discovering them still in foolish mirth, Parker looked himself all over carefully, then turned to his wife. "We seem to be affording these young ladies a great deal of hearty pleasure, Mrs. Parker."

Mrs. Parker was not so dense. "What is the matter?" she asked, sharply. "What has happened? This laughter is not natural—you are both hysterical."

Both girls instantly became as grave as they had been hilarious a moment before.

"Now I *know* something is wrong," said Mrs.

Parker. "Where is the Captain? What made you laugh that way? Have the savages broken out?"

Jennie met Parker's eyes fairly popping from his head, and went off into another shout. At last she paused and said, breathlessly: "Oh, you are funny! Come into the house. We've been entertaining a lynching party—all the Indians are in the hills and the sheriff's in the office throttling the agent."

While the Parkers consumed their crusts of bread and scraps of cold meat, Jennie told them what had happened.

Parker rose to the occasion. "We must get out o' here—every one of us! We should never have come in here. Your brother is to blame; he deceived us."

"He did not!" replied Jennie. "You shall not hold him responsible!"

"He knew the situation was critical," Parker hotly retorted. "He knew an outbreak was likely. It was criminal on his part."

"Jerome Parker, you are a donkey," remarked Elsie, calmly. "Nothing has really happened. If you're so nervous, go home. You can't sculp an Indian, anyway—grasshoppers and sheep are in your line." She had reverted to the plain talk of the studios. "Your nervousness amused us for a while, but it bores us now. Please shut up and run away if you are afraid."

"You're not very nice," said Mrs. Parker, severely.

"I don't think it's very manly of your husband when he begins to blame Captain Curtis for an invasion of cowboys."

"You admitted you were scared," pursued Parker.

"Well, suppose we were, we didn't weep and complain; we set to work to tide over the crisis."

Jennie put in a word. "If you'd feel safer in the camp of the enemy, Mr. Parker, we'll set you down the valley with the settlers. I intend to stay right here with my brother."

"So do I," added Elsie; "if there is danger it is safer here than with the cowboys; but the mob is gone, and the Captain and Osborne will see that we are protected."

Meanwhile the office resounded with the furious argument of the sheriff. "The whole western part of the State is disgusted with the way in which these Indians escape arrest. They commit all kinds of depredations, and not one is punished. This has got to stop. We intend to learn this tribe it can't hide thieves and murderers any longer." He ended, blustering like a northwest wind.

"Produce your warrants and I'll secure the men," replied Curtis, patiently. "You shall not punish a whole tribe on a pure assumption. You must come to me with a proper warrant for a particular man, and when you receive him from me you must prove his guilt in court. As the case now stands, you haven't the slightest evidence that an Indian killed this herder, and I will not give over an innocent man to be lynched by you."

As the sheriff stormed up and down the floor Lawson said, in a low voice: "Delay—delay."

Curtis, who had been writing a note, slipped it to Lawson, who rose and went out of the door. Curtis continued to parley.

"I appreciate your feeling in this matter, Mr. Sheriff, and I am willing to do what is right. I have called a council of my head men to-night, and I will ask them to search for the murderer. If one of the Tetongs killed your herder he will tell someone of it. I again suggest that you go back to your people and assure them of my willingness to aid in this affair. Give me three days in which to act."

"That crowd will not be satisfied unless we bring an Injun with us. We've got to do that or they'll come rompin' in here and raise hell with you. I propose to take old Crawling Elk himself and hold him till the tribe—"

"If you attempt such a crime I will put you off the reservation," replied Curtis, sharply.

"Put me off! By——, I think I see you doing that! Why, the whole State would rise and wipe you and your tribe out of existence." He turned threateningly and towered over Curtis, who was seated.

"Be quiet, and keep your distance, or I'll put you in irons! Sit down!"

These words were not spoken loudly, but they caused the sheriff's face to blanch and his knees to tremble. There was a terrifying, set glare in the officer's eyes as he went on:

"What do you suppose would be the consequences of firing upon a captain of the United States army in the discharge of his duty, by a sheriff acting outside the law? You have only three men out there, and one of them is my friend, and you know the quality of Calvin Streeter. I am still in command of this reservation, Mr. Sheriff."

Lawson re-entering at this moment, Curtis said: "Ask Streeter to come in, will you, Mr. Lawson?"

Calvin entered smilingly. "Well, what's the upshot?" he asked.

"It is this, Calvin. The sheriff has no warrant for anybody, not even for a suspect. I have asked him to go back and wait till I can find some clew to the murderer. Do you consider that reasonable?"

"It sounds fair," admitted Calvin, growing grave.

"Now the question of whether the State or county authority covers a federal reservation or not is too big a question for us to settle. You see that, Calvin?"

Calvin scratched his head. "It sure is too many fer me."

"Now I'll compromise in this case, Mr. Sheriff. You discharge the rest of your deputies and send them away, while you and Calvin remain with me to attend a council—not to arrest anybody, but to convince yourself of my good-will in the matter. I will not permit you to be armed nor to arrest any of my Indians until we know what we are doing. When we secure evidence against any man I will arrest him myself and turn him over to you. But I insist that you send away the men in the outer office."

Calvin spoke up. "I reckon the Major's right, sheriff. How ye goin' to arrest a man if you don't know who he is? I reckon you better do as he says. I ain't a-lookin' fer no fuss with the agent, and the United States army only fifty miles off."

The sheriff growled surlily. "All right, but there ain't no monkey business about this. I get my man sooner or later, you bet your heart on that." As he went out into the general office and announced the agent's demand, Green blurted out defiant phrases.

"I'll be damned if I would! No—stick it out! Do? Why, take old Elk and hold him till the tribe produces the right man—that's the way we always done before."

The arguments of Calvin could not be heard, but at last he prevailed, and the sullen deputies withdrew. The sheriff scrawled a hasty note to the county attorney to explain his failure to bring his man, and the three deputies went out to saddle up. Their cursing was forceful and varied, but they went.

Parker, seeing them come forth, met them, inquiring anxiously.

"Well, what do you think of the situation?"

Green looked at him surlily. "You belong here?"

"No, I'm just a visitor."

"Well, you better get out quick as God'll let ye."

"Why, what is going to happen?"

"Just this: we're goin' to have the man that killed Cole or we'll cut this whole tribe into strips. That's all," and they moved on, cursing afresh.

Parker fell back aghast, and watched them in silence as they saddled their horses and rode off. He then hurried to the office. Wilson, after going in to see his chief, came back to say: "The Major will see you in a moment. He's sending out his police."

A few moments afterwards six of the Indian policemen came filing out, looking tense and grave, and a couple of minutes later Curtis appeared.

"What is it, Parker?"

"What is going on, Captain? I am very anxious."

"You need not be. We've reached a compromise. Wait a moment and I will go over to the house with you."

When he reappeared, Lawson was with him. Nothing was said till they were well in the middle of the road. Then Curtis remarked, carelessly:

"You attended to that matter, Lawson?"

"Yes, Crane's Voice is ten miles on his way."

"There go two dangerous messengers," said Curtis, lifting his eyes to the hill-side, up which the sullen deputies were climbing.

Parker was importunate—he wished to understand the whole matter. Curtis became a little impatient. "I will explain presently," he replied, and nothing more was said till they entered the library, which was filled with the women of the agency. Jennie had reassured them as best she could, but they were eager to see the agent himself. Miss Colson, the kindergarten teacher, was disposed to rush into his arms.

Curtis smiled round upon them. "What's all this—a council of war?"

Miss Colson seized the dramatic moment. "Oh, Major, are we in danger? Tell us what has happened."

"Nothing much has happened since dinner. I have persuaded the sheriff to discharge all his deputies except Calvin, and they are to remain over. I have sent for the head man to come in, and we are going to council to-night. The trouble is practically over, for the sheriff has given up the attempt to arrest Elk as a hostage. Now go back to your work, all of you. You should not have left your children," he added, rather sternly, to Miss Colson. "They need you now."

The women went out at once, and in a few minutes Curtis was alone with the members of his own little circle. "Now I have another story for you," he said, turning to Elsie. "While I am sure the worst of the sheriff's work is over, I realize that there are two hundred armed men over on the Willow, and that it is better to be on the safe side. Therefore I have sent to Fort Lincoln for troops. Crane's Voice will reach there by sundown—the troops should arrive here by sunrise to-morrow. Meanwhile I will talk with Elk—"

"Suppose Elk don't come?" asked Jennie.

Curtis looked grave. "In that case I shall go to find him."

Elsie cried out, "You wouldn't do that?"

"Yes, it would be my duty—I have promised—but he will come. He trusts me. I have ordered him to bring all his people and camp as usual just above the agency store. Now, of course, no one can tell the precise outcome of all this, and if you, Miss Brisbane, and Mr. and Mrs. Parker, want to go down to the white settlement, I will send you at once. Mr. Lawson will go with you, or I will ask the sheriff to take you—"

"The safest place on the reservation is right here!" said Lawson. "Suppose the ranchers return—they will take control here, and use the agency as a base of supplies; the fighting will take place in the hills. Besides, our going would excite the settlers uselessly, and put Captain Curtis deeper into trouble. I propose that we stay right here, and convince the employés and the Indians that we are not alarmed. I don't want to assume the responsibility of a panic, and our going this afternoon might precipitate one."

Curtis was profoundly grateful to Lawson for this firm statement. "I think you are right, Mr. Lawson," he said, formally. "You see my position clearly. I feel sure I can control the sheriff by peaceable means—and yet my responsibility to you weighs upon me." He looked at Elsie again. "I think you can trust me. Will you stay?"

"Of course we will stay," she replied, and Parker sank into his chair as if resigned to his fate.

Curtis went on: "I am not speaking to reassure myself. Perhaps I am too positive, but my experience as an officer in the army has given me a contempt for those six-shooter heroes. The thing I really fear is a panic among the settlers. Naturally, I am disinclined towards the notoriety I would gain in the press; but the troops will certainly be here tomorrow, and that will settle the turmoil. The sheriff is less of an embarrassment, now that he has only Calvin as deputy."

"Send the sheriff over here—we'll entertain him by showing him the photograph album," called Jennie. "We helped out this forenoon, and we can do it again."

"I don't think such heroic methods are necessary; an extra good dinner will do quite as well," replied Curtis, smiling. "I'm sorry, Mr. Parker, that your expedition for material is coming to this grewsome end."

Elsie interposed. "It is precisely what he wants; he will know from positive knowledge how a Tetong brave dresses for war. I have always claimed that no Indian ever wore that absurd war-bonnet."

Lawson added: "And *you* will gain valuable information as to the character of white settlers and 'Indian outbreaks.' "

"I ought to telegraph papa."

"I have already done so," replied Lawson—"in anticipation of the hullabaloo that will break forth in the papers of the State to-morrow."

"I shall wire the department a full statement to-night," said Curtis. "But we must be careful what we say at this point."

"Isn't it a foolish thing not to have a telegraph line connecting the fort and the agency?" cried Jennie. "The troops could have been half-way here by this time."

"It's the same penny-wise and pound-foolish method by which the Indian service is run," responded Lawson.

"Here comes one of my scouts," said Curtis, as a young Tetong galloped up to the gate, threw himself from his reeking pony, and strode into the hallway without knocking, his spurs clattering, his quirt dangling from his waist. As he stood before his chief, delivering his message with shadowy silence and swiftness, Elsie thrilled with the dramatic significance of the scene. The stern, almost haughty face of the young man was in keeping with his duties.

Curtis dismissed the boy and translated his message. "He says the settlers below us have fled towards Pinon City, taking all their goods with them. White Wolf's band are all in camp except the young men, who are scouting for the chiefs to see what it all means. That mob of cowboys took delight, no doubt, in scattering consternation as they passed. The settlers are in stampede."

"Wilson is coming across the street," said Jennie, "and has an Indian with him."

"Another scout," said Curtis. "Now I will let you know all that goes on, but I must ask you all, except Mr. Lawson, to leave me the library to transact this business in." As Elsie passed him, she drew towards him with a little, shrinking movement which moved him deeply. It was as though she were clutched by a force greater than her will.

"It's like being at army headquarters," she said to Jennie.

"It is a little like a commander's tent in the field. I wish we dared to throw that old sheriff off the reservation. He has no right to be snooping around here."

Parker slumped deep in a big rocker, and Mrs. Parker sat beside him and put her hand on his arm.

"Don't worry about me, Jerome."

He looked up gloomily. "I got you into this, dearest, and I must get you out. If the soldiers come tomorrow I will ask for an escort to the fort, and then we can reach the railway and get out of the cursed country. I'd as soon live in a den of hyenas and rattlesnakes."

Elsie laughed. "Parker, you are too amusing. You are pathetic. When I think of you as you pranced about the camp-fire two days ago and look upon you now, my heart aches for you."

"I don't think it generous of you to make fun of us at this time, Bee Bee," Mrs. Parker replied, reproachfully.

"Oh, let her go on. Her Latin Quarter English doesn't disturb me," Parker answered, savagely.

Curtis at this moment appeared. "My message was from the farmer at Willow Spring. He says all his employés, with one or two exceptions, have disappeared; that the band of Crawling Elk was threatened by a mob of white men early this morning, and that they are all breaking camp in order to flee to the hills. All the settlers on the Willow are hurrying their women and children down towards Piñon City. The whole country has been alarmed by the menace of the coroner's inquest, which is camped below the agency at Johnson's ranch, waiting the sheriff's return. The deputies had not reached there when this letter was written," added Curtis. "The sheriff's message will disperse the crowds, and I am sending a note of reassurance to the farmers and to the settlers."

"It's getting mighty serious, don't you think so?" asked Parker. "I wish the troops were here. Can't we hurry them up?"

"No, all that can be done has been done. I am telling you all that goes on, and I must request you not to repeat it. I wish you would all be specially guarded in the presence of the sheriff. You might engage him in a game of 'cinch' after dinner. Anything to keep him out of my way."

"We'll absorb him," said Jennie.

One by one Curtis called in his most trusted employés, and, quieting their fears, put them to their duties. Special policemen were uniformed and sent to carry messages to the encampments on the hills, asking the head men of each band to come at once to the agency for council, and to order their people into camp. The tranquillizing effort of the agent's bearing made itself felt immediately. The threads of the whole tangle were soon in his hands and made straight, and when he received the sheriff at six o'clock he was confident and serene of bearing.

Two Horns came down from the hills, and at the agent's order gathered his band close around his own tepee to camp until the trouble was ended. Together they made a tour of the village, and Curtis made it plain that he would protect them, and that no more armed men would come among them to incite violence.

"They have turned back, for fear of the Little Father and of Washington," said Two Horns to the old men, and they were glad of his words.

Curtis was by no means at ease. As he recalled the threats of the cattlemen, the encroachments of their flocks, the vicious assaults made on Crow Killer and Yellow Hand, he divined a growing antagonism which could go but little further without producing war. His mind dwelt on the hurrying figure of Crane's Voice. Much depended on him. He saw him as he faced the sentry. "If he should fail to reach the Colonel! But he will not fail, and troops will be instantly despatched."

From these considerations he turned to the growing trust and confidence which Elsie was displaying. That movement towards him, slight as it was, and the softened look in her eyes, quickened his breath as he allowed his inward self to muse on their meaning. She was looking to him for protection, and this attitude was not only new, it was disturbing; and the soldier found it necessary to put away his pipe and fall savagely upon some work to keep his mind from ranging too far afield.

CHAPTER XXII

A Council at Night

THE SHERIFF came to dinner rather shamefacedly, but Calvin, being profoundly pleased, was on his very best behavior. "This being deputy suits me to the ground," said he to Wilson, as he rose in answer to the call to dinner.

As they were crossing the road he said, confidentially: "Now see here, you mustn't talk politics round the ladies over there, sheriff."

"Politics?"

"You know what I mean. You keep to the weather and the crops, and let this murder case alone for a minute or two, or I'll bat you one for luck."

Winters took this threat as a sign of their good understanding, and remarked, jocosely, "You damned young cub, I'll break you in two for a leather cent."

"That's all right, but what I say goes," replied Calvin. And remembering old Joe Streeter's political pull, the sheriff did not reply.

Jennie kept the talk pleasantly inconsequential

during dinner by a cheery tale of the doings of a certain Chinaman she had once tried to train into a cook, and Calvin, laughing heartily, matched her experience with that of his mother while keeping house in Pinon City one winter. This left Elsie to a little conversation with Curtis.

"You must let me see this council to-night," she said, and her request had the note of a command.

"I know how you feel," he said, "and I wish I could do so; but I can't make an exception in your favor without offending the Parkers."

"Are you not the general?" she asked, smilingly. "If you see fit to invite me and leave them out, they can only complain. I'm going to stay here with Jennie, anyhow."

"In that case we can manage it."

"Do you know what I think? You've instigated this whole affair to convert me to your point of view. Really, the whole thing is like a play. I'm not a bit frightened—at least, not yet. It's precisely like sitting in a private box and seeing the wolves tear holes in Davy Crockett's cabin. You are the manager of the show."

"Well, why not? When the princess tours the provinces it is customary to present historical pageants in her honor. This drama is your due." And as he spoke he observed for the first time the absence of the ring from her significant finger. The shock threw him into a moment's swift surmise, and when he looked up at her she was flushed and uneasy. She recovered herself first, and though her hand remained on the table it had the tremulous action of a frightened small animal—observed yet daring not to seek cover.

"I hope this council to-night will not fail. I am eager to see what you do with them," she hastened to say.

"They will come!" he replied.

Calvin was relating a story of a mountain-lion he had once treed for an Eastern artist to photograph.

"Just then the dern brute jumped right plum onto the feller and knocked him down, machine and all; for a minute or two it was just a mixture o' man and lion, then that feller come up top, and the next thing I seen he batted the lion with the box, and that kind o' stunted the brute, and he hit him again and glass began to fly; he was game all right, that feller was. When the lion stiffened out, he turned to where I was a-rollin' on the pine-needles, and says, quiet-like, 'Give me your revolver, please.' I give it to him, and he put it to the lion's ear and finished him. When he got up and looked at his machine he says, 'How much is a mountain-lion skin worth?' 'Bout four dollars, green,' I says. He looked at the inwards of his box, which was scattered all over the ground. Says he, "You wouldn't call that profitable, would you—a seventy-dollar instrument in exchange for a four-dollar pelt?'"

Everybody laughed at this story, and the dinner came to an end with the sheriff in excellent temper. Lawson offered cigars, and tolled him across the road to the office, leaving Curtis alone in his library.

He resolutely set to work to present the situation of the sheriff's presence concisely to the department in a telegram, and was still at work upon this when Jennie entered the room, closed the curtains, and lit the lamp.

Elsie came in a little later to say, sympathetically:

"Are you tired, Captain Curtis?"

He pushed his writing away.

"Yes, a little. The worst of it is, I keep saying: *If so and so happens, then I must do thus and thus,* and that is the hardest work in the world. I can deal with actual, well-defined conditions—even riots and mobs—but fighting suppositions is like grappling with ghosts."

"I know what you mean," she replied, quickly. "But I want to ask you—could father be of any help if I telegraphed him to come?"

He sat up very straight as she spoke, but did not reply till he turned her suggestion over in his mind. "No—at least, not now. What troubles me is this: the local papers will be filled with scare-heads to-morrow morning; your father will see them, and will be alarmed about you."

"I will wire him that I am all right."

"You must do that. I consider you are perfectly safe, but at the same time your father will think you ought not to be here, and blame me for allowing you to come in; and, worst of all, he will wire you to come out."

"Suppose I refuse to go, would that be the best of all?" Her face was distinctly arch of line.

His heart responded to her lure, but his words were measured as he answered: "Sometimes the responsibility seems too great; perhaps you would better go. It will be hard to convince him that you are not in danger."

She sobered. "There really is danger, then?"

"Oh yes, so long as these settlers are in their present mood, I suppose there is. Nothing but the life of an 'Injun' will satisfy them. Their hate is racial in its bitterness."

"You think I ought to go, then?"

He looked at her with eyes that were wistful and searching.

"Yes. It is a sad ending, but perhaps Captain May-nard will be here to-morrow with a troop of cavalry, and—I—think I must ask him to escort you to the railway."

"But the danger will be over then."

"To your father it will seem to be intensifying."

"I will not go on that account! I feel that the safest

place will be right here with you, for your people love you. I am not afraid when I am near you."

Curtis suddenly realized how dangerously sweet it was to sit in his own library with Elsie in that mood seated opposite him. The sound of a tapping on the window relieved the tension of the moment.

"Another of my faithful boys," he said, rising quickly. Then, turning to her with a tenderness almost solemn, he added: "Miss Brisbane, I hope you feel that if danger really threatened I would think of you first of all. You will stay with Jennie tonight?"

"If you think best, but we want to know all that goes on. I can't bear to be battened down like passengers in a storm at sea; there is nothing so trying to nerves. I want to be on deck with the captain if the storm breaks."

"Very well. I promise not to leave you in ignorance," and, raising the curtain, he signed to the man without to enter. It was Crow, the captain of the police, a short man with a good-humored face, now squared with serious dignity.

"Two Dog has just come in from Willow Creek," he reported. "He says the cattlemen are still camped by Johnson's ranch. They all held a council this afternoon."

"Are any of the head men here?"

"Yes, they are all at my tepee. They want to see you very bad."

"Tell them to come over at once; the council will take place here. I want you, but no more of the police. I want only the head men of each band."

After the officer went out Curtis moved the easy-chairs to the back of the room and set plain ones in a semicircular row at the front. Hardly was he settled when Elk, Grayman, and Two Horns entered the room, and, after formally shaking hands, took the seats assigned them. Their faces, usually smiling, were grave, and Grayman's brow was knotted with lines of anxiety. He was a small man, with long, brown hair, braided and adorned with tufts of the fine feathers which grow under the eagle's wings. He was handsome and neatly dressed, the direct antithesis to Crawling Elk, who was tall and slovenly, with a homely, grandfatherly face deeply seamed with wrinkles, a face that would be recognized as typical of his race. He seemed far less concerned than some of the others.

Two Horns, also quite at his ease, unrolled his pipe and began filling it, while Curtis resumed his writing.

Jennie, looking in at the door, recognized the chiefs, and they all rose politely to greet her.

"I'm coming to the council," she said to Two Horns.

He smiled. "Squaws no come council—no good."

"No, no, heap good," she replied. "We come. Chiefs heap talk—we catchim coffee."

"Good, good!" he replied. "After council, feast."

One by one the other chiefs slipped in and took their places, till all the bands were represented save that of Red Wolf, who was too far away to be reached. Curtis then sent for the sheriff and Calvin and Elsie and Lawson, and when all were seated began his talk by addressing the chieftains. He spoke in English, in order that the sheriff could hear all that was said, and Lawson interpreted it into Sioux.

"You know this young man"—he pointed at Calvin. "Some of you know this man"—he touched the sheriff. "He is the war chief of all the country beyond where Grayman lives. He comes to tell us that a herder has been killed over by the Muddy Spring. He thinks it was done by an Indian. The white people are very angry, and they say that you must find the murderer. Do you know of any one who has threatened to do this thing?"

One by one the chiefs replied: "I do not know

who did this thing. I have heard no one speak of it as a thing good to be done. We are all sad."

Two Horns added a protest. "I think it hard that a whole tribe should suffer because the white man thinks one redman has done a wrong thing."

Grayman spoke sadly: "My people have had much trouble because the cattlemen want to drive their herds up the Willow, and we are like men who guard the door. On us the trouble falls. It is our duty—the same as you should say to a policeman, 'Do not let anybody come in my house.' Therefore we have been accused of killing the cattle and stealing things. But this is not true. I remembered your words, and I did nothing to make these people angry; but some of my young men threw stones to drive the sheep back, and then the herder fired at them with revolver. This was not our fault."

"He lies!" said the sheriff, hotly, when this was interpreted. "No one has fired a gun but his reckless young devils. His men were riding down the sheep, and the herder rocked 'em away."

"You admit the sheep were on the reservation, then?" asked Curtis.

"Well—yes—temporarily. They were being watered."

"Well, we won't go into that now," said Curtis, turning to the chiefs and speaking with great solemnity, using the sign-language at times. And as he sat thus fronting the strongly wrought, serious faces of his head men he was wholly admirable, and Elsie's blood thrilled with excitement, for she felt herself to be in the presence of primeval men.

"Now, Grayman, Elk, Two Horns, Standing Elk, Lone Man, and Crow, listen to me. Among white men it is the law that when any one has done a wrong thing—when he steals or murders—he is punished. If he kills a man he is slain by the chief, not by the relatives of the man who is slain. As with you, I am here to apply the white man's rule. If a Tetong has shot this herder he must suffer for it—he and no one else. I will not permit the cattlemen to punish the tribe. If you know who did this, it is your duty to give him up to the law. It is the command of the Great Father—he asks you to go back to your people and search hard to find who killed this white man. When you find him bring him to me. Will you do this?"

No one answered but Two Horns, who said, "Ay, we will do as you say," and his solemnity of utterance attested his sincerity.

"Listen to me," said Curtis again, fixing their eyes with his dramatic action. "If my only brother had done this thing, I would give him up to be punished. I would not hesitate, and I expect you to do the same."

"It is always thus," Standing Elk broke out. "The cattlemen wish to punish all redmen for what one bad young warrior does. We are weary of it."

"I know it has been so, but it shall not be so again, not while I am your chief," Curtis responded. "Will you go home and do as I have commanded? Will you search hard and bring me word what you discover?"

One by one they muttered, "Ay!" and Curtis added, heartily: "That is good—now you may go."

"I want to say a word," said the sheriff.

"Not now," replied Curtis. "These people are in my charge. Whatever is said to them I will say," and at his gesture they rose, and Crow, Standing Elk, and Lone Man went soberly out into the night.

Grayman approached Curtis and took his hand in both of his and pressed it to his breast. "Little Father, I have heard your words; they are not easy to follow, but they have entered my heart. No white man has ever spoken to me with your tongue. You do not lie; your words are soft, but they stand like rocks—they do not melt away. My words shall be like yours—they will not vanish like smoke. What I have promised I will fulfil." As he spoke his slight frame trembled with the intensity of his emotion, and his eyes were dim with tears, and his deep, sweet voice, accompanying his gestures, thrilled every soul in the room. At the end he dropped the agent's hand and hastened from the house like one afraid of himself.

Curtis turned to Lawson to hide his own emotion. "Mr. Lawson, I assume the sheriff is as tired as the rest of us; will you show him the bed you were kind enough to offer?"

"Sheriff Winters, if you will come with me I'll pilot you to a couch. It isn't downy, but it will rest a tired man. Calvin, you are to bunk alongside."

"All right, professor." Calvin rose reluctantly, and as he stood in the door he said, in a low voice, to Jennie. "Now if you want me any time just send for me."

"Hold the sheriff level—that's what you do for us."

"I'll see that he don't get gay," he replied, and his hearty confidence did them all good.

After the sheriff and his deputy went out, Elsie said: "Oh, it was wonderful! That old man who spoke last must be the Edwin Booth of the tribe. He was superbly dramatic."

"He took my words very deeply to heart. That was Grayman, one of the most intelligent of all my head men; but he has had a great deal of trouble. He comprehends all too much of the tragedy of his situation."

Elsie sat with her elbows on the table, gazing in silence towards the empty fireplace. She looked weary and sad.

Curtis checked himself. "I regret very deeply the worry and discomfort all this brings upon you."

"Oh, I'm not thinking of myself this time, I am thinking of the hopeless task you have set yourself. You can't solve this racial question—it's too big and too complicated. Men are simply a kind of ferocious beast. They go to work killing each other the way chickens eat grasshoppers."

"Your figure is wrong. If our Christian settlers only killed Indians to fill their stomachs they'd stop some time; but they kill them because they're like the boy about his mother—tired of seeing 'em 'round."

There was a time when Elsie's jests were frankly on the side of the strong against the weak, but she was becoming oppressed with the suffering involved in the march of civilization. "What a fine face Grayman has; I couldn't help thinking how much more refined it was than Winters! As for the cowboys, they were hulking school-boys; I was not a bit afraid of them after they were dismounted."

"Unfortunately they are a kind of six-footed beast, always mounted; there isn't a true frontiersman among them. It angered me that they had the opportunity to even look at you."

His intensity of gaze and the bitterness of his voice took away her breath for an instant, and before she could reply Jennie and Lawson came in.

Lawson was smiling. "Parker is righteously incensed. He tried to enter the council an hour ago and your minions stopped him. He is genuinely alarmed now, and only waiting for daylight to take flight."

"Jerome is a goose," said Elsie.

"He's a jackass at times. A man of talent, but a bore when his yellow streak comes out." Turning to Curtis he said, very seriously, "Is there anything I can do for you, Captain?"

"You might wire your version of the disturbance to the Secretary along with mine. We can safely look for an avalanche of newspaper criticism, and I would like to anticipate their outbreak."

"Our telegrams will be at once made public—"

"Undoubtedly, and for that reason we must use great care in their composition. I have mine written; please look it over."

Jennie, who had dropped into a chair, checked a yawn. "Oh, dear; I wish it were morning."

Curtis looked at her and laughed. "I think you girls would better go to bed. Your eyes are heavy-lidded with weariness."

"Aren't you going to sleep?" asked Jennie, anxiously.

"I shall lie down here on the sofa—I must be where I can hear a tap on the window. Good-night."

Both girls rose at his word, and Elsie said: "It seems cruel that you cannot go properly to bed—after such a wearisome day."

"You forget that I am a soldier," he said, and saluted as they passed. He observed that Lawson merely bowed when she said "Good-night" politely. Surely some change had come to their relationship.

Lawson turned. "I think I will turn in, Captain; I have endorsed the telegram."

"I must go at once." He tapped on the pane, and almost instantly a Tetong, sleeping under the window, rose from his blanket and stood with his face to the window, alert and keen-eyed. "Tony, I have a long ride for you."

"All right," replied the faithful fellow, cheerfully.

"I want you to take some letters to Pinon City. Come round to the door."

As he stepped into the light the messenger appeared to be a boy of twenty, black-eyed and yellow-skinned, with thin and sensitive lips. "Take the letters to the post-office," said Curtis, speaking slowly. "You understand—and these despatches to the telegraph-office."

"Pay money?"

"No pay. Can you go now?"

"Yes, go now."

"Very well, take the best pony in the corral. You better keep the trail and avoid the ranches. Good-night."

The young fellow put the letters away in the inside pocket of his blue coat, buttoned it tightly, and slipped out into the night, and was swallowed up by the moonless darkness.

"Aren't you afraid they will do Tony harm if they meet him?"

"Not in his uniform."

"I wouldn't want that ride. Well, so long, old man. Call me if I can be of any use."

After Lawson went out Curtis sank back into his big chair and closed his eyes in deep thought. As he forecast the enormous and tragic results of the return of that armed throng of reckless cattlemen he shuddered. A war would almost destroy the Tetongs. It would nullify all he had been trying to do for them, and would array the whole State, the whole Indian-hating population of the nation, against them. Jennie re-entered softly and stood by his side. "It's worrisome business being Indian agent, after all, isn't it, George?" she said, with her hand in his hair.

He forced himself to a cheerful tone of voice. "Oh, I don't know; this is our first worry, and it will soon be over. It looks bad just now, but it will be—"

A knock at the outer door startled them both. "That is a white man—probably Barker," he said, and called, "Come in."

Calvin Streeter entered, a little abashed at seeing Jennie. Meeting Curtis's look of inquiry, he said, with winning candor, "Major, I been a-studyin' on this thing a good 'eal, and I've come to the conclusion that you're right on all these counts, and I've

concluded to ride over the hill and see if I can't argue the boys out of their notion to kill somebody."

Jennie clapped her hands. "Good! That is a splendid resolution. I always knew you meant right."

Curtis held out his hand. "Shake hands, my boy.
There isn't a moment to be lost. If they are coming
at all, they will start about sunrise. I hope they have
reconsidered the matter and broken camp."

Calvin looked a little uneasy. "Well, I'll tell ye, Major, I'm afraid them lahees that we sent back home
will egg the rest on; they sure were bilun mad, but
I'll go and do what I can to head 'em off. If I can't
delay 'em, I'll come along with 'em, but you can
count on me to do any little job that'll help you after we get here. Good-night."

"Good-night. Don't take any rest."

"Oh, I'm all right. Nobody ain't huntin' trouble
with me."

After he went out Jennie said: "I call that the
grace of God working in the soul of man."

Curtis looked at her keenly. "I call it the love of
woman sanctifying the heart of a cowboy."

She colored a little. "Do we women go on the pay-
rolls as assistant agents?"

"Not if we men can prevent it. What kind of a report would it make if I were forced to say, 'At this
critical moment the charming Miss So-and-so came
to my aid, and, by inviting the men in to dinner with
a sweet smile, completely disarmed their hostility.
Too much honor cannot be given,' etc."

"I guess if history were written by women once in
a while those reports wouldn't be so rare as they
are."

CHAPTER XXIII

The Return of the Mob

CURTIS WAS awakened about four o'clock by Wilson at his window. "Are you awake, Major?"

"Yes; what is it?"

"Two of the scouts have just come in from the hills. They are sure the ranchers are coming to make war. Bands of white men are crossing the county to join the camp. It certainly looks owly, Major."

Curtis rose and went to the window. "The troops will be here by nine o'clock at the furthest, and the mob will not move till sunrise, and can't reach here, even by hard riding, before eleven."

"Shall I send a courier out to meet the troops and hurry them on?" asked Wilson, whose voice was untouched of fear.

"It might be well. Send Two Horns to me if you can find him. Keep silent as to these reports."

"All right, Major."

Curtis did not underestimate the dangers of the

situation. If the troops did not arrive, and if the armed posse of the settlers should come and attempt to arrest Elk, war would follow, that was certain. Meanwhile he was one day's hard riding from either the fort or the telegraph line, with the settlers between, and no news could reach him for twenty-four hours.

At that very moment the morning papers were being distributed bearing a burden of calumny. The department would open his telegram in a few minutes, but the Secretary's reply could not reach him before sunset at the earliest, "and by that time I will be master of the situation or there will be war. I must parley—delay them, by any means, till the troops arrive. Colonel Daggett will forward the men at once—I hope under Maynard—and Jack is no sluggard. He will be here if only the Colonel takes action."

The sun rose as usual in a cloudless sky, but the wind was again in the northwest, and as he stood on the little porch looking up the valley he could see the smoke of the camp-fires in Grayman's camp, and beyond him the Crawling Elk and his people occupied a larger circle of shining tepees. The two villages seemed as peaceful as if the people were waiting for their rations, but as he lifted his eyes to the hills he could see the mounted sentinels patiently waiting the coming of the sun, and he knew that beyond and to the east every butte was similarly crested with spies. These people of the wide spaces had their own signal service and were not to be taken unawares. Each movement of the enemy would be flashed from hill to hill, miles in advance of the beat of their horses' hoofs.

As he was returning to his library Elsie met him. "Good-morning, Captain. Did you sleep?"

"Oh yes, indeed!" He spoke as lightly as he could.

"But my messengers reporting disturbed me a little during the early morning.'

"With bad news?"

"Oh no, quite the contrary. I think we are well out of our difficulty."

"I'm sure I hope so. You look tired."

"I'm ashamed of it. You must have slept well—you are radiant. I am sorry I cannot promise you the Elk for a sitter to-day."

"I like him better as the leader of his people. Do we breakfast with the sheriff this morning?"

"That affliction is bearing down upon us," he replied. "He is even now moving morosely across the road. I fear he is in bad temper."

"I think I will be late to breakfast in that case," she said, with a little grimace, and fled.

Curtis greeted his guest pleasantly. "Good-morning, sheriff."

"Good-morning, Major. Have you seen anything of my deputy?"

"No; has he left you?"

"I didn't miss him till this morning," replied Winters, sourly. "But he's gone, horse and all."

"Well, the loss is not serious. Come in and break an egg with me."

Jennie was distinctly less cordial than before, but she made her unwelcome guest comfortable, and asked after his health politely. She was just pouring his second cup of coffee when the furious clanging of the office bell made them all start.

Curtis looked at his watch. "Good Heavens! It can't be the eight-o'clock bell. What time have you?"

"Seven thirty-three."

Curtis sprang up. "It's a signal of fire!"

At the word "fire" Jennie turned white and rose. Elsie came flying down-stairs, crying:

"The Indians are running!"

A wild shout arose, "Stop that bell!" and a moment later Wilson burst in at the door—"Major, the Indians are signalling from the buttes—everybody is taking to the hills—the mob is coming."

Curtis gave Elsie one piercing look. "I hope you will trust me; you are in no danger, even if this alarm is true. I think it is a mistake. I will return soon and let you know. I beg you not to be alarmed."

The alarm was true. On the buttes horsemen were riding to and fro excitedly crossing and re-crossing the same ground—the sign which means an approaching enemy. On every hill-side mounted warriors were gathering and circling. Boys with wild halloos were bringing in the ponies. The women busy, swarming like bees, were dropping the tepees; even as the agent mounted the steps to the office and looked up the valley, the white canvases sank to the ground one by one as though melted by the hot sun. War times were come again, and the chanting cries of the old women came pulsing by on the soft west wind.

A grim smile settled on the agent's lips as he comprehended these preparations. He knew the history of these people and admired them for their skill and their bravery. War times were come again!

"Our cowboy friends have set themselves a memorable task in trying to wipe out this tribe. The ranchers never fight their own battles; they always call upon the federal government; and that is their purpose now, to stir up strife and leave the troops to bear the burden of the war."

"I don't see our fellers," said the sheriff, who was deeply excited. "I'll ride to meet them."

"They are a long way off yet," said Curtis. "The Tetong sentinels have only signalled their start. I hope the troops are on the way," he said to the two girls who had followed and now stood close beside him as if for protection. Then he called to the sheriff, who had started for his horse: "I depend on you to keep off this invasion, sheriff. I warn you and your men that this entrance here at this time is a crime against Washington."

Winters did not reply, and Curtis knew that he would join the majority; being a candidate for re-election, he could not afford to run counter to the wishes of his constituents. Hastily mounting his horse, he galloped furiously away.

Curtis strained his eyes down the valley, hoping for a sight of the guidons of the —th.

"What can you do?" asked Elsie.

"Nothing but await the issue," he replied. "I have sent another courier to hasten the troops; it is now a race between the forces of law and of order. If the mob arrives first, I must delay them—prevent their advance if possible. There is nothing else to be done."

"Can we help?"

"I'm afraid not. There will be two or three hundred of the invaders this time, if the sheriff is to be believed. I am afraid to have you meet them. I think it better for you all to keep within doors."

"I wish my father knew—he could stop this!" wailed Elsie, in sudden realization of her helplessness. "He could wire the authorities in Pinon City. I know they would listen to him."

"Here come the Parkers!" said Jennie. "Now look out for squalls."

"I had forgotten them," said Curtis, with a comic look of dismay.

Parker was running, half dragging his poor, breathless wife, while in their rear Lawson appeared, walking calmly, quite irreproachable in a gray morning suit, and the sight of him was a comfort to Curtis, for his forces were practically reduced to Wilson and four or five clerks.

"Now, Captain, what are you going to do?" called Parker. "You let us into this—"

Being in no mood for squalls, Curtis cut Parker short. "Be quiet; don't be uselessly foolish. Try and conduct yourself like a reasonable human being. Jennie, go into the house, and take the ladies with you. You'll have all the women of the agency to look after in a few minutes. Lawson, I can depend on you—will you go over to the office with me?"

When they reached the office Lawson threw back his coat and displayed two wicked-looking revolvers. "I've been known to fight when pushed too far," he said, smilingly.

In the space of an hour the panic had become preparation. On a low butte to the southwest a dark mass of armed and resolute warriors waited on their swift ponies ready for whatever came, while behind them on a higher ridge a smaller group of dismounted chieftains sat in council. Up the slopes below and to the right the women and old men were leading the ponies, laden with their tepees, children, and supplies, precisely as in the olden times. The wagons of the white men were of no use where they were now climbing. The ways of the wheel were no longer desirable. They sought the shelter of the trail.

"I am confident that the troops will arrive first," said Curtis.

"If the powers of evil have found a leader, it will be hard to control them even with a troop of cavalry," Lawson replied, soberly. "The sheriff will go with the mob when it comes to a show down."

"Oh, of course. I do not count on him; but Calvin is loyal."

Before the office stood two or three of the white employés of the agency with their wives and children about them. Two policemen alone remained of all the throng of red employés usually to be seen about the yards; the rest were out on duty or had joined their people in the hills.

"What shall we do?" cried Miss Colson, a look of mortal terror on her face. She crowded close to Curtis and laid her hands on his arm. "Let us stay near you."

"You are in no danger," he replied. "Those poor devils on the hill-side are the ones who will suffer. Where are your children?" he asked, sharply.

"They all disappeared like rabbits at sound of the bell; only the kindergarten class remains."

"Go and help take care of them," he commanded. "Sing to them—amuse them. Wolf Robe," he called to one of the policemen—he of the bow-legs—"go to the people on the hill and say to them to fear nothing, Washington protects them. Tell them they must not fight. Say to the mothers of the little ones that nothing shall hurt them. Go quick!"

Wolf Robe handed his sombrero, his coat, and his revolver to his friend, Beaver Kill, and ran away towards the corral, agile as a boy.

"What did he do that for?" asked Jennie.

Curtis smiled. "He is Indian now; he doesn't want to be mistaken for a cowboy."

When he reappeared on his pony, his long, dark hair streaming, a red handkerchief bound about his head, he looked like a warrior stripped for battle. "There isn't a faithfuler man in the world," said Curtis, and a lump rose in his throat. "He has been riding half the night for me, but he charges that hill as if he were playing a game."

"I don't understand how you can trust them to do such things," said Elsie. "Perhaps he will not come back. How do you know he will do as you commanded?"

"Because that ugly little bow-legged Tetong is a man!" replied Curtis. "He would die in performance of his duty." And something in his voice made the tears start to Elsie's eyes.

The sentinels on the hills were quiet now—facing the northeast, motionless as weather-vanes. The camps had disappeared as if by magic; nothing remained but a few wagons. Wolf Robe, diminishing to the value of a coyote, was riding straight towards the retreating women. Even as Curtis watched, the chieftains on the higher hill rose, and one of them started downward towards the warriors on the rounded hill-top. Then a small squad detached itself from the main command and slid down the grassy slope to meet the women. As they rode slowly on, the moving figures of those leading the camp horses gathered round them. Curtis understood some command was being shouted by the descending squad.

Separating themselves from the led ponies, these scouts swept on down the hill directly upon the solitary and minute figure of Wolf Robe, whose pony climbed slowly and in zigzag course.

"They will kill him," said a woman.

Wolf Robe halted and waited till the skirmishers rode up to him. They massed round him closely, listening while he delivered his message.

"When he returns we will know all that his people have learned of the invaders," said Curtis. "They will tell him what they have seen."

"It is strange," exclaimed Elsie, in a low voice, standing close beside him. "But I'm not afraid. It is like a story—a dream. That I should stand here watching Indians preparing for war and waiting for United States troops is incredible."

"I wish it were not true," he replied. "But it is. I have no fear of my people, only of the rash act of a vicious white man."

"Which way will the cattlemen come from?" asked Jennie.

"Probably down that trail." He pointed to the northeast. "Part of them may come up the valley road. Wolf Robe has started on his return."

The little squad of warriors returned to the group of chieftains, while the loyal Wolf Robe came racing down the slope, his hair streaming, his elbows flapping. In a few minutes he dropped rein at the gate and re-entered the yard. Standing before his chief, he delivered his message.

"Their hearts are very glad at your good words, but the women are crying for their babies. They ask that you send them away before the bad white men come. Send them out towards the hills and they will come down and get them—this they said."

"What did the scouts say?"

"They said that the sentinels on the hills saw the white men break camp and come this way—many of them—so they say."

"Where are they now?"

"They are hidden in the pines of the valley. They will soon be here—so they say."

"Take a fresh pony and ride back and tell all who have children here to come down and talk with me. Tell them I will turn the white men away. No one shall be harmed. The children are safe. There will be no war. I will meet them in the old camp. I keep repeating there is no danger because I believe it," he said to the silent group around him, after Wolf Robe rode away. "There is nothing to be done but wait. So go about your duties," he added, with a note of command.

One by one the employés dropped away till only Wilson remained. His only sign of nervousness was a quiver of the muscles of one cheek, where he held his quid of tobacco. His bright blue eyes were fixed on the sentinels, while he leaned negligently against the fence. Lawson, smoking a German pipe, was watching the warriors on the hills, a rapt expression on his face, as if he were working out some problem in ethics which demanded complete concentration and absorption of thought. The two girls had drawn close together as if for comfort, their nerves a-quiver with the strain.

"Are you waiting for something to go off?" suddenly asked Curtis.

Each one started a little, and all laughed together.

"I think I was," confessed Elsie.

"You seemed to be holding your breath. I wish you'd both go in and rest," he pleaded. "It is no use—"

"They're coming!" interrupted Lawson.

"Where? Where?"

"The sentinels are signalling again."

All turned to the east, but nothing could be seen—no smoke, no dust, no sign of horsemen—yet the swift circling of the sentinels and the turmoil among the warriors on the butte indicated the menace of an approaching army. Another little band detached itself from the huddle of the camp and came down the hill, slowly and in single file.

"The squaws are coming for their children, even before Wolf Robe reaches them," said Lawson.

"And there's the mob!" said Curtis, and at his words a keen thrill of fear ran through the hearts of the women. With set, pale faces they looked away beneath levelled finger.

"That's right," said Wilson, "and two hundred strong."

The sad-colored horsemen were pouring over a high, pine-clad ridge some two miles to the east, and streaming down into a narrow valley behind a sharp intervening butte.

"Now, girls, you *must* go in!" commanded Curtis, sharply. "You can do no good—"

"George, let us stay!" pleaded Jennie. "We saved you yesterday, and we may help to-day."

"What is the use of shutting us in the house? I'm not afraid," added Elsie. "These men will do us no harm."

"I beg you will not interfere," he said, looking at Jennie, but Elsie knew he included her as well. "It isn't a bit impressive to have an agent flanked with women—in a council of war."

"Hang the looks! they're mighty effective sometimes," remarked Lawson.

"That's right!" chimed in Wilson. "By the Lord! they look sassy," he added, referring back to the cowboys.

They formed a sinister cavalcade as they came streaming down the rough road, two and two, like a monstrous swift serpent, parti-colored, sinuous, silent, save for the muffled clatter of their horses' hoofs. Curtis nerved himself for the shock, and, though weakened and embarrassed by the presence of Elsie and Jennie, he presented a soldierly breast to the mob. Had it been a question of protecting the women, the case would have been different, but to argue a point of law with them at his elbow exposed him to ridicule and to interruption.

As the horsemen debouched upon the valley road, a prodigious cloud of dust arose and sailed away on the wind, completely hiding the rear ranks so that they could not be numbered. As they drew near, the sheriff could be seen riding at the head of the column side by side with a big man in a blue shirt. They approached at a shacking trot, which was more menacing than a gallop would have been—it was steady, inexorable, self-contained as a charge of cavalry.

As they reached the issue-house, Curtis opened the gate and stepped out into the road and faced them alone, and Elsie grew cold with fear as the sheriff and his formidable following rode steadily up. When almost upon the agent the leader turned, and, pushing his limp hat away from his eyes, shouted:

"*Halt!*" As the men pulled in their horses he added, "Keep back there!"

The mob had found a leader, and was organized for violence. Curtis, with folded arms, seemed small and weak as the army of invasion came to a stand, filling the lane between the office and the agency house with trampling horses and cursing men.

"Good-morning," growled the leader, surlily. "We're come for old Elk, and I want to say we get him this time. No monkey business goes with old Bill Yarpe. Women can't fool me."

Calvin Streeter rode out of the throng and pushed his way to the front.

Yarpe yelled: "H'yar! Keep in line there!"

"Go to hell!" replied Calvin, as he rode past him. "I'm no fool. I want to hear what goes on, and I tell ye right now you treat these people fair or you'll hear from me."

"I'll shoot you up a few if you ain't keerful, young feller," replied the old ruffian.

"That's right, General, he's too fresh," called some one.

Calvin spurred his horse alongside Yarpe's and looked him in the eye with a glare which made the older man wince. "You be decent before these women or I'll cut the heart out o' ye. You hear me!"

Curtis stepped forward. "Careful, Streeter—don't provoke trouble; we'll protect the women."

The sheriff rode between the two men. "Cal, git away—you're my deputy, remember."

As Cal reined his horse away, Curtis went to him and said, in a low voice: "I appreciate your chivalry, Calvin, but be careful; don't excite them."

As he looked into the big, red, whiskey-bloated face of Yarpe, Curtis was frankly dismayed. The old ruffian was not only inflamed with liquor, he was intoxicated with a subtler elixir—the pride of command. As he looked back over his followers he visibly expanded and a savage glare lit up his eyes. "Keep quiet, boys; I'll settle this thing."

Curtis again stepped towards the sheriff. "What do you propose to do, Mr. Sheriff?"

Yarpe broke in boisterously. "We want old Elk. Bring him out or we go after him." A chorus of applause followed.

"On what authority do you make this demand?" asked Curtis, facing Yarpe.

"On the authority of the sheriff of Pinon City," replied Yarpe, "and we come along to see he does his duty."

"The sheriff is present and can speak for himself. He was my guest last night and made an agreement with me, which, as an honorable man, he is disposed to keep."

The sheriff avoided Curtis's eye, but Yarpe replied:

"He showed the white feather. He let you fool him, but you can't fool this crowd. Bring on your Injun, or we go get him."

"Have you a warrant?"

"Oh, damn the warrant!"

The sheriff cleared his throat. "Yes. I have a warrant for Crawling Elk and Grayman," he said, and began searching his pockets. The decisive moment had arrived.

CHAPTER XXIV

The Gray-Horse Troop

CURTIS MINUTELY studied the crowd, which was made up very largely of reckless young men—cowboys from all over the range, together with the loafers and gamblers of the cow-towns. The sheriff's deputies were all well to the front, but were quiet; they seemed to be a little abashed by the gaze of the women to whom they were indebted for their dinner of yesterday. Each member of the gang was burdened with ammunition and carried both rifle and revolver.

The sheriff dismounted and handed a paper to Curtis, who took plenty of time to read it. It was manifestly bogus, manufactured for use as a bluff, and had not been properly sworn out; but to dispute it would be to anger the cattlemen. There was only one chance for delay.

"Very well," he said, at last. "This warrant calls for two of the head men among the Tetongs. Of course, I understand your motives. You do not intend to

charge these chiefs with the crime, you only wish to
force the tribe to yield some one else to your vengeance. In face of such a force as this of yours, Mr.
Sheriff, I can only yield, though I deny your right to
lay hand on one of my charges. I do all this under
pressure. If your men will retire a little I will call a
messenger and communicate with the chiefs named,
and ask—"

Yarpe glared. "Communicate hell! Sheriff, say the
word and we'll go and get 'em."

Curtis fixed a calm gaze upon him. "You are a
brave man, Mr. Yarpe, but you'll need all your resolution when you charge up that hill in the face of
those desperate warriors." As he swept his arm out
towards the west all eyes were turned on the
swarming mass of mounted Tetongs. The women
had moved higher, and were halted just on the eastern brow of the high ridge, behind and to the right
of the fighting men. "Now what will you do, Mr.
Sheriff?" pursued Curtis; "act with me through the
head men, or make your demand of the whole
tribe?"

A dispute arose among the crowd. A few shouted,
noisily, "Say the word and we'll sweep the greasy
devils off the earth." But the larger number, like the
sheriff's posse of the day before, found it not easy
to overawe this quiet soldier.

Calvin harangued the leader. "No, I will not button my lip," he shouted again, confronting Yarpe,
"for you nor no other man. You let the sheriff and
the Captain fix this thing up. What are you in this
thing for, anyhow? You don't own a foot of land nor
a head o' stock. You're nothing but a bum! You can't
get trusted for a pound of tobacco. Nice man to
lead a mob—"

"Shut him up, Bill," shouted one fellow.

"Cal's right," called another.

"Don't let 'em fool ye, Bill; we come fer a redskin, and we'll have him or burn the town."

Calvin had a revolver in each hand, and on his face was a look that meant war.

Curtis called to Lawson. "Take the women in, quick!" He feared shooting among the leaders of the mob. "Don't shoot, Calvin. Keep the peace."

With tears of impotent rage filling her eyes, Elsie retreated towards the office under Lawson's care. Curtis stepped to the side of the leader. "Silence your gang," he said.

Yarpe raised his bellowing voice. "Keep quiet, there! I'll settle this thing in a minute."

"Keep back!" commanded the sheriff.

The crowd fell back a little, with Calvin crowding them hard, revolver in hand. "No more funny business with me," he said, and death blazed from his eyes. "Get back!"

Quiet having been restored, the sheriff, Curtis, and Yarpe were revealed in animated argument. Curtis was talking against time—every moment was precious.

"If you give in, your chances for re-election ain't worth a leatherette," Yarpe said to the sheriff.

"You crazy fool! You wouldn't charge that hill?" asked the sheriff.

"That's what I would, and that's what the boys come for."

"But what good would it do?"

"It would learn these red devils a lesson they wouldn't forget, and it would make you an' me the most popular men in the county. If you don't do it, you're dead as the hinges of hell."

"If you charge that hill, some of you will stay there," put in Curtis.

Yarpe turned and roared: "Boys, the sheriff has weakened. Will you follow me?"

"We will!" shouted the reckless majority.

At this precise moment, while looking over the sheriff's head towards the pinon-spotted hill to the west, Curtis caught the gleam of something white bobbing down the hill. It disappeared, but came into sight lower down, a white globe based in a splash of blue. It was a white helmet, topping the uniform of a cavalry officer. A sudden emotion seized Curtis by the throat—his heart warmed, swelled big in his bosom. Oh, the good old color! Now he could see the gauntleted gloves, the broad shoulders, the easy seat of blessed old Jack Maynard as he ambled peacefully across the flat.

"Look there!" he cried, turning to the group inside the gate, his finger pointing like a pistol. His voice rang out joyous as a morning bugle, and the girls thrilled with joy.

Yarpe looked. "Hell! The cavalry! We're euchred—clean."

Over the hill behind the officer appeared a squadron of gray horse, marching in single file, winding down the trail like a long serpent, spotted with blue and buff, the sun sparkling fitfully from their polished brass and steel. When Curtis turned to the sheriff his face was pale with excitement for the first time, quivering, exultant. "You'll have the federal troops to deal with now," he said. "At least we are on equal terms."

A deep silence fell on the mob. Every ruffian of them seemed suddenly frozen into immobility, and each sat with head turned and eyes wide-staring, watching the coming of the blue-shirted horsemen.

As the officer approached he was distinguishable as a powerful, smooth-faced young man in a captain's uniform. As his eyes rested on Curtis his plump, red face broke into a broad smile. It was plain that he was Irish, and not averse to a bit of a shindy.

Riding straight up to the agent, he formally saluted, and in a deep, dry, military voice, said:

"Colonel Daggett presents his compliments to Captain Curtis and tenders Squadron B, at your service. Captain Maynard in command."

With equally impersonal decorum Curtis acknowledged the courtesy.

"Captain Curtis returns the compliment, and thanks Captain Maynard for his prompt and most opportune arrival—Jack, I'm mighty glad to see you."

Maynard dismounted and they shook hands. "Same to you, old man. What's all the row?"

A clear, distant, boyish voice cried, "By columns of four into line!" and the bugle, breaking voice, caused the hair of the agent's head to stand; turning, he saw the squadron taking form as it crossed the stream. It required his most heroic effort to keep the tears from his eyes as his ear heard the dull rattle of scabbards and he watched the splendid play of the gray horses' legs and broad chests as they came on, weary but full of spirit yet. There was something inexorable in their advance. In their order, their clean glitter, their impersonal grace, was expressed the power of the general government.

Turning to the sheriff, he said: "Sheriff Winters, this warrant is bogus—forged this morning by some one of your lynching-party; the ink is hardly dry. I decline to serve it," and he tore it into strips and flung it on the ground.

"Halt!" cried the on-coming commander, and with creak of saddle and diminishing thunder of hoofs the Gray Squadron stopped within fifty feet of the agency gate, and out of the dust a young lieutenant rode forward and saluted.

"Hold your position, Mr. Payne," commanded Maynard.

"I just *love* Captain Maynard!" said Jennie, fervently.

"I'll tell him," said Lawson.

"Now," said Maynard, "what's it all about? Nice gang, this!"

The mob that had been so loud of mouth now sat in silence as profound as if each man had been smitten dumb. It was easy to threaten and flourish pistols in the face of an Indian agent with a dozen women to protect, but this wall of Uncle Sam's blue was a different barrier—not to be lightly overleaped. The cowboys were not accustomed to facing such men as these when they shot up towns and raced the Tetongs across the hills.

"Now what is it all about?" repeated Maynard, composing his comedy face into a look of military sternness.

Curtis explained swiftly in a low voice, and ended by saying: "This is, in effect, a lynching-party on federal territory. What would you do in such a case?"

"Order them off, instanter!"

"Precisely. I have done so, but they refuse to go."

"Do they?" Maynard turned and remounted his horse. Saluting, he said:

"Captain Curtis, I am ready to execute any order you may choose to give."

Curtis saluted. "You will see that these citizens, unlawfully assembled, leave the reservation at once. Sheriff Winters, with all due respect to your office, I request you to withdraw. Captain Maynard will escort you to the borders of the reservation. When you have a warrant properly executed, send or bring it to me and I will use every effort to serve it. Good-morning, sir."

Captain Maynard drew his sword. " *'Tention, squadron!'* " The tired horses lifted their heads as the dusty troopers forced them into line.

Maynard's voice rang out: *"Left wheel, into line—march!"*

"You'll hear from this!" said the sheriff. "You'll find the State won't stand any such foolishness."

Yarpe's ferocity had entirely evaporated. " 'Bout face, boys; we're not fightin' the United States army—I had enough o' that in '63. Clear out! Our bluff don't go."

The cowboys, cursing under breath, whirled their ponies and followed Yarpe, the redoubtable. The sheriff brought up the rear, still contending for the rights of the county, but he retreated. Small as the dusty squadron looked, it was too formidable, both because of its commanders and because of the majestic idea it embodied.

Calvin was the last to leave. "I done my best, Major," he said, loudly, in order that Jennie might hear.

"I know it, Calvin; come and see us again in your civil capacity," replied Curtis, and waved a cordial salute.

As the squadron fell in behind and was hidden by the dust of the passing cattlemen, Curtis turned to where Elsie still stood. He was smiling, but his limbs were stiffened and inert by reason of the rigidity of his long position before the posse.

"We are saved!" he said, in mock-heroic phrase.

"Oh, wasn't it glorious to see the good old blue-and-buff!" cried Jennie, the tears of her joy still on her cheeks. "I could have hugged Captain Maynard."

"There is chance yet," said Curtis. "He's coming back."

Elsie did not speak for a moment. "What would you have done if they had not come?" she asked, soberly.

"I could have delayed them a little longer by sending couriers to Elk and Grayman; but let's not think of that. Let's all go into the house; you look completely tired out."

Elsie fairly reeled with weakness, and Curtis took her arm. "You are trembling," he said, tenderly.

"I haven't stirred for a half-hour," she said. "I was so tense with the excitement. I feared you would be shot, and the tribe isn't worth the sacrifice," she added, with a touch of her old spirit.

"I was in no physical danger," he replied. "But I should have felt disgraced had the mob had its way."

"The people are coming back," said Lawson. "They have seen the soldiers."

"So they are!" exclaimed Curtis. "They are shouting with joy. Can't you hear them? The chiefs are riding this way already; they know the army will protect them."

The thick mass of horsemen was breaking up, some of them were riding towards the women with the camp stuff, others were crossing the valley, while a dozen head men, riding straight towards the agency, began to sing a song of deliverance and victory. Joyous shouts could be heard as the young men signalled the good news.

"The cattlemen are going—the soldiers have come!"

CHAPTER XXV

After the Struggle

Upon reaching the library each member of the party sank into easy-chairs with sighs of deep relief, relaxed and nerveless. The storm was over. Jennie voiced the feeling as she said, "Thank the Lord and Colonel Daggett." Elsie was physically weary to the point of drowsiness, but her mind was active. Mrs. Parker was bewildered and silent. Even Parker was subdued by the grave face of the agent.

Lawson, with a curious half-smile, broke the silence. "There are times when I wish I owned a Gatling gun and knew how to use it."

Curtis started up. "Well, it's all over but the shouting. I must return to the office and set things in order once more."

"You ought to rest a little," said Elsie. "You must feel the strain."

"I am a little inert at the moment," he confessed, "but I'm Hamlet in the play, you know, and must be at my post. I'll meet you all at lunch. You need have no further worry."

The employés responded bravely to his orders. The cheerful clink of the anvil broke forth with tranquillizing effect. The school-bell called the children together, the tepees began to rise from the sod as before, and the sluggish life of the agency resumed its unhurried flow, though beneath the surface still lurked vague forms of fear. Parker returned to his studio, Lawson sought his den, and there stretched out to smoke and muse upon the leadings of the event, while Jennie planned a mid-day dinner for a round dozen. "It will be a sort of love-feast to Captain Maynard," she said, roguishly.

"Will he return so soon?" asked Elsie.

"Oh yes, he'll only go a little way. Jack Maynard can smell a good dinner across a range of foothills. Didn't he look beautiful as he smiled? I used to think he grinned, but to-day—well, he looked like a heavenly cherub in the helmet of an archangel as he rode up."

Elsie was genuinely amused. "What is the meaning of this fervor. Has there been something between you and Captain Maynard in the past?"

"Not a thing! Oh, I always liked him—he's so good-natured—and so comical. Can you peel potatoes?"

"I never did such a thing in my life, but I'll try."

About one o'clock Maynard came jogging back, accompanied by a sergeant and a squad of men, dusty, tired, and hungry.

Curtis met him at the gate. "Send your horses down to the corral, Captain. You're to take potluck with us."

Maynard dismounted, slowly, painfully. "I've been wondering about those girls," he said, after the horses were led away. "One is your sister Jennie, of course; but who is the other? She's what the boys would call a 'queen.' "

"You've heard of Andrew J. Brisbane?"

"You mean the erstwhile Senator?"

"Yes; this is his daughter."

"Great Himmel! What is she doing here?"

"She's an artist and is making some studies of Indians."

"I didn't suppose a man of Brisbane's blood and brawn could have a girl as fine as she looks to be."

"Oh, Brisbane has his good points— But come over to the house. Of course the mob gave no further trouble?"

"Not a bit, only the trouble of keeping them in sight; they rode like Jehu. I left the chase to Payne—it was what Cooper used to call a 'stern chase and a long chase.' Your quarters aren't so bad," he added, as they entered the library.

Jennie came in wearing an apron and looking as tasty as a dumpling. "How do you do, Colonel Maynard?" she cried out, most cordially.

He gave his head a comical flirt on one side. "I beg your pardon! Why Colonel?"

"I've promoted you for the brave deed of this morning."

He recovered himself. "Oh!—oh—yes!— Hah! I had forgotten. You saw me put 'em to flight? I was a little late, but I gave service, don't you think?"

"You were wonderful, but I know you're hungry; we're to have dinner soon—a real dinner, not a lunch."

He looked a little self-conscious. "Well—I—shall be delighted. You see, I was awake most of the night, and in riding one gets hungry—and, besides, breakfast was a little hurried. In fact, I don't remember that I had any."

"Why, you poor thing! I'll hurry it forward. Cheer up," and she whisked out of the room.

Maynard flecked a little dust from his sleeve and inquired, carelessly: "Your sister isn't married?"

"No, she sticks to me still. She's a blessed, good girl, and I don't know what I should do without her."

"You mustn't be selfish," remarked Maynard, reflectively. "But see here, I must knock off some dust, or I will lose the good impression I made on the ladies."

"Make yourself at home here and we'll have something to eat soon," said Curtis at the door.

The dinner was unexpectedly merry. Every one felt like celebrating the army, and Maynard, as the representative of the cavalry arm, came near blushing at the praise which floated his way on toasts which were drunk from a bottle of sherry, a liquor Jennie had smuggled in for cooking purposes.

"I admit I did it," he rose to say, "but I hold it not meet to have it so set down."

Parker was extravagantly gay. "I'm going to do a statue of Maynard on his horse rushing to our rescue," he said. "It will be a tinted piece like the ancients used to do. That white helmet shall flash like snow. Sheridan will no longer be the great equestrian."

"Leave off the broad smile," interrupted Lawson. "Captain Maynard's smile made light of our tragic situation."

"I don't think so; it was the smile of combat," exclaimed Elsie. "It was thrilling."

Maynard bowed. "Thank you, Miss Brisbane."

"It was Jack Maynard's murderin' grin," said Curtis; "It was the look the boys used to edge away from at the Academy. I must tell you, Jack nearly got shunted into the ways of glory. He could whip any man in West Point in his day, and a New York sporting man offered to back him for a career. Thereupon Jack wrestled with the tempter and 'thrun 'im.' He now sees his mistake. He might have been 'Happy Jack, the Holy Terror,' by this time, earning two hundred thousand a year like the great O'Neill."

Maynard sighed. "Instead of which, here I am rescuing beleaguered damsels, like the hero of a dime novel, on two thousand a year."

Jennie spoke up sharply. "I will not have Captain Maynard made fun of any more. It was a noble deed, and he deserves better treatment for it."

Maynard bowed. "I have one defender," he said, soberly.

"Here's another," cried Elsie.

"With two such faithful defenders I defy the world!" he shouted, valorously. Thereupon they left off joking him.

As they rose from the table, Curtis turned to Elsie: "Would you like to go with me to make a tour of the camp?"

Her eyes lighted up. "I should like it exceedingly."

"Very well, about three o'clock we will go. You will have time for a *siesta*. You must be tired."

"Oh no, I am quite rested and ready to go any time," and her bright eyes and warm color confirmed her words.

With military promptness the horses were brought round, and, accompanied by Maynard and Jennie, Curtis, with Elsie by his side, led the way to the camp. She was a confident horsewoman and rode a fine brown pony, and Curtis, who had never ridden with her before, glowed with pleasure in her grace and skill.

As they galloped off up the road a keen twinge of remorseful pity for Lawson touched Elsie's heart. He was grown suddenly older, it seemed to her, as though he had definitely given up the attempt to remain young, and this thought made her rather sober. He was being left out of her plans now almost unconsciously, while the other—

"One of the real heroes in this affair," Curtis was saying, "is Crane's Voice. He has been in saddle nearly thirty-six hours, and is willing to start again to Pinon City if I ask it."

"Of course you will not?"

"No. I will send a white man. The settlers might do even Crane's Voice an injury."

All was quiet in the camps, with little sign of the precipitate flight of the morning, either in the faces of the men or in the disposal of the tepees. The old men and some of the women came out to greet their Little Father and the soldier of the good heart, and Curtis gave out a tranquillizing message and asked, "Have you called the council?"

"Ay, for sunrise to-morrow," answered Elk and Two Horns.

"That is good," he replied. "Where are your young men?"

"Some are in the hills, some are gone as messengers, others are watching the ponies."

"Call them all in. I don't want them riding about to-night. Keep them in camp, close by the soldiers—then no harm will come to them."

So, scattering greetings and commands, he rode through the two circles of tepees. The redmen were all eager to shake hands with Maynard, in whom they recognized a valiant friend as well as an old-time enemy.

They found the camp of Grayman less tranquil, for the stragglers were still coming in from the hills, and scores of women were busy resetting their tepees. Grayman himself came forth, nervous and eager. "Ho, Little Father, my heart is glad that the soldiers have come."

"We are all glad," replied Curtis. "Where is your son?"

Grayman looked trouble. "I do not know. He is away with Cut Finger, my sister's son."

"Cut Finger is bad company for your son."

"I know it; but they are blood-brothers, as is the way of young men. Where one is, there the other is also."

Maynard and Jennie were not as deeply interested in the camp as they had given out to be at starting. He was recalling to her mind some of the parties they had attended together at Fort Sibley. "Really, Captain Maynard," she was saying, as they rode up, "you would have it appear that we saw a great deal of each other in those days."

"That's my contention entirely," he replied, "and it is my *in*tention to continue this Indian outbreak indefinitely in order to go into cantonment here."

"You always were susceptible to good dinners, Captain Maynard."

"Say good company, and you'll be right entirely."

Curtis, having caught Maynard's last remark, called out in the biting tone of the upper classman at West Point.

"Are you on special duty, Captain Maynard, or riding in the park?"

He saluted imperturbably. "By good luck I am doing both, at your service."

"Merely cast your eye around so that you can report the Tetongs peaceful and in camp, then you may ride where you please."

Maynard swept his eyes over the village. "It is done! Now, Miss Curtis, let's try for the top of that hill?"

"No, no, you have been riding all night."

"Why, so I have! In the charm of your presence I'd forgotten it. I'm supposed to be fagged."

"You don't look it," remarked Curtis, humorously, running his eyes over the burly figure before him. "At the same time, I think you'd better return. Your commissariat wagons will be rumbling in soon."

Maynard again saluted. "Very well, 'Major,' it shall

be so," and, wheeling his horse in such wise as to turn Jennie's pony, they galloped off together, leaving Curtis and Elsie to follow.

"It's hard to realize that disaster came so near to us," he said, musingly, and Elsie shaded her eyes with her hand and looked up at the hills.

"There is a wonderful charm in this dry country! I have never seen such blinding sunshine. But life must be difficult here."

"You begin to feel that? I expect to stay here at least five years, providing I am not removed."

She shuddered perceptibly. "Five years is a long time to give out of one's life—with so little to show for it."

He hesitated a moment, then said, with deep feeling, "It's hard, it's lonely, but, after all, it has its compensations. I can see results. The worst side of it all is—I can never ask any woman to share such a life with me. I feel guilty when I consider Jennie—she ought to have a home of her own; she has no outlook here."

She looked straight ahead as she replied. "You would find life here intolerable without her."

"I know it; but in my best moments I realize how selfish it is in me to keep her."

"Suppose you were to resign, what would you do?"

"I would try to secure a chance at some field-work for the Ethnologic Bureau. It doesn't pay very well, but it would be congenial, and my proficiency in the sign language would, I think, make me valuable. I have determined never to go back to garrison life without some special duty to occupy my mind."

"Life isn't a bit simple when you are grown up, is it?"

"Life is always simple, if one does one's duty."

"That is a soldier's answer; it is not easy for me

to enter into that spirit. I have my art, and no sense of duty at all."

"Your position is equally strange to me; but duties will discover themselves—later. A life without duties is impossible."

"I know what you mean, but I do not intend to allow any duty to circumscribe my art." This she uttered defiantly.

"I don't like to hear you say that. Life is greater than art."

She laughed. "How different our points of view! You are Anglo-Saxon, I am French. Art counts far more with us."

"Was your mother French? I did not know that."

"Yes—a Canadian. I have her nature rather than that of my father."

"Sometimes I think you are your father's daughter. Did your mother live to enjoy her husband's success?"

"Not to the full. Still, she had a nice home in Alta, where I was born. She died before he was elected Senator." They had nearly reached the agency now, and she shook off her sober mood. "Shall we go in with a dash?"

"I'm agreed."

She put quirt to her horse and they entered the lane at a flying gallop. As he assisted her to alight at the studio door he said:

"I hope your father will not require you to join him in the East. It is a great pleasure to have you here." His voice touched something vibrant in her heart.

"Oh, I don't think he will when he fully understands the situation. I'm sure I don't want to go. I shall write him so."

Curtis rode away elate as a boy. Something which he did not care to define had come to him from her, subtle as a perfume, intangible as light, and yet it had entered into his blood with most transforming effect. He put aside its analysis, and went about his duties content with the feeling that life was growing richer day by day.

Wilson, seeing his shining face, sighed and said to himself: "I guess the Major has found his girl. He's a lucky dog. I wish I could pick up even a piece of plain calico, I'd be satisfied." And he ran through a list of the unmarried women within reach, to no result, as usual.

Meanwhile the supply-wagons had arrived, and Captain Maynard was overseeing the laying-out of the camp just below the agency. Lieutenant Payne and his command returned at five o'clock, and in a short time the little village of white tents was in order. Curtis came over to insist that the officers take dinner with them at "the parsonage," and, as Captain Maynard had already spoken of the good company and the excellent dinner he had enjoyed in the middle of the day, Lieutenant Payne was quite ready to comply, especially as his lunch had been as light as his breakfast.

The meal was as enjoyable as the mid-day dinner, and the Parkers derived much comfort from the presence of the soldiers.

"I guess I'm not fitted to be a pioneer artist," Parker confessed, and the hearty agreement he met with quite disconcerted him.

Mrs. Parker was indignant at the covert ridicule of her husband, and was silent all through the meal; indeed, the burden of the conversation fell upon Jennie and Maynard, but they were entirely willing to bear it, and were not lacking for words.

"It is good to hear the bugles again," Jennie remarked, as one of the calls rang out on the still air, sweet and sad and as far removed from war as a love song.

"They're not so pleasant when they call to the

same monotonous round of daily duties," said Mr. Payne.

Curtis smiled. "Here's another disgruntled officer. What would you do—kill off the Indians and move into the city?"

"To kill off a few measly whites might insure completer peace and tranquillity," replied Maynard.

"You fellows couldn't be more righteously employed," put in Lawson. "You might begin on the political whoopers round about."

"What blasphemy!" cried Jennie. "These 'noble pioneers!' "

"Founding a mighty State," added Curtis.

"Founding a state of anarchy!" retorted Lawson. "They never did have any regard for law, except a law that worked in their favor."

Parker got in a word. "Lawson, do you know what you are? You're what Norman Bass used to call 'a blame a-riss-to-crat.' " This provoked a laugh at Lawson's expense.

"I admit it," said Lawson, calmly. "I am interested in the cowboy and the miner—as wild animals—as much as any of you, but as founders of an empire! The hard and unlovely truth is, they are representatives of every worst form of American vice; they are ignorant, filthy, and cruel. Their value as couriers of the Christian army has never been great with me."

Maynard was unusually reflective as he stared at Lawson.

"That's mighty plain talk," he observed, in the pause that followed. "You couldn't run for office on speeches like that."

"Lawson's living doesn't depend on prevarication," remarked Curtis. "If it did—"

"If it did I'd lie like the best—I mean the worst of you," replied Lawson.

"In a few years there will not be an Indian left," Parker remarked.

"The world will be the poorer."

"They will all be submerged," continued Parker.

"Why submerge them? Is the Anglo-Saxon type so adorable in the sight of God that He desires all the races of the earth to be like unto it? If the proselytizing zeal of the missionaries and functionaries of the English-speaking race could work out, the world would lose all its color, all its piquancy. Hungary would be like Scotland, Scotland would be Cornwall, Cornwall would duplicate London, and London reflect New York. Beautiful scheme for tailors, shoemakers, and preachers, but depressing to artists."

"You must be one of those chaps the missionaries tell about, who would keep men savage just to please your sense of the picturesque."

"Savage! There's a fine word. What is a savage?"

"A man who needs converting to our faith," said Jennie.

"A man to exercise the army on," said Maynard.

"A man to rob in the name of the Lord," said Parker.

"You're stealing all my oratorical thunder," complained Lawson. "When a speaker asks a question like that he doesn't want a detailed answer—he is pausing for effect. Speaking seriously—"

"Oh!" said Maynard, "then you were *not* serious."

Lawson went his oratorical way. "My conviction is that savagery held more of true happiness than we have yet realized; and civilization, as you begin to see, does not, by any construction, advance the sum of human happiness as it should do."

"What an advantage it is to have an independent income!" mused Maynard, looking about the table. "There's a man who not only has opinions, but utters them in a firm tone of voice."

"I am being instructed," remarked Elsie. "I used

to think no one took the Indian's side; now every one seems opposed to the cattlemen."

"When we are civilized enough to understand this redman, he will have disappeared," said Curtis, very soberly.

"Judging from the temper of this State at present, I reckon you're about right," replied Maynard. "Well, it's out o' my hands, as the fellah says; I'm not the Almighty; if I were I'd arrange things on a different basis."

"We are all transition types," remarked Curtis, harking back to a remark of Lawson's making.

"Even these settlers are immortal souls," said Parker.

"Consider!" exclaimed Lawson. "How could we live without the Indian question? Maynard would be like Othello—occupation gone. Curtis would cease to be a philanthropist. Elsie Bee Bee would go sadly back to painting 'old hats' and dead ducks. I alone of all this company would be busy and well paid. I would continue to study the remains of the race."

Jennie rose. "Put a period there," said she, "till we escape, and, remember, if we hear any loud talk we'll come out and fetch you away," and she hurried out into the sitting-room, where Elsie and Mrs. Parker yielded up valuable suggestions about dress.

As the Parkers rose to go, Lawson approached Elsie and asked in a low voice: "*Are* you going home to the mess-house to-night? If you are, I want to go with you."

"I'll be ready in a moment," she replied, but her eyes wavered. As they stepped out together quite in the old way, he abruptly but gently began:

"It is significant of our changed relations when I say that this is the first time I've had an opportunity for a private word since our camping trip. There is no need of this constraint, Elsie. I want you to be your good, frank self with me. I'll not misunderstand it. I am not charging anything up against you. In fact, I can see that you are right in your decision, but it hurts me to have you avoid me as you have done lately."

There was something in his voice which brought the hot tears to her eyes and she replied, gently: "I'm very sorry, Osborne. I hoped you wouldn't care—so much, and I didn't mean—"

"I've tried not to show my hurt, for my own sake as well as yours, but the fact is I didn't realize how deeply you'd taken root in my thoughts till I tried to put you away. It is said that no two lovers are ever equal sharers in affection—one always gives more than the other—or one expects more than the other. I was perfectly sincere when I made that bargain with you, and I know you were; but you are younger than I, and that has changed the conditions for you. I am older than you thought, and I find myself naturally demanding more and more. I think I understand better than I did two days ago why you gave me back the ring, and I do not complain of it. I shall never again refer to it, but we can at least be friends. This cold silence—"

She put out her hand. "Don't, please don't."

"I can't bear your being stiff and uncomfortable in my presence, Bee Bee! You even called me Mister Lawson." There was a pathetic sort of humor in his voice which touched her. "Let us be good comrades again."

She gave him her hand. "Very well, Osborne. But you are mistaken if you think—"

"Time will tell!" he interrupted, and his voice was strenuously cheerful. "Anyhow, we are on a sound footing again. Good-night."

The presence of Maynard and the troop was a greater relief to Curtis than he realized. He laid down for a moment's rest on his couch and fell into a dreamless sleep at once, and Jennie, deciding not to arouse him, spread a light shawl over him and withdrew softly. Maynard's coming brought a deeper sense of security than a stranger could have given with twice the number of troops. "Jack Maynard is so dependable," she said, and a distinct note of tenderness trembled in her voice.

CHAPTER XXVI

The Warrior Proclaims Himself

THE MESSENGERS from both Riddell and Pinon reported to Curtis about daylight, laden with papers and telegrams. The telegrams naturally received first reading. There was one filled with instructions from the Secretary of the Interior, and one from the Commissioner, bidding him stand firm. Several anxious ones from various cities, all of this tenor: "Is there any danger? my niece is one of your teachers," etc. In the midst of the others, Curtis came upon a fat one for Elsie, plainly from her father. This he put aside till after breakfast, when he permitted himself the pleasure of carrying it to the studio. He found her at work, painting a little brown tot of a girl in the arms of her smiling mother.

"I have a telegram for you—from your father, no doubt."

She rose quickly and opened the envelope. As she read she laughed: "Poor papa; he is genuinely alarmed. Read it."

He took it with more interest than he cared to show, and found it most peremptory in tone.

"Reports from Fort Smith most alarming. Come out at once. Have wired the agent to furnish escort and conveyance. Shall expect you to reply immediately, giving news that you have left agency. You should not have gone there. I will meet you at Pinon City if possible; if I do not, take train for Alta. Wire me your plans. Country is much alarmed. I must hear from you at once or shall be worried."

Curtis looked up with an amused light in his eyes. "He's a little incoherent, but sufficiently mandatory. When will you start?"

"I will send a telegram out at once that I am safe, and all danger over. He will not want me to leave now."

"Very well. A messenger will start at once with all our letters and messages. Anything you wish to send can go at the same time."

"What news have you?"

"I only had time to glance at my mail, but the papers are all that Lawson has predicted. If you would know how important a criminal I am, read these"—he pointed at a bundle on a chair. "I must go back to the office now, but I will wait for your letters and telegrams before despatching a messenger. If you think it better to go than to stay, I will ask Captain Maynard to escort you to the station."

"I will stay," she replied.

She wrote a brief telegram to her father, saying: "I am quite safe and hard at work. All quiet; don't worry," and also composed a letter giving vital details of the situation and taking strong ground against the way in which the cattlemen had invaded the reservation. In conclusion she added: "I have a fine studio, plenty of models, and am in fine health; I cannot think of giving up my work because of this foolish panic. Don't let these settlers influence you against Captain Curtis; he's right this time."

As she ran through the papers and caught the full significance of their precipitate attack on the agent, her teeth clinched in hot indignation. At the first breath, before they were sure of a single item of news, they leaped upon an honorable man, accusing him of concealing stolen cattle and of harboring murderers and thieves. "As for the Indians, it is time to exterminate these vermin! Let the State wipe out this tribe and its agency, and send this fellow Curtis back to his regiment where he belongs," was the burden of their song.

As she read on, tingling with wrath at these vulgarly written and utterly un-Christian editorials, the girl caught an amazing side-glimpse of herself and the views she once held. She remembered reading just such reports once before, and joining with her father in his desire to punish the redmen. Was Lawson right? Had her notions of the "brave and noble pioneers fighting the wild beast and the savage" arisen from ignorance of their true nature? Had they always been as narrow, as bigoted, as relentless, and as greedy as these articles hinted at? Some of Lawson's clean-cut, relentless phrases came back to her at the moment, and she began to believe that he was nearer right than she had been. And her father? Would he sanction such libels as these? At last the essential grandeur of the position held in common by both Curtis and Lawson—of the right of the small people to their place on the planet—came to her, and in opposition to their grave, sweet eyes she saw again the brutal, leering faces of the mob, and comprehended the feelings of a chief like Grayman, as he confronts the oncoming hordes of a destroying race.

Meanwhile, in the grassy hollow between two round-top hills the bands of Elk and Grayman were gathered in extraordinary council. No one was in gala-dress, no one was painted, all were serious or sad or morose. Upon their folded blankets the head men sat in a small circle on the smooth sod, exposed to the blazing sun. Behind them stood or knelt a larger circle, the men and boys on one side, the women on the other, while in the rear, mounted on their fleetest ponies, some two hundred of the young men were ranked, enthralled listeners to the impassioned speeches of the old men.

Crawling Elk made the first address, repeating the story which the agent had told and calling upon all those who sat before him to search for the guilty one and report to him if they found him. His words were received in silence.

Then Grayman rose, and, stepping into the circle, began to speak in a low and sorrowful voice. Something in his manner as well as in his words enlisted the almost breathless interest of the crowd. There was a tragic pathos in his voice as he called out:

"You see how it is, brothers; we are like a nest of ants in a white man's field, which he is ploughing. We are only a few and weak, while all around us our enemies press in upon us. We have only one friend—our Little Father. We must do as he says. We must give up a man to the war chief of the cowboys. They will never believe that any one else killed the sheepman. The cattlemen and sheepmen are always quarrelling, but they readily join hands to do the Tetongs harm."

"It is death to us to fight the white man; I know it. Unless we all wish to be shot, we must not become angry this time; we must do as the Little Father says, and if we cannot find the man who did this thing, I will go and give myself into the hands of the white war chief." A murmur of protest and anger ran round the circle. "It is better for one to suffer than many," he said, in answer to the protest, "and

I am old. My wife is dead. I have but one son, and he is estranged from me. I say, if we cannot find who did this thing, then I am willing to go and be killed of the white people in order to keep the peace. I have said it."

Standing Elk leaped to his feet, tall, gaunt, excitable. "We will not do this," he said. "We will fight first." And among the young warriors there was applause. "The Tetongs are not dogs to be always kicked in the ribs. I have fought the white man. I have met 'Long Hair' and 'Bear Robe' in battle. I am not afraid of the cattlemen. I am old, but my heart is yet big. Let us do battle and die like brave men."

Then Crawling Elk rose, and his broad, good-humored face shone in the sun like polished bronze as he turned his cheek to the wind.

"The words of my brother are loud and quick," he said, slowly. "In the ancient time it was always so. He was always ready to fight. I was always opposed to fighting. We must not talk of fighting now; all that is put away. It belongs to the suns that have gone over our heads. We must now talk of cattle-herding and ploughing. We must strive always to be at peace with the cowboys. I, too, am old. I have not many years to live; but you young men have a long time to live, and you cannot be always quarrelling with the settlers; you must be wise and patient. Our Little Father, Swift Eagle, is our friend; you can trust him. You can put your hand in his and find it strong and warm. His heart is good and his words are wise. If we can find the man who did this evil deed, we must give him up. It is not right that all of us should suffer for the wickedness of one man. No, it is not right that we who are old should die for one whose hands are red."

This speech was also received in silence, but plainly produced a powerful effect. Then one of the men who found the body rose and told what he knew of the case. "I do not think a Tetong killed the man," he said, in conclusion.

In this wise the talk proceeded for nearly two hours, and then the council rose to meet again at sunset, and word of what had been said was carried to Curtis by Crawling Elk and Grayman.

To them Curtis said: "I am pleased with you. Go over the names of all your reckless young men, and when you reach one you think might do such a deed, question him and his people closely. The shells of the rifle were the largest size—that may help you. Your old men would not do this thing— their heads are cool; but some of your young men have hot hearts and may have quarrelled with this herder."

The old men went away very sorrowful. Grayman was especially troubled, because he could not help thinking all the time of Cut Finger, his nephew.

Running Fox, or "Cut Finger," as the white people called him, he knew to be a morose and reckless young man, and probably possessed by some evil spirit, for at times he was quite crazy. Once he had forced his pony into the cooking-lodge of Bear Paw for no reason at all, and Bear Paw, in a rage, had snatched up his rifle and fired, putting a bullet through the bridle hand of Running Fox, who lost two fingers and gained a new name. At another time the mad fool had tried to force his horse to leap a cliff; and once he had attempted to drown himself; and yet, between these obsessions, he could be very winning, and there were many among Elk's band who pitied him. He was comely withal, and had married a handsome girl, the daughter of Standing Wolf. It was easy to imagine that Cut Finger was the guilty one, and yet to think of him was to think of his son's intimate friend.

When he reached his tepee Grayman lit his pipe and sat down alone and remained in deep thought for hours. He feared to find Cut Finger guilty, for his own son was Cut Finger's friend, or fellow, and that means the closest intimacy. There are no secrets between a Tetong and his chum. "If Cut Finger is guilty, than my son knows of it. That I fear."

When any one came to the door he motioned them away; even his daughter dared not enter, for she saw him in meditation. As he smoked he made offering to the Great Spirit, and prayed that he might be shown the right way, and his heart was greatly troubled.

Crawling Elk, with a half-dozen of his head men, was seated in his tepee, calmly discussing the same question. The canvas of his lodge was raised, as much to insure privacy as to let the wind sweep through. It was not easy to accuse any man of this crime, or even to suggest the name of any one as capable of such a foolish deed of blood. For relationships were close; therefore it was that he, too, narrowed the investigation down to Cut Finger. It is easier to accuse the son of a neighbor than your own son, especially if that other is already a marked man among reckless youths.

At five o'clock Grayman called his daughter and said, "Send my sister, Standing Cloud, to me."

Standing Cloud came and took a seat on the outside of the tepee—on the side where the canvas was fastened up—and there sat with bent head, her fingers busy with blades of grass, while her brother questioned her. She was a large and comely woman of middle age. Her expression was still youthful, and her voice had girlish lightness. She was at once deeply moved by her brother's questions. She did not know where her son was; he had not been to see her for several days. She understood whereto the questioning tended, and stoutly denied that her son would do so evil a deed. Nevertheless, Grayman was compelled to say:

"You know he has a bad head," and he made the confused, wavering sign of the hand which signifies crazy or foolish, and the mother rose and went away sobbing.

Then Grayman recalled the words of the Little Father. "If my own brother should do wrong, I would give him up to the war chief," he therefore said. "If my son and my sister's son are guilty, I will give them up," and he rose and sought out Crawling Elk and told him of his fears, and repeated his resolution as they sat together while the sun was going down and the crier was calling the second council.

"It is right," said Elk. "Those who are guilty must be punished; but we do not know who fired the shot."

The people were slow in coming together this second time, and darkness was falling as the head men again took their seats. A small fire was being built in the centre of the circle, and towards this at last, like nocturnal insects, the larger number of the people in the two camps slowly concentrated.

The wind had gone down and the night was dark and still and warm. The people gathered in comparative silence, though the laugh of a girl occasionally broke from the clustering masses of the women, to be followed by a mutter of jests from the young men who stood close packed behind the older members of the bands. Excitement had deepened since the morning, for in some way the news had passed from lip to lip that Grayman had discovered the evil-doer.

On their part the chieftains were slow to begin their painful task. They smoked in silence till the fire was twice replenished, then began talking in low tones among themselves. At last Crawling Elk arose and made a speech similar to that of the morning. He recounted the tale of the murdered white man, and the details of finding the body, and ended by saying: "We are commanded by the agent to find the ones who have done this evil deed. If any one knows anything about this, let him come forward and speak. It is not right that we should all suffer for the wrong-doing of some reckless young warriors."

"Come forth and speak, any one who knows," called the head men, looking round the circle. "He who remains silent does wrong."

Two Horns rose. "We mean you, young men—you too," he said, turning to the women. "If any of you have heard anything of this matter, speak!"

Then the silence fell again on the circle of old men, and they bent their heads in meditation. Crawling Elk was just handing the pipe to Grayman, in order to rise, when a low mutter and a jostling caused every glance to centre upon one side of the circle, and then, decked in war-paint, gay with beads and feathers, and carrying a rifle, Cut Finger stepped silently and haughtily into the circle and stood motionless as a statue, his tall figure erect and rigid as an oak.

A moaning sound swept over the assembly, and every eye was fixed on the young man. "Ahee! Ahee!" the women wailed, in astonishment and fear; two or three began a low, sad chant, and death seemed to stretch a black wing over the council. By his weapons, by his war-paint, by his bared head decked with eagle-plumes, and by the haughty lift of his face, Cut Finger proclaimed louder than words: "I am the man who killed the herder."

Standing so, he began to sing a stern song:

"I alone killed him—the white man.
  He was a thief and I killed him.
  No one helped me; I alone fired the shot.
  He will drive his sheep no more on Tetong
    lands.

This dog of a herder.
He lies there in the short grass.
It was I, Cut Finger, who did it."

As his chant died away he turned: "I go to the hills to fight and die like a man." And before the old men could stay him he had vanished among the young horsemen of the outer circle, and a moment later the loud drumming of his pony's hoofs could be heard as he rode away.

Curtis was sitting alone in the library when a tap at his window announced the presence of Grayman.

Following a gesture, the chieftain came in, and, with a look on his face which expressed high resolution and keen sorrow, he said:

"The man who killed the herder is found. He has proclaimed himself at our council, and he has ridden away into the hills."

"Who was he?"

"Cut Finger."

"Ah! So? Well, you have done your duty. I will not ask you to arrest him. Crow will do that. I hope"—he hesitated—"I hope your son was not with him?"

" 'I alone did it,' he says. My son is innocent."

"I am very glad," replied Curtis, looking into the old man's tremulous face. "Go home and sleep in peace."

With a clasp of the hand Grayman said good-night and vanished.

There was nothing to be done till morning, and Curtis knew the habits of the Indians too well to be anxious about the criminal. Calling his faithful Crane's Voice, he said:

"Crane, will you go to Pinon City?"

Crane's Voice straightened. "To-night?"

"Yes, to-night."

"If you will let me wear a blue coat I will go."

Curtis smiled. "You are a brave boy. I will give you a coat. That will protect you if you are caught by the white men. Saddle your pony."

With a smile he turned on his heel and went out as cheerfully as though he were going on an errand to the issue-house.

In his letter to the sheriff Curtis said: "I have found the murderer. He is a half-crazy boy called Cut Finger. Make out a warrant for him and I will deliver him to you. You will need no deputies. No one but yourself will be permitted to cross the line for the present."

After Crane had galloped off, Curtis laid down his pen and sat for a long time recalling the events of the evening. He remembered that Lawson and Elsie went away together, and a pang of jealous pain took hold upon him. "I never had the privilege of taking her arm," he thought, unreasonably.

CHAPTER XXVII

Brisbane Comes for Elsie

AMONG OTHER perplexities which now assailed the agent was the question of how to secure Cut Finger without inciting further violence. He confidently expected the police to locate the fugitive during the day, probably in the camp of Red Wolf, on the headwaters of the Elk.

"He cannot escape. There is no place for him to go."

"He may have committed suicide," said Wilson, discussing the matter with his chief the following morning.

"He may, but his death will not satisfy the ranchers unless they are made the instrument of vengeance. They would feel cheated and bitterer than ever," replied Curtis, sombrely. "He must be taken and delivered up to the law."

On his return to the office after breakfast Curtis stopped at the door of Elsie's studio, his brain yet tingling with the consciousness that no other man's claim stood between them now.

She greeted him joyously. "I am starting a big canvas this morning," she said. "Come in and see it."

He stepped inside to see, but the canvas only had a few rude, reddish lines upon it, and Elsie laughed at his blank look as he faced the easel.

"This thing here," she pointed with her brush, "is a beautiful purple butte; this yellow circle is the sun; these little crumbly looking boxes are trees; this streak is a river. This jack-in-the-box here is Crow Wing on his horse."

Her joking helped to clear his brain, though his blood was throbbing in his ears.

"Ah! I'm glad to know all that. Will you tag each anomalous hump?"

"Certainly. You will recognize everything by number or otherwise." She turned a suddenly serious face upon him. "I am determined to get back to work. These last few days have been so exciting. Is there any news?"

"Yes. The murderer proclaimed himself at a big council last night."

"He did! Oh, tell me about it! When?"

"I don't know exactly the hour, but the chieftains came to me about nine o'clock. I know him well; he is a reckless, handsome, half-crazy young man——" He broke off suddenly as Heavybreast, one of the policemen, profoundly excited, darkened the doorway. "Cut Finger is on the hill," he signed, and pointed away with trembling finger to a height which rose like a monstrous bee-hive just behind the school-house. On the rounded top, looking like a small monument on a colossal pedestal, sat a mounted warrior.

"What is he there for?" asked Curtis.

"He wants to die like Raven Face. He wants to fight the cowboys, he says. He don't want to hurt any one else, he says; only the cowboys and their war chief, so he says."

"Where is Crow? I want this man arrested and brought to me."

"Now he will shoot any one who goes up the hill; he has said so. All the people are watching."

Curtis mused a moment. "Can you send word to him?"

"Yes; his wife is here."

"Then tell him I will not let him fight. Tell him that shooting will do no good, and that I want him to come down and see me."

The officer trotted away.

"What did he say?" asked Elsie. "What is that man on the hill for?"

"That is Cut Finger, the guilty man. He proclaimed himself the murderer last night and now he is willing to die, but wants to die on his horse."

The whole agency was again tremulous with excitement. The teachers, the scholars, the native employés were all gathered into chattering groups with eyes fixed on the motionless figure of the desperate horseman, and in the camps above the agency an almost frenzied excitement was spreading. The stark bravery of the boy's attitude had kindled anew the flame of war, and behind Cut Finger on the hills two groups of mounted warriors had gathered suddenly. Several of the more excitable old women broke into a war-song, whose wail came faintly to the ears of the agent.

"Two Horns, silence those singers," said Curtis, sternly.

Elsie and Jennie and the Parkers joined the group around the agent, and Miss Colson, the missionary, came flying for refuge at the side of her hero.

"What are you going to do?" asked Parker. "If the fellow really means to shoot, of course no man can go up to him. You might send some soldiers."

"Silence in the ranks!" commanded Maynard, and, though he smiled as he said it, Parker realized his mistake. He turned to Elsie and his wife. "I tell you, we'd better get out of here. I feel just like a man sitting on a powder-mine. There's no telling what's going to happen next."

Lawson turned towards him with a sarcastic grin. "I wish I'd realized the state of your nerves, Parker; I should have invited you to Asbury Beach instead of the Indian country."

Maynard brought his field-glasses to bear on the desperado. "He has dismounted," he said. "He is squatted beside his horse, the bridle-rein on his arm, a rifle across his knees, and is faced this way. His attitude is resolute and 'sassy.' "

Curtis quietly said: "Now, friends, I wish you would all go in and pay no further attention to this man. Miss Colson, go back to your work. So long as he sees us looking at him he will maintain his defiant attitude. He will grow weary of his bravado if ignored."

"Quite right, Captain," replied Lawson, and the little knot of visitors broke up and dispersed to sheltered points of observation.

Under the same gentle pressure the employés went back to work, and the self-convicted warrior was left to defy the wind and the sky. Even the Tetongs themselves grew tired of looking when nothing seemed likely to happen, and the forenoon wore away as usual, well filled with duties. Maynard's men got out for drill an hour later, and their bugle's voice pulsed upward to the silent and motionless watcher on the hill like mocking laughter. The clink of the anvil also rose to him on the hot, dry air, and just beneath him the children came forth at recess to play. He became tired of sitting on the ground at last, and again mounted his horse, but no one at the agency seemed to know or to care. The sun beat remorselessly upon his head, and his throat became parched with thirst. Slowly but surely the exaltation of the morning ebbed away and a tremulous weakness seized upon him, so that, when his wife came bringing meat and water, he who had never expected to eat or drink again seized upon the food and ate greedily.

Then, while she sat on the ground and repeated the agent's message, he stood beside his horse, sullen and wordless. The bell rang for noon, and as the children came rushing out they pointed up at him again, and the teachers also stood in a group for a moment, with faces turned upward, but only for a moment, then went carelessly away to their meals.

An hour passed, the work-bell rang, the clerks returned to their duties, and the agent walked slowly across the road towards the office. Cut Finger lifted his rifle and pointed it. "I could shoot him now," he muttered. "But he is a good man; I do not want to kill him." Then the heat and silence settled over hill and valley, and no sound but the buzzing of flies and the clatter of grasshoppers broke the hot, brooding hush of the mid-day. The wind was from the plain and brought no coolness on its wings.

But he was not entirely forgotten. Elsie, from her studio door, kept close watch upon him. "There's something fine about him after all," she said to Curtis.

"It's like the old Mosaic times—an eye for an eye. He knows he must die for this, but he prefers to die gloriously, as a warrior dies."

A dust down the road caught Curtis's attention. "The mail will soon be in and then we will see how all this affects the press of the State; the Chicago dailies will not reach us for a couple of days yet."

"Send the papers over here, please!" cried Elsie, "I'm wild to see them."

"Why not all assemble at 'the parsonage' and I'll bring them there?"

"Very well; that will do as well," she replied. "It will be such a joy to read our obituaries."

As he entered the library with his armful of papers a half-hour later Curtis exclaimed: "Well, now, here is a feast! The commotion on the outside is prodigious. Here are the Copper City and Alta papers, and a dozen lesser 'lights and signals of progress' in the State. Help yourselves." He took out a handful of letters and telegrams. "And here are the prayers of anxious relatives. A telegram for you, Miss Brisbane; and two for you, Lawson."

Elsie's message from her father was brief. "Have no word from you; am en route for Pinon City. Not finding you there will cross to agency at once. Why do you not come out?"

Looking at the date she said: "Papa is coming; he is probably on his way to the agency at this moment."

Curtis looked a little troubled. "I hope not; the roads are dusty and the sun is hot."

"By George! this is fierce stuff," said Parker, looking up from his paper.

"Cut Finger has left the hill," announced Jennie from the door-way; "he is nowhere to be seen."

"Now he will submit to arrest," exclaimed Curtis. "His fine frenzy is gone."

"I'm sorry," Elsie soberly exclaimed. "Must you give him up to that stupid sheriff?"

"Yes, it must be done," replied Curtis. "My only claim to consideration lies in executing the law. I fought lawlessness with the promise that when the sheriff came with proper warrant I would act."

As the young officer went back to his duties the head-lines of the papers he had but glanced at began to burn into his brain. Hitherto his name had been most inconspicuous; only once or twice had it achieved a long-primer setting; mainly it had kept to the security and dignity of brevier notices in the *Army and Navy Journal*. Now here it stood, blazoned in ill-smelling ink on wood-pulp paper, in letters half an inch in height:

CURTIS CULPABLE

THE AGENT SHIELDS HIS PETS

while in the editorial columns of the Copper City papers similar accusations, though adroitly veiled, were none the less apparent. He had smiled at all this in the presence of his friends, but inwardly he shrank from it just as he would have done had some tramp in the street flung a handful of gutter slime across the breast of his uniform. A gust of rage made his teeth clinch and his face burn hot, and he entered his office with lowering brows.

Wilson looked up with a grin. "Well, Major, the politicians are getting in their work on us."

"This is only the beginning. We may expect an army of reporters to complete the work of misrepresentation."

"The wonder is they haven't got here before. They must be really nervous. Crane says the people in town have very bad hearts. As near as I can make out they faced him up and threatened his life. He says the mob is hanging round the edge of the reservation crazy for blood. He got shy and took to the hills."

"Did he see the sheriff?"

"Yes, the sheriff is on the way."

"Is Crane still asleep?"

"Yes. He didn't wait for grub; he dropped like a log and is dead to the world."

"Poor chap! I shouldn't have sent him on this last trip. Where is Tony?"

"Tony's out in the hills to keep an eye on Cut Finger. Will you go after him to-night?"

"No, not till morning. The police will locate him and stay with him to-night, and to-morrow morning I will go out and get him myself. I don't want any shooting, if it can be avoided. What is it, Heavy-breast?" he asked of a large Tetong who entered at the moment, his eyes bright with information.

"White man coming," signed the redman.

Curtis rose and went to the door and looked down the road.

Three carriages were passing the issue-house—one a rather pretentious family surrey, the others ordinary mountain wagons. In the hinder seat of the surrey, and beside the sheriff, sat a gray-haired man.

"It is Senator Brisbane!" said Curtis to Wilson, and a keen pang of anticipated loss came to him, for he knew that Brisbane had come to take his daughter away. But his face was calm as he went down to the gate to meet his distinguished and powerful enemy.

The ex-Senator was hot, weary, and angry. He had arrived in Pinon City on the early train, just as the county attorney and the sheriff were about to set forth. A few words with these officials assuaged his anxiety for his daughter but increased his irritation towards Curtis. Leaving orders for another team to follow, he had taken passage with the sheriff, an action he regretted at once. The seats were too low and too narrow for his vast bulk, and his knees grew weary. The wind came from the plain hot and insolent, bringing no relief to the lungs; on the contrary, it filled his eyes and ears with dust and parched the skin like a furnace blast. Altogether the conditions of his ride had been torturing to the great man, and he had ridden the latter part of it in grim silence, mentally execrating both Lawson and

Curtis for luring his daughter so far from civilization.

No one spoke till the agent, pacing calmly down to the gate, stepped into the road and said:

"Good-evening, gentlemen, will you get out and come in?"

Even then Brisbane made no reply, but the sheriff spoke up: "I suppose we'll have to. This is Senator Brisbane, Major. He was very anxious about his daughter and so came in with me. This is Mr. Grismore, our county attorney."

Curtis bowed slightly. "Mr. Grismore I have seen. Senator Brisbane I have met. Send your horses down to the corral, sheriff, and come in; you can't return to-night."

As the sheriff got out he said: "This second team is the Senator's, and the reporter for the Associated Press is in there with Streeter."

Brisbane got out slowly and painfully, and a yellow-gray pallor came into his face as he stood beside the carriage steadying himself by resting his hand on the wheel. The young county attorney, eager to serve the great politician, sprang out and offered a hand, and Curtis, with sudden pity in his heart, made a step forward, but Brisbane put them both aside harshly.

"No, no! I'm all right now. My legs were cramped—that's all. They'll limber up in a minute. The seats were too low for a man of my height. I should have stayed in the other carriage."

After all he was Elsie's father, and Curtis relented: "Senator, if you'll take a seat in my office, I'll go fetch your daughter."

"I prefer to go to her myself," Brisbane replied, menacingly formal. "Where is she?"

"I will show you if you will permit," Curtis coldly replied, and set out to cross the road.

The old man hobbled painfully at first, but soon

recovered enough of his habitual power to follow Curtis, who did not wait, for he wished to have a private word with Elsie before her father came. She was lying down as he knocked, resting, waiting for the dinner call.

"Your father is here," he said, as she opened the door.

Her face expressed surprise, not pleasure.

"Here! Here at the agency?"

"Yes, and on his way to the studio. Moreover, he is very dirty, very disgusted, very crusty, and not at all well."

"Poor old father! Now he'll make it uncomfortable for us all. He has come for me, of course. Who is with him?"

"The sheriff, the county attorney, and some reporters."

She smiled. "Then he is 'after you,' too."

"It looks that way. But you must not go away without giving me another chance to talk with you. Will you promise that?" he demanded, abruptly, passionately. "I have something to say to you."

"I dare not promise," she responded, and her words chilled him even more than her action as she turned away to the door. "How slowly he walks! Poor old papa! You shouldn't have done this, popsey," she cried, as she met him with a kiss on his cheek.

Curtis walked away, leaving them alone, a hand of ice at his heart.

Brisbane took her kiss without changing to lighter mood.

"Why didn't you follow out my orders?" he demanded, harshly. "You see what I've had to go through just because you are so foolishly obstinate. That ride is enough to kill a man."

Her throat swelled with anger, but she choked it

down and replied very gently. "Come into the studio and let me clean off the dust. I'm sorry."

He followed her in and sank heavily upon a chair. "I wouldn't take that journey again for ten thousand dollars. Why didn't you come to the railway as I ordered?"

"Because I saw no good reason for it. I knew what I was doing. Captain Curtis assured me—"

"Captain Curtis!" he sneered. "You'd take his word against mine, would you?"

"Yes, I would, for he is on the ground and knows all the conditions. He has the outbreak well in hand. You have seen only the outside exaggeration of it. He has acted with honor and good judgment—"

"Oh, he has, has he? Well, we'll see about that!" His mind had taken a new turn. "He won't have anything in his hand six months from now. No West Point dude like him can set himself up against the power of this State and live."

"Now, papa, don't start in to abuse Captain Curtis; he is our host, and it isn't seemly."

"Oh, it isn't! Well, I don't care whether it is or is not; I shall speak my mind. His whole attitude has been hostile to the best interests of the State, and he must get off his high horse."

As he growled and sneered his way through a long diatribe, she brought water and bathed his face and hands and brushed his hair, her anger melting into pity as she comprehended how weak and broken he was. She had observed it before in times of great fatigue, but the heat and dust and discomfort of the drive had reduced the big body, debilitated by lack of exercise, to a nerveless lump, his brain to a mass of incoherent and savage impulses. No matter what he said thereafter, she realized his pitiable weakness and felt no anger.

As he rested he grew calmer, and at last consented to lie down while she made a little tea on an alcohol lamp. After sipping the tea he fell asleep, and she sat by his side, her mind filled with the fundamental conception of a daughter's obligation to her sire. To her he was no longer a great politician, no longer a powerful, aggressive business man—he was only her poor, old, dying father, to whom she owed her every comfort, her education, her jewels, her art. He had never been a companion to her—his had been the rule absolute—and yet a hundred indulgences, a hundred really kind and considerate acts came thronging to her mind as she fanned his flushed face.

"I must go with him," she said; "it is my duty."

Curtis came to the door again and tapped. She put her finger to her lips, and so he stood silent, looking in at her. His eyes called her and she rose and tiptoed to the door.

"I came to ask you both to dinner," he whispered.

Her eyes filled with quick tears. "That's good of you," she returned, in a low voice. "But he would not come. He's only a poor, old, broken man, after all." Her voice was apologetic in tone. "I hope you will not be angry." They both stood looking down at him. "He has failed terribly in the last few weeks. His campaigning will kill him. I wish he would give it up. He needs rest and quiet. What can I do?"

Curtis, looking upon the livid old man, inert and lumpish, yet venerable because of his white hairs—and because he was the sire of his love—experienced a sudden melting of his own resolution. His throat choked, but he said:

"Go with him. He needs you."

At the moment words were unnecessary. She understood his deeper meaning, and lifted her hand to him. He took it in both his. "It may be a long time before I shall see you again. I—I ought not—" he struggled with himself and ceased to speak.

Her eyes wavered and she withdrew her hand.

"My duty is with him now; perhaps I can carry him through his campaign, or dissuade him altogether. Don't you see that I am right?"

He drew himself up as though his general-in-chief were passing. "Duty is a word I can understand," he said, and turned away.

CHAPTER XXVIII

A Walk in the Starlight

HAVING NO further pretext for calling upon her, Curtis thought of Elsie as of a strain of music which had passed. He was rather silent at dinner, but not noticeably so, for Maynard absorbed most of the time and attention of those present. At the first opportunity he returned to his papers, and was deep in work when Jennie came in to tell him that Elsie was coming over to stay the night.

"She has given up her bed to her father, and so she will sleep here. Go over about nine and get her."

If she knew how deeply this command moved him, she was considerate enough to make no comment. "Very well, sis," he replied, quietly. "As soon as I finish this letter."

But he did not finish the letter—did not even complete the sentence with which his pen was engaged when Jennie interrupted him. After she went out he sat in silence and in complete immobility for nearly an hour. At last he rose and went out into the warm and windless night.

When he entered the studio he found her seated upon one trunk and surveying another.

"This looks like flight," he said.

"Yes; papa insists on our going early to-morrow morning. Isn't it preposterous! I can only pack my clothing. He says the trouble is only beginning, and that I must not remain here another day."

"I have come to fetch you to Jennie."

"I will be ready presently. I am just looking round to decide on what to take. Be seated, please, while I look over this pile of sketches."

He took a seat and looked at her sombrely. "You'll leave a great big empty place here when you go."

"Do you mean this studio?"

"I mean in my daily life."

She became reflective. "I hate to go, and that's the truth of it. I am just beginning to feel my grip tighten on this material. I know I could do some good work here, but really I was frightened at papa's condition this afternoon. He is better now, but I can see that he is failing. If he insists on campaigning I must go with him—but, oh, how I hate it! Think of standing up and shaking hands with all these queer people for months! I oughtn't to feel so, of course, but I can't help it. I've no patience with people who are half-baked, neither bread nor dough. I believe I like old Mary and Two Horns better."

"I fear you are voicing a mood, not a conviction. We ought not to condemn any one;" he paused a moment, then added: "I don't like you to even *say* cruel things. It hurts me. As I look round this room I see nothing which has to do with duty or conviction or war or politics. There is peace and beauty here. You belong in this atmosphere; you are fitted to your environment. I admit that I was fired at first with a desire to convert you to my ways of thought; now, when a sense of duty troubles you, takes you away from the joy of your art, I question myself. You are too beautiful to wear yourself out in problems. I now say, remain an artist. There is something idyllic about your artist life as I now understand it. It is simple and childlike. In that respect it seems to have less troublesome questions of right or wrong to decide than science. Its one care seems to be, 'What will produce and preserve beauty, and so assuage the pain of the world?' No question of money or religion or politics—just the pursuit of an ideal in a sheltered nook."

"You have gone too far the other way, I fear," she said, sadly. "Our lives, even at the best, are far from being the ideal you present. It seems very strange to me to hear you say those things—"

"I have given the matter much thought," he replied. "If I have made you think of the woes of the world, so you have shown me glimpses of a life where men and women are almost free from care. We are mutually instructed." He rose at this point and, after hesitation, said: "When you go I wish you would leave this room just as it is, and when I am tired and irritable and lonely I'll come here and imagine myself a part of your world of harmonious colors, with no race questions to settle and no harsh duties to perform. Will you do this? These few hangings and lamps and easels are unimportant to you—you won't miss them; to me they will be priceless, and, besides, you may come back again some time. Say you will. It will comfort me."

There was a light in his eyes and an intensity in his voice which startled her. She stammered a little.

"Why, of course, if it will give you the slightest pleasure; there is nothing here of any particular value. I'll be glad to leave them."

"Thank you. So long as I have this room as it is I

shall be able to persuade myself that you have not passed utterly out of my life."

She was a little alarmed now, and hastened to say: "I do not see why we should not meet again. I shall expect you to call when you come to Washington—" she checked herself. "I'm afraid my sense of duty to the Tetongs is not strong. Don't think too hardly of me because of it."

He seemed intent on another thought. "Do you know, you've given me a dim notion of a new philosophy. I haven't organized it yet, but it's something like this: Beauty is a sense of fitness, harmony. This sense of beauty—call it taste—demands positively a readjustment of the external facts of life, so that all angles, all suffering and violence, shall cease. If all men were lovers of the beautiful, the gentle, then the world would needs be suave and genial, and life harmoniously colored, like your own studio, and we would campaign only against ugliness. To civilize would mean a totally different thing. I'm not quite clear on my theory yet, but perhaps you can help me out."

"I think I see what you mean. But my world," she hastened to say, "is nothing like so blameless as you think it. Don't think artists are actually what they should be. They are very human, eager to succeed, to outstrip each other; and they are sordid, too. No, you are too kind to us. We are a poor lot when you take us as a whole, and the worst of it is the cleverest makers of the beautiful are often the least inspiring in their lives. I mean they're ignorant and spiteful, and often dishonorable." She stopped abruptly.

"I'm sorry to hear you say that. It certainly shatters a beautiful theory I had built up out of what you and other artists have said to me." After a little silence he resumed: "It comes down to this, then: that all arts and professions are a part of life, and life is a compromise between desire and duty. There are certain things I want to do to-day, but my duties for to-morrow forbid. You are right in going away with your father—I'm not one to keep you from doing that—but I must tell you how great has been the pleasure of having you here, and I hope you will come again. If you go to-morrow morning I shall not see you again."

"Why not?"

"I start at dawn to arrest Cut Finger."

"Alone?"

"No. The captain of the police goes with me."

Her face paled a little. "Oh! I wish you wouldn't! Why don't you take the soldiers?"

"They are not necessary. I shall leave here about four o'clock and surprise the guilty man in his bed. He will not fight me." He rose. "Are you ready to go now?"

"In a moment," she said, and softly crossed the floor to peep into the bedroom. "Poor papa, he looks almost bloodless as he sleeps."

As they stepped out into the darkness Curtis realized that this was their last walk together, and the thought was both sweet and sad.

"Will you take my arm?" he asked. "It is very dark, though there should be a new moon."

"It has gone down; I saw it," she replied, as she slipped her hand through his elbow. "How peaceful it all is! It doesn't seem possible that to-morrow you will risk your life in the performance of duty, and that I will leave here, never to return. I have a curious feeling about this place now. It seems as though I were settled here, and that I am to go on living here forever."

"I wish it were true. Women like you—you know what I mean; there are no women like you, of course—come into my life too seldom. I dread the empty futility of to-morrow. As an Indian agent, I must expect to live without companionship with such as you. I have a premonition that Jennie is going to leave me—as she ought."

"You will be very lonely then; what will you do?"

"Work harder; do more good, and so cheat myself into forgetfulness that time is flying."

"You are bitter to-night."

"Why shouldn't I be when you are going away? It wouldn't be decent of me to be gay."

"Your methods of flattery are always effective. At one moment you discuss the weightiest matters with me—which argues I have brains—and then you grow gloomy over my going and would seem to mean that I am charming, which I don't think is quite true."

"If I weren't a poor devil of an army officer I'd convince you of my sincerity by asking you not to go away at all."

"That *would* be convincing," she said, laughingly. "Please don't do it!"

His tone became suddenly serious. "You are right, I can't ask you to share a life like mine. It is too uncertain. I may be ordered back to my regiment next winter, and then nothing remains but garrison duty. I think I will then resign. But I am unfitted for business, or for any money-getting, and so I've decided that as an honorable man I must not imperil the happiness of a woman. I claim to be a person of taste, and the girl I admired would have other chances in life. I can't afford to say to her, 'Give up all your comfort and security and come with me to the frontier.' She would be foolish to listen—no woman of the stamp I have in mind could do it." They were nearing "the parsonage" gate, and he ended in a low voice: "Don't you think I am right?"

"The theory is that nothing really counts in a woman's life but love," she replied, enigmatically.

"Yes, but theory aside—"

"Well, then, I can conceive of a girl—a very *young* girl—leaving wealth and friends, and even her art, for the man she loved, but—"

He waited a moment as a culprit listens to his judge. "But then—but in case—"

"If the girl were grown up and loved luxurious living, and shared an enthusiasm—say for art—then—" She broke off and said, wearily, "Then she might palter and measure values and weigh chances, and take account of the future and end by not marrying at all."

They had reached the gate and he spoke with perceivable effort: "I've no right to ask it, of course, but if you take pity on my loneliness at any time and write to me, your letters will be more welcome than it is seemly in me to say, and I'll promise not to bore you with further details of my 'Injines.' Will you be kind to me?"

"I will be glad to write," she replied, but in her voice was something he did not understand. As they entered the house Elsie said: "Captain Maynard, Captain Curtis is going out to-morrow morning to arrest that crazy Indian. Do you think he ought to go alone?"

"Certainly not! It would be too dangerous. He shall have an escort," replied Maynard, emphatically.

"No, no!" said Curtis, decisively. "I am safer to go unarmed and alone."

"George!" protested Jennie, "you shall not go out there alone. Why don't you send the police?"

Maynard here interposed. "Don't take on worry; I'll go with him myself."

This last hour in Elsie's company was a mingled pain and pleasure to Curtis, for she was most charming. She laid aside all hauteur, all perversity, and gave herself unreservedly to her good friends. They were all at high tension, and the talk leaped from jest to protest, and back to laughter again, agile and inconsequent. The time and the place, the past and the future, counted for little to these four, for they were young and they were lovers.

At last Jennie rose. "If you people are to rise at dawn you must go to sleep now. Good-night! Come, Elsie Bee Bee."

Maynard followed Jennie into the hall with some jest, and Curtis seized the opportunity to delay Elsie. He offered his hand, and she laid hers therein with a motion of half-surrender.

"Good-night, Captain. I appreciate your kindness more than I can say."

"Don't try. I feel now that I have done nothing—nothing of what I should have done; but I didn't think you were to leave so soon. If I had known—"

"You have done more than you realize. Once more, good-night!"

"Good-night!" he said, in an unsteady voice; "and remember, you promised to write!"

"I will keep my promise." She turned at the door. "Don't try to write around your Indians. I believe I'd like to hear how you get on with them."

"Defend me from mine enemies within the gates, and I'll work out my problem."

"I'll do my best. Good-bye!"

"No, not good-bye—just good-night!"

For a moment he stood meditating a further word, then stepped into the hall. Elsie, midway on the stairs, had turned and was looking down at him with a face wherein the eyes were wistful and brows perplexed. She guiltily lowered her lashes and turned away, but that momentary pause—that subtle interplay of doubt and dream—had given the soldier a pleasure deeper than words.

Jennie was waiting at the door of the tiny room in which Elsie was to sleep, her face glowing with admiration and love. "Oh, you queenly girl!" she cried, with a convulsive clasp of her strong arms. "I can't get over the wonder of your being here in our little house. You ought to live always in a castle."

Elsie smiled, but with tears in her eyes. "You're a dear, good girl. I never had a truer friend."

"I wish you were poor!" said Jennie, as they entered the plain little room; "then you could come here as a missionary or something, and we could have you with us all the time. I hate to think of your going away to-morrow."

"You must come and see me in Washington."

"Oh no! That wouldn't do!" said Jennie, half alarmed. "It might spoil me for life out here. You must visit us again."

There was a note of honest, almost boyish suffering in Jennie's entreaties which moved the daughter of wealth very deeply, and she went to her bed with a feeling of loss, as though she were taking leave of something very sweet and elementally comforting.

She thought of her first lover, and her cheeks burned with disgust of her folly. She thought of two or three good, manly suitors whose protestations of love had left her cold and humorously critical. On Lawson's suit she lingered, for he was still a possibility should she decide to put her soldier-lover away. "But I *have* done so—definitely," she said to some pleading within herself. "I can't marry him; our lives are ordered on divergent lines. I can't come here to live."

"Happiness is not dependent on material things," argued her newly awakened self. "He loves you—he is handsome and true and good."

"But I don't love him."

"Yes, you do. When you returned Osborne Lawson's ring you quite plainly said so."

She burned with a new flame with this confession;

but she protested, "Let us be sensible! Let us argue!"

"You cannot argue with love."

"I am not a child to be carried away by a momentary gust of emotion. See how impossible it is for me to share his work—his austere life."

And here entered the far-reaching question of the life and death of a race. In a most disturbing measure this obscure young soldier represented a view of life—of civilization antagonistic to her faith, and in stern opposition to the teachings of her father. In a subtle fashion he had warped the word *duty* from its martial significance to a place in a lofty philosophy whose tenets were only just beginning to unfold their inner meaning to her.

Was it not true that she was less sympathetic with the poor brown peoples of the earth than with the animals? "How can you be contemptuous of God's children, whom the physical universe has colored brown or black or yellow—you, who are indignant when a beast is overburdened? If we repudiate and condemn to death those who do not please us, who will live?"

She felt in herself some singular commotion. Conceptions, hitherto mere shells of thought, became infilled with passion; and pity, hitherto a feeble sentiment with her, expanded into an emotion which shook her, filled her throat with sobs, discrediting her old self with her new self till the thought of her mean and selfish art brought shame. How small it all was, how trivial, beside the consciousness of duty well done, measured against a life of self-sacrifice, such as that suggested by this man, whose eyes sought her in worship!

Could there be any greater happiness than to stand by his side, helping to render a dying, captive race happier—healthier? Could her great wealth be put to better use than this of teaching two hundred

thousand red people how to meet and adjust themselves to the white man's way of life? Their rags,
their squalor, their ignorance were more deeply depressing to her lover than the poverty of the slums,
for the Tetongs had been free and joyous hunters.
Their condition was a tragic debasement. She began
to feel the arguments of the Indian helpers. Their
words were no longer dead things; they had become electric nodes; they moved her, set her blood
aflame, and she clinched her hands and said: "I will
help him do this great work!"

CHAPTER XXIX

Elsie Warns Curtis

BRISBANE WAS early awake, abrupt and harsh in command. "Come! we must get out o' here," he said. "I don't want to be under the slightest obligation to this young crank. I intend to break him."

She flamed into wrath—a white radiance. "When you break him you break me," she said.

"What do you mean?"

"I mean I've changed my mind. I think he's right and you are wrong."

The entrance of the sheriff prevented a full accounting at the moment, but it was merely deferred. Once in the carriage, Brisbane began to discredit her lover. "Don't tell me Curtis is disinterested; he is scheming for some fat job. His altruistic plea is too thin."

"You are ill-fitted to understand the motives of a man like Captain Curtis," Elsie replied, and every word cut. "What have you—or I—ever done that was not selfish?"

"I've given a thousand dollars to charity for every cent of his."

"Yes, and that's the spirit in which you gave—never to help, only to exalt yourself, just as I have done. Captain Curtis is giving himself. He and his sister have made me see myself as I am, and I am not happy over it. But I wish you would not talk to me any more about them; they are my friends, and I will not listen to your abuse of them."

It was a most fatiguing ride. Brisbane complained of the heat and the dust, and of a mysterious pain in his head; and Elsie, alarmed by his flushed face, softened. "Poor papa, I'm so sorry you had to come on this long ride!" Lawson was also genuinely concerned over the Senator's growing incoherency, and privately told the driver to push hard on the reins.

When they rounded the sharp point of the Black Bear Mesa, and came in sight of the long, low, halfway house, Lawson sat up with a jerk. "There is the mob—camped and waiting for the sheriff."

As Elsie looked at the swarming figures of the cowboys her mind forecasted tragic events. The desperadoes were waiting to lynch Cut Finger—that was plain. Curtis had said he would not surrender his prisoner to be lynched. He was coming; he would be met by this mob.

She clutched Lawson by the arm. "We must warn him!"

He merely nodded; but a look in his eyes gave her to understand that he would do his duty.

The cattlemen, seeing the wagon whirling round the mesa, mounted and massed in stern array, believing that the carriage contained the sheriff and his prisoner. They were disappointed and a little uneasy when they recognized Brisbane, the great political boss; but with ready wit Johnson rode along in front of the gang, saying, with a wink: "Put up your guns, boys. This is a meeting in honor of Senator Brisbane." Then, as a mutter of laughter ran down the line, he took off his hat and lifted his voice:

"Boys, three cheers for Senator Brisbane—hip, hip, hurrah!"

After the cheers were given the horsemen closed round the carriage with cries for a speech.

Brisbane, practised orator and shrewd manipulator, rose as the carriage stopped, and removed his hat. His eyes were dim and the blood seemed about to burst through his cheeks, but he was not without self-possession.

"Gentlemen, I thank you for this demonstration, but I must ask you to wait till I have rested and refreshed myself. With your permission I will then address you."

"Right—right!"

"We can wait!" they heartily responded, and opened a way for the carriage.

Elsie shuddered as she looked into the rude and cruel faces of the leaders of this lynching party. They no longer amused her. She saw them now from the stand-point of Captain Curtis and his wards, and realized how little of mercy they would show to their enemies. On Lawson's lips lay a subtly contemptuous smile, and he uttered no word—did not lift a hand till the carriage was at the door.

Streeter helped the Senator out, and with unexpected grace presented his hand to Elsie. "I do not need help," she said, coldly, and brushed past him into the little sitting-room, which swarmed with excited, scrawny, tired, and tearful women.

"What is goin' on out there? Have the soldiers put down the pizen critters?" asked one.

"You're Miss Brisbane—we heerd you was all killed at the agency. Weren't you scared?"

Almost contemptuously Elsie calmed their fears, and by a few questions learned that this house had

been made a rallying-point for the settlers and that
the women were just beginning to feel the depressing effects of being so long away from their homes
without rest and proper food.

"*Do* you think we can go home now?"

"Certainly. Captain Curtis will see that you are
not harmed," she replied, and she spoke with all a
wife's sense of joy and pride in her husband.

"We've been camping here for almost a week,
seems like, an' we're all wore out," wailed one little
woman who had three small children to herd and
watch over.

Brisbane, inspirited by an egg-nog and a sand-
wich, mounted a wash-tub on the low porch and began a speech—a suave, diplomatic utterance,
wherein he counselled moderation in all things. "We
can't afford at this time to do a rash thing," he said,
and winked jovially at Johnson. "The election coming on is, after all, the best chance for us to get
back at these fool Injun apologists. So go slow,
boys—go slow!"

As these smooth words flowed from his lips Elsie
burned with shame and anger. Some newly acquired
inward light enabled her to read in the half-hearted
dissuasion of her father's speech a subtle, heartless
encouragement to violence *after* election. While the
cheers were still ringing in her ears, at the close of
the address, Elsie felt a touch on her shoulder and
turned to face Calvin, standing close beside her,
timid and flushed.

She held out her hand with a swift rush of confidence.

"Why, how do you do, Mr. Streeter?"

"I'm pretty well," he said, loudly, and added, in a
low voice, "I want to see you alone." He looked
about the room. The corner least crowded was occupied by a woman nursing a wailing baby. "Come

this way; she's Norwegian; she can't understand us."

Elsie followed him, and when he spoke it was in a rapid, low mutter. "Is the Major goin' to come with Cut Finger?"

"I'm afraid so."

"He mustn't. You know what this gang's here for?"

"What can we do? Can't we warn him?"

"Well, I'm goin' to take a sneak and try it. It's all my neck is worth to play it on the boys; but it's got to be done, for the Major is a fighter, and if this mob meets him there will be blood on the moon. Now don't worry. I'm going to slide right out through the first gate I see and head him off; mebbe you'd like to write a word or two."

"You are a real hero," she said, as she put a little slip of paper into his hand, and pressed it there with both of hers.

"Don't do that," he said, hurriedly; "they'll think something's up. I'm doin' it for the Major; he's treated me right all the way along, and I'll be derned if I let this gang do him."

A pain shot through her heart. Putting her hand to her bosom, she said: "It means everything to me, Calvin. Good-bye. I am trusting you—it's life or death to me. Good-bye!"

CHAPTER XXX

The Capture of the Man

THE EAST was saffron and pale-blue as Crow and the agent drove out of the corral and up the road to the south. Two Horns was the driver. Crow alone was armed, and he wore but his official revolver. Maynard had been purposely left out of the expedition, for Curtis did not wish to seem to question in the slightest degree the obedience of his people. He preferred to go unarmed and without handcuffs or rope, as a friend and adviser, not as an officer of the law.

The morning was deliciously cool, with a gentle wind sliding down from the high peaks, which were already glowing with the morning's pink and yellow. From some of the tepees in Grayman's camp smoke was already rising, and a few old women could be seen pottering about the cooking lodges, while the morning chorus of the dogs and coyotes thickened. There was an elemental charm in it all which helped the young soldier to shake off his depression.

Passing rapidly through the two villages, Two Horns turned to the left and entered upon a road which climbed diagonally up the side of a long, low ridge. This involved plodding, and by the time they reached the summit the sun met them full-fronted. In the smaller valley, which lay between this ridge and the foot-hills, a rough trail led towards the mountains. This way Two Horns took, driving rapidly and silently, and soon entered the pines and piñons which form the lower fringe of the vast and splendid robe of green which covers the middle heights of the Rocky Mountains.

After an hour of sharp driving, with scarcely a word or gesture, Crow turned and said: "Cut Finger there. Black Wolf, his tepee."

The trail here took a sharp curve to the left to avoid a piece of stony ground, and from a little transverse ridge Curtis could look down on a small, temporary village, the band of Black Wolf, who had located here to cut hay on the marsh.

"We must surprise him if we can," said Curtis to Crow. "We must not shoot. I will talk to him. If he cocks his gun kill him; but I don't think he will want to fight."

The lads could be heard singing their plaintive songs as they climbed the hills for their ponies. Smoke was rising from each lodge, and children, dogs, and hens were outdoing each other in cheerful uproar as Two Horns drove up to where Black Wolf stood, an old man with thin, gray hair, shielding his eyes with the scant shadow of his bony wrist.

"Ho, agent!" he cried. "Why do you come to see us so early?"

"Is Cut Finger here?"

"Yes; he is in there." He pointed to a tepee near.

"Be silent!" commanded Curtis, as he alighted swiftly, but without apparent haste or excitement.

Crow instantly followed him, alert and resolute. As they entered the tepee Cut Finger, still half asleep on his willow hammock, instinctively reached for his rifle, which lay beneath him on the ground, dangerous as a half-awakened rattlesnake.

Curtis put his foot on the weapon, and said, pleasantly: "Good-morning, Cut Finger; you sleep late."

The young man sat up and blinked stupidly, while Crow took the gun from beneath the agent's foot.

Curtis signed to Black Wolf. "This boy has killed a herder and I have come for him. You knew of his deed."

"I have heard of it," the old man replied, with a gesture.

"It is such men who bring trouble on the tribe," pursued Curtis. "They must be punished. Cut Finger must go with me down to the agency. He must not make more trouble."

The news of the agent's mission brought every soul hurrying to the tent, for Cut Finger had said, "I will fight the soldiers if they come."

Curtis heard them coming and said: "Crow, tell all these people outside that Cut Finger has done a bad thing and must be punished. That unless such men are cast out by the Tetongs they will always be in trouble."

Crow lifted up his big, resounding voice and recounted what the agent had said, and added: "You shall see we will take this man. I, Crow, have said it. It will be foolish for any one to resist."

The agent, sitting before Cut Finger, addressed him in signs. "I am your friend, I am sorry for you. I am sorry for any man who does wrong and suffers punishment; but you have injured your people, you made the white man very angry; he came ready to shoot—you saw how I turned him away. I said: 'I will find the man who shot the herder. I will bring him—I do not want any one else to suffer.' Then you proclaimed yourself. You said: 'I alone did this thing.' Then you went on the hill to fight—I cannot allow that. No more blood will be shed. I will not lie; I have come to take you. You will be punished; you must go with me to the white man's strong-house."

A whimpering cry arose, a cry which ended in a sighing moan of heart-piercing, uncontrollable agony, and Curtis, turning his face, saw the wife of Cut Finger looking at him from her blanket on the opposite side of the tepee. A shout of warning from Crow made him leap to his feet and turn.

Cut Finger confronted him, his eyes glowing with desperate resolution.

"Sit down!" commanded the Captain, using his fist in the sign, with a powerful gesture. The fugitive could not endure his chief's eyes; he sank back on his couch and sat trembling.

"If you touch the Little Father I will kill you," said Crow, gruffly, as he stood with drawn revolver in his hand. "I, Crow, have said it!"

Black Wolf was looking on with lowering brow. "He says the white man was driving his sheep on our land."

"So he was," replied Curtis, "but it is bad for the Tetongs when a white man is killed. It is better to come and tell me. When an Indian kills a white man the white men say: 'Let us kill *all* the Tetongs— spare no one.' Cut Finger said he was ready to die. Well, then, let him go with me, and I will make his punishment as light as I can. I am his friend—a friend to every Tetong. I will tell the war chief at Piñon City how it was, and he will say Cut Finger was not alone to blame—the white man was also to blame. Thus the punishment will not be so heavy. Cut Finger is a young man; he has many years to live if he will do as I tell him. He will come back to his tribe by-and-by and be a good man."

So, by putting forth all his skill in gesture he conveyed to Cut Finger's mind a new idea—the idea of sacrificing himself for the good of the tribe. He also convinced the members of Black Wolf's band that their peace and safety lay in giving him up to their agent, and so at last the young desperado rose and followed his chief to the wagon wherein Two Horns still sat, impassive and unafraid.

As he put his hand on the carriage-seat a convulsive shudder swept over Cut Finger. He folded his arms and, lifting his eyes to the hills, burst forth in a death-song, a chant so sad, so passionate, and so searching, that the agent's heart was wrenched. Answering sobs and wails broke from the women, and the young wife of the singer came and crouched at his feet, her little babe in her arms, and this was his song:

> "I am going away.
> I go to my death.
> The white man has said it—
> I am to die in a prison.
> I am young, but I must go—
> I have a wife, but I must go
> To die among the white men
> In the dark.
> So says the soldier chief."

Curtis, looking into the eyes of Black Wolf, perceived that the old man wavered. The wailing of the women, the young man's song, had roused his racial hatred—what to him was the killing of a "white robber"?

"Be quiet!" commanded Curtis, and the song ceased. "Get in, quick! No more singing."

The ending of the song left the prisoner in a mood of gloomy yet passive exaltation. He took the place indicated and sat with bowed head, his hands limply crossed.

"Go on!" commanded Curtis, and Two Horns brought the whip down on the horses. As they sprang forward a wail of agony burst from the lips of the bereaved young wife. At this cry Cut Finger again turned upon the agent with hands opened like the claws of a bear—his face contorted with despair. Curtis seized him in a grip whose crunching power made itself felt to the marrow of the Tetong's bones, and his eyes, piercing with terrible determination, shrivelled the resolution of the half-crazed man. He sank back into his seat, a hopeless lump of swaying flesh, his face a tragic mask, and uttered no further word till the sound of a galloping horse made them all turn to see who followed.

"My wife!" the prisoner said. "She carries my baby."

This was indeed true. The sad little wife was galloping after, riding a strong bay pony, the reins flapping loose, while across the pommel of her saddle she held her small pappoose, whose faint wailing told of his discomfort and terror.

"Wait—me take papoose," the prisoner said, in English, with a note of command.

Curtis was deeply touched. He ordered Two Horns to halt, and Crow got out and took the babe and handed it to Cut Finger, who received it carefully in his long arms. No woman could have been tenderer.

As they drove on, a big lump rose in the soldier's throat. It seemed a treacherous and sinful thing to hand this man over to a savage throng of white men, perhaps to be lynched on the road. "I will not do it," he said; "I will take him to Pinon City myself. He shall have trial as if he were white. I will yield him to the law, but not to vengeance."

Cut Finger thereafter spoke no word, did not even

look back, though Curtis detected him turning his head whenever the sound of the galloping horse grew faint or died away for a few moments. The baby ceased to wail, and on the rough ground, when the wagon jarred, the father held the little one high as in a sling.

Upon entering the camp of Crawling Elk they found all the people massed, waiting, listening, and their presence excited the prisoner greatly, and he began again to sing his death-chant, which now seemed infinitely more touching by reason of the small creature he cradled so lovingly in his arms.

"Be silent!" commanded Curtis. "You must not sing. Drive fast, Two Horns!"

Answering wails and fragments of chanting broke from the women; one or two cried out, "Take him from the agent!" But the men shook their heads and sadly watched them pass. "He has done a foolish thing; he must now suffer for it," said Crawling Elk.

As they drew up before the door of the parsonage Curtis sprang out and said to Cut Finger:

"Give me the baby; he shall be well cared for."

The father gave up the child passively, and Curtis called to Jennie:

"Here is a babe that is tired and hungry—be good to it."

"Where is the mother?" asked Jennie, as she tenderly received the little brown boy.

"She is coming," he said, and the mother galloped up in a few moments and fairly tumbled off her horse. "See!" Curtis said to her and to the father: "My sister will give the baby milk, and its mother shall also be fed. You need not fear; both will be taken care of. We are your friends."

Cut Finger watched Jennie as she carefully carried the baby into the house, and as he turned away, a look of apathetic misery, more moving than any cry, settled on his face.

Maynard, who had been standing in the door, said, in a tone of astonishment, "Did that wild Injun carry his papoose all the way down?"

"Yes, and was as tender of it as a woman, too."

"Well, I'll be hanged! There's a whole lot for me to learn about Injuns yet. Want a guard?"

"Yes; I think it safer. There is a good deal of sympathy for this poor chap."

"I don't blame 'em very much," said Maynard. "Take him right down to our guard-house, and I'll have Payne detail a squad of men to take care of him."

"I intend taking him to Pinon myself. I can't find it in my heart to give him over into the hands of these whites—they'd lynch him, sure."

"I believe it," replied Maynard, with conviction.

As they passed the agency gate, Winters and the county attorney stepped out as if they expected to receive the prisoner; but the savage grin on the sheriff's face died out as Curtis nodded coldly and drove past.

"That fellow is a wolf. Did you have any trouble?" asked Maynard.

"Not a bit. We surprised him in bed, as I planned to do."

"Nice thing, your leaving me out in this way!"

"Have the Brisbanes gone?"

"Yes. Got away about eight o'clock. Lawson went with them, though he's coming back to see you clear of this war. He's a crackerjack, is Lawson; but the old man has you marked for slaughter."

It was good to be able to turn his prisoner over to the blue-coats and feel that he would not be taken away except properly and in order. Lynching does not flourish under the eyes of a commander like Maynard. As Curtis led his man into the guard-house and motioned him to a seat, he said, in signs:

"You are safe now from the cattlemen. I am your

friend, remember that. I myself will take you to the white chief's big village. I will not let the war chief have you. I will turn you over to the wise man—the man who will judge your case. I will let your wife and your little son go with you. So you see I am still your Little Father. I am very sorry you have shot this man, but you must be punished. I cannot prevent that."

As he met the sheriff he said, quietly, "I have decided to accompany you to Pinon City."

The sheriff was not greatly surprised.

"Oh, very well. But I don't see the need of it."

"I do!" replied Curtis, and his tone silenced opposition.

Going immediately to the house, Curtis flung himself down in his chair and submitted to Jennie's anxious care. She brought him some coffee and biscuit, and stood with her hand on his shoulder while he ate. "Well, they're gone—Lawson and all. I never saw a greater change in any one than in that girl. Do you remember how she was last fall? I never supposed I should come to love her. I hated her for the treatment of you then, but—I think she has a different feeling towards us now—not excepting you. I think—she was crying because she was—going—away—from—you."

He looked up at her and smiled incredulously. "Your loyalty to me, sis, is more than I deserve!"

Curtis seized a moment to cross the square to Elsie's studio, eager to see whether she had regarded his wishes or not. It was an absurd thing to ask of her, and yet he did not regret having done so. It would serve as a sort of test of her regard, her sympathy. Now as he stood at the door he hesitated—if it should be bare!

He turned the knob and entered. The effect of the first impression was exalting, satisfying. All was in order, and the air was deliciously cool and fragrant, infilled with some rare and delicate odor. Each article was in its place—she had taken nothing but the finished pictures and some sketches which she specially needed. Scraps of canvas covered with splashes of color were pinned about on the walls, the easel stood in the centre of the room, and her palette and brushes were on the table. The young soldier closed the door behind him and took a seat in deep emotion. At that moment he realized to the full his need of her, and his irreparable loss. All he had suffered before was forgotten—swallowed up in the empty, hungry ache of his heart. The curtains and draperies were almost as much a part of her as her dress, and he could not have touched them at the moment, so intimately personal did they seem.

It appeared that he had not fully understood himself, after all. This empty temple, where she had lived and worked, these reminders of her beautiful self, were not to be a solace and a comfort, after all, but a torture. He felt broken and unmanned, and the aching in his throat grew to an intolerable pain, and with a reaction to disdain of himself he rose and went out, closing and locking the door.

CHAPTER XXXI

Outwitting the Sheriff

MAYNARD CAME over just as the wagon was being brought round, and with a look of concern on his big, red face, began: "Now see here, Curtis, you'd better take an escort. Those devils may be hanging round the edge of the reservation. Say the word and I'll send Payne and a squad of men."

"I don't think it at all necessary, Maynard. I don't want to excite the settlers, and, besides, the troops are all needed here. I have no fear of the mob while daylight lasts. They will not attempt to take the man from me. I leave you in command. Wilson will keep the police out on the hills and report any movement of the mob."

Maynard saluted. "Very well, Major; when may I look for you to return?"

"Not before to-morrow night. I shall get in by sundown to-day, for it is all the way down hill; the return will be slower."

"I don't like to see you go away with that cut-throat sheriff."

"I am not alone," said Curtis. "I have two of the faithfulest men in the world—Two Horns and Crow—both armed and watchful. Don't worry about me, Jack; keep yourself alert to-night."

The wagon was now standing before the guard-house, and the prisoner was being brought forth by Crow. Cut Finger, blinking around him in the noon-day glare, saw his wife already in the wagon, and went resignedly towards the agent, who beckoned to him.

"You may sit beside her," Curtis signed, and the youth climbed submissively to his seat. "Mr. Sheriff, you are to take a place beside the driver."

Winters, swollen with rebellion because of the secondary part he had to play, surlily consented to sit with Two Horns.

"Crow, you camp here," called Curtis, and the trusted Tetong scrambled to his seat. "Drive on, Two Horns."

For an hour and more no one spoke but Two Horns, gently urging the horses to their best pace. Curtis welcomed this silence, for it gave him time to take account of many things, chief of which was Brisbane's violent antagonism. "He overestimates my importance," he thought. "But that is the way such men succeed. They are as thorough-going in destroying the opposition as they are in building up their own side."

He thought, too, of that last intimate hour with Elsie, and wished he had spoken plainer with her. "It would have been definite if I had secured an answer. It would have been a negative, of course, and yet such is my folly, I still hope, and so long as there is the slightest uncertainty I shall waste my time in dreaming." His mind then turned to the question of the mob. There came into his mind again the conviction that they were waiting to intercept the sheriff at the boundary of the reservation; but he was perfectly certain that they would relinquish their designs when they found the sheriff reinforced by three determined men—one of them an army officer and the agent. He had no fear on that score; he only felt a little uneasy at leaving the agency.

A sharp exclamation from Crow brought his dreaming to an end, and, looking up, he saw a horseman approaching swiftly, his reins held high, his elbows flapping. "That's young Streeter," he said, on the impulse.

"So it is," replied Winters, hot with instant excitement. "I wonder what's his hurry?"

Calvin came up with a rush, and when opposite set his horse on his haunches with a wrench of his powerful wrist, calling, in lazy drawl: "Howdy, folks, howdy. Well, I see you've got 'im," he remarked to Curtis.

"You've been ridin' hard," said Winters; "what's your rush? Anything doin'?"

Calvin looked down at his panting, reeking horse, and carelessly replied: "Oh no. I'm just takin' it out o' this watch-eyed bronco." He exchanged a look with the sheriff. "I thought I'd ketch ye 'fore ye left the agency. I'd like a word with you, sheriff; tumble out here for a minute. You'll wait a second, won't you, Major?"

Curtis looked up at the sun. "Yes; but be quick."

Calvin slid from his horse, and while the sheriff was climbing stiffly down on the opposite side slipped a note into Curtis's hand.

As the sheriff listened to Calvin's low-voiced report Curtis glanced at the paper. It was in pencil, and from Elsie. "The mob is waiting at the half-way house, cruel as wolves—turn back—for my sake."

Curtis crumpled the paper in his hand and called

out imperatively: "Come, Sheriff Winters, I cannot wait."

Winters turned away smilingly. "That's all right, Cal. I didn't understand, that's all. I'm glad the boys went home. Of course the troops settled everything."

Curtis caught Calvin's eye, and a nod, almost imperceptible, passed between them, and the cowboy was aware that the soldier understood the situation. "Where did you leave the Senator?"

"At the half-way house."

"How was he?"

"Feeling well enough to make a speech," replied Calvin.

The other team, containing Grismore and the reporters, was by this time but a few rods away, and, watching his opportunity, Curtis signalled: "Stop that wagon—hold them here." Calvin again nodded. "Drive on," called Curtis. And Winters smiled with rare satisfaction.

Some miles before reaching the border of the reservation, Two Horns, at a sign from Curtis, left the main road and began to climb a low ridge to the east.

The sheriff turned and called sharply: "Where is he going?"

"He has his orders, Mr. Sheriff."

"He's taking the wrong road. It is five miles farther that way."

"He is following my orders."

"But I don't see the sense of it."

"You are only a passenger. If you don't care to ride with us you can walk," replied Curtis, and the sheriff settled back into his seat with a curse. The second wagon had been left far behind, and would undoubtedly keep the main road, a mishap Curtis had calculated upon.

An hour or two of extra travel would not matter,

especially as the mob was being left safely on the left.

The warning from Elsie had a singular effect upon the soldier. He grew almost gay at the thought of her care of him. In some occult way the little card meant a great deal more than its few words. If they were delayed at the half-way house they might not reach Pinon in time for the afternoon train, and so—"I may see her again."

As he neared the boundary of the reservation the sheriff gained in resolution. Looking backward, he saw his own team following, outlined like a rock against the sky, just topping a ridge, and reaching over he laid his hand on the reins and pulled the horses to a stand.

"Right here *I* take charge!" he growled. "I'm on my own ground. Get out o' there!" he said to the prisoner, and as he spoke he drew his revolver and leaped to the ground.

Cut Finger turned towards Curtis, whose face was set and stern. "Sit still!" he commanded, with a gesture. "Put up your gun!" he said to Crow, who had drawn his revolver, ready to defend his prisoner.

Winters flew into bluster. "Do you defy my authority now? I'm sheriff of this county!" he shouted. "Your control ends right here! This is State territory."

Curtis eyed him calmly. "I started out to give this man safe convoy to the prison, and I'm going to do it! Not only that—he is a ward of the government, even when lodged in the county jail, and it is my duty to see that he has fair trial; then, and not till then, will I abandon him to the ferocity of your mob. I know your plan, and I have defeated it. Do you intend to ride with us?"

The sheriff's courage again failed him as he looked up into the direct, unwavering eagle gaze of the young officer. He began to curse. "We'll have your hide for this! You've gone too far! You've defied the laws of the county!"

"Drive on," said Curtis, and Two Horns touched his ponies with the whip.

"Halt, or I fire!" shouted Winters.

"Drive on!" commanded Curtis, and Two Horns laid the whip hard on the back of his off horse.

Winters fired, but the bullet went wide; he dared not aim to kill. Cut Finger rose as if to leap from the wagon, but Crow seized him with one great brown paw and thrust his shining gun against his breast. "Sit down, brother!" he said, grimly. "We'll care for you."

The prisoner sank back into his seat trembling with excitement, while the wife began to cry piteously.

Curtis, looking back, saw the sheriff waving his revolver maniacally, but his curses fainted on the way. A sudden reaction to humor set in, and the young agent laughed a hearty chuckle which made his faithful Tetong aides break into sympathetic grins.

Nevertheless, the case was not entirely humorous. In a certain sense he had cut athwart the law in this last transaction, though in doing so he had prevented an act of violence which would have still further embittered the tribe. "I am right," he said, and put away all further doubt.

The drive now settled into a race for the jail. "The sheriff, after being picked up by his own party, will undertake to overhaul us," reasoned Curtis, but that did not trouble him so much as the thought of what lay before him.

The road ran along Willow Creek, winding as the stream itself, and Curtis could not avoid the thought of am ambuscade. On the right were clumps of tall willows capable of concealing horsemen, while on the left the hot, treeless banks rose a hundred feet above the wagon, and the loopings of the track prevented a view of what was coming. If the mob should get impatient, or if they should suspect his trick, it would be easy to send a detachment across the hills and intercept him. "Push hard!" he signed to Two Horns.

The road was smooth and dusty and descended rapidly, so that the horses had little to do but guide the tongue. As the wagon rocked and reeled past the ranch houses, the settlers had hardly time to discern what manner of man was driving, but they were thrown into fierce panic by the clatter of fleeing horses and the cloud of prophetic dust. The sheriff was not in sight, and no sound of him could be detected in the whiz of their own wheels.

At last Two Horns, with his moccasined foot on the brake, broke through the hills out upon the valley land, with Pinon City in sight. The mob and the sheriff were alike left behind. Ambush was now impossible.

"Easy now, Two Horns," called Curtis, with a smile and an explanatory gesture. "We're safe now; the angry white men are behind," and the reeking, dusty, begrimed horses fell into a walk.

The hour for their arrival in Pinon City was fortunate. The town was still at supper, and in the dusk Curtis and prisoner escaped notice. They hurried across the main street and on towards the jail, which stood on a little knoll just outside the town.

As they drew up before the door a young man came out and stared with inquiring gaze.

Curtis spoke first. "Are you the turnkey?"

"I'm in charge here; yes, sir."

"I am Captain Curtis, the agent. This is Cut Finger, charged with the murder of a white man. I have brought him in. The sheriff is just behind." He turned to the prisoner and signed. "Get down! Here is the strong-house where you are to stay!"

Cut Finger clambered slowly down, his face rigid, his limbs tremulous with emotion. To go to the dark room of the strong-house was the worst fate that could overtake a free man of the hills, and his heart fluttered like a scared bird.

"It would be a good plan to let his wife go in with him," suggested Curtis. "It will save trouble."

The poor, whimpering girl-wife followed her culprit husband up the steps and into the cold and gloomy hall to which they were admitted, her eyes on the floor, her sleeping child held tightly in her arms. When the gate shut behind him Curtis signed to the prisoner this advice:

"Now be good. Do not make any trouble. Do what these people tell you. Eat your food. I will ask the sheriff to let your wife see you in the morning, and then she will go home again. She can come once each month to see you." He touched the wife on the arm, and when she comprehended his gesture she uttered again that whimpering moan, and as she bent her head in dumb agony above her babe, Curtis gently led her to the door, leaving Cut Finger to the rigor of the white man's law.

CHAPTER XXXII

An Eventful Night

AT THE railway station Curtis alighted. "Go to Paul Ladue's," he said to Two Horns. "Put the horses in his corral and feed them well. Sit down with Paul, and to-morrow morning at sunrise come for me at the big hotel. Be careful. Don't go on the street to-night. The white men have evil hearts."

"We know," said Crow, with a clip of his forefinger. "We will sleep like the wolf, with one eye open."

As they drove away, Curtis hurried into the station, and calling for a blank, dashed away at a brief telegram to the Commissioner. While revising it he overheard the clerk say, in answer to a question over the telephone: "No, Senator Brisbane did not get away on 'sixteen.' He is still at the Sherman House."

Curtis straightened and his heart leaped. "Then I *can* see Elsie again!" he thought. Hastily pencilling two or three shorter messages, he handed them in and hurried up the street towards the hotel, eager to relieve her anxiety.

By this time the violet dusk of a peaceful night covered the town. The moon, low down in the west, was dim, but the stars were beginning to loom large in the wonderful deep blue to the east. The air was windless. No cloud was to be seen, and yet the soldier had a touch of uneasiness. "I wish I had brought my faithful men with me to the Sherman House. However, there is no real cause to worry. Paul is more Tetong than borderman—and will protect them—if only they keep off the street."

He began to meet men in close-packed groups on the sidewalk—roughly clad citizens who seemed absorbed in the discussion of some important event. A few of them recognized him as he passed, and one called, in a bitter tone, "There goes the cur himself!" Curtis did not turn, though the tone, more insulting than the words, made his heart hot with battle. It was plain that the sheriff and his party had already entered and reported their defeat. A saloon emptied a mob of loud-voiced men upon the sidewalk before him, and though he feared trouble he pushed steadily forward. The ruffians gave way before his resolute feet, but he felt their hate beating like flame upon his face. He dared not turn a hair's-breadth to the right nor to the left; nothing was better than to walk straight on. "They will not shoot me in the back," he reasoned, and beyond a volley of curses he remained unassaulted.

The rotunda of the hotel was filled with a different but not less dangerous throng of excited politicians and leading citizens, who had assembled to escort Brisbane to the opera-house. The talk, though less profane than that of the saloon loafers, was hardly less bitter against the agent. Mingled with these district bosses were a half-dozen newspaper men, who instantly rushed upon Curtis in frank and boyish rivalry. "Captain, what is the news?" they breathlessly asked, with pads and pencils ready for his undoing.

"All quiet!" was his curt reply.

"But—but—how about—"

"All lies!" he interrupted to say, and pushed on to the desk. "Is Senator Brisbane and party still here?" he asked, as he signed his name in the book.

The clerk applied the blotter. "Yes; he is still at supper."

The young soldier took time to wash the dust from his face and hands and smooth his hair before entering the dining-room. At the threshold he paused and took account of his enemies. Brisbane and three of his most trusted supporters, still sitting at coffee, were holding a low-voiced consultation at a corner table, while Lawson and Elsie sat waiting some distance away and near an open window. The Parkers were not in view.

Elsie, at sight of her lover, rose impulsively, and her face, tired and pale, flushed to a beautiful pink. Her lips formed the words. "Why, there is Captain Curtis!" but her voice was inaudible.

He hastened forward with eyes only for her, and she met him with both hands outstretched—eager, joyous!

"Oh, how good it is to see you! We were so alarmed—Calvin warned you?"

"Yes. He met me just before I left the reservation."

"But I expected you to bring soldiers; how did you escape? Did you find the cattlemen gone?"

"I flanked them." His face relaxed into humor. "Discretion is a sort of valor sometimes. I took the Willow road."

Lawson now joined them, and in his hand-clasp was a brother's regard for the soldier. His smile was exultant. "Good work! I knew Calvin could be trusted. It looked bad for Cut Finger when we reached the half-way house."

"You must be hungry!" exclaimed Elsie. "Sit here and I will order something for you."

"I *was hungry* an hour ago," he said, meaningly, "but now I am not. But I am tired," he added. "Where are the Parkers?"

Elsie laughed. "On their way to civilization. They fled on the up-train."

"The town is aflame," said Lawson. "You and your Tetongs are an issue here to-night. A big meeting is called, and the Senator is to speak. He has just discovered you," he added, glancing towards Brisbane, who had risen and was glaring at Curtis, his small eyes hot as those of an angry bear.

"Excuse me, won't you?" pleaded Elsie, rising hastily. "I must go to him!"

Curtis also rose and looked soberly into her eyes. "May I not see you again?"

She hesitated. "Yes. I'm not going to the meeting. Come to our parlor when you are finished supper."

He remained standing till she joined her father and passed from the room, then he turned towards Lawson, who said:

"Seriously, my dear Curtis, you are in danger here. I hope you will not go out this evening. Even Uncle Sam's blue might not prove a protection in the dark of a night like this. Where did you house your men?"

"At Ladue's, with orders not to leave the corral."

"Quite right. Where is the sheriff?"

This question brought a humorous light into the young soldier's eyes. "When I saw him last he was on Sage-hen Flat swinging his revolver and cursing me," and he told the story.

Lawson grew grave. "I'm sorry you had to do that; it will give your enemies another grip on you. It's a mere technicality, of course, but they'll use it.

You must watch every one of your clerks from this on; they'll trump up a charge against you if they can, and secure a court-martial. This election is really the last dying struggle of the political banditti of the State, and they will be defeated. Take to-night as an example. The reckless devils, the loud of mouth are alone in evidence, the better class of citizens dare not protest—dare not appear on the streets. But don't be deceived, you have your supporters even here, in the midst of this saturnalia of hate. You are an issue."

Curtis grimly smiled. "I accept the challenge! They can only order me back to my regiment."

"As for Brisbane, he is on the point of collapse. He has lost his self-control. He has attained a fixed notion that you are his most dangerous enemy; the mention of your name throws him into fury. I lost patience with him to-day, and opened fire. 'You are doomed to defeat!' I said to him. 'You represent the ignoble, greedy, conscienceless hustler and speculator, not the peaceful, justice-loving citizen of this State. Your dominion is gone; the reign of order and peace is about to begin.' If it were not for Elsie I would publicly denounce him, for his election would work incalculable injury to the West. But he can't fill the legislature with his men as he did twelve years ago. He will fail of election by fifty votes."

"I hope so," responded Curtis, with a sigh, as Lawson rose. "But I have no faith in the courage of the better element; virtue is so timid and evil is always so fully organized."

After Lawson left him Curtis hurriedly finished his supper and went his way to his room for a moment's rest. Through the open windows he could hear the cheering which greeted Brisbane's entrance into the opera-house, which faced upon the little square before the hotel. The street was thronging with noisy boys, and at intervals a band of young herders clattered into the square. Their horses thickened along the hitching-poles, and the saloons swarmed with men already inflamed with drink. The air seemed heavy, oppressive, electrical, and the shrill cheers which rose above the dull rumble of pounding boot-heels in the hall possessed a savage animal vehemence. Again a sense of impending disaster swept over the young officer. "I am tired and nervous," he thought. "Surely law and order rules in a civilized community like this."

He put away all thoughts of war as he followed the boy up the stair-way to the Brisbane private parlor, and became the lover, palpitant with the hope that he was about to see Elsie alone.

She met him at the door, her face a-quiver with feeling, a note of alarm in her voice. "Have you heard the cheering? They are denouncing you over there!"

"I suppose so. But let's not talk of such unimportant matters; this is our last evening together, and I want to forget the storm outside. Since I left you last night I have had a most remarkable experience, and I—"

"Oh, you mean catching the murderer; tell me about it!"

"No. Oh no; that is not worth telling. I mean something more intimately personal." Shrill yells from across the way interrupted him, and Elsie rose and shut the window. "I hate them; they are worse than savages," she said. "Please don't mind them."

He went on: "I was about to say I had a deal of time to think on my long ride this morning, and I reached some conclusions which I want to tell you about. When my prisoner was safe in the guardhouse, I went over to see how my little temple of art looked—I mean your studio, of course. I closed the door and dropped into one of the big chairs, hoping to gain rest and serenity in the beauty and quiet of the place. But I didn't; I was painfully depressed."

She opened her eyes very wide at this. "Why?"

"Because everything I saw there emphasized the irrevocable loss I had suffered. I couldn't endure the thought of it, and I fled. I could not remain without weeping, and you know a man is ashamed of his tears; but when I got your note of warning I flung conscience to the winds! 'It is not a crime to love a woman,' I said. 'I will write to her and say to her "I love you, no matter what happens;"' and, now I find you here, I tell it to you instead of writing it."

She was facing him with a look of perplexity and alarm. One hand laid upon her throat seemed to express suffering. When she spoke her voice was very low.

"What do you expect me to say; you make it so hard for me! Why do you tell me this?"

"Because I could not rest till I had spoken. For a long time I thought you were bound to Lawson, and since then I've tried to keep silent because of my poverty and—no one knows better than I the unreason of it all—I do not ask you to speak except to say, 'I am sorry.' When I found you were still within reach, the desire to let you know my feeling overcame every other consideration. I can't even do the customary thing and ask you to wait, for my future is as uncertain as my present, but if you could say you loved me—a little—" he paused abruptly, as though choked into silence by a merciless hand.

Elsie remained silent, with her eyes turned towards the window, her hands in her lap, and at last he went on:

"If your father is a true prophet, I shall be ordered back to my regiment. That will hurt me, but it won't ruin me exactly. It would be a shameful thing if the department sacrificed me to expediency; but politicians are wonderful people! If you were not so much an artist and Andrew Brisbane's daughter, I would ask you to come to me and help me do my work, but I can't quite do that—yet; I can only say you are more to me now than any other soul in the world. I do this because I can't keep from it," he repeated, in poor ending.

"I've heard that the best way to make a woman love a man is to persecute the man," she replied, smiling a little, though her eyes were wet. "When you were apparently triumphant I hated you—now—" she hesitated and a sudden timidity shook her.

He sprang up. "Can you carry out the figure? I dare you to finish the sentence. Do you care for me a little?" His face, suddenly illuminated, moved her powerfully.

"I'm afraid I do—wait, please!" She stopped him with a gesture. "You mustn't think I mean more than I do. My mind is all in a whirl now; it isn't fair to hurry me; I must take time to consider. Your being poor and an Indian agent wouldn't make any difference to me if I— But I must be sure. I respect you—I admire you very much—and last night when I said good-bye I felt a sharp pain here." She put her hand to her throat. "But I must be sure. There are so many things against it," she ended, covering her eyes with her hand in piteous perplexity.

His eyes were alight, his voice eager. "It would be such a glorious thing if you could join me in my work."

The mention of his work stung her. "Oh no! It is impossible. I should die here! I have no sense of duty towards these poor vagabonds. I'm sorry for them—but to live here—no, no! You must not ask it. You must go your way and I will go mine. You are only torturing me needlessly."

"Forgive me," he pleaded. "I did not mean to do so."

She continued, wildly: "Can't you see how crazy, how impossible, it is? I admire you—I believe in your work—it is magnificent; but I can't live your life. My friends, my art, mean too much to me."

There was a tremulous, passionate pleading which failed of finality: it perplexed her lover; it did not convince him.

"You are right; of course you are right," he said again; "but that does not help me to bear the pain of your loss. I can't let you go out of my life— utterly—I can't do it—I will not— Hark! What is that?"

A faint, far-off, thundering sound interrupted him. A rushing roar, as of many horsemen rapidly approaching. Hastening to the window, Curtis bent his head to listen. "It sounds like a cavalry charge. Here they come! Cowboys—a mob of them! Can it be Yarpe's gang? Yes; that is precisely what it is. Yarpe leading them into some further deviltry."

Whooping and cursing, and urging their tired horses with quirt and spur, the desperadoes, somewhat thinned of ranks, pouring by in clattering, pounding rush—as orderless as a charging squad of Sioux warriors—turned up a side street and disappeared almost before any one but Curtis was aware of them.

"They are bent on mischief," said the soldier as he turned upon the girl, all personal feeling swept away by the passing mob. "They have followed me in to force the jail and hang Cut Finger." He caught up his cap. "I must prevent it!"

"No! No!" cried Elsie, seizing his arm. "You must not go out in the street to-night—they will kill you— please don't go—you have done your duty. Now let the mayor act, I beg of you!"

"Dear girl, I *must* thwart this lynching party. I would be disgraced! Don't you see? They have seized the moment when the citizens are all in the hall away from the jail to do this thing. I must alarm the town and prevent them."

Even as he pleaded with her the tumult in the hall broke forth again, roared for a moment in wild crescendo, and then ceased instantly, strangely. A moment's silence followed, and a confused murmur arose, quite different from any sound which had hitherto emanated from the hall. A powerful voice dominated all others, and through the open windows the words of command could be distinctly heard. *"Keep back there! Keep your seats!"*

"The meeting is breaking up!" exclaimed Curtis. "Some one has alarmed them. See, they are pouring out to prevent this crazy mob from carrying out its plan."

The shouting ceased, but the trample of feet and the murmur of voices thickened to a clamor, and Elsie turned white with a new fear. "They are rushing across the square! Perhaps they are coming for *you!*"

"I don't think so; they would not dare to attack me—they hate me, but—"

Her over-wrought nerves gave way. A panic seized her. "Hide! Hide! They will kill you!" she cried out, hoarsely.

"No; I am going to help them defend the jail."

"For my sake!" she pleaded, "don't leave me! Listen! they are coming!" she whispered. The sound of many feet could be heard in the lobby below, the roar of a hundred voices came up the stair-way, but even the excited girl could now detect something hushed and solemn in the sound—something mournful in the measured footsteps up the stairs.

"It is father!" she cried, with a flash of divination. "Something has happened to him!" And with this new terror in her face she hurried out into the hall.

Curtis reached her side just as the head of the procession topped the stair-way.

Brisbane, up-borne by Lawson and a tall young stranger, first appeared, followed by a dozen men, who walked two and two with bared heads and serious faces, as if following a hearse. The stricken man's face was flushed and knobby, and his eyelids drooped laxly like those of a drunkard. He saw nothing, and his breathing was labored.

"Father,, what has happened?" called Elsie. "Tell me—quick!"

"A touch of vertigo," answered Lawson, soothingly. "The doctor says nothing serious."

"Are you the doctor?" she turned to the young man.

"Yes. Don't be alarmed. The Senator has overtaxed himself a little, that is all, and needs rest. Show me his bed, and we will make him comfortable."

Elsie led the way to the bedroom, while Curtis stood helplessly facing the crowd in the hall. Lawson relieved the situation by coming out a few moments later to say:

"Gentlemen, the doctor thanks you, and requests you to leave the Senator to rest as quietly as possible."

After this dismissal had dispersed the on-lookers, Lawson turned to Curtis. "The old man's work as a speaker is done. Rather tragic business, don't you think? He was assailing you with the utmost bitterness. His big, right fist was in the air like a hammer when he fell; but it was his last effort."

Curtis seized his hand and said: "I envy you your chance to go with her and serve her." His voice changed. "The mob! Did you hear Yarpe and his men pass?"

"No; when?"

"Not ten minutes ago. I fear some mischief."

The doctor appeared. "Mr. Lawson, a moment."

As Lawson hurried into the sick-room a far-off,

faint volley of pistol-shots broke the hush that had settled over the square. Distant yells succeeded, accompanied by a sound as of some giant hammering. The young soldier lifted his head like a young lion listening to a battle-call. "They are beating in the gates!" he said. For a moment he hesitated, but only for a moment. "She is safe!" he thought, with a glance towards Elsie's door. "My man and the poor little wife are not," and he rushed down the stairway and out into the street with intent to find and defend his faithful men.

CHAPTER XXXIII

Elsie Confesses Her Love

As HE paused on the steps to the hotel, a gust of bitter rage swept over him. "What can I do against this implacable town? Oh, for a squad of the boys in blue!"

The street and square were filled with men all running, as to a fire, from left to right—a laughing, jesting throng. Along the hitching-poles excited and jocular cowboys were loosing their ponies and leaping to their saddles. Some excitable citizen had begun to ring the fire-bell, and women, bareheaded and white with fear, were lining the sidewalks and leaning from windows. The town resembled an ant-hill into which a fleeing bison has planted a foot.

"Oh, sir!" cried one young mother as she caught sight of Curtis, "are the Injuns coming?"

"No," he replied, bitterly, "these marauders are not Indians; they are noble citizens," and set off at a run towards the corral in which Two Horns and Crow were camped. The tumult behind him grew

fainter, and at last died to a murmur, and only one
or two houses showed a light.

Ladue's was an old ranch on the river, around
which the town of Pinon had for twenty years been
slowly growing. The cabin was of stone, low and
strong, and two sides of it formed the corner of a
low corral of cottonwood logs. In this enclosure
teamsters (for two bits) were allowed to camp and
feed their horses. A rickety gate some fifty feet
south of the house stood ajar, and Curtis entered
the yard, calling sharply for Crow Wing and Two
Horns. No one replied. Searching the stalls, he
found the blankets wherein they had lain, but the
tumult had undoubtedly called them forth into danger.

Hurrying to the house, he knocked most vigor-
ously at the door—to no effect. The shack was also
empty. Closing the door with a slam, the young officer, now thoroughly alarmed, turned back towards
the hotel. A vast, confused clamor, growing each
moment louder, added edge to his apprehension.
The crowd was evidently returning from the jail, ju-
bilant and remorseless. Upon reaching the corner of
the square Curtis turned to the left with the design
of encircling it, hoping to find the two redmen looking on from a door-way on the outskirts of the
throng.

He had crossed but one side of the plaza, when a
band of cowboys dashed in from the opposite corner with swinging lariats, whooping shrilly, in close
pursuit of a flying footman. A moment later a rope
looped, the fugitive fell, and the horsemen closed
round him in joyous clamor, like dogs around a fox.

With a fear that this was one of his men, Curtis
raised a great shout, but his voice was lost in the
rush and roar of the throng pouring in towards the
fugitive. In fierce rage he rushed straight towards
the whirling mass of horsemen, but before he had

passed half the intervening space a horseman circled the pavilion, and the popping of a revolver, swift yet with deliberate pauses, began. Wild yells broke forth, the pursuers scattered, other revolvers began to crack, and as the press of horsemen reeled back, Curtis perceived Calvin, dismounted and bareheaded, with his back against the wall of the little wooden band-stand, defiant, a revolver in each hand, holding the mob at bay, while over his head a light sputtered and sizzled.

A lane seemed to open for Curtis as he ran swiftly in towards the writhing, ensnared captive on the ground. It was Two Horns, struggling with the ropes which bound him, and just as his Little Father bent over him the big Tetong freed himself, and, with a sliding rush, entered the shadow by Calvin's side. Instantly his revolver began to speak.

Curtis, left alone in the full light of the lamp on the pavilion, raised his arms and shouted: "Hold! Cease firing!" The crowd recognized him and fell silent. The army blue subdued them, and those who had done the shooting began to edge away.

For a moment the young soldier could not speak, so furious was he, but at last he found words: "Cowards! Is this your way of fighting—a hundred to one? Where is your mayor? Have you no law in this town?" He turned to Calvin, who stood still, leaning against the pavilion. "Are you hurt?"

Calvin lifted one dripping hand. "I reckon I'm punched a few. My right arm feels numb, and the blood is fillin' my left boot. But I'm all here, sure thing." But even as he spoke he reeled. Curtis caught him; he smiled apologetically: "That left leg o' mine, sure feels like a hitchin'-post; reckon some one must o' clipped a nerve somewhere."

Two Horns seized him by the other arm, just as Winters blustered into the circle. "What's going on here; who's doin' this shootin'?"

"This is a good time to ask that," remarked Curtis. "Where were you twenty minutes ago?"

Calvin struggled to get his right hand free. "Let me have a crack at the beast!" he pleaded. "I saw you," he said to Winters: "you were in the lynching crowd, you sneak! You hung round in the shadow like a coyote."

Curtis tried to calm him. "Come, this won't do, Calvin; you are losing blood and must have a doctor; come to the hotel."

As they half-carried him away the young rancher snarled back, like a wounded wolf: "I disown the whole cowardly pack of ye; I put my mark on some of ye, too."

The crowd was now so completely with Calvin that Winters hastened to explain: "Cal is my deputy; he was acting inside his duty! He was trying to keep the peace and you had no business fightin'," and proceeded to arrest some fairly innocent bystanders, while the wounded desperadoes were being swiftly hidden away by their friends, and the remaining citizens of the town talked of what should have been done.

Calvin continued to explain as they hurried him through the excited throng. "I tried to stand 'em off at the jail," he said, "but I couldn't get near enough; my cayuse was used up. Oh, you was there!" he called to a tall man with a new sombrero. "I saw you, Bill Vawney, and I'll get you for it; I've spotted you!"

He was enraged through every fibre of his strong, young body, and only the iron grip of the persistent men kept him from doing battle.

As they neared the hotel, Curtis, looking up, glimpsed Elsie's white face at the window and waved his cap at her. She clapped her hands in joy of his return, but did not smile. The hotel lobby was packed with a silent mass of men, but the landlord, with authoritative voice, called out: "Clear the way, gentlemen!" and a lane opened for them. "Right in here," he added, and led the way to the parlor bedroom. The Captain and Calvin were now most distinguished of citizens; nothing was too good for them.

"Bring a physician," said Curtis.

"Right here," replied a cool, clear voice, and Doctor Philipps stepped to Calvin's side and relieved Two Horns.

The young rancher sank down on the bed limply, but smiled as he explained: "I'm only singed a little, doc. They had me foul. You see, I was in the light, but I handed one or two of them something they didn't like. I left a keepsake with 'em. They won't forget me soon."

The physician pressed him back upon the bed and began to strip his clothes from him. "Be quiet for five minutes and I'll have you in shape. We must close up your gashes."

Curtis, relieved of part of his anxiety, then asked: "How is the Senator?"

"Pretty comfortable; no danger."

"Don't leave me, Major," called Calvin, as Curtis turned away to seek Elsie. "Don't let this chap cut me up. I'm no centipede. I need all my legs."

There was genuine pleading in the boy's voice, and Curtis came back and took a chair near him while the doctor probed the wounds and dressed them. The officer's heart was very tender towards the reckless, warm-hearted young rancher as he watched his face whiten and the lips stiffen in the effort to conceal his pain. "Calvin, you've been loyal all through," he said, "and we won't forget it."

At last, when the wounds were bandaged and the worst of the pain over, Curtis turned to Two Horns and signed:

"Where is Crow and the wife of Cut Finger?"

"I do not know."

"I will go find him; you remain here. Do not fear;

you are safe now. Sit down by Calvin's bed. You will sleep here to-night."

As he made his way through the close-packed mass of excited men in the lobby and before the hotel, Curtis met no hostile face. It seemed that all men were become his friends, and eager to disclaim any share in the mob's action. He put their proffered hands aside and hurried back to Ladue's, which he found close-barred and dark.

"Who's there?" called a shaking voice as he knocked.

"Captain Curtis. Where is Crow?"

"In here!" was the answer, in joyful voice. As he opened the door, Ladue reached his hand to the agent. "My God, I'm glad it is you! I was afraid you'd been wiped out. Where is Two Horns?"

Crow, with his revolver still gripped in his hand, stepped forward, his face quivering with emotion. "Little Father, it is good to see you; you are not hurt? Where is Two Horns?"

"Safe in the big house with me. The evil white men are gone; you will camp here, you and the wife of Cut Finger," he signed as he saw the cowering form of the little wife.

Ladue, a big, hulking, pock-marked half-breed, began to grin. "I was a-scared; I sure was. I thought we was all goin' to hang. Old Bill Yarpe was out for game."

"The better citizens are in control now," replied Curtis. "You are safe, but you'd better remain in the house till morning."

As Curtis made his way through the crowd someone raised a cheer for "Major Curtis," and the cry was taken up by a hundred voices. Indignant citizens shouted: "We'll stand by you, Major. We'll see justice done."

Curtis, as he reached the stair-way, turned and coldly said: "Make your words good. For four days a mob of two hundred armed men have menaced the lives of my employés and my wards, and you did nothing to prevent them. I am glad to see you appreciate the horror and the disgrace of this night's doings. If you mean what you say, let no guilty man escape. Make this night the memorable end of lawlessness in your country."

"We will!" roared a big, broad-faced, black-bearded man, and the crowd broke into another roar of approval.

Elsie was waiting at the top of the stairs, tense and white. Her eyes burned down into his with a singular flame as she cried out:

"Why didn't you come to me sooner? Why do you walk so slowly? Are you hurt? Tell me the truth!"

"No, only tired," he answered, as he reached her side.

She put out her hand and touched his breast. "You are; you are all bloody. Take off your coat; let me see!"

"No, it's not mine; it is poor Calvin's; he was badly wounded; he leaned against me."

"But I saw you standing in the pistol-fire; take it off, I say!" Her voice was almost frenziedly insistent.

He removed his coat in a daze of astonishment, and she cried out, triumphantly: "See! I was right; your shirt is soaked. You are wounded!"

"True enough!" he replied, looking down in surprise at a big stain on his shoulder. "I've been 'singed,' as Calvin calls it. It can't be serious, for I have not felt it."

A sudden faintness seized upon Elsie as she gazed fixedly upon the tell-tale stain. A gray whiteness passed over her face. "Oh, God! suppose you had been killed!" she whispered.

In that shuddering whisper was the expression of the girl's complete and final surrender, and Curtis

did not question, did not speak; he took her in his
arms to comfort her.

"My sweetheart, you *do* love me! I doubt no more.
My poverty, your wealth, what do they matter?"

She suddenly started away. "Oh, your wound!
Where is the doctor? Go to him!"

"The touch of your lips has healed me," he protested, but she insisted.

"Go! You are bleeding!" she commanded; and so,
reluctantly, lingeringly, with most unmilitary sloth,
he turned away, made numb to any physical pain by
the tenderness in her voice.

As the young surgeon was dressing the gash, he
said: "Well, Captain, things happen in the West."

"Yes, the kind of things which ought not to happen anywhere. I suppose they lynched poor Cut Finger?"

"No; they merely shot him and dragged him to
death, as near as I can learn."

Curtis clinched his fists. "Ah, the devils! Where is
the body?"

"Back in the corridor of the jail."

Curtis pondered the effect of this news on the
tribe. "It's a little difficult to eliminate violence from
an inferior race when such cruelty is manifested in
those we call their teachers."

He sent for Ladue, who was deep in discussion of
the evening's events with Crow and Two Horns, and
said to him: "Do not tell the wife of Cut Finger of
the death of her husband; wait till morning. What
the sheriff will do with the body I do not know. To-
morrow say to her, 'All is over; go with the agent.'
It will do her no good to remain here. Good-night!"

It was hard to realize in the peaceful light of the
following morning that the little square had been
the scene of so much cruelty and riot. The towns-
people came forth yawning and lax, and went about

their duties mechanically. Crow Wing and Two Horns, who would camp nowhere but on the floor of Curtis's room, were awake at dawn, conversing in signs, in order not to disturb the Little Father.

He, waking a little later, called to them in greeting and said: "Now all is quiet. The white men are sorry. You are safe. Go to Paul's, eat and get ready. We must start at once for the agency. Cut Finger did an ill deed, and brought trouble on us all. Now he is dead, but good may come out of it. Go, tell the little wife; be gentle with her; say to her I wish her to go home with us."

Silently, soberly, the two redmen left the room, and Curtis dressed and went at once to find Calvin. The boy looked up as Curtis entered and cheerily called: "Hello, Major, I've had a lively dream. I dreamed there was some gun-play goin' on out in the square and you and I were in it. Was that right?"

"I've a sore place here on my shoulder that says you are. How do you feel? Can you travel? If you can, I'll take you home in my buckboard."

"I can travel all right, but I haven't any home to go to. The old man and I haven't hitched very well for a year, and this will just about turn me out on the range."

"Well, come home with me, then; Jennie will soon have you all right again; she's a famous nurse, and will look out for you till your mother comes over, as she will. Mothers don't go back on their boys."

A curious dimness came into the bold, keen eyes of the wounded youth. "Major, that'll suit me better than anything else I know."

"Very well, if the doctor says you can travel, we'll go along together," replied Curtis.

He was eager to see Elsie and was pacing impatiently up and down the hall when Lawson met him, smiling, imperturbable. "Well, Captain, how are you this morning?"

"Have you seen Miss Brisbane?"

"No; she is still asleep, I hope. The Senator is conscious, but in a curious state; seems not to know or care where he is; his troubles are over."

Even as he spoke a maid came from Elsie's room to say that her mistress would breakfast in her own parlor, and wished both Mr. Lawson and Captain Curtis to join her in half an hour.

Lawson, in discussing the events of the night, was decidedly optimistic. "This outbreak will bring about a reaction," he said, with conviction. "You will find every decent man on your side to-day."

"I hope so," responded Curtis. "But last night's mob made me long for my Gray-Horse Troop."

When they entered the little parlor Elsie rose and passed straight to Curtis without coquetry or concealment. "How is your wound? Did you sleep?"

He assured her that he was almost as well as ever, and not till she had convinced herself of the truth did she turn to Lawson. "Osborne, I can never thank you enough for your good, kind help."

Osborne protested that he had done nothing worth considering, and they took seats at the table—a subdued and quiet group, for Lawson was still suffering from his loss, and the lovers could not conceal from themselves the knowledge that this was their last meeting for many long months. Elsie was a being transformed, so tender, so wilful, so strangely sweet and womanly was she in every smile and in every gesture.

They dwelt upon impersonal topics so long as Lawson remained; but he, being ill at ease, hastened with his coffee, and soon made excuse to withdraw, leaving them alone. For a moment they faced each other, and then, with a wistful cadence in his voice, Curtis said: "Dear girl, it's hard to say good-bye now, just when I have found you, but I must return at once."

"Oh, must you? Can't you wait till we go—this afternoon?"

"No; I must be the first to carry this dreadful news to my people."

"You are right, of course; but I'll miss you so, and you need me. Say you need me!"

"Need you! Of course I do; but you cannot stay with me and I cannot go with you."

"I know, I know!" she sighed, resignedly. "But it hurts all the same."

"This tumult will die out soon," he went on, in the effort to comfort her, "and then I can come on to Washington for a visit. I warn you I've lost all my scruples; seventeen hundred million dollars are as straws in my path, now that I know you really care for me."

"I don't feel rich now; I feel very poor. You must come to Washington soon."

"I warn you that when I come I will ask hard things of you!" He rose and his face darkened. "But my duty calls!"

She came to him and yielded herself to his embrace. "My queenly, beautiful girl! It is sweet to have you here in my arms; but I *must* say good-bye—good-bye."

In spite of his words he held her till she, with an instinctive movement, pushed from his arms. "Go—go quick!" she exclaimed, in a low, imperative voice.

Not staying to wonder at the meaning of her strange dismissal, he turned and left the room without looking back.

Only after he had helped Calvin into the wagon, and had taken his seat beside him, did the young soldier lift his eyes in search of her face at the window. She was looking down upon him, tears were on her cheeks, but she blew a kiss from her finger-tips, not caring if all the world were there to see.

CHAPTER XXXIV

Seed-Time

As Lawson predicted, the very violence of this out-burst of racial hatred was its cure. A reaction set in. The leaders of Brisbane's party, with loud shouts, ordered their harriers back to their lairs, while the great leader himself, oblivious to daylight or to darkness, was hurried home to Washington. The Tetongs returned to their camps and hay-making, the troops drilled peacefully each afternoon in the broiling heat, while Curtis bent to his work again with a desperate sort of energy, as if by so doing he could shorten the long, hot days, which seemed well-nigh interminable after the passing of Elsie and her friends.

In a letter announcing their safe arrival in Washington, Elsie said:

"I am going to see the President about you, as soon as he returns from the mountains. Papa is gaining, but takes no interest in anything. He is pitifully weak, but the doctor thinks he will recover if he will only rest. His brain is worn out and needs complete freedom from care. Congress has adjourned finally. I am told that your enemies expect to secure a court-martial on the charge of usurping the authority of the sheriff. Osborne says not to worry, for nothing will be done now till the President returns, and he is confident that the department will sustain you—the fact that the violence you feared did actually take place has robbed your enemies of their power."

Nevertheless, the fight against the Tetongs and himself went on with ever-increasing rancor during July and August, and each Congressional candidate was sharply interrogated as to his attitude towards the removal bill. The anti-administration papers boldly said: "If we win (and we will) we'll cut the comb of this bantam. We'll break his sabre over his back."

To this the opposition made answer: "We're no lovers of the redman, but Captain Curtis is an honorable soldier, doing his duty, and it will not be easy for you, even if victorious, to order a court-martial."

This half-hearted defence gave courage to those who took the high ground that the time for lynching had gone by. "The Tetongs have rights which every decent man is bound to respect, no matter how much he personally dislikes the redskin."

During the last days of August a letter came from Elsie, full of comforting assurances, both public and private, being more intimate and tender in tone than any that had preceded it, and full of sprightly humor too. It began:

"MY DEAR SOLDIER,—I've been so busy fighting your enemies I couldn't write a letter. I've met both the Secretary and the commissioner—their desks are said to be full of screeds against you—*and I've been to see the President!* He wasn't a bit gallant, but he listened. He glowered at me (not unkindly) while I told your story. I'm afraid I didn't phrase it very well, but he listened. I brought out all the good points I could think of. I said: 'Mr. President, Captain Curtis is the most disinterested man in the Indian service. He is sacrificing everything for his plans.' 'What are his plans?' he asked, so abruptly that I jumped. I then spoke learnedly of irrigating ditches and gardens; you would have laughed had you heard me, and I said: 'If he is ordered back to his regiment, Mr. President, these poor people will be robbed again.' 'Does Mr. Blank, of New York, endorse Captain Curtis?' he asked. I didn't see what this led to, but I answered that I did not know. 'He's a friend of yours, isn't he?' he asked. 'Whom do you mean?' I said, and my cheeks burned. Then he smiled. 'You needn't worry,' he said, banging the table with his fist. 'I'll keep Captain Curtis where he is if every politician in the State petitions for his removal.' I liked his wooden cuss-word, and I thanked him and jumped up and hurried home to write this letter. The Secretary told Osborne that the bill for buying out the settlers would certainly go through next winter, and that your plans were approved by the whole department. So, you see, you are master of the situation, and can plan as grandly as you wish—the entire reservation is yours.

"It is still hot here, and now that my 'lobbying' is done, I am going to the sea-shore, where papa is, and I know I shall wish you were with me to enjoy it. I am so sorry for you and Jennie, my heart aches for you. Think of it! The cool, beautiful ocean will be singing me to sleep to-night. I wish I could send you some fruit and some ices; I know you are longing for them.

"I wonder how it will all turn out? Will you be

East this winter? Perhaps I'll help you celebrate the opening of your new gardens, next spring. Wouldn't you like me to come out and break a bottle of wine over the first plough or water-gate or something? If you do, maybe I'll come. If you write, address me at the Brunswick, Crescent Beach. I wish you could come and see me here—you look so handsome in your uniform."

The soldier's answer was not a letter, it was a packet! He began by writing sorrowfully:

"Dearest Girl,—I fear I shall not be able to get away this winter. There is so much here that requires my care. If the bill passes, the people will be stirred up; if it doesn't pass, the settlers will be uneasy, and I shall be most imperatively necessary here. Nothing would be sweeter to me than a visit to you at the beach. As a boy I knew the sea-shore intimately, and to wall the sands with you would be to revive those sweet, careless boy memories and unite them with the deepest emotions of my life—my love for you, dear one. It almost makes me willing to resign. In a sense it would be worth it. I *would* resign only I know I am not losing the delight forever—I am only postponing it a year.

"I have thought pretty deeply on my problem, dearest, and I've come to this conclusion: When two people love each other as we do, neither poverty nor riches—nothing but duty, should separate them. Your wealth troubled me at first. I knew I could not give you the comforts—not to say luxuries—you were accustomed to, and I knew that my life as a soldier would always make even a barrack a place of uncertain residence. I must stand to my guns here till I have won my fight; then I may ask for a transfer to some field where life would not be so hard. If only there were ways to use your great wealth in helping these people I would rejoice to be your agent in the matter.

"I am a penniless suitor, but a good soldier. I can say that without egotism. I think I could have acquired money had I started out that way; of course I cannot do it now. Perhaps my knowledge and training will come to supplement and give power to your wealth. I must work. I am not one to be idle. If I go on working—devising—in my own way, then my self-respect would not be daunted, even though you were worth ten millions instead of one. I am fitted to be the head of a department—like that of Forestry, or Civil Engineering. After my work here is finished I may ask for something of that kind, but I am resolved to do my duty here first. I like your suggestion about the water-gate. I hold you to that word, my lady. One year from now, when my gardens are ready for the sickle, I will have the criers announce a harvest-home festival, and you must come and dance with me among my people, and then, perhaps, I will take a little vacation, and return with you to the East, and be happy with you among the joyous of the earth for a little season. Beyond that I dare not plan."

The administration was sustained, and Brisbane's forces were beaten back. The better elements of the State, long scattered, disintegrated, and without voice, spoke, and with majesty, rebuking the cruelty, the barbarism, and the blatant assertion of men like Musgrove and Streeter, who had made the State odious. Even Winters, the sheriff, was defeated, and a fairly humane and decent citizen put in his place, and this change, close down to the people, was most significant of all. "Now I have hope of the courts," said Curtis to Maynard.

If the Tetongs did not at once apprehend the peace and comfort which the defeat of Brisbane's gang and the passage of the purchase bill assured to them, they deeply appreciated the significance of the immediate withdrawal of the settlers. They rejoiced in full-toned song as their implacable and sleepless enemies drove their heavily laden wagons across the line, leaving their farms, sheds, and houses to the government for the use of the needy tribe.

The urgency of the case being fully pleaded, the whole readjustment was permitted to be made the following spring, and the powers of the agent and his employés were taxed to the uttermost. When the order actually came to hand, Curtis mounted his horse and rode from camp to camp, carrying the good news; calling the members of each band around him, he told the story of their victory.

"Your days of hunger and cold will soon be over," he said. "The white man has gone from the reservation. The water of the streams, the ploughed fields, are all yours. Now we must set to work. Every one will have good ground; all will share alike, and every one must work. We must show the Great Father at Washington that we are glad of his kindness. Our friends will not be ashamed when they come to see us, and look upon our corn and wheat."

Every man, woman, and child did as they had promised. They laid hands to the duties appointed them, and did so merrily. They moved at once to the places designated. A mighty shifting of dwellings took place first of all, and when this was finished they set to work. They built fences, they dug ditches, they ploughed and they planted, cheery as robins. Even the gaunt old women lifted their morose faces to the sun and muttered unaccustomed thanks. The old men no longer sat in complaining council, but talked of the wonderful things about to be.

"Ho! have you heard?" cried one. "Grayman lives

in the house the white man has left; Elk too. Two Horns sleeps in the house above Grayman, and is not afraid. Ah, it is wonderful!"

The more thoughtful dwelt in imagination on the reservation completely fenced, and saw the hills swarming with cattle as in the olden time it swarmed with the wild, black buffalo. They helped at the gardens, these old men, and as they rested on their hoes and listened to the laughter of the women and children, they said one to the other: "Our camp is as it was in the days when game was plenty. Every one is smiling. Our worst days are over. The white man's road is very long, and runs into a strange country, but while Swift Eagle leads we follow."

There was commotion in every corral, where long-haired men in leggings and with feathered ornaments in their hats, were awkwardly breaking fiery ponies to drive, for teams were in sharp demand. The young men who formerly raced horses, for lack of other things to do, and in order not to die of inertness, now became the hilarious teamsters of each valley. Every person, white or red, who could give instruction in ditching and planting, was employed each hour of the day. The various camps were as busy as ant-hills, and as full of cheer as a flock of magpies.

Curtis was everywhere, superintending the moving of barns, the building of cabins, and the laying out of lands. Each night he returned to his bed so tired he could not lie flat enough, but happy in the knowledge that some needed and permanent improvement had that day been made. Lawson, faithful to his post, came on from Washington, and was a comfort in ways less material than wielding a hoe. He went about encouraging the people at their work, and his words had the quality of a poem.

"You see how it is!" he said. "You need not despair. It is not true that the redmen are to vanish from the earth. They are now to be happy and have plenty of food. The white people, at last, have found out the way to help you."

Maynard got a short leave of absence, and came over to see "the hustle," as he called it, and to visit Jennie, who still refused to leave her post, though she had practically consented to his proposal. "We will see," she had said. "If George marries, then I will feel free to go with you; but not now."

Maynard expressed the same astonishment as ever. "A man may fight a people a lifetime and never really know 'em. Now I consider it marvellous the way these devils work."

Calvin, after his recovery, came seldom to the agency. He recognized the power and the fitness of Captain Maynard's successful courtship, and though Jennie wrote twice inviting him to call, he did not come, and did not even reply till she had almost forgotten her own letters. In a very erratic and laborious screed he conveyed his regrets. "I'm powfle bizzy just now. The old man is gone East, an' that thros all the work of the ranch onto me. Ime just as mutch obliged." Jennie did not laugh at this letter; she put it away with a sigh—"Poor boy!"

CHAPTER XXXV

The Battle with the Weeds

BETWEEN THE planting and the reaping lay the sun-smitten summer-time and a battle with the weeds! It was a period demanding patience and understanding in Curtis, for as the first flush of enthusiasm over the sowing died away, apathy and indifference sprang up naturally as thistles. These childlike souls said: "Behold we have done our part, now let Mother Earth and the Father Sun bring forth the harvest. We cannot ripen the grain; we can only wait. Besides, we are weary."

To them harvest should follow seeding without further effort. They were like boys wearied with waiting for the trees to grow. The seed and the apple were too far apart. Curtis, understanding this lack of training in their lives, did not allow himself to express the impatience he sometimes felt. He told them that the new life they were to lead involved constant care, but care would bring a reward. "In the old days when you hunted, these things were not so." He also made honorable examples of men like Two Horns and Crane's Voice, who kept their gardens clean of all noxious plants.

He organized mimic war-parties. "To-day," he said, "the warriors of Elk will go forth with me against these evil ones, the weeds. Each man will be armed with a bright hoe. Elk, old as he is, will lead, and I will go by his side. We will work busily till the sun has climbed half-way to his hill; then we will smoke."

His knowledge of their needs, their habits, their modes of thinking, made all that he did successful. He allowed the women to bring cool drinks, flavored with herbs, and to build little bowers to shade their sons and husbands from the fierce sun while they rested. There was grumbling, there was envy, naturally, but less than he expected.

On the first day of July he was confident of a big crop, and wrote to Elsie, saying: "The potatoes are in bloom, the wheat is waving in the wind like a green sea. I am waiting."

To this she replied: "Papa's mind turns to the mountains these hot days, and so we are coming; also my heart yearns for a certain soldier in the West—a commander of shining hoes and a leader of destructive red ploughmen. I ought, for my own peace and comfort, to forget this singular creature; but, alas! I cannot. My perplexity grows daily. I long to see him, yet I am afraid!"

These words made him tireless and of Job-like patience. "You need not wait till the harvest is ended," he wrote, in reply. "Come and watch the grain ripen, so that you will be garmented duly and ready for the feast. Moreover, we will snatch so many more days of joy out of the maw of devouring time."

To this she answered: "Your expressed reasons are not overwhelming, but as the sun is scorching now, we leave soon. We will reach Pinon City in about ten days. Father is quite well, but restless with the heat. I am well, but restless, for other reasons. I don't see that the problem of our lives is any nearer solution, do you? What can I do? What can you do? Is there any common ground?"

"There are no problems now that you are coming," he replied.

It was with a deep surprise and joy that she found herself trembling before each of his letters. All the old-time ecstasy and breathless passion of her girlhood came back to her, but enlarged, and based deeper, a woman's care and introspection giving it greater significance and power.

The next day after Elsie's definite promise Curtis rode over to the first camp and called the people round him and said:

"Next week we will hold our feast to give thanks for the good things the earth has given to us, and after we have councilled together we will feast and have a dance. Let everything be in order. Come in your finest dress. Let every garment be as it was of old. Let the young girls be very beautiful in whitened buckskin and beads. I do not despise your old-time dress; I like it. Hereafter, when you work you will need to wear white man's clothes, for they are more comfortable; but when you wish to have a good time, then your old dress will be pleasant. I do not ask you to forget the old time. It is past, but it is sweet to you. I want you to be happy, for I am happy."

CHAPTER XXXVI

The Harvest-Home

THE HAY-HARVEST was still going on when Curtis and Jennie drove down the valley to meet Elsie and Lawson at Piñon City. "Father is much changed," Elsie had written. "You will hardly know him now. He has forgotten all about his campaign; he remembers you only momentarily, so that you need not feel any resentment. He will probably meet you as if he had never seen you before. Please do not show any surprise, no matter what he says."

Curtis expected to find Brisbane a poor shambling wreck of a man, morose and sorrowful to look upon, and his astonishment was correspondingly profound as the ex-Senator descended from the train. His step was vigorous, and his face was placid and of good color; thus much the young soldier took in at a glance, then he forgot all the world in the radiant face of his heart's beloved.

As she put up her lips to be kissed, Elsie's eyes were dim with tears, and she hurried to Jennie as if for relief from her emotion. When she turned, her father was shaking hands urbanely with Curtis.

"Glad to meet you, sir," he said, in the tone of the suave man of position. "I didn't catch the name."

A spasm of pain crossed Elsie's face. "This is Mr. Curtis, papa. Don't you remember Captain Curtis?"

"Ah, yes, so it is," he replied. "I remember you spoke of him once before. I am very glad to make your acquaintance—very glad indeed, sir."

To meet this calm politeness in a man who, in his right mind, would have refused to shake hands, was deeply moving to the young officer. To all outward appearance the great promoter was the same, and on all matters concerning his first campaign and first term, and especially on the events of his early life, he spoke with freedom, even with humor, but of the incidents of the later campaign he had no recollection. That he had been defeated and humbled seemed also to have left no lasting mark upon his mind.

"The fact is, my memory has grown very bad," he explained. "I can remember faces in a dim way, but anything that is said to me I forget instantly."

For a time the thought of Brisbane's mental decay threw a gloom over the party, but Elsie said: "Please don't mind him. I have reached a certain philosophic calm in the matter. I can do him no good by sorrowing. I have, therefore, determined to be as happy as I can."

Curtis cheerfully called: "We must start at once. Will your father go with us?"

"Oh no! I am afraid to have him undertake that. He will go on to Copper City with his secretary."

"Of course, that is best," replied Curtis, vastly relieved.

Brisbane parted with Elsie quite matter-of-factly, and his urbanity remained unbroken as he shook hands with Curtis. "Pleased to have met you, sir," he said, and, in spite of her resolution, the tears filled the daughter's eyes. The old warrior's smiling forgetfulness of feuds was tragic.

As they rode homeward, Curtis and Elsie sat as before on the forward seat, and he detailed what had taken place at the agency, and she listened, genuinely absorbed. She laughed and she wept a little as his story touched on the pathetic incidents of the year.

"You are like a father confessor," she said. "You hold in your hands the most intimate secrets of your people. I don't understand your patience with them. Do you feel that you have made your demonstration?"

"What I have done is written in lines of gold and green on the earth. The sky is too bright to remember my gray days," he replied, most exultantly.

She looked at him quizzically. "You are developing new and singular powers."

"I have a new and singular teacher."

"New?" she queried.

"New to me," he answered, and in such enigmatic way they expressed their emotion while Lawson and Jennie chatted gayly and in clear prose behind. Part of the time Elsie drove, and that gave Curtis an excuse to lay his hand on her wrist when he wished her to drive slow. At the half-way house she shuddered and made a mouth of disgust. "Let's hurry past here; I have a bad heart when I think of those horrible men."

"They are thinning out, and this ranch has 'changed hands' as they say on restaurant signs in Chicago. Here's our north line of fence," he said, as they came to a big, new gate. "I hastened to build this at once before anything happened to prevent. This keeps the stock of the white man out, and has stopped all friction."

As they came in sight of the flag-pole, Elsie cried

out: "Just think! This is the third time I have driven up this road in this way. Twice with you."

"I know it is wonderful. I don't intend you to go away without me."

She was ignoring every one of his suggestions now, but the flush of her cheek and a certain softness in her eyes encouraged him to go on.

As they alighted at the door, Jennie remained to look after her bundles, and Curtis and Elsie entered the library together. He who had waited so eagerly for this moment turned and folded her close in his arms. "I need you, sweetest! I'll never let you go again. Never!"

This was her moment to protest; but she was silent, with her face against his shoulder.

Jennie bounced into the hall with a great deal of premonitory clatter and hurried Elsie to her room to rest.

"And now you're to be my really truly sister," she said, closing the door behind her.

"I think—George," she hesitated a little, and blushed before speaking his name, "expects it—rather confidently."

"Then give me a good hug, you glorious thing!"

CHAPTER XXXVII

The Mingling of the Old and the New

EARLY ON the morning of the great day—before the dawn, in truth—the Tetongs came riding in over the hills from every quarter of the earth, bringing their finest clothing, their newest blankets, and their whitest tepees, all lashed on long poles between which the patient ponies walked as in the olden time. Every man, woman, and child able to sit a horse was mounted. No one wore a white man's hat or shoes or vest; all were in leggings and moccasins, fringed and painted, and they carried their summer blankets as they once carried their robes of the buffalo-skin. Even the boys of six and seven wore suits cunningly fashioned and decorated like those of their elders. The young warriors, painted, and with fluttering feathers, rode their fleetest ponies, with shoulders bare and gleaming like bronze in the sun.

With all due form, without hurry or jostling, the whole tribe camped in a wide ellipse, each clan in its place, each family having a fixed position in the circle. The tepees rose like magic, and their threads of smoke began to creep up into the clear sky like mysterious plants, slender and wavering.

Greetings passed from camp to camp, the head men met in council, and, as the sun rose higher, swarms of the young men galloped to and fro, laying out a racing-course and making up for a procession under Wilson's direction.

Curtis said: "I am not interdicting any of their customs merely because they belong to their old life, but because some of them are coarse or hurtful. Their dance is not harmful unless protracted to the point of interfering with their work. That they are all living somewhat in the past, to-day, is true; but they will put away this finery and go to work with me tomorrow. To cut them off from all amusement is cruel fanaticism. No people can endure without amusement."

"How appropriate their gay colors seem in this hot, dun land!" remarked Elsie. "They would look gaudy in a studio; but out here they are grateful to the sense."

In the centre of the wide circle of tepees a huge bower of pines was being erected for the dance, and pulsing through the air the voice of the criers could be heard, as they rode slowly round the circle publishing the programme of the day.

"Looking over the camp towards the hills it is not difficult to imagine one's self back in the old days," said Maynard. "I saw Sitting Bull camped like this. See, here is the 'Soldier Lodge' or chief's headquarters," and he pointed to a large, handsome tepee set in one of the foci of the big ellipse.

Everywhere they went Curtis and his friends met with hearty greeting. "Hoh-hoh! The Little Father!" the old men cried, and came to shake hands, and the women smiled, looking up from their work. The little children, though they ran away at first, came out again when they knew that it was the Captain who called. Jennie gave hints about the cooking, and praised the neat tepees and the pretty dresses, while Elsie, looking upon it all with reflective eyes, could not help thinking, "Such will be my work if I do my duty as a wife."

Once she looked at the firm, bold, facial outlines of the man she had learned to love, and snuggled a little closer into his shelter; he would toil to make every hardship light, that was certain; but, oh! the dreary winters! There were moments when she took to herself a part of the love and obedience this people showed Curtis. Here was a little kingdom over which Curtis reigned, a despotic monarch, and she, if she did her duty, would reign by his side. It had, at least, the virtue of being an unconventional self-sacrifice. And then, again, she smiled to think that Elsie Bee Bee should feel a touch of pride in being the wife of an Indian agent!

Driving his guests back to the agency, Curtis returned to the camp and moved about on foot among his people. Wherever he went he seemed to give zest to the sports, and knowing this he remained with them till noon, and only came in to rest his weary feet and aching eyes for half an hour before lunch.

It was unutterably sweet to stretch out in his big, battered easy-chair, in the shaded coolness of the library, and feel Elsie's smooth, light hand in his hair.

"And you are never to leave me," he said, dreamily. "I can't realize it yet." After a pause he added: "I am demanding too much of you, sweetheart."

"You are demanding nothing, sir; if you did you wouldn't get it. If I choose to *give* you anything, you are to be grateful and discreetly silent."

"Can't I say, 'Thank you'?"

"Not a word."

"I am content," he said, and closed his eyes again to express it, and she, being unasked, bent and kissed his forehead.

Rousing up a few minutes later, he said, "I have a present in keeping for you."

"Have you? What is it? Is it from you? Why didn't you let me see it before?"

He rose and opened a closet door. "Because the proper time had not come. Before I show it to you I want you to promise to wear it."

"I promise," she instantly replied.

"Don't be so ready; I intend it to be a symbol of your change of heart."

"Well, then, I don't promise," she said, backing away.

"I don't mean your change of heart towards me; I have a ring to express that; this is to express your change of heart towards—"

"Towards Injuns?"

"No; towards all 'the small peoples of the earth.' "

"Well, then, I can't wear it; I haven't changed. Down with them!" she shouted, in smiling bravado.

He closed the door. "Very well, then, you shall not even see the present; you are not worthy of it."

"Oh, please! please! I'll forgive all the heathens of Africa, if you will only let me see."

"I don't believe I like that, either," he replied. "You are now too flippant. However, I'll hold you to the word. If you don't mean it now you will by-and-by."

Elsie clapped her hands with girlish delight as he held up a fine buckskin dress, beautifully adorned with beads and quills. It was exquisitely tanned, as soft as silk, and a deep cream color.

"Isn't it lovely! I'll wear it whether my heart is changed or not."

"Here are the leggings and moccasins to match."

She gathered them all up at a swoop. "I'm going to put them on at once."

"Wait!" he commanded. "Small Bird, who made these garments, is out in the kitchen. I want to call her; she can be your maid for this time."

As Small Bird sidled bashfully into the hall Elsie cried out in delight of her. She was dressed in the old-time Tetong dress, and was exceedingly comely. Her face was carefully painted and her hair shone with much brushing and oil. Her teeth were white and even.

"Can she speak English?" asked Elsie.

"Not very well; but she understands. Small Bird, the lady says, thank you. She thinks they are very fine. Her heart is glad. Go help her dress."

"Come!" cried Elsie, eagerly, and fairly ran up the stairs in her haste to be transformed into a woman of the red people.

When she returned she was a sister to Small Bird. Her dark hair was braided in the Tetong fashion, her face was browned, and her little feet were clothed in glittering, beaded moccasins.

"You look exactly like some of the old engravings of Mohawk princesses," cried Curtis. "Now you are ready to sit by my side and review the procession."

"Are we to have a procession?"

"Indeed we are, as significant as any mediæval tournament. I am the resident duke before whom the review takes place, and I shall be in my best dress and you are to sit by my side—my bride-elect."

"Oh no!"

"Oh yes. It is decided." He drew himself up haughtily. "I have said it, and I am chief to-day. It is good, Small Bird," he said, as the Tetong girl started to go. "My wife likes it very much."

Elsie ran towards the girl and took her by the

shoulders as if to make her understand the better. "Thank you; thank you!"

Small Bird smiled, but surrendered to her timidity, and, turning, ran swiftly out of the room.

Curtis hooked Elsie in his right arm. "Now all is decreed. You have put on the garb of my people," and his kiss stopped the protest she struggled to utter.

Surely the day was a day strangely apart. Everything that could be done to make it symbolic, to make it idyllic, was done. Curtis appeared after lunch in a fine costume of buckskin, trimmed with green porcupine quills and beads, and for a hat he wore a fillet of beaver-skin with a single feather on the back. Across his shoulder he carried the sash of a finely beaded tobacco pouch, and in his hand a long fringed bag, very ancient, containing a peace-pipe, which had been transmitted to Crawling Elk by his father's father, a very precious thing, worn only by chieftains.

"Oh, I shall paint you in that dress," cried Elsie.

So accoutred, he led the way to the canopied platform under the flag-pole, where the reviewing party were to sit. In order that no invidious distinctions might be drawn, two or three of the old chiefs and their wives had been given seats thereon, and they were already in place. Not many strangers were present, for Curtis had purposely refrained from setting a day too long ahead, but Lawson's friends and some relatives of the employés, and several of the young officers from the fort made up the outside representation. Maynard was in his brightest uniform, and Jennie, looking very nice in a muslin gown, and a broad, white hat, sat by his side.

From the seats in the stand, the camp, swarming with horsemen, could be seen. Wilson, as grand marshal, was riding to and fro, assisted by Lawson, who had entered into the game with the self-sacrificing devotion of a drum-major. His make-up was superb, and when at last he approached, leading the cavalcade, Elsie did not recognize him. His lean face, dark with paint, was indistinguishably Tetong, seen from a distance, and he sat his horse in perfect simulation of his red brethren. He was but re-enacting scenes of his early life. His hunting-shirt was dark with use, and his splendid war-bonnet trailed grandly down his back. He rode by, looking neither to the right nor the left, singing a new song.

> "We are passing.
> See us passing by.
> We are leaving the old behind us.
> The new we seek to find. We are passing,
>   passing by."

Crawling Elk followed, holding aloft a spear with a green plume; it was a turnip thrust through with a sharp-pointed, blackened stick, and behind him, two and two, came fifty of his young warriors carrying shining hoes upright, as of old they carried their lances, while at their shoulders, where quivers of arrows should have swung, dangled trim sheaves of green wheat and golden barley. The free fluttering of their feather-ornamented hair, the barbaric painting on their faces and hands, symbolized the old life, as the green arrows of the grain prefigured the new. Behind them rode their women, each bearing in her left hand a bunch of flowers. Those who could read wore on their bosoms a small, shining medal, and in their hair an eagle feather. No Tetong woman had ever worn a plume before.

Standing Elk, quaint and bent, rode by, singing a war-song, magnificent in his dress as war chief, leading some twenty young men. His hands were

empty of the signs of peace, and his face was rapt
with dreams of the past, but his young men carried
long-handled forks which flamed in the sun, and
bracelets of green grass encircled their firm, brown
arms. They, too, were painted to signify their clan
and their ancestry, and the "medicine" they affected was on their breasts. Their wives were close
behind, each bearing a stalk of corn in bloom; their
beaded saddles and gay blankets were pleasant to
see. Every weapon bespoke warfare against weeds.
Every ornament represented the better nature, the
striving, the aspiration of its wearer.

Then came the school-children, adding a final
note of pathos, poor little brown men and women
trudging on foot to symbolize that they must go
through life, plodding in the dust of the white man's
chariot wheel—their toes imprisoned in a shapeless
box of leather, their hair closely clipped, their clothing hot and restrictive. Each carried a book and a
slate, and their faces were very intent and serious
as they paced by on their way from the old to the
new. They were followed by the school-band playing
"The Star-Spangled Banner," with splendid disre-
gard of the broken faith of the government whose
song it was.

And so they streamed by, these folk, accounted
the most warlike of all red men, genially carrying
out the wishes of their chief, illustrating, without
knowing it, the wondrous change which had come
to them; the old men still clinging to the past, the
young men careless of the future, the children already transformed, and, as they glanced up, some
smiling, some grave and dreaming, Elsie shuddered
with a species of awe; it seemed as if a people were
being disintegrated before her eyes; that the evolu-
tion of a race having proceeded for countless ages
by almost imperceptible degrees was now and here
rushing, as by mighty bounds, from war to peace,

from hunting to harvesting, from primitive indolence to ordered thrift. They were, indeed, passing, as the plains and the wild spaces were passing; as the buffalo had passed; as every wild thing must pass before the ever-thickening flood of white ploughmen pressing upon the land.

Twice they circled, and then, as they all massed before him, Curtis rose to sign to them.

"I am very proud of you. All my friends are pleased. My heart is big with emotion and my head is full of thoughts. This is a great day for you and also for me. Some of you are sad, for you long for the old things—the big, broad plain, the elk, and the buffalo. So do I. I loved those things also. But you have seen how it is. The water of the stream never turns back to the spring, the old man never grows young, the tree that falls does not rise up again. So the old things come never again. We have always to look ahead. Perhaps, in the happy hunting-ground all will be different, but here now we must do our best to live upon the earth. It is the law that, now the game being gone, we must plough and sow and reap the fruit of the soil. That is the meaning of all we have done to-day. We have put away the rifle; we here take up the hoe.

"I am glad; my heart is like a bird; it sings when I see you happy. Listen—I will tell you a great secret. You see this young woman," he touched Elsie. "You see she wears the Tetong dress, the same as I; that means much. It signifies two things: Last year her heart was hard towards the Tetongs; now it is soft. She is proud of what you have done. She wears this dress for another reason; she is going to be my wife, and help me show you the good way." At this moment a chorus of pleased outcries broke forth. "Now, go to your feast. Let everything be orderly. To-night we will come to see you dance."

With an outburst of jocular whooping, the young

men wheeled their horses and vanished under cover of a cloud of dust, while the old men and the women and the children moved sedately back to camp; the women chattering gayly over the day's exciting shows, and in anticipation of the dance which was to come.

There were tears in Elsie's eyes as she looked up at Curtis. "They have so far to go, poor things! They can't realize how long the road to civilization is."

"I do not care whether they reach what you call civilization or not; the road to happiness and peace is not long, it is short; they are even now entering upon it. They can be happy right here, and so can we," he ended, looking at her with a tender wistfulness. "Can't you understand?"

"You have conquered," she said, with deep feeling. "Under the spell of this day, I feel your work to be the only thing in the world worth doing." Her words, her voice, so moved him that he bent and laid a kiss upon her lips. When he could speak, he said: "Now I want to ask something of you. I have a leave of absence for six months. Show me the Old World."

She sprang up. "Ah! Can you go?"

"When the crops are garnered and sifted, and my people clothed and sheltered."

"I'd rather show you Paris than anything else in the world!" she cried. "I'd almost marry you to do that."

"Very well, marry me; we will spend our honeymoon there; perhaps then you will be willing to spend one more year here with me, and then— well— Never cross the range till you get to it is a maxim of the trail."

READING LOG		
1		82